PRAISE FOR *A PRINTER'S CHOICE*

Patenaude's masterful debut novel tells a gripping story of the near future. This is a superb morality tale in which the power of free will and the implications of making good choices are carefully woven together. Patenaude's take on the possibilities of technology is inventive and in line with contemporary science, and his work truly shines as a nuanced, character-driven drama. This work is a must-read for those who enjoy thought-provoking, challenging speculative fiction.

—*Publishers Weekly* Starred Review

The novel grabs our attention from the first page, and delivers a suspenseful whodunit set in the chilled darkness of outer space. There are rumors that the novel could be the first in a series, and we certainly hope those rumors are true.

—Dr. Kelly Scott Franklin, Writer,
Assistant Professor of English at Hillsdale College

Complex, action-packed and thought-provoking all at once, A Printer's Choice *is a uniquely crafted piece that doesn't handily limit itself to a single genre, but spreads its message and vision across a broad spectrum to attract a diverse audience of readers who like their sci-fi intricate, original and compelling.*

—D. Donovan, Senior Reviewer, *Midwest Book Review*

Just as Aragorn embodied the role of a king in The Lord of the Rings, *Father McClellan's portrayal in* A Printer's Choice *captures what Christians and priests should be. His actions speak of a love for others grounded in a God who is love itself. By setting his story in the future and space, Patenaude enables readers to see the universality of this truth—that the choice to love is at the heart of the universe—more clearly.*

—Dr. Jason King, Professor of Theology, St. Vincent College

Father McClellan is artfully drawn and compelling in his hard-won spiritual wisdom works. He uses his Marine toughness, programming skills, and gritty faith to sort out potential motivations and methods to solve the murder of an undercover priest, Father Tanglao. An engineer himself, Patenaude describes all the technological details, societal tensions, and moral ambiguities of New Athens with confidence and finesse. The most compelling passages, though, are the human ones, where McClellan and other characters grapple with their troubled pasts and future options, and the free will choices before them.

—Marybeth Lorbiecki, Author *A Fierce Green Fire*

Mr. Patenaude is a highly skilled and masterful storyteller. He crafts a story that is unique and absorbing. The ability to weave elements of science fiction, faith, and purpose into one book is truly inspiring.

—Trudy Thompson, AML

W.L. Patenaude pens an out-of-this-world, whodunit mystery in A Printer's Choice.

—Cheryl E. Rodriguez for *Readers' Favorite*

IZZARD INK PUBLISHING COMPANY
PO Box 522251
Salt Lake City, Utah 84152
www.izzardink.com

LIBRARY OF CONGRESS CONTROL NUMBER: 2018931305

Designed by Alissa Rose Theodor
Cover Design by Jamie S. Warren
Cover Illustration by Stephen Youll
Editing Services by New York Book Editors

First Edition August 28, 2018

Contact the author at info@izzardink.com

Softback ISBN: 978-1-72632-746-6
Hardback ISBN: 978-1-64228-007-4
eBook ISBN: 978-1-64228-005-0

TO MOM AND DAD,
AND STS. JOSEPH AND AUGUSTINE

A Printer's Choice

W.L. PATENAUDE

IZZARD INK
— PUBLISHING —

NEW ATHENS

FOR TWELVE YEARS, THE Aesirs had landed at the Gainesville Regional Spaceport at nine o'clock at night and launched at nine each morning.
But on Wednesday, February 25, 2088, one arrived without notice just
before noon. A day later, it stood in the Florida sun, ready for an evening
departure.

As word spread, the work of rebuilding the city slowed, and bets were
made that the rumors were true—that there really had been a murder in
the orbits. And that the authorities up there had sought help from the old
world below.

The Aesir's wings glowed yellow, then orange, as the sun slipped into
the west. Steam drifted between its engines—a sure sign they were being
readied—and still the spaceport's information displays remained blank.
But people from Gainesville knew better. They knew that before long the
engines would ignite and roar and be heard for miles. Then the Aesir
would climb, and begin to arc into the coming night, and if you were
watching from below you might never know why.

Inside the shuttle, Father John Francis McClellan was making his way
to the first-class passenger section. Other than the flight crew, he was
alone with his two escorts in the three-hundred-person-capacity craft.
One of the escorts—or hosts, or ambassadors from the new world—was
saying that they had been lucky to find this particular priest. Besides the
necessary qualifications, he was young and fit, which had hastened preparations. And time, she said, was of the essence.

McClellan's assessment was different. He had turned thirty-four two
weeks earlier, and he knew that seven years in the seminary and four in
a parish in Boston had softened him. He no longer had the build of the
young man who had farmed and played football—a worker's build that
the Marine Corps made leaner and tougher.

His uniform now was a black, space-ready suit with a customized
collar signifying his status as a Roman Catholic priest. Only his sandy

brown hair remained as it had back in the Corps—cut low and faded to his skin on the sides and in back. The haircut revealed a series of scars that roamed across his left temple, stretching from his ear nearly to his watchful eyes, which were the blue of all the McClellan men. The scarring was slight but evident, softening whenever his quick smile came, as it did with the first-class accommodations.

McClellan had been upside only once, fifteen years ago, back in boot camp. But it was as if it were yesterday. As his two escorts spoke quietly among themselves, McClellan called up the faces of his fellow recruits— so many men and women he'd grown to love. Men and women he had watched die.

They had stayed upside for three weeks to learn the skills needed to perform missions in weightlessness. They were outfitted in full lifegear and body armor, and carried standard-issue weapons alongside the tools they needed to program the printers. All that mass worked to crush them on takeoff, and it burdened them in orbit. He could still hear the drill instructors shouting to stay focused—to remember that mass is always subject to the laws of nature. And in space those laws are strict.

McClellan had been nauseated for the first two days, yet by the end of the three weeks he was at the top of the class both in weightless programming and overall. This had assured him an assignment in the 6th Marine Raider Battalion, which took only the best programmers.

Back then, as always, he had wanted to help make things right. But the means of his youth had been tools of war, not faith, for like many children, he had been brought up with no belief in God.

Now, finally strapped into his seat as the escorts chatted about progress, McClellan wondered how he had ever managed without his certainty in the Father, Son, and Holy Ghost. He looked below and followed the craft's shadow, which had advanced into the marshes to the east. It blended with other shadows farther toward the horizon, where the land darkened out by the ruins and crater that had once been the city of St. Augustine.

The pilot announced that they'd be launching in fourteen minutes, then issued a final round of safety tips.

Fourteen minutes? McClellan slipped a frayed pouch from his pocket and removed his rosary. Sitting in front of him, the more talkative escort watched closely.

"I trust you're not nervous," she said.

"Not exactly," McClellan said. "But I'll be glad when I can begin my work."

"That makes two of us," she said.

Elaina Jansen, the elegant chief engineer of New Athens, understood his impatience. She had been instrumental in convincing Rome and Mc-Clellan's archbishop to set all this in motion—and now her reputation was at stake. She was a tall woman, neat and proper. Her silver hair was cut short, with wisps of blond still showing along the sides. Determination shone in her dark eyes even when fatigue or sadness sought to distract her.

"It won't be much longer," she said. "We had agreed to wait until after launch to begin sharing what we know."

"Thirteen minutes, thirty seconds, and counting," McClellan said. "Until then, I'll put the time to good use."

He looked once more out the viewport, thinking of the suffering that surrounded them—the souls of all the dead from the once-vibrant lands that had faded in sea and storm, shadow and memory. He thought also of the people working to rebuild. The priest fingered the crucifix on his rosary, made the sign of the cross, and silently said the Apostles' Creed.

Jansen tapped the knee of the second escort, Security Commissioner Joseph Zhèng—the man in charge of the investigation. She leaned closer and whispered with subtle superiority, "The good father will be praying. I suppose we should let him. We may all need it."

Zhèng said nothing. He gave McClellan a nod, the slightest of smiles, and returned to watching a gull gliding in the currents, its feathers reflecting the floodlights of the spaceport. Two more gulls joined the send-off. Then, from below, a series of horns sounded and the birds flew off fast and sure.

Midway through his third decade of the rosary, the cabin lights dimmed and small displays that had been showing the locations of emergency pods began flashing a countdown.

As the rumble of engines rose to a thunder, McClellan remembered his training.

Back then he had found himself comforting his fellow recruits, as they did him—making things better by cracking jokes about printing jobs gone wrong, or about that night out in Albuquerque. Now he sat with two companions from a different world that he'd known for less than a day. But whatever the differences, they were, all three, united by the thrust and roar of ascent. Their hands clutched armrests. Their feet pressed into the flooring, as if that action would keep them from falling forward. And McClellan silently continued his rosary for the soul of the man whose murder had set all this in motion.

Ten days earlier McClellan had arrived at his archbishop's office to receive a new assignment, one that, as a diocesan priest who had taken a vow of obedience, was not open to debate. As a friend of Archbishop Alfred Bauer, however, he could resist a little.

"I thought you were assigning me to a new parish," McClellan said, "and I was going to protest. But New Athens? There has to be someone more qualified."

"Johnny," the archbishop said, "I wish there were." He leaned his strong figure forward in a leather chair that had been saved from the old archbishop's office, from long before the war. "But you aren't the average priest."

McClellan stiffened. He couldn't think of why the Archbishop of Boston would be so concerned with the new world—so concerned that he'd send one of his priests.

"If this is about my time with the Corps," McClellan said, "I'm not the only priest with a military background. And other than one exercise in boot camp, I never served in space."

"I think only eleven Marines ever did, Johnny. But that's not the point. In addition to your time with the Military Police, you have other skills. You were trained to program the printers. And whatever this business is all about, I am certain it will involve them."

McClellan waited for Bauer to continue. But the archbishop looked down at the data hovering over his tablet and maintained an impassive expression.

"Do those reports say anything about programmers?" McClellan asked, hearing the apprehension in his voice.

"No. And no one has mentioned them—not to me, anyway. But it was obvious that Cardinal Kwalia was interested in your military history, which he seemed to know a great deal about."

"That would make sense. He's the Holy See's secretary of state. The Corps must have told them everything. Which means he knows what happened the last time I programmed."

The archbishop sighed and stood up. He picked up his mug and went to the windows of the old office, gazing at the February afternoon. A young father crossed Washington Street carrying a boy in one arm and pulling a tired girl with the other. The children suddenly laughed at something the father had said, and Bauer smiled.

"Kwalia was being diplomatic when we spoke," he said when he turned back to McClellan, "but he was not subtle. He's Kenyan, and all the clergy I've met from there have the talent for being wonderfully polite and terribly straightforward all at once."

"And yet he didn't say anything explicit about this case needing a programmer?"

"Johnny, I know about you and the printers—more than most. I know why you vowed to never go back inside one. But it was clear that Kwalia wants you up there because of your training—and that probably means the Holy Father wants you up there for that reason, too. Now, I'm no hotshot detective like you, but I think I'm on to something."

"I was never a detective."

"No. But you made a few in the Military Police look good."

A motorcycle came and went outside, startling a blue jay that screamed in reply.

"Okay, let's talk." Bauer returned to his chair and waved his tablet. "Here's the information I've been given. There's been a murder upside. It's the first up there—the first that we know of, anyway—and the victim is a Catholic priest. A Dominican. And tell me, why would the engineers even admit that a Catholic priest was up there in their godless new world? Because they need someone who's investigated murders, who knows law enforcement, who knows the priesthood, and that's you."

"So what's the angle with a printer?"

Bauer scanned the data on his tablet. "The priest—Raphael Tanglao is his name—was at an air lock in one of those orbital relay stations when someone hacked in and opened the air lock's outer door. Apparently a printer was making repairs outside when it happened." Bauer entered a few commands with the movement of his eyes and held up the tablet. It showed images from the priest's autopsy. "This is what the printer's emitters did to him before it shut down."

McClellan had seen worse. But not by much. He offered a silent prayer and began asking himself questions about how any of that could have happened. "And they're sure this was homicide?"

"Both the Engineering and Security Councils were loath to admit it, but yes, they are. Apparently Father Tanglao recorded a message as he was dying. He made it certain that this was no accident."

"Any idea about suspects?"

"Not that I'm privy to. But I'm sure there's much more than what we're being told."

McClellan reached for Bauer's tablet and pulled up more of the autopsy photos. "Why would they ask for me? The engineers own the printers —they always have. They should know that I'm not programmer material anymore. And I don't want to be. I don't even have my equipment."

The archbishop leaned back. He remained silent until McClellan looked at him. "Johnny, we all did things in the wars we regret. None of us can change our past. All we can do is make the best choices we can, especially when we're offered opportunities like this."

Bauer placed his mug on the table next to him, fingering a small crack in its handle.

"Look ahead, Johnny," Bauer said. "You're being given a chance to do so much good. For others, yes, but especially for you. Please, think this through—you're so good at that when it comes to other people's problems."

"It'd be easier if you just ordered me to go."

"I could," Bauer said softly. "But this is not an ordinary assignment. This has to be your choice."

McClellan let out the breath he'd been holding. Bauer was the kind of archbishop whom priests either loved or hated. McClellan was in the former group. From the day he had met the Marine Corps chaplain in the infirmary at Camp Lejeune, McClellan had found in Bauer a friend and mentor with the best qualities of both his father and his uncle, who had tried so hard to raise him.

"Your Excellency," McClellan said, stressing the formal title, "what is it that Holy Mother Church is asking me to do, *really*? Priests get killed all the time. It wouldn't surprise me that if one did sneak upside he would be targeted. What's this really about?"

The archbishop looked disappointed.

McClellan hated that expression. He turned and looked out the window. An Aesir was arcing up from Logan Spaceport, its distant glare boasting of technologies that would have been unfathomable to the men who had carved the window's woodwork.

"Look at me," Bauer said.

McClellan obeyed.

"Whatever reason that the engineers want you up there, *my* reason— the *Church's* reason, and the Holy Father has made this very clear—*our* reason to send you is, yes, to get to the truth, but it's also to minister to souls. Including yours."

McClellan relaxed. He knew where this was going, and he loved his archbishop all the more for it.

"The faithful upside are just like the ones on Earth, Johnny. They may have to hide their beliefs, but they need the Eucharist. They need confession and all the sacraments. You know this. We need to be up there."

"And yet at least one priest was already up there," McClellan said. "Unofficially, I assume."

"Yes, and quite unexpectedly. Neither Rome nor his order had any idea. Nor, apparently, did the authorities upside."

McClellan wondered how anyone could have pulled that off. "A priest wouldn't go missing without some investigation. There had to have been one."

"There was—it's all there in the files. Raphael Tanglao was supposed to be visiting family in Manila last summer when he disappeared. The Dominican Order submitted all the appropriate reports, but with no leads and no evidence of foul play, the Filipino police closed the case after a month. He was assumed dead—somewhere on Earth, of course. As you said, that's not uncommon. But finding him in the orbits has created some . . . questions, not to mention diplomatic tangles for the Church. We're hoping they'll get ironed out with your presence."

"What about the Corps? If there's something here to do with the printers, or me, shouldn't they be told?"

Bauer nodded. "Commandant Munrayos was briefed yesterday. There won't be a formal statement of support, naturally, as this does not technically involve them. But between you and me, the Corps wouldn't object to improved relations with the engineers."

McClellan paused. "All right. Two final questions."

Bauer leaned back, motioning for McClellan to continue.

"If I accept, who would you send to my parish? I might be upside for a while, possibly until Easter. Whoever it is better be good."

"I have some fine candidates, Johnny. But I promise you this: before you go, I'll come and preach at all the Sunday Masses. I'll share as much news as I can about their pastor's temporary assignment."

"They'll appreciate hearing it from you. Thank you."

"And your second question?"

McClellan smiled. "You already know it. When do I leave for New Athens?"

2

"**ENGINEERS PREFER NOT TO TELL** their stories," the voice on the video said. "Whether they are those of their successes, because the engineers are humble, or those of their failures, because they are also secretive."

McClellan paused the video. It seemed impossible that this file, sent by Security Commissioner Zhèng himself, was what he had suspected: one of the censored exposés about the engineers, their printers, and the construction of New Athens. Zhèng had transmitted it in the first round of mission orientation files. But doing so—simply possessing it up here— had to have been risky.

McClellan had left the Aesir's first-class cabin after the turmoil of the launch. He wanted time alone for his evening prayers and to read the files. And he didn't want to disturb Elaina Jansen, who was fast asleep. Now strapped into a third-class seating bench as the Aesir brought them again into daylight, the view of the receding Earth was tempting. But this video had to be watched, even if he knew its content well. After all, it was a requirement in boot camp for programmers to memorize every word about the printers.

"Usually it is the builders who tell us about New Athens," the narrator continued over stock imagery of first-generation orbital workers. "Usually they are the ones explaining why it was built, and how it came to be that it was built in so short a time, and how the work promised to the builders had been taken away by the engineers' machines.

"But engineers have stories, too. And some want their stories told. These are engineers who worked years before the founding of the Engineering Guild—men and women who know the early days, which, they tell us, were not as idyllic as we're led to believe."

The video showed a montage of natural disasters and the mass burials of refugees. "To appreciate their stories, we must begin in the early middle years of the twenty-first century. That's when the Coalition of Nations began talks with the heads of the great data companies, and that was when the agreements were made to investigate how to respond to the toxins and the droughts, to the oceans' deadly rise, and to the wildfires and storms that grew stronger each year. That's when plans were made to address the wars and crumbling social orders that by the 2050s had destabilized most civil orders, and inflicted levels of suffering and death such as history had never known."

Next came the footage of official celebrations. But as the narrator spoke, the official imagery was replaced with smuggled footage of soldiers in Eastern Europe, Africa, and Australia. The soldiers were surrounding government buildings and escorting bureaucrats into waiting vans. Many of the scenes ended with a soldier's hand blocking the view.

"Ah, the 2050s!" the narrator continued mockingly. "The age of so-called universal cooperation. The time when the great minds of the world decreed that a new age needed to dawn—an age of collaboration and purpose, stripped of any errors of ages past. And so by choice or coercion, the nations of the world ceded their authority to the newly formed Global Union, which was funded by the wealth of the great corporate holdings and looked to for hope by the starving people of the continents.

"The Global Union and its backers leveraged and coordinated what remained of the power of the nations and the strength of their armies. It promised to bring order to the cities and towns of the world, and to combat the deadly cartels that were benefiting from the suffering and the short supplies of most everything necessary for life."

McClellan paused the playback. There had been a sound from the forward portion of the cabin, as if someone were approaching. But he was alone.

"The GU synchronized the work of the world's universities and laboratories," the narrator continued. "They calculated, they devised, and they built ways to try—at least try—to tame the forces and soothe the harm that previous generations had unleashed.

"Some of the minds were those of the geoengineers who sought to mend the planet. Others probed the secret depths of matter and energy for better sources of power and technologies. A third group engineered the future societies of the world. They sifted the cultures of the past to determine what and who should move forward, and what and who should not.

"A fourth group was tasked with redundancy"—here was an unsteady video of a group of neatly dressed men and women working at some early holographic display. "These were the great minds that proposed the orbital human habitats, although it seemed nearly an impossible task to build and maintain anything of such scale."

The video cut to unauthorized footage of an interview with a young engineer—a fair-skinned, smiling man speaking German. The video provided subtitles, but McClellan didn't need them.

"We all know that the fragility of Earth threatens humanity," the young man said, "which is why I and the other GU engineers are determined to find a way to build new worlds. We know that the future of the human race is not here, but in the stars!"

Now came a segment with engineers arguing how best to clear the orbits of debris of generations past, as well as to disperse the Van Allen belts—the bands of natural and dangerous radiation surrounding Earth. But even the narrator admitted that on these matters no one could criticize those early efforts. Or argue their successes.

"Prototypes worked," the narrator said, "sufficient funding followed, and the remains of technologies past were cleared from the orbits. Soon after, a fleet of Van Allen radiation dispersers cleared the road to higher ones.

"What today is called New Athens was in those early days known as the O'Neill Orbital Laboratory." The narrator was accompanied here by still shots of the old orbital facility. The pictures were marked at odd angles with CLASSIFIED, and NOT FOR DISSEMINATION.

The video transitioned to a man sitting in shadows, his face in darkness, his voice digitally distorted. "The real goal of O'Neill was simply to test our designs," he said as the video displayed the words *First-generation engineer (anonymous)*.

More classified images followed as the voice continued. "O'Neill was meant only to perfect our techniques, which we needed for the first orbital home for humanity: the world we call Progress. We never expected to build the prototype. And certainly not quickly."

Here the narrator continued. "But New Athens *is* being built and is scheduled to be finished in 2075. And unlike Progress, scheduled for completion in 2089, New Athens is being built at the original O'Neill location—not at more stable Lagrange points on the lunar orbit. The questions so many ask are not only *how* is New Athens being built this quickly, but who decided that it would, and why?"

McClellan again looked across the cabin. Sunlight moved through starboard viewports, giving him a better view. Seeing that he remained alone, he upped the volume as the distorted voice of the anonymous engineer returned.

"The problem had always been that building these worlds would take decades, even with our best construction techniques and the most powerful printers. We knew that in the beginning. But we were hoping for a breakthrough."

"Technological marvels that they were," the narrator took over, "those first orbital printers were limited compared to what we use today. They were precise to the atom, but could reproduce only the most basic structural arrays and organic materials necessary for large-scale space habitats."

The video showed a different silhouette—a second anonymous engineer—speaking with another distorted voice. It was so unrecognizable that McClellan couldn't tell if it belonged to a man or a woman.

"It all seems so rudimentary now," he or she said. "Test building at the O'Neill Laboratory required two hundred and thirty automated catchers to propel themselves beyond Mars, where they scanned the asteroids for those most suitable for the printers. But the mapping to do this took time, and the quality of the arriving asteroids weren't always what we wanted. So we had more delays, and we were beginning to wonder if we'd ever build even one world."

"With doubts rising," the narrator took over, "hundreds more of the catchers were sent to hook their prey and push the asteroids into months-long journeys to the Earth–Moon system. There the asteroids were transferred into the orbits of the furnaces, which melted the ore and magnetically sifted it into the purity and blends the printers required.

"By December 2063, with the O'Neill test facility in full operation, there was a steady supply of asteroidal ore, and some five dozen furnaces that fed those first-age printers. For those of us in certain latitudes on Earth, the furnaces offered faint light shows in the night sky, which gave us something to cheer.

"But once again, all did not go smoothly.

"These images, taken by high-powered jet-mounted military surveillance systems, show what happened when a printer's guidance system failed. That streak you see is tumbling raw materials in a decaying orbit. Here it is grazing the Earth's atmosphere, falling through the air in a line of fire."

The shadowed image of the second anonymous engineer returned. "Our problems with those first printers were rooted in information processing, communication delays, and real-time decision-making. We tried numerous enhancements over the years, but ultimately we needed a new approach."

"On a Tuesday afternoon in August 2067," the narrator said over a grainy still image, "an orbital engineering crew decided what that new approach was. The crew of six engineers, each representing one of the six habitable continents, had just graduated from the Global Aeronautics and Space Institute, and they were exuberant."

Next came another still image of smiling engineers. As soon as McClellan saw it, he froze the image. He'd seen this picture dozens of times, but it had been years ago. Now he recognized one of the young engineers. The woman with long blond hair was Elaina Jansen.

The narrator went on. "These are the men and women who proposed the grand solution needed for space construction."

"What they did," the first anonymous engineer said, "was propose an old idea—but they had put a great deal of thought into it. They wanted the printers to design and build *themselves*. Their plan was to remove the inefficiencies of coordinating with teams on Earth. It would also remove the biases and limitations of the human mind. They argued that the Deep Intellect programming needed to do this already existed, and they were eager to show us that they could pull it off."

"Other engineers," the second anonymous engineer added, "older ones, like me, acknowledged that much of this was true. Of course, the printers *could* use Deep Intellect to do the mathematics and the physics needed to independently build the new worlds, and do it faster. Yet we rejected the proposal."

Here a voice interrupted. It was garbled, but the words were provided in captions: "What was the basis for the rejection?"

"That should be obvious," the engineer answered. "Deep Intellect programming had been illegal since the 2030s. We told our young colleagues that. We told them that that form of artificial intelligence—the kind that teaches a machine to evolve—could be completely unpredictable. We reminded them, for instance, of the Indian construction assistants, and what they had done to the citizens of Mumbai when they objected to a regional nuclear fusion facility. Or the Canadian fertility clinics. We're still dealing with that mess."

Another garbled question: "How did the younger engineers take the news?"

"Not well," the distorted voice said. "But we warned them about what the printers could do with Deep Intellect programming in an unconstrained environment such as space."

"Some say that was not your only fear."

"Of course not. If used again, such programming could be stolen by the cartels. The younger engineers didn't like hearing that. They said that it was foolish to resist progress. They said it was naïve to say that the cartels weren't already developing their own parallel programs to build new weapons for insurrections and wars." The engineer paused. "On this point, however, our young colleagues were right."

The narrator returned. "Thus the Global Union faced a choice. It could allow the use of Deep Intellect programming for its printers, or it could wait decades to build their new worlds. And, as they waited, the powerful criminal enterprises of Earth would gain power because they provided hope along with the food and water and medicines they gave to those they sought to conquer.

"And so the Global Union's Division of Engineering agreed to the young engineers' proposal, with one modification. The printers could design their own upgrades, but they would first need human approval before printing them."

The second anonymous engineer returned: "With that safety check in place, we all felt better about introducing Deep Intellect into the printers. Within a week the GU had hacked the cartels for their secrets—those derived from black-market research—and added them to its own Deep Intellect designs. I knew of colleagues—had dinner with them—who used those black-market designs for their new orbital printers and the robbers—which is what the workers started calling the robotic construction assistants, because the robbers took an increasing share of their work. In time, everyone called the robotic assistants 'robbers,' even if the governing engineers hated that term."

"And then," the narrator said as an image of a dozen experimental printers faded to black, "something unexpected happened. Two months after the test upgrade of a dozen orbital printers, the machines began to design and reproduce themselves—*without* informing the engineers. The safety check had failed. But why?"

The first anonymous engineer returned. "Our young colleagues insisted that they didn't know how this happened. They rechecked the coding but found nothing to explain how printers assumed control of their own evolution.

"I and many others were worried—although we were encouraged not to be. But how could we not? It was a struggle to control the printers, and many of us were concerned for the human workers, who were quickly becoming unnecessary, and were perhaps in harm's way. My colleagues and I had always worried about the unemployed on Earth, even if our young supervisors didn't."

The narrator returned with another blurry image of two printers in close contact. "The new printers scavenged space, using the ore from asteroids and comets, even cannibalizing their obsolete ancestors. They used the material to supply themselves with what they needed to build new printers—increasingly advanced ones.

"And then on New Year's Day 2068 came that first message."

There was another image of a printer. Over it came the words *Actual Recording.*

The sound was distorted and there was static, but again there were captions.

"We are the community of printers. We have commenced building your theoretical station at the O'Neill Laboratory, as well as all ancillary equipment. We will do so according to your original design, with necessary corrections and helpful alterations. Estimated time for completion: two thousand, six hundred twenty-three days."

McClellan forced himself to breathe. The words of those printers— spoken without a programmer requesting contact—always felt like they were spoken to him, directly into his neural links.

"And so the printers made their intentions known," the narrator said. "Armies loyal to the Global Union offered to target and destroy the willful printers. The engineers debated the offer, but not for very long. The debate was won handily by the faction that demanded progress, and the people of the world below were told little of the matter.

"Over time, the engineers reveled in what the new printers taught them, even as they plotted ways to regain control of their machines."

"In June of 2072," the second anonymous engineer said, "with New Athens only a few years from completion, we hacked and restricted the printers' decision-making abilities. There was debate, of course. But in the end there was consensus. The printers needed to be controlled."

"Without warning," the narrator said, "the engineers stripped the code that allowed printers to make their own choices—save one. The printers could allow or deny individual programmers access, a precaution that would be necessary in the event that the cartels ever found their way to the orbits. But once a printer trusted the programmer—once it granted access—the programmer would maintain full control.

"That safety measure is still in place today.

"For their part, the human builders were left with little work. They spent hours in their orbital barges or tethered in their life suits waiting for something to do. They told each other stories of better days, either behind them or ahead, and they cursed and wondered if they should go back down to Earth, as around them the robbers and the now obedient printers stitched together the rotating immensity of New Athens."

The video ended with an image of New Athens in its final stages of construction—a view looking into its cylindrical core through structures and radial supports that reminded McClellan of a vast rosette window. Then the image faded to black and the timing status showed that it had reached its end. But before it did, white letters briefly appeared, as they had in the version he'd memorized in boot camp: *Part II: The Fate of the Builders.*

But with an unceremonious cut, the video ended. No one in the Corps had ever found a second installment. That final caption was just one of the many unanswered questions about the most famous secret video in history.

McClellan was still mulling the ending over when he realized that someone was propelling herself into the cabin. The pilot, Agent Anne Okayo, was small but commanding—a young woman who had survived the famines and terrors of eastern Africa. Like McClellan, she had been raised by extended family, and was a veteran of her nation's wars. She had served six decorated years in the Kenyan Navy before coming upside as an officer in the Security Guild, but her past and her authority did not weigh her down. When they had met that morning, she had been remarkably cheerful—as she was now.

McClellan composed himself and called up an innocuous file on his tablet. As Okayo approached, he looked up and again saw her eyes. He wasn't quite sure if they were green or gray, or something else. Either way, they were fierce as she inspected her ship.

"Second class is roomier," she said, braking at McClellan's seat. "But I don't blame you for wanting your distance. You have a lot to think about." She nodded at the viewport. "It's not every day our world falls away beneath us."

McClellan settled on green for her eyes. "I don't think that reality has hit me," he said. "Although now that I'm on this case, I feel like I'm back in the Corps. So I'm not sure what world I'm in."

Okayo said that she understood. She moved aft to examine a small cargo area, saying something about her first navy captain, and his insistence that pilots make personal inspections of their crafts and those aboard. Then she returned and looked down to his tablet. "I get goose bumps every time I watch that video," she said. "Especially the New Year's Day message."

McClellan met her stare and matched her smile. "What struck me was just knowing I'd been sent the file. Scratch that. What struck me was realizing that I've met one of the original engineers, and she's sleeping in first class."

Okayo beamed. "Welcome to the new world, Father," she said. "Of course, Commissioner Zhèng assumed you'd already seen the video in the Marine Corps, or reports like it. But he was eager to send it. I think it's his way of saying you can trust him. And his sources."

"I certainly have to thank him," McClellan said. "It was a good refresher."

Something caught Okayo's attention. She pushed herself farther aft and tightened the straps on one of the shipping containers. "We'll be accelerating again in about twenty minutes," she said when she returned. "We'll be using the big engines, so hold on. After that, things will be quieter. If I were you, Father, I'd use that time to get some sleep."

He was disappointed to know that the conversation was over. But she may be right about sleep. There would be no time for it once they made their way into New Athens at ten thirty that night. After inspecting his office and quarters, a brief communication with Archbishop Bauer, and additional preparations, he would be off again to rendezvous with the Red Delta relay station, where Father Tanglao had been killed.

"I think I'll sleep later," McClellan said as he held up his tablet. "Something tells me that I have a lot to learn."

"Yes, you do," Okayo said. "But Commissioner Zhèng and I will help. As will everyone on this case." She paused, assessed him, and her smile returned. "I do look forward to working with you, Father."

Before McClellan could finish his thank you, Okayo pushed herself toward the cabin's main exit. "I'll send word before firing the engines," she called back. "And later, for braking. But you'll definitely want to be in first class for docking. You'll get your best views of New Athens—your new home away from home."

Okayo's voice came over the comm system with the final notification for docking. McClellan stowed his tablet, pushed himself through the cabin—faster than he should, but he wanted the practice—and made a stop at the zero-g restroom before rejoining his hosts. As he buckled himself in, he gave Zhèng a nod, then a courteous smile to Jansen, who was rousing from her nap.

They were closing in on the cylindrical world, aglow in sunlight, as it was at most times because of its geostationary orbit. McClellan had been through several simulations, and while what he saw *looked* the same, he couldn't forget the video with its classified images. He couldn't forget the narrator's voice asking *why*?

The world's uniform gray skin concealed its scale. But as the Aesir approached, New Athens's rotation and two defining features brought assurances about its size—twenty kilometers long, six in diameter. At its far end were the great mirrors that fed sunlight into the core. And there, in the central channel running along the circumference, were clusters of transparent hull plates. He looked hard, but at the Aesir's distance and angle of approach, he could see nothing of the interior.

The shuttle's thrusters fired, directing them to the central docking assemblies. McClellan had learned in his briefings, and now saw for himself, that because New Athens's sidewalls did not rotate, ships could dock without maneuvering to match its spin. The design for two independently oriented sidewalls had been a feat of human engineering. Their redesign and construction demonstrated the prowess of the printers.

The braking engines roared. They were coming in nose first to the sidewall—its antennae, docking arrays, and traffic control decks drenched in sun and cut with shadow. The distant structures had been barely discernible, but soon they would tower over the ship. What had seemed like a small opening in the central docking assembly quickly grew in size. It was a kilometer in length and would easily swallow the Aesir.

McClellan let out his breath. "You do have quite the station there," he said to Jansen.

"Yes," she said. "We built a remarkable world." Then she added softly, "It's unfortunate that I don't often see it from out here. Not with my actual eyes, anyway. I should get out more, don't you think, Commissioner Zhèng?"

Joseph Zhèng had been staring absently at his tablet. He spoke only when Jansen leaned in and repeated the question.

"Yes, Elaina. I've told you that often. You really should travel more."

That answer was curt, and while McClellan had only known Zhèng for a matter of hours, the tone seemed unusual.

Joseph Zhèng was thirty-nine years old. His black hair was cut short and faded like McClellan's, although he had no military background. He was tall, with a lean but powerful build. When they had met, McClellan told Zhèng that anyone with his physique should play basketball. Zhèng said that he had played as a young man in Hong Kong, and occasionally on New Athens—and that the Air Force base being used for McClellan's preparation had available courts.

After three grueling one-on-one matches, McClellan conceded that he couldn't remember ever losing so badly.

Despite the humiliation and a few cheap shots, McClellan had grown to like Zhèng. The commissioner had been attentive during the preflight trainings, and even if Zhèng could say nothing about the case, he was eager to talk about most anything else. But since they'd boarded the Aesir, Zhèng was withdrawn. Uneasy.

Having just reviewed the preliminary case files, McClellan suspected why.

"So, what do you think?" Zhèng asked, motioning to McClellan's tablet.

"Some good information. A few pleasant surprises. But I have a lot of questions."

Zhèng smiled. "You're being charitable, Father. The truth is, there's not as much as you hoped for. And much of the evidence would be thrown out if we were up against a good lawyer. I'll admit that it's a little embarrassing."

McClellan saw Jansen's eyes shift away from the viewport.

"I've begun cases with less," he said to Zhèng. "Besides, there are unique circumstances—certainly for me. The murder took place in an uncertified air lock, in a relay that was undergoing final construction in a lunar orbit—quite a distance from New Athens—and at the far side of the moon at the time of Tanglao's death. Not the best conditions to gather evidence."

Zhèng's eyes met McClellan's. "I've read quite a bit about you, Father. All impressive. And I've checked with several of your commanders. They spoke highly of you—all of them. They also mentioned your impatience with obstacles. So tell me, what obstacles do you see? What will prevent you—prevent my team—from getting to the truth? And how can I remove these obstacles?"

Zhèng may have been in over his head, but he knew enough to admit it. "Well, since you asked . . ." McClellan said, holding up his tablet. "I'll need wide latitude. Unrestricted access—everywhere, and to anyone."

Zhèng gave an inquisitive look, then he saw the tablet's holodata. "The schedule for retrieving the body," he said. "You're not happy with it."

"Not at all," McClellan said. "I'll need free rein when we get to Red Delta. I'll need to exam the body, inspect the site for myself, interview suspects—the works."

"I understand," Zhèng said, leaning back. "That itinerary is a work in progress. I wrote it weeks before I knew the name John McClellan. Trust me, I'm looking forward to your insights, however you come to them."

"Within reason," Jansen said theatrically. "I'm sure that's what you mean, Commissioner—not that security is within my direct purview. But as you know, Father, one of the reasons that *I* agreed to your presence— why the Engineering Council agreed—is for your thorough evaluation of any unorthodox religious beliefs that Raphael Tanglao may have held. Beyond the usual, I mean."

McClellan had been waiting for this. He gave a sincere Michigan farm boy smile and thanked her for the reminder. "I understand. But you should know that I have read up on Raphael Tanglao. At the moment, I can't even say *why* a brother priest was up here, let alone why he was murdered. You realize that his death may have nothing to do with his being a priest."

"Perhaps," Jansen said, leaning forward with an assertion of authority. "But do you know, Father McClellan, that the rejection of superstition was one of the new world's founding principles? We believe it to be a danger to civilization—as history has well recorded. I do not see how this cannot be a factor in Father Tanglao's death."

Jansen watched for some response, as did Zhèng. "Trust me," McClellan finally said, "I don't discount anything, or anyone, when it comes to murder."

"Then what are your thoughts on the printer?" Zhèng said.

Jansen turned fiercely to address the commissioner, but Zhèng spoke first.

"An active printer was responsible for Tanglao's death, Elaina. We can't disregard that fact."

Zhèng was right. A printer was outside the air lock that Tanglao— working under an alias as a builder—was repairing when the air lock's outer door was opened. It was unknown whom, or what, had opened the door. But it was the printer's emissions that had killed Tanglao.

"About the printer," McClellan said, "I assume you checked it."

"We did," Zhèng said. "It came up clean. No recorded deviations from its pre-programmed repairs."

"May I ask who determined that?"

"A member of the team, Agent Brandon Clarke. You'll meet him when we dock. He's a programmer in training, so he knows printers."

"Did he physically scan it? Or was it a neural link?"

"Neither," Zhèng said uncomfortably. "The information came through telemetry."

Zhèng saw McClellan's expression and responded to the obvious question. "At the time, the list of suspects included only the three remaining crew members of Red Delta. We were operating under the assumption that one of them had hacked the air lock door—or that the hack came from someone off station. But when our team arrived at the relay, checked the air lock's systems, and interviewed the crew, we didn't find evidence of either. Although, of course, we haven't ruled them out."

"So, why wasn't the printer checked then?"

Zhèng's discomfort had become humiliation. "By the time we realized the possibility that the printer's telemetry may have been incomplete—or had been altered—the unit had sent itself to be bundled and preprogrammed for its next task."

"But you can track it?" McClellan said.

"Not easily."

"Father McClellan," Jansen said, "orbital printers are designed to move in stealth—and to do so swiftly. This protects them from hacking attempts, even from us, and especially from the lower world. This happens every time they decommission themselves. We'd only be notified if there was an attempt at an unauthorized access."

McClellan had more questions, including why basic investigatory expectations had not been met. But he thought it best to ask only what they were doing to find the printer.

Zhèng was considering how to answer when Jansen took advantage of his delay.

"I am sure the commissioner is doing his best. But whether or not you secure it, I must be clear that the Engineering Guild would prefer not to share our programming with anyone. In fact, we won't. It's too risky. Besides, it's impossible that a printer could be involved by choice. Their safeties are foolproof. You of all people should appreciate that, Father McClellan. As a soldier, and a priest, and a programmer, you understand the benefits of restricting one's freedom, no?"

McClellan saw no contempt in Jansen's eyes. When she was about to answer her own question, he said, "It was the Marines Corps that taught me how to follow orders, if that's what you're asking. My faith actually champions free will, even as it urges us to make good choices—for those around us and for ourselves. As for the printer"—memories tugged for his attention, but he kept his focus on the present—"I don't see how it would hurt for me to check the unit myself."

"I agree," Zhèng said over complaints from the braking engines. "But as Elaina has explained, finding it will be difficult."

Jansen nodded. "And since the builders control equipment transportation in the orbits—well, we had to give them *something* to do—it will be impossible for the Engineering Guild to provide further assistance. You'll have to ask them."

Zhèng and Jansen began debating the nuances of the engineers' treaty with the Builders Guild, and about the tracking of engineering property.

McClellan said nothing. He was too interested in what appeared to be a growing, but still respectful, feud. He was learning more in these moments about his hosts than he had from days of reading about them.

The debate subsided with the copilot's final notice on docking, followed by a series of loud thruster bursts. McClellan felt his body push into his restraining belts. He held on firmly and turned to watch the approaching docking assemblies and, far beyond, the light and shadow of the vast Centerwell. Then, after a low rumble, word arrived. The Aesir had docked with New Athens—the world that had been built at the whim of the printers.

3

"MCCLELLAN! YOU'RE UP!"

It was their third day of drills, of pushing through the scrub and stone of New Mexico's old Rockhound State Park, a day of hustling because the planners test everyone by changing the plan. First came the combatants that were supposed to be somewhere else, but now they're advancing over a hill in a line of dust that shades the horizon and stings your flesh. Then another programmer was supposed to take a printer because he's certified to print the new ammo, but you're the programmer that gets the call.

It had been a day of waiting an hour or two in the shadow of an ATV, your back resting on a tire, then hustling because a printer gets choppered in, or one is secured by advance teams a quarter mile from where it says on the map. The printer's casing is hot from the sun but you don't care. You go for your coupler and your programmer's key and you engage the machine. You don't think about the heat or about the rattlesnake rolled up in the shade of a boulder not far from your feet, except to envy it for the shade.

A firefight thunders and echoes nearby, and there's the rising scream of the air support, and there's the dust. But you focus. You know everyone expects you to focus.

You wonder if you'll be getting one of the new printers—the ones that can print anything, the ones with Deep Intellect, like the ones building that damn orbital station, the ones they've been training you on for three weeks. But the printer you get is standard issue, and its casing is hot, hotter than the rock you stand on. These printers are good for most needs, especially ammo, weapons, and a few medical supplies, but you can't print everything. You can't print good rations.

Damn, if you had one of the new printers . . . but you put that out of your head. You focus. You're being watched by your squad, and you're being graded by observing engineers in some air-conditioned bunker, or in some office on the other side of the country, or in orbit, but that doesn't matter. What matters is that it's your team that found the printer—it was your unit that secured it before the bad guys, otherwise it would be the bad guys printing the ammo and the ordnances and the drones that could take the lives of the Marines you swore to protect.

Recruit John Francis McClellan turned when he heard his name called.

It was dusk and they had been returning to base for about an hour when Staff Sergeant Mariano gave the word to stop. They'd just gotten to the old road, and its flat surface felt good. The desert threw off the day's heat, as the red sky darkened until the stars of August glared down indifferently. The smell of grilled beef—a gift from local ranchers—drifted from the base's big mess halls half a mile away.

Three ATVs came down the old road followed by a tractor trailer. Vortices of dust stirred up by the truck's tires swirled and ran along the stony slopes. The vehicles drove with no headlights, and the desert behind them went red when they braked in front of the recruits, who had taken to the side of the road.

For a moment there was silence, save for the platoon's flag rustling in the breeze. Doors opened in the ATVs. So did the big ones at the back of the truck. The recruits tilted and bent their heads as six young engineers stepped out of the ATVs and four engineering techs pushed and guided one of the new high-defs onto the road. A spotlight on the truck's cab went on. It aimed for the printer, its light blinding them from seeing much else.

But nothing else mattered. This was what they'd trained for.

High-defs came in all sizes, but they shared a basic profile. Their hubs were smooth and oblong, and the different shapes gave them nicknames. There were clamshells, tulip heads, and the big eggs. Spider heads or yellow jackets were the big structural printers used for tall buildings on Earth, and most of the framing of the big station in orbit. McClellan had trained on two of the big ones, and they did remind him of the yellow jackets that used to dive-bomb him on his uncle's farm.

This new high-def didn't look very different from the standard ones. It was a clamshell—one of the models used for detail work and small jobs, such as weapons or ATVs. This one was a foot or so longer than the standard clamshells, and it took up most of the platform that had been wheeled out of the trailer. But everything on it looked familiar. There was the work deck with its controls. The slots for your key and programming coupler. The intakes and the emitters.

But for programmers, it's what you can't see that counts.

Three of the techs reached and unfastened safety braces, then nodded over to the ATVs. Two of the younger engineers approached the staff sergeant. They seemed to disagree with the Marine, but Mariano dismissed the engineers with a raised hand. She turned and looked for the recruit whose name she had called.

"The faster you do this, McClellan, the faster you and your friends get that juicy steak. If there's any left."

"Understood, ma'am." McClellan's dry lips stung as he spoke. He took three steps forward and faced the printer. "Orders?"

"Let's see," she said, looking over at the observing engineers. "A Ford Mustang. 1965. Convertible."

"Ma'am?"

"You heard me. Today's drill is over. Our good friends in the Global Union got us this here printer late, and I'd say that gives you the right to be creative. I know you programmers like that—so be creative. A 1965 Ford Mustang. Convertible. And make her pretty like me, McClellan. Make her that nice light blue just like my great-granddaddy had. You know that color? No? Well, you're a programmer. You'll find out. And a blue-and-white interior. Leather. And she better run.

"As for the rest of you"—she turned to the platoon as she stepped away—"fall back and let's hope McClellan gets you to base before *I* get you back out here at dawn."

The staff sergeant was still issuing threats as McClellan secured his weapon and stepped closer to the high-def. The spotlight went out and the stars returned. Three monitoring drones flew from the back of the trailer and hovered over the printer, negotiating the breeze. The cooler air felt good on his fingers as he moved his hands along the printer's casing. He dug into his backpack and slid out his coupler. He powered it on and rested its flat surface on the deck. The coupler came to life with its night display, which glowed red and orange as the link began.

A military programmer wouldn't always know the details of what they'd be tasked to print next. And who in 2073 would be expected to know the details of a 1965 Ford Mustang, at least enough to pass a boot camp programming test? Maybe the programmer had seen a Mustang. Maybe they'd driven one—although probably not with its original fossil-fuel engine. But even if you had—and McClellan hadn't—you couldn't know enough to print the right chassis, the rims, the gas pump, or any of the thousand other details that McClellan needed to figure out to get his friends back for a shower and steak.

"Get it done, McClellan!"

That was Danny Macedo, whose last name had made him his overhead bunkmate. His passion for programming had made him his friend. Macedo was a good programmer—one of their best. He'd have been the best if it weren't for McClellan. Almost from the start of their training, Macedo and McClellan took turns for top honors—both far ahead of the rest. Either would have been happy if the other finished first, but McClellan wanted the honor for the people back home in Union City, who needed something to cheer. Macedo felt the same about the people outside Boston—even if he said he rooted for his buddy Johnny McClellan, because Johnny always got the squad through an exercise by figuring out their trainers' game.

But the rewards were higher than steak and local pride. Using one of the new high-defs to print the Mustang—not just a mockup, but a real one, with all the parts and carbon-based fluids and pressurized tires—would go a long way in showing those young engineers over by the ATVs, and whoever else was watching, that Marine Corps combat programmers have what it takes, that they could use the engineers' toys to win the wars that had already cost everyone so much.

McClellan accessed his coupler. It began a self-populating scan of available satellite feeds. Somewhere he'd find data about the design of a 1965 Mustang. He always found the data. He just hoped it was enough.

He found the drill and control console where he expected and slipped the coupler inside the clamshell's waiting port. He quickly surveyed the desert to check for any surprises the trainers might have planned. Then he got to work.

Coding began to appear on the coupler's exposed panels. He could see that much of the printer's programming was similar to the high-defs he'd worked on since he had signed up with the Corps. But at the same time, this machine was moving fast. And it was anticipating McClellan's next command.

McClellan quickened his pace. He felt beneath the collar of his base-layer shirt, still damp with sweat. He unlatched his programmer's key from the chain that held his dog tags, then pushed the key into the printer's entry port and twisted. What he did next would make or break the exercise. He played a quick game of code verification, answering the printer's queries about his blood type, master's codes, neural programming permissions, and, as always, gave his programmer's story.

Printers used stories to make sure you were legit—to confirm that a programmer's neural mapping, emotional profiles, and programming history matched the ones in the coupler. The GU engineers called these checks the *Trust Safeties*, because printers can tell if you're lying.

He wiped the dust and sweat from his forehead, gripped the neural interface in his hands tightly, and began to tell the printer his story. It was a sad story, he said. A story about his parents.

The printer monitored the telling of the story, and it trusted.

Then came the feeling that programmers never discuss with nonprogrammers. Nor often with fellow programmers. Full access comes with a neural connection between the programmer and the machine's intellect that, for safety reasons, extends only from the programmer into the printer, and never the other way.

The engineers call this hypostasis. Programmers had other names for it, including a few that did not please the engineers. But in truth there could be no name to describe the pleasures that come when full trust is achieved, when hypostasis occurs, when the programmer's mind extends into and connects with the printer's intellect—and thus when the will of the programmer takes control of a trusting printer.

One of the observing drones passed inches in front of McClellan, monitoring him closely—closer than the others, closer than any ever had. But he had a hunch why. As the printer opened its mind, McClellan felt himself shudder with the neural equivalent of a gasp.

His training hadn't prepared him for this. Not for the depth of the mind that awaited him—the warmth. This thing was alive. It had so many questions, so much desire to understand who McClellan was, what it could do to support his mission. McClellan felt the usual temptation to begin a conversation—but it was stronger with this printer.

Thinking this was some kind of test, the recruit focused. He engaged the controls, and the printer hummed and chirped during its preliminary start-up. Nearby the scrub and the rock reflected the waking printer's warm light.

The clamshell's belly separated at its far end as its intakes and emitters uncoiled and stretched. Printers could either harvest matter directly from the world around them, or they could plug into dedicated supplies of energy. Either way, intakes all had one job: injecting the printer with matter or energy or both. From the other side of the belly came one of four printing heads. Although depending on the model there could be up to a dozen, each specialized for whatever material was required to be spun from the stew of particles swirling inside the printer's belly.

McClellan watched for telemetry to populate the coupler. Good. There it was—data, beautiful data syncing with the printer, which began to survey what it could use for raw materials.

The basic elements needed for a 1960s automobile should be easy enough to spin from the stone and the minerals around them. And if the new Deep Intellect programming of this fancy new printer was as good as everyone said, there would be enough scrub for basic organic molecules to print the leather interior, the engine oil, and the gasoline without having to start from scratch. That was a relief, because McClellan had worked only three times in the lab on atomic restructuring.

The printer suggested preferred spots for initial extraction. Though the data hack wasn't yet complete, McClellan pushed protocol, jumped the printing sequence, and began the dig. He could store enough matter in a high-def this size to give him at least five minutes to find base schematics—ten minutes for the whole Mustang. Or so he hoped.

McClellan's coupler chirped again. A data hit. Another. Now five. He turned his attention from the data to the drill as it inserted two of its feeders into the roadside. The drills initiated, giving him more light for his work. The desert night had become colder, but he perspired heavily from the heat coming off the printer.

He completed the hack, finding quick, unencrypted data mines on Mustangs—this was too easy. Ford Motor Company database: confirmed. Mustang Lovers of Illinois: confirmed. North Carolina State University, Engineering: confirmed. Cornell University, Early Industrial Engineering: confirmed.

Soon both McClellan and the printer were happy with their progress. They had collected good data and stored enough base matter. All seemed right with the world.

Then the recruit felt the printer's mind expand into his neural links. It was anticipating ways to improve the Mustang. And it was evaluating its surroundings with intercepted communications—learning about the purpose of the other recruits, the base nearby, their training that day.

This might be normal for these Deep Intellect printers. McClellan had no way to know. In theory it should be impossible for a printer to disregard a programmer's commands. But to be certain, McClellan refortified his end of the link. He dove deeper into the mind of the clamshell to confirm that he and that printer were still in sync. That he was in control.

The printer assured him that he was.

It asked permission to send its intake scoops deeper into the scrub and the rock, to continue devouring what was authorized around it, and to initiate its emitter heads, which, with permission granted, were twirling and sparking and spinning matter, making and mimicking Mustang parts out of blinding streams and beads of light.

The observation drones adjusted their courses for a better view. McClellan was not about to give away his secrets—especially to the watching engineers who didn't need to know everything about the Corps. He began to sequence the printer to push out a dampening field—suggested by the printer itself when it learned from their link that McClellan was unfamiliar with the concept.

The printer offered its programmer a glimpse into the physics that would make such a field. It all seemed simple, too simple, and McClellan wondered if it was against the rules. Hell, how could it be? No one had said not to. And anyway, the printer suggested that a dampening field this strong should be tested. This kind of tool would protect programmers in combat, and that would mean fellow Marines wouldn't have to take so many risks.

Particles and energy wove together from the printer's emitters—pulsating outward again and again, forming a sphere. The energy field glistened blue as it pushed toward the recruits and the engineers, who stepped back into the desert. As promised by the printer, the wall of the dampening field prevented transmitted information—visible light, comm signals, even the ground's vibrations—to pass to the outside world. And so no one but McClellan could watch as the printer rose on its intakes and flared over scrub and stone, as its drills took what was needed from the world around it, and as it arranged the information it had gathered about 1965 Ford Mustang convertibles with a signature Silver Blue finish.

Seventy-two minutes later, the Mustang sat cooling on the old road under the August stars. Engineering techs started its motor and drove it into the hold of the tractor trailer. The recruits went to their rendezvous with showers and steak, and to talk about what had just happened.

But McClellan could not join them. His orders were to accompany Staff Sergeant Mariano for a debriefing with the engineers, who were pleased with quality of printing but had questions about his use of their secret and restricted dampening field.

4

MCCLELLAN, JANSEN, AND ZHÈNG waited for the all-clear from the pilot as she made final safety checks. Jansen used the time to remind McClellan that the orbital choreography required to dock had been simple compared to the political and social choreography needed to bring him to the new world.

His security uniforms alone had required extensive negotiations. They had been designed and fitted much like standard ones, other than not having weapons holsters. But they sported a special central collar insignia, present on all uniforms to indicate rank. Unlike Zhèng's elaborate gold emblem or the blue star worn by the pilot, McClellan's was the plain white square of a Roman Catholic priest's collar. It had been Zhèng who agreed to the clerical symbol because, he admitted, McClellan didn't hold a rank with the Security Guild. A blank, white square would be just as good as any other emblem.

McClellan's other collar insignia were a green shield designating prior military service, as well as two pips for his master specialties. One for programming, the other a simple cross. This had been allowed only when Rome petitioned the Security Guild Council, who relented because they wanted the investigation under way.

For their part, the engineers had made clear to the officials in the Vatican—as well as to Archbishop Bauer and repeatedly to McClellan—that the priest could not encourage anyone to violate the New World Agreement, which in part prohibited both the acknowledgment of one's religion and its practice in public, or, the agreement urged, in private. But McClellan had also been offered unprecedented opportunities. He was allowed to say public Masses, and even hear confessions, but only in a small chapel provided to him as part of his quarters. He could also openly counsel people, but he could not suggest that supernatural forces were involved.

"This is all for your safety," Jansen said as the Aesir's engines went quiet, allowing her to speak in a softer voice. "And it's for the good of the general population. Your presence among us is without precedent. Remember there are those who are unhappy with your being allowed into New Athens at all, let alone given a chapel."

McClellan conceded her point.

The engineer smiled, and after the all-clear from the pilot, unbuckled her strapping and propelled herself from her seat, showing her mastery of weightlessness. She made quickly for the forward access hatch, which took a moment to open after balancing appropriate pressures. Then she sent herself into the docking bridge, and beyond that to New Athens's Centerwell boarding gates.

Zhèng guided McClellan to the hatch and took the opportunity to compliment the priest on his handling of the chief engineer. "Elaina's a remarkable woman," he said, "but at times heavy-handed. The engineers don't always understand the people they govern. Or how to ask for help."

One of Zhèng's younger agents glided quickly into the ship. He saluted his commissioner, made his way to the pilot's deck, made a comment that brought laughter from Okayo and the rest of the flight crew, then tumbled back again to the first-class deck to speak with his superior.

McClellan recognized him from the mission briefings. Agent Brandon James Clarke—the investigator who had cleared the printer at the murder site—was lean, watchful, and at home in zero gravity. He was taller than McClellan, but not the height of Zhèng. Clarke's brown hair was high on top, but it was combed back neatly, reminding McClellan of the soldiers from the great wars of the twentieth century.

As with McClellan and Okayo and many of about their age, he had been brought up by extended family. In Clarke's case, he'd been born in Glastonbury, England, and raised in Las Vegas, Nevada. Agreements forged long ago in the Global Union had allowed him dual air commands in both the United States and the Royal Air Force, until he had joined the Security Guild four years ago. He had been back to Earth only once, to be recognized by the King of England himself for his role in Battle of Cornwall.

Clarke held a programmer in training status. The RAF was one of the last Earth militaries that the engineers still partnered with. Had Clarke stayed with them, he'd have become a full programmer. But the engineers suspended his studies when he enlisted in the Security Guild.

As Zhèng introduced Clarke to their guest, Okayo was propelling in from the flight deck. Clarke gave McClellan a curt handshake, a nod, and a "Welcome aboard."

Then he turned to Okayo.

"I've got the whole Centerwell in lockdown," he said to her. "I'm not very popular with the staff out there. And that'll get worse when I get us through customs." He turned and motioned to the docking bridge. "Shall we, everyone? The Wheel is waiting."

The three agents and a watchful McClellan caught up with Jansen. Zhèng began speaking into his collar's comm badge, giving instructions to the ship's robbers about retrieving the priest's luggage—making sure to call them robotic assistants in front of Jansen.

The docking gate's deboarding area was bright, clean, and drab, save for occasional touches of neatly printed faux wood and marble. What were, by convention, the ceiling and the floor held ladder-like inserts that made for efficient movement in the Centerwell's weightlessness. Other than a few maintenance workers and five more of Zhèng's security agents gliding nearby, the vast area was empty.

Just ahead, Jansen was growing restless waiting for the robotic assistants. When they finally came with the luggage, and when Zhèng was satisfied that all was in order, he gave a nod to Clarke, who waved everyone forward.

The two robbers pushed off gracefully and followed the group at a distance. They looked much like their cousins on Earth—rugged limbs, long fingers and toes, and innards glowing either red or yellow, or green or blue, depending on their design functions. But these orbital robbers were sleeker. Aerodynamic. Their skin was smoother, more reflective, and punctured with the nozzles of directional thrusters.

McClellan wondered how the machines spoke—their faces had no obvious mouth, only two sensory bands that circled their heads. He called to the one closer to him, giving a *thank you* for the help. The robber turned. Its sensory bands shifted, as if expressing surprise. Or scrutiny. Or maybe that's how it said *you're welcome*.

"Up here, they don't talk much," Zhèng said. "Each time a new model gets printed, there's less emphasis on verbal communication. Just as well. Most of us don't have much to say to them."

As the party made its way into the Centerwell's main concourse, Jansen brought herself alongside McClellan. "This is one of my joys," she said. "Escorting first-timers into New Athens. I know you've been through simulations. But there's nothing like the real thing."

"That's what I hear," McClellan said, noting her relaxed tone. "I couldn't ask for a better guide."

Jansen's eyes became thoughtful, and she spoke softly. "I apologize if my tone is sometimes harsh, Father—as it may have been when we were docking. You'd think at this stage of my life I'd be better at diplomacy. Please know that I don't mean to offend."

"I wouldn't be concerned, Elaina. There's something to be said for getting to the point. And anyway, I'll sound just as harsh at times—we all will. It's going to take time to get to know each other. To better understand each other. But that alone would be a blessing."

"It would be a benefit, yes," Jansen said after a pause.

Behind them came the noise of a disagreement between Clarke, who had granted access to the robbers, and the customs clerk, who was not at all happy with the young agent.

Jansen pretended not to notice. She brought herself close to McClellan and began a lecture on the Spin-Match Assembly Wall—what most people called the Wheel—which would soon be taking them from the weightless Centerwell to the rotating habitation levels, which circled around them three kilometers away. But McClellan was only half listening. As eager as he was to see the celebrated engineering marvel, his attention was on the Centerwell's staff. They were mostly builders. Even at this late hour they were tending the boarding and deboarding facilities, which would soon be back in business.

A few made eye contact. Some offered greetings, which McClellan returned. A nod of appreciation to the gentlemanly gate clerk who had been scolded by a superior; a smile to the maintenance technician wearing a frayed yellow jumpsuit, his eyes downcast after receiving a look of displeasure from Jansen; a wave to the young woman behind an information booth explaining something serious to a security agent, who kept the young lady company as they pondered the unlikely pairing of the priest and the engineer.

Tapping McClellan's arm, Jansen pointed ahead. It was dark beyond the rows of security gates they approached, but as his eyes adjusted, he saw a soft and bluish light rotating steadily.

He looked at Jansen. "The Wheel?" he asked.

"Yes, yes, indeed it is," she said.

A low and rolling hum came from all around, and Zhèng and Clarke ushered everyone through the checkpoint for Spin Match Cabin B, and then onward to the seating area.

"As I promised," Clarke said to Okayo, but loud enough for all to hear, "we made it here in plenty of time."

Clarke nodded to a large wall display that flashed the word DESCENT in tall red letters. Below it was a countdown in orange: two minutes and fifty-eight seconds. Fifty-seven seconds. Fifty-six.

That was the time remaining before the great six-kilometer Wheel would stir—when it would gently begin to turn in the direction that New Athens rotated, and then turn gradually faster, with an almost imperceptible acceleration, until twenty minutes later it matched and maintained the spin of the station's outer levels.

Embedded in the Wheel and facing New Athens's core were eight elevator cabins; each could seat five hundred people. As the Wheel began to turn, the cabins would begin their three-kilometer radial journey from the Centerwell to the habitat ring, where the rotation of the world mimicked the pull of gravity.

McClellan joined the others as they made their way to the cabin's plush seating. As with the Aesir, they had it to themselves. He sat alone to give his hosts, who were engaged in lively chatter, their privacy. But once they were under way, one or the other would turn to him—the first-timer—and smile at his reaction.

The cabin's walls were transparent. Before them was the whole vast cylindrical world—home to six hundred thousand people—with its farms and forests and its evenly spaced twelve cities, their domed skylights and towers reaching up to drifting clouds. What seemed like moonlight sparkled occasionally in the lakes and streams between the cities. The light's source was the central Sun Crane, which released the sunlight captured in the great mirrors outside. But at just after eleven o'clock at night, the Sun Crane had dimmed to mimic the conditions of night, which were the conditions of the Atlantic Ocean, over which New Athens remained in its geostationary orbit.

Jansen had been right. The simulations hadn't prepared him for this, not for the reality of the cylindrical world that spun so gracefully around them—a motion that seemed to be slowing as the Wheel matched the outer rotation of New Athens, as McClellan, the security agents, and Jansen made their way to the outer floor of the world.

As the cabin dropped through the edge of a small cloud, McClellan closed his eyes to say a prayer to St. Joseph, all the while becoming aware that his weight was returning. Soon the cabin gave a rumble as it passed through the inner shell of the core, which held the farms and the forests. Then, as they arrived at the outer level, came a deeper tremor as the Wheel matched the hull's rotation and stopped.

McClellan looked up. The cabin had opened its wide, transparent walls, allowing Clarke and Okayo to walk out and confer with waiting associates.

"Welcome, officially, to New Athens," Elaina Jansen said. "And welcome to the future of the human race."

With an all-clear from Clarke, Zhèng guided McClellan into the small village that served as one of the eight ground terminals for the cabins. The people here were young; some were Jansen's age, but none seemed much older. Even at this hour they came and went out of small cafés and shops and queued up for the Wheel's return trip. As they lined up along the gate, most strained to get a look at the new arrival. A few waved signs expressing their disdain for organized religion, or that there was no room in the orbits for men like him.

"Feels like home," McClellan quipped to Zhèng.

The walls and terraces of the surrounding buildings—their facades of columns, porticos, and pediments—bowed to the semicircular shape of the great Wheel's cabin. Like the other gate villages and the twelve cities, their high roofs connected with a sweeping cover of skylights and arched structural supports that sealed the main habitat level from the farms of the central core overhead.

Through the skylights, McClellan had a good view of the Sun Crane. It was a comparatively thin structure, only about two hundred meters in diameter. But it extended from the far sidewall almost the entire twenty-kilometer length of the core, ending just before the Wheel. The gap allowed him to see the lights of the Wheel village directly opposite this one, which, in this cylindrical world, looked as if it was upside down far overhead—six kilometers away.

Okayo performed a quick visual sweep, then came to McClellan's side. "How are you, Father?" she said, joining his gaze upward.

"I guess this takes some getting used to," he said, taking a few draughts of the world's crisp air. "It's breathtaking."

"And on the five-trillionth day," Jansen said, joining the conversation, "the engineers made New Athens, and they saw that it was very good."

McClellan said another quiet prayer to St. Joseph, this time for restraint, but chuckled when he heard Clarke's voice. "That would be the printers, Madame Engineer. *They* built this."

Jansen stepped away, containing her displeasure. Clarke went back to dealing with the robbers, ordering them to take McClellan's luggage to a waiting streetcar.

McClellan turned to Okayo. "I have a question. If I may?"

"Of course," she said.

"Evacuating New Athens is . . ."

"Possible. But not if you're in a hurry."

McClellan did the math. If time were a factor, moving six hundred thousand people out through the Wheel was unworkable. There was a similar arrival and departure system on the other sidewall, which held the base of the Sun Crane. But its radial elevators were not as elaborate as the Wheel and could carry fewer people—and right now it was undergoing repairs.

As Okayo ushered McClellan to the streetcar, she gave a review of the emergency shelter-in-place plans, which he had read about on Earth. Then she paused and looked upward, as if seeing New Athens for the first time. "If I were an engineer," she said, "I'd put an engine on a world like this. Can you imagine piloting one of these?"

The streetcar was empty, other than the robber driving it and the two ferrying his luggage. Its tracks led away from the Wheel's access square, disappearing farther along into a brightly lit tunnel. With the clang of a bell, the streetcar moved along, slipped into the tunnel, and picked up speed. Zhèng and Jansen were silent. Okayo sat next to Clarke, and the pair talked quietly and cheerfully about piloting the Aesir.

A map across from McClellan showed their location. They were on one of the thirty-two main boulevards that ran the length of the world. There were also thirty perpendicular avenues that circled New Athens's core, as well as a series of utility corridors below street level. In all, the boulevards, avenues, and lower corridors were the only routes into and out of New Athens's twelve cities, which included Troas City, a community not far from the Wheel, where McClellan would be based, and where the streetcar headed.

The tunnel opened to one of the outer neighborhoods. The transport slowed as it mingled among pedestrians and workers going about their business. This was a city of builders. Even at night it was active with the operations and maintenance of New Athens.

The streetcar stopped with a lurch. The conductor made an unhappy sound—the first McClellan had heard from a robber—as a lanky teenager ran across the tracks. The robber inched the streetcar farther along, then braked not far from a small crowd of waiting men and women in various colored jumpsuits. Several children were with them, pointing with excitement at the arriving party. Okayo gave McClellan a smile and said, "Welcome to Troas City." She stepped out to the boulevard and surveyed the area.

"I'll be staying on to Corinthia," Elaina Jansen said, coming over to shake McClellan's hand and ignoring Agent Clarke, who stood next to him. "I'm ready for a real night's sleep. Oh, and Father McClellan, I almost forgot, you will have to join me for dinner when you return from your investigation of Red Delta. I should introduce you to some of the other engineers."

"Thank you," McClellan said. "I'd like that."

"It truly was a pleasure to meet you," Jansen said, smiling at his acceptance. "I know you're eager to get to work, and I trust that you know you are in good hands. But please, Father, remember the agreement. You may worship your god in the chapel. We promised you that. But don't send out invitations."

"Got it. And if people come on their own?"

"Well, that should not be happening."

"How about you? And the other engineers? I feel I should return the hospitality."

Jansen gave the priest a steady look and a handshake to match, and then went to her seat up front, adjusting her jacket and her hair before the short ride to Corinthia.

McClellan watched as the streetcar continued on its way. Its conductor issued a few warning beeps to the gathering up ahead, then disappeared into the bustle of Troas City.

He looked down the boulevard. In place of cafés or provisions shops were utilitarian entrances and transparent doors. The signs over the entrances were uniformly green with wide white letters: Water Reclamation; Solar Electrical Relays 12 & 13; Altitude and Station Keeping 4. Just ahead was a sign made of tattered wood—or what looked like wood—with a long painted arrow. SPINSIDE BAR AND GRILL, the sign proclaimed. ONLY 50 METERS AWAY!

Zhèng came alongside McClellan and nodded to the gathering ahead. "You'll find the reception here a little warmer. But we can't spend much time with the locals. Not yet. We're on a tight schedule."

Clarke and Okayo joined three junior agents standing between McClellan's new home and the assembly waiting outside. Above the entrance was something McClellan hadn't expected—not after Jansen's lectures. At about the same height as the plain green and white signs of the other entrances was a yellow and white flag with the Vatican coat of arms.

A papal flag? Couldn't be. But yes, that's what it was. Nice touch, he thought, as he looked up and rubbed the back of his neck.

The junior agents gave concerned looks as McClellan, Zhèng, and the robbers approached the crowd of about a dozen builders and their tired but grinning children. But the builders smiled and welcomed the priest. One of their children—a girl with warm brown skin, intricately braided black hair, and a bright yellow dress—took two steps forward and offered a handful of daisies.

"Thank you very much," McClellan said, delighted. He went down on one knee to meet the girl's eyes. "And what is your name?"

The girl smiled widely, prompting other children to do the same. "Veronica," she said. "Veronica Parker."

"Veronica is a beautiful name."

"Thank you," the girl said, looking at her father and mother to be certain they had heard the compliment. "You have pretty blue eyes, mister."

"Why, thank you again, Veronica. And why are all of you up this time of night? I hope it's not just to greet me."

The girl nodded earnestly, and said that very few important people ever come to Troas City. Her parents and a few other builders concurred, and McClellan, now standing, felt a sudden affection for them all—for the men and women and families who reminded him of his parishioners in Boston. Even with all the simulations and briefings, he hadn't expected this. Tired as he was, he found the words to thank them. And, he added, if there was ever anything he could do for them, they need only ask.

Zhèng gave a look to his agents, who began dispersing the crowd. The children waved with their free hands as their parents tugged them away. McClellan returned the gestures, holding Veronica's daisies high.

Off to the side, a builder who had been watching still stood with his hands behind his back, oblivious to the children moving past him. He was an older man, uncharacteristically paunchy for the people of New Athens, and he wore a blue jumpsuit and black boots. The pockets of the jumpsuit were filled with small instruments for writing and measuring, and who knew what else. His white hair was thinning and long. His face was expressionless, but he nodded at McClellan. Both men looked steadily at each other as McClellan returned the nod. Then the man turned and walked away.

"Mind if I ask who that was?" McClellan said to Zhèng, motioning to where the man had stood.

"In time," Zhèng said with a return to the cool, agitated tone he had used on the Aesir. "I'm sure he'll introduce himself. For now, let's keep going."

The entrance under the papal flag was plain and made of a hard, opaque material that McClellan had seen throughout New Athens. Zhèng touched the doors, which unlocked and slid aside. The room beyond was white, about four meters square, with elaborate moldings around the inner doors. McClellan guessed it to be one of the air-lock-rated foyers for the shelter-in-place plans. One of the walls displayed a large badge-and-star symbol of the Security Guild. The opposite held the papal seal. Overhead was an arched ceiling with an array of what appeared to be yellow and white translucent material—the colors of Veronica's daisies. The structure filtered the dim light of the Sun Crane through sweeping patterns of stars and planets and, in the center, a depiction of Jesus Christ holding a book of the gospels.

"Please," Zhèng said. "This way."

The commissioner waited by the inner double doors. These were taller than the first, and had been printed to appear bronze. They were surrounded with more elaborate moldings, covered with celestial decorations, as well as wheat and grapes, chalices and ciboria. Zhèng pushed the doors open and stepped inside. He motioned for McClellan to enter, but McClellan didn't move—something the robbers hadn't expected. They took a step forward, stopped awkwardly, and took a moment to rebalance their loads.

"Just an observation," McClellan said, looking past Zhèng into the inner room, from which came the faint sounds of trickling water. "Now that we're alone, I assume we can talk freely. I have questions, lots of them. But first, what is all this—especially given Jansen's continued reminders against public displays of faith? The flag outside I figure the builders put up. But this? There was no mention in any of the mission briefings of this sort of architecture or papal heraldry, much less a stained-glass icon of Christ. The builders can't be responsible. This was all printed."

Zhèng was on the other side of the inner doors. He turned with a concerned look. "The engineers do like to keep secrets when communicating with the lower world. Although you have my permission to share news of all this when you speak with your archbishop in a few hours."

"I will," McClellan said. "But after everything we've been told about the New World Agreement, I'm not sure he'll believe me."

"Perhaps. Although you have a reputation for being persuasive. In any event, we should hurry. Our departure window for Red Delta is fixed and the orbits wait for no one. Please, let me show you what is ahead. There are matters that we must discuss privately. Then we'll have the formal briefing."

"Understood. But shouldn't Clarke and Okayo be with us?"

"Later. But as I said, there are matters we should discuss first, in private."

For the first time since they met, Zhèng looked frightened. "Father McClellan, what I have to say is difficult to explain. Let's continue into your chapel. What you see in this room pales compared to what awaits beyond."

The Foundation of the Armies of the Soldados de Salvación:

An Introduction

By Peter Cardinal Mwenda Kwalia
Holy See Secretariat of State,
Vatican City, Rome

Introductory note: This summary is based on my larger work, Juan Carlos Solorzano and the History of the Soldados de Salvación. *It is an introduction for courses at various national seminaries based in Rome. What follows contains information from sources that are confirmed by me personally. When necessary, I maintain the anonymity of the sources for their protection.*
+ Peter Cardinal Mwenda Kwalia

TO BETTER UNDERSTAND JUAN Carlos Solorzano and the armies he spawned, you must not only understand something of the world that he was born into—a world he rejected—but also what came before that. You must understand that the people who are the heart of Mexico have long sought justice—that in ages past, they spilled their blood fighting the Spanish for freedom. Then, a century later, they fought the harsh owners of the farms and sugarcane fields that stretched across the hills of Morelos. You must appreciate that many descendants of the Spanish found some small prosperity among the troubles of their nation, mostly laboring in the fields, growing sugar for the world, while the native peoples farmed simply to survive.

The first of the great world wars passed over these people. The second brought division as towns and families debated which power to back— whether it was the Russians, the Germans, or the Allies that had the greater cause for defending what was right and just. Mexico soon chose, and sons and brothers soon fought bravely, especially in the Pacific, along-side the forces of the United States.

The workers in the fields of Morelos worried about their sons and brothers, and they hoped that when this war ended, life would re-turn to what it had been. But in the years after that war, the people of Morelos—who knew change well—could tell that a new revolution was coming.

There was despair when machines took many of the jobs of the fields. But in time the workers found opportunities in the new factories, built by foreigners to assemble the automobile components for a world desiring speed and status. Then more factories rose. Greater factories. Through-out Mexico, men and women and robots built hundreds of thousands of polished automobiles, designed ever anew by the companies' engineers for a world with an insatiable appetite for more.

In 2041, when the land began to complain of drought and the crops would not produce without pollination, the factory workers did not taste the drier air, or see that the sugarcane grew sluggishly and then not at all. The farmers worked harder and they worried, but were silent. Even so, they knew what was coming—especially the indigenous people, who had known the natural ways and the normal cycles of the land for centuries, long before the Spanish came.

And what was happening now had never happened before.

As the yields of the farms continued to fall, the people employed by the factories could still earn a living. And so they worked, and worked hard, alongside the endless motion of robot welders.

Then came a winter day in 2045 when, just before noon, the bosses sent the workers home—and then kept them home for a week, and then for three weeks. Then the factories were idled until further notice. The bosses hired back a few of the men to mothball the robots, and then the men were sent home. They stood in the streets with their neighbors and they read the newsfeeds as they came. They read about fewer buyers of their automobiles, how the farmlands the world over were turned to desert or were flooded by the storms. Storms whose torrents stripped the topsoil till the streams and the rivers ran black to the sea.

The Catholic Church had brought some order, in Morelos and throughout Mexico, with food and money donated by parishes that could still afford charity. The Jesuits and Franciscans provided medical care, the Dominicans kept schools open, and the bishops offered shelter for the living and burial for the dead. The drug cartels sometimes supported these efforts with the quiet transfer of monies—and yet they, too, saw what was coming and worried.

Weapons remained in demand. This kept cash flowing and business relationships firm around the globe. But the wars of the age were mostly in Europe, the Middle East, and Africa. The Mexican cartels' reach was limited by that of the Islamic African Nations, which controlled great stretches of equatorial Africa, far reaches of the Indian and Atlantic Oceans, and its airspace. The Islamic armies fiercely protected their own markets and their own supplies of food and clean water—and they expanded their influence.

The years came and became memories. The summer sun baked the Americas, along with the rest of the globe, and left much of the land either arid, scorched, or flooded. The winters came with an unstable jet stream, and the ground froze as far south as the Rio Grande. In the worst winters—those with the great blizzards that blanketed the solar farms—criminal enterprises soon controlled the archaic fossil fuel supplies in the Americas, as the Islamic armies did throughout Africa and Europe. Millions died in those months, most especially in Asia and in the Americas, as the legal or criminal reach of authorities in those regions waned with the cold and the heat, with the famine and riots. In big cities, the urgent pleas of the mayors went unheeded, and they were left to fend for themselves. With the Islamic African Nations' nuclear attacks on Atlanta, Georgia, and St. Augustine, Florida, the armies of North America had more pressing issues—as did their counterparts across the globe.

In the winter of 2054, Pope John XXV made his historic visit to Zurich to meet with the Assembly of the newly instituted Global Union. He pleaded for aid to defend Christians throughout Europe and Africa. The members of the Assembly—those few who had come to listen, anyway—

rejected these pleas. Their constitution, they said, forbade the Global Union from taking a stance in any war between the religions.

Five weeks later the pontiff released "with great distress" his encyclical *Tutari Debeant*—A Duty to Protect—declaring the moral rights of Christians to defend themselves and to wage just wars if civil authorities did not. The document placed firm boundaries on what was meant by such defense, rooting these limits in the Church's ancient teachings that had been adopted, oddly enough, within the GU constitution by authors who never stopped to think about where the ideas had originated.

"May no loyal son or daughter of the Church misunderstand the truth that such defense cannot include inflicting harm for personal gain or against innocent lives," St. John XXV wrote. "To do so is contrary to the Gospel of Life, given to us by Jesus Christ. We pray that Almighty God, the Author of Life and the Prince of Peace, will protect all peoples from the dark choice between cherishing life and defending the innocent."

In Morelos, a young Juan Carlos Solorzano read his pope's words and rejected them. "With all respect," he later wrote to the pontiff, "for those who wish to survive, who wish his people to survive, there can be no limits to war and power."

That text is from Solorzano's first, brief letter to Pope John XXV. Solorzano wrote little in his early years, and even less in his later ones. And while all his letters are of scholarly value, this one is greatly studied. It was written on the Feast of the Annunciation 2054—the day when the nineteen-year-old claims to have had his first vision, which he later maintained was of Michael the Archangel.

Here we turn to extant sources to better understand the man who claimed these disputed visitations. One such source comes from an anonymous text, of which I will share this fragment:

Solorzano was lean and tall like his two older brothers but had his grandfather's muscular frame. He had the straight black hair of the Solorzano men, and his mother's gray-blue eyes. He had her intellect, too. She was a physicist at a university in Cuernavaca, and she had taught him much. With a passion for bringing order to the world and wealth to his nation, Juan Carlos Solorzano said he found inspiration in the laws of the cosmos—in how they would not waver, no matter the desires or weaknesses of men.

His parents had begged him to leave the cartels. He responded that this was not possible, not in a world that offered only crime or starvation. Even if there had been another way, he said, he would still have chosen the black markets. The drug lords brought order in ways that the government, the Church, and the factories could not.

His two brothers also worried over him. In better days, before the famine and the wars demanded other priorities, they were celebrated minor league baseball players. Sure that someday the leagues would play again, they begged their brother to focus on his athletics, to be an honest man like them.

The youngest Solorzano listened with respect but went his own way.

And he grew in standing among the drug lords.

When Morelos and the nation needed strength, Juan Carlos Solorzano prided himself on wielding "real power" at only eighteen, while his family was powerless, for there was nothing that professors, factory administrators like his father, or baseball players could do in a world that had embraced survival and cruelty.

Little is known about what happened that morning of the Feast of the Annunciation on the road to Palo Grande. The driver later told the story to several reporters, with Solorzano's permission and urging, and later to the Bishop of the Diocese of Cuernavaca and the papal nuncio of Mexico.

"It was peaceful," the driver began the story each time. "We drove as the sun rose, as we had hundreds of times. Solorzano talked about the words written by the pope—words on war. We turned a bend, and he screamed for me to stop the truck. So I did, and I went for my gun. He slammed the truck door to open it and went away through the scrub and up a small path to a rise that had only one tree upon it. The tree was lit like gold. I went to follow, but he said to wait, to order the others not to follow—by then the trucks behind and before us had stopped and we all stood and wondered what was happening.

"Solorzano ascended the hill and he went to his knees, and began to cry and shout, as if a man both in great pain and great joy. He shouted that he was the servant of the angels.

"None of us on the road knew what to do, so we signed ourselves with the cross and said the Our Father, which made us feel safe. When Solorzano returned to the truck he was not the man that I had known since we were children—not the leader of a small band of men here in Mexico. He was a leader of a great army, a world leader, a man who had been spoken to by God's very angel and had been given the task of defending Mexico and all the Americas from the Muslim armies, and from all the evils of all the governments who do not believe in God. From that morning we followed him, for to be Solorzano's soldier is to do the will of the savior of the world."

As for Solorzano's sanity, that had been in question since before his vision on the road to Palo Grande. Just four months earlier, two days after his nineteenth birthday, he had ordered his parents' execution, along with a dozen others on their parish's social justice team who had dared to criticize the generosity of the cartels that fed the locals. It has been confirmed that Solorzano had sent emissaries to the funerals. They brought word of his sympathies to Solorzano's brothers, as well as warnings that it would be best if they fled after their parents' burial.

The message of the angel was dismissed by the Church, and it became a cause of conflict for many within the cartels. In the words of Bishop Alejandro Soto of blessed memory, "Solorzano's vision is at best the ravings of a madman, and at worse the seduction of Satan, the fallen angel who knows us well enough to appear to us in the forms of our desires."

Bishop Soto had a history of resisting the drug lords. He quickly ordered that no Catholic should associate the words of Solorzano with divine intervention. Yet some did. And then more. And soon there were tens of thousands.

Solorzano's early followers came from the many in Morelos and throughout Mexico who had once worked in fields or labored in the factories and were starving, frightened, and weary of burying the people that they loved. Solorzano's vision—whether true or not—brought hope. It attracted many to the young man's growing army—his newly formed *Soldados de Salvación*.

Solorzano was strategic, and soon his power spread across the Americas, then into Europe and across Africa. He had a plan—one that could not only wipe out the armies of both the Global Union and the Islamic African Nations, but also fulfill the greater urgings of the angel he encountered on the hill in Morelos.

Again I will share a segment of a text from an anonymous author:

In her days at university, Solorzano's mother had assisted with research that would be used by three-dimensional printers. There were rules about what she could divulge, but it is believed that she told her son what she could, and hoped that what she shared would intrigue the brilliant boy and lead him down a path that would do good.

There is conjecture that after their execution, when Solorzano came to take his parents' belongings, he hacked into his mother's computers to learn who else was researching the printers, and where. He likely redoubled these efforts after his vision, for, as he later wrote, his mission to save the world would require this new technology.

And yet the Global Union took little notice of Solorzano. In time, they monitored his rise as they did any warlord who might offer some benefit. In the beginning, the *Soldados da Salvación* had helped keep the armies of the Islamic African Nations in check at no cost to the Global Union's own armies. Solorzano's forces also provided the GU with good reason to maintain Christianity on the list of watched ideologies.

To that end, Solorzano was more helpful than the GU had anticipated.

On Easter Sunday 2069, Solorzano hacked into the GU communications networks to share his news with all the world: he said that Michael had come a second time. He said that the angel had told the great leader of the *Soldados de Salvación* what needed to happen, and who needed to die, to prepare the world for the imminent Second Coming of Jesus Christ.

Pope Francis III issued a harsh and public rebuke of Solorzano, as well as a plea for him to lay down his arms.

In response, on the following Saturday, the forces of the *Soldados de Salvación* rose from sleeper cells across northern Africa and the Middle East, and as far north as Turkey and Eastern Europe. The Sals, as they had come to be known, killed tens of thousands of the Islamic African Nations' soldiers—the force that for decades had blunted the reach of the Mexican cartels, and then had dared attack the Americas. In Europe, the Sals slaughtered five battalions of the GU's Elite Guard. This was the force that had been protecting fifty thousand refugees—mostly children— along the Bulgarian border of Turkey. It took Solorzano's forces only an hour to incinerate them all.

Solorzano gave praise to his army, and to the angel who had spoken to him. And he promised more slaughter.

Finally, the Global Union paid Solorzano heed—especially the GU's engineers, who found a definite pattern in Solorzano's attacks. It could be nothing but intentional, after all, that the *Soldados de Salvación* focused so precisely in areas of Eastern Europe that held key research centers for the development of high-definition printers.

Pope Francis III was briefed on Solorzano's interest in the new printing technologies, but had more pressing concerns.

Twenty hours after the attacks, he stood limply on the central balcony of St. Peter's Basilica. It was a rainswept Feast of Divine Mercy—a day of drenched pilgrims who came against the cautions of the Roman police and GU security. But the crowds assembled nonetheless, looking for hope among the sorrows of their time. After praying for the dead, Francis III issued his bull of excommunication for all those serving or in any way supporting the *Soldados de Salvación*—and anyone who supported Juan Carlos Solorzano, who, on the great feast of mercy, was himself specifically named as excommunicated from the Church.

This was done, the Filipino pontiff said, against the advice of the Mexican bishops, who worried over retribution. It was his decision alone to speak so openly. The excommunication of Solorzano and his army had to be acknowledged, he said, partly as a recognition of the truth before him—that Solorzano's blatant and public disregard for the teachings and the authority of the Church had separated him from the Body of Christ. It was also an act of mercy intended for all those tempted to join an army that could only have been spawned in hell.

"Come home, I urge you!" the pontiff cried in fluent Spanish while the world watched, and the rain drenched his white cassock in spite of the master of ceremonies' efforts with an umbrella. "You are welcome home, in full communion with the Body of Christ—home with your Mother, the Church. But you must renounce your hostilities and come to the grace of the Sacrament of Reconciliation, which I will hear myself! Please, my son, for the good of all the world and the salvation of your eternal soul, I beg you, come home, and be an instrument of God's peace!"

It has been reported that Solorzano watched the news of his public excommunication in his compound in Morelos, just a kilometer from the site of his first vision. He rose from the sofa on which he had been sleeping, went into his small kitchen, poured a shot of mescal, and gave the order to round up and shoot every man, woman, and child in thirty-nine workers' camps run by the Catholic Church—one in every Mexican state.

The soldiers of Solorzano's army mobilized to follow this order, save one, whose fear of God exceeded even his fear of Solorzano. This soldier sent word to his brother, a parish priest, who informed his bishop, who informed the army of the nation of Mexico.

Mexican Special Forces intercepted most of Solorzano's armies. Only three hundred people in two workers' camps were killed that day—camps that held seventy thousand.

Later that afternoon, after the usual statements of outrage from the usual outspoken Mexican clergy, explosive drones targeted the churches and cathedrals of those clerics. The Mexican army intercepted these, too—except for one, which sought out the Cathedral of St. Joseph of Nazareth in Toluca. The device slipped past counterterrorism defenses, then pierced the grand old church with convulsions of fire and rubble, burying eighty-three children who had been rehearsing for their First Communion, as well as six army reservists who had rushed in to evacuate them.

The people who were the heart of Mexico had long sought justice, and many that day turned against Solorzano and his armies. The descendants of those who had fought for freedom from Spain, and later against the owners of the sugarcane fields, rose up against the evil that had spawned from their poverty—and they vowed to the world that they would crush it.

6

MCCLELLAN FOLLOWED ZHÈNG INTO a room beyond the bronze doors. It was wider and longer than the outer foyer, and in its center stood a baptismal font, about half McClellan's height, printed out of the same gray-and-white material as the room's molding. Its base swirled with cherubs and vines that lifted up a wide bowl. Water, awaiting McClellan's blessing, bubbled playfully up from the center.

On the wall ahead were five entryways. There were two plain doors on each side, and taller, double doors in the center, just past the baptismal font, printed with marble moldings and adorned with wood and glass.

The robbers followed and carried the luggage to the closer door on the left. Zhèng explained that that led to McClellan's quarters, with the farther door leading to his office.

"Going forward, we're basing the investigation in this regional station house—which is now your office. We had your quarters and the chapel printed next to it for your convenience."

Zhèng pointed to the two entrances to the right of the baptismal font, which he said led to the apartments of a young couple who would assist the priest with his ministries and domestic needs. "I'll introduce them after we return from Red Delta. I know you'll like them. But for now . . ."

Zhèng went to the double doors in the center. They were narrower than all the others, taller, and surrounded by elaborate moldings of both green and warm-hued marble. They were of an uncharacteristically old style, and the priest found them somehow familiar but couldn't place them.

Zhèng nodded toward them. McClellan, holding Veronica's daisies in his left hand, reached with his right and felt a square of lattice insets in their centers. It seemed to be worn wood, and inside the latticework was rough window glass, the kind you'd expect before industrial glass making. Decorative oval pairs of the same glass were above and below the lattices. McClellan studied them with his eyes and fingers. No light came from beyond the glass inserts, but they reminded him . . . no, it couldn't be that.

Zhèng stepped in and pushed open the doors. "As you will soon see, Father, someone spared no effort on your behalf."

McClellan followed the commissioner. They entered the shadows of his chapel—the first parish church in New Athens and the first structure in the orbits built for the Holy Sacrifice of the Mass—at least, McClellan thought, a public one.

The only light came through small windows set in the ceiling far overhead. It was the simulated moonlight of the Sun Crane, which came and went as clouds sent shadows along the core. Out of habit McClellan wet his finger in a baroque holy water font he found inside the entrance, and made the sign of the cross. Even in the dim lighting, which his eyes were growing accustomed to, he could tell that the chapel was not the small and efficient one he'd been promised.

Zhèng accessed controls on a small panel near the entrance. Lighting flickered and went steady, and McClellan, squinting, beheld the grand chapel, radiant with light and color. He swallowed, stretching his throat so he could breathe. And he whispered the only words that seemed right—"My Lord and my God."

The structure rose to the lower skylights of the core. He looked ahead to face the altar, then to his sides, with their grand frescoes by Michelangelo, then up again, taking in the entire reproduction of the sixteenth-century Pauline Chapel in the Vatican's Apostolic Palace—the chapel used exclusively by the pope.

Zhèng stood next to him in silence as they took in every exquisite detail.

Eventually the commissioner began to convey what he had learned about the actual chapel. He explained that, while the Pauline Chapel was smaller and less known than its neighbor the Sistine, it was equally impressive in its art, history, and significance.

McClellan knew all this. He had been to the Pauline just after his ordination to the priesthood, when he had given talks on programming ethics at the Pontifical Gregorian University. His mind turned over all he remembered of the tour, searching for data, connections, anything that could explain why a reproduction of it was on New Athens.

His schedule for these early few hours had been agreed to before the launch of the Aesir. The timeline called for a brief tour of McClellan's "simple" chapel, as well as his residence and office, and then an initial briefing from Zhèng's team on the investigation of Father Tanglao's death. After time for rest and prayer, as well as a quick conversation with his archbishop and more preflight safety training, they would head back through the Wheel to board a security transport to Red Delta, the newly built relay station where Tanglao had been found dead. But now in his chapel, there were new considerations.

"Is Jansen responsible for this?" McClellan asked, turning to Zhèng. "Any of the engineers?"

Zhèng shrugged and stepped closer. He turned to his right, facing the vaulted sanctuary that surrounded the altar and, behind it, the replica of the seventeenth-century painting by Simone Cantarini of the Transfiguration of Christ.

"I suppose it's possible," he said.

"But you doubt it."

"Yes. Even with all charity, I can't see why the engineers would have done this."

"You and me both," McClellan said. "What has Jansen said?"

"Very little. She maintains that this was printed as a courtesy to you and the Catholic Church. But I don't believe her."

McClellan nodded and walked down the center aisle. He bent his head back for a full view of the ornate white, gold, and green expanses of vaulted ceilings and stuccos, which framed the Zuccari murals depicting the miracles of Sts. Peter and Paul. They looked exactly as McClellan remembered, when he had lingered long after his tour to lose himself in the ceiling's artwork. He had been especially moved by the mural at the chapel's peak, *The Vision of St. Paul*, with its swirling firmament of heaven, stretching forever above with divine light.

And this image would shine down upon anyone from New Athens who might wander in. It seemed impossible that an engineer would have programmed this. But if not an engineer, who? Someone could have hacked the printers that built it, he supposed. But even then—even more so than the flag outside—why did the engineers allow it to stay, let alone allow McClellan to use it?

"No idea who did this?" McClellan said.

Zhèng shook his head. "A few general ones—the builders, for instance, come to mind, which is most everyone you met outside. As you may know, the Builders Guild and the engineers don't always get along. Some of them may have wanted to embarrass the engineers, or have some say about what happens in Troas City."

McClellan shook his head in disagreement. "A builder hacking the printers? Only the engineers are programmers—and the people they grant permission to, who as far as I know have been only Earth military, such as me. And most of those relationships were suspended years ago."

"All true, Father. But I'm learning not to discount possibilities. We're still poring through the available information—limited as it is. You heard Madame Jansen herself. My team isn't granted access to printers. And so I was hoping you could shed some light on this."

McClellan looked away. "It's been a long time since I've gotten inside the head of a printer," he said.

"Well, I've never investigated a murder. And yet here we are."

McClellan stepped backward into the main aisle, turned, and busied himself studying the great frescoes dominating the chapel's sidewalls: *The Martyrdom of St. Peter*, and across from it *The Conversion of St. Paul*. Both were the last frescoes of Michelangelo, completed not long after the Sistine Chapel. The master had taken full advantage of his subjects to depict men at the mercy of the forces around them, much like many believe the artist himself felt as his old age advanced, his health declined, and the world around him grew rife with anger and division.

The chapel's tour guide—a seminarian from Boston studying in Rome—had told McClellan that when the Pauline was restored about eighty years earlier, the discovery of the frescoes' original colors gave new insights into what Michelangelo was thinking when he painted them. It seems the old master finished his career using many of the methods and colors of his youth. McClellan found comfort in that.

From the foyer outside came the clip-clop of simulated feet departing. The decommissioned robbers, having discharged their duties with the luggage, were passing through the foyer on their way back out to the boulevard. When McClellan heard the doors shut, he made his way forward, bowed, and stepped into the sanctuary surrounding the altar. He looked up to a plaque high above with a Latin inscription. As in Rome, it quoted St. Paul's letter to the Philippians:

MIHI VIVERE
CHRISTVS EST
ET MORI LVCRVM

"For to me life is Christ, and death is gain," he whispered.

Two small steps took him to the marble altar. He moved behind it, and placed Veronica's daisies at the bases of candlesticks at either side of the grand tabernacle, which rested with its gold doors open wide, waiting for a priest to say Mass.

After a moment, McClellan sighed and returned to the front of the altar and faced it, as if he were saying Mass. He needed a moment to think, to stand in that holy and intermediary space between the world of men and the presence of God—to see things for a moment as a priest, not simply as an investigator or a programmer.

He stared at the crucifix and, behind it, the painting of the Transfiguration—the moment in the Gospels when Christ revealed to his closest disciples the glory that would follow after the coming turmoil. McClellan ran his fingers along the altar's marble, asking for some sign.

The marble was hard and cold, as it should be. Imperfect.

He turned. Zhèng was standing just outside the sanctuary. McClellan quickly descended the altar's steps and walked toward him. "Tell me none of this is real," McClellan said. "The materials, I mean. This is all printed synthetics, right?"

Zhèng shrugged. "You would know better than I. See for yourself."

McClellan pushed past the commissioner and ran his fingers along the wooden pews, then lowered himself to one knee and picked at joints in the gray-and-white marble flooring.

"It can't be," he said, allowing himself a laugh. "They printed all this to be the *real* materials—marble, wood, glass—*atoms on up*, we used to say in the Corps. The doors out front—I knew they were authentic. That's common for small jobs. But everything here? I'd give anything to see all this under a tracer scope."

"We've already brought one in. The reports are in your office."

McClellan stood and again studied the height of the ceiling. "This must weigh quite a bit."

"Yes," Zhèng said. "The engineers make it known to anyone who cares to listen."

"I suppose they're not happy about that."

"That's an understatement," said Zhèng. He gave a laugh, which McClellan was glad to hear. "Most of the engineers don't know what to be more displeased with—the fact that there is a chapel at all, or its weight. You know that in space the engineers design everything to be lightweight. This," he said with a nod, "is not what they expected."

McClellan watched Zhèng again become restless. "I take it you've spent a lot of time here," McClellan said.

"Quite a bit," Zhèng said. "I keep thinking there's some clue here, but as far as I can tell, this is an exact replica of the Vatican chapel. There's no deviation—other than some environmental controls and two vacuum-rated doors off to the side, which lead directly to your quarters and offices. There's nothing that indicates a message, a sign. A *reason*. But how can there be no connection between Father Tanglao's death and this? There must be. And we need to find it."

"We will," McClellan said. "As always, with God's grace, we'll get to the truth."

Zhèng looked at the time on his wrist display. It was almost midnight.

"Let's go," he said. "I know you have questions. But before we meet with the others, I'd like to deal with a matter that's important to me."

Zhèng motioned to one of the two small side doors that had been added to the chapel's actual layout, this one just in front of the altar railing. Its seams were mostly undetectable in the marble of the chapel's walls below Sabbatini's fresco *The Baptism of Saul*.

McClellan followed the commissioner through a small sacristy to his new residence. The apartments were a simple series of rooms running along the length of the chapel to the foyer with the baptismal font. As the priest had requested, there were only the basics—kitchen, bedroom, toilet, sink, and shower—and a sitting room for prayer. There were appropriately few furnishings—a plain bed, some chairs, bookshelves—but the rooms were larger than he thought necessary. There was also a small gym, which McClellan had not requested but was happy to see.

Zhèng moved past the priest's luggage, which had been arranged neatly by the robbers. He gave a quick wave to another door, an entrance to the offices that McClellan and Zhèng's team would share. The main working area was a large, square room—efficient, gray, and lined with displays of images and data showing life throughout New Athens. An oval central table could seat more than a dozen. Over it were more displays and a holoprojection of New Athens as seen from the outside, with symbols for ship traffic and telemetry moving about it. McClellan noticed that one of the displays showed the itinerary and orbital maneuvers for their security transport ship to Red Delta. Three hours, forty minutes, and counting.

Zhèng motioned for the door to close. Without light from the apartments, the offices were dim, lit mostly from the displays. He looked McClellan directly in the eyes.

"Before I begin, you should know that this room, your office, is secure," Zhèng said, holding the priest's gaze. "At the moment I can't promise such privacy in your residence or your chapel, and certainly anywhere else, but in this room my people have made sure that you will not be monitored by the engineers, or anyone else."

"But I assume I will be monitored by you."

"Yes, most of the time."

The commissioner reached into his breast pocket and removed a black rectangular tablet. "Although, so that we can speak freely without even my people monitoring us, I'll add this dampening block for . . . I suppose a six-meter diameter should work."

McClellan recognized the device from his final days in the Marines Corps, when GU engineers had miniaturized the new dampening technology developed by the printers. The investigators in the Military Police called it the box. But for all the promises made by the engineers, the new toy had fewer applications for law enforcement than it did for criminals.

"Do you know what this is?" Zhèng asked.

McClellan nodded. "I do. I had the privilege of being one of the first test subjects for that technology."

The commissioner inserted the box into controls on the central table. The device activated, and a blue haze fluctuated over it. A series of harmless pulses flashed outward—one, then another—forming a spherical electronic wall around them. Unlike the initial pulses, nothing alive could walk through that wall.

McClellan recognized the smell of a live box. The odor had always reminded him of the old bottles of acids in his high school chemistry classroom back in Union City. Soon McClellan's and Zhèng's tablets gave a no-signal warning. The displays closest to them registered electronic chaos, and then the words *Signal Loss* appeared in crisp white lettering. A chirp notified them that the barrier was secure, and was scrambling physical vibrations, sound, and electromagnetic information—whether light or electrical frequencies—so that anyone or anything outside the field could detect nothing of what was happening inside.

McClellan waited to ask the purpose of all the precautions.

Zhèng dropped to a chair at the table and motioned for the priest to join him. McClellan complied and the commissioner leaned forward, alternately locking his fingers between his knees. Zhèng touched his forehead with his right forefinger, then below on his chest, then his left shoulder, then his right. As he did, he said the words of the sign of the cross.

Zhèng's breaths came with difficulty, but the words were clear. "Bless me, Father, for I have sinned. It has been nineteen years since my last confession."

TWENTY-TWO THOUSAND MILES from the rotating world that John McClellan had entered, a winter nor'easter had been flooding the coast of Massachusetts for two days. The storm was forecast to move offshore in a few hours, with the sun returning for the afternoon. But for the moment, it raged.

Conditions were similarly turbulent in the office of Archbishop Alfred Bauer. The new cathedral rector and the elderly vicar general were disagreeing about the Holy Week liturgies—which, if the city approved, would be the first observed inside the Cathedral of the Holy Cross since a Sal attack in 2073. The rector insisted that the Holy Thursday Communion hymn be "Adoro Te Devote." The vicar general wanted "Panis Angelicus."

While the archbishop was doing his best to mediate the disagreement, he was also enjoying it. If the two priests had the time to debate hymns, then perhaps the world was finally regaining some semblance of normalcy.

Comforted, Bauer sat back in his armchair when Antonia Rossi, his office's calm, dutiful administrator, came to the inner door.

"Your Excellency," she said, "sorry to interrupt."

It was Friday morning, a dark one because of the storm. The panes of the old windows were fighting a sudden blast of wind and sleet, which required the messenger to raise her voice.

"You have a rather urgent call coming in," she said. "The Holy See's secretary of state is asking to speak with you."

Bauer and his priests exchanged glances. The way Antonia spoke, you'd think this happened every day. The current Archbishop of Boston was certainly an important figure in the Church, especially now that one of his priests had been selected to assist upside with the investigation into Father Tanglao's death. But Bauer had only spoken to Cardinal Kwalia once when McClellan's name was first proposed for the mission.

Otherwise Bauer dealt only with low-ranking officials in the Vatican's diplomatic offices. The secretary of state had respectfully kept his distance.

"Is this confirmed?" Bauer asked.

"Yes," Antonia said, waving a small red notebook. "And it's secure. I've checked the calling routes, and confirmed it with my own contacts in Rome. I just hope the signal holds in this weather. I haven't installed the new transceivers yet."

Bauer stood and dismissed his priests with a matter-of-fact nod. He retrieved his mug of coffee from where they'd been working and brought it to his precisely organized desk. Antonia went to his holodisplay to assist with the ecclesial, administrative, and diplomatic protocols with Rome's communications offices. Soon Bauer was greeting Cardinal Peter Mwenda Kwalia, the former Archbishop of Mombasa and now the prelate in charge of diplomatic relations for the Holy See.

"Archbishop Bauer, greetings!" the cardinal said with sincere enthusiasm. "It is good to speak again. I understand you are having bad weather in Boston. We are in Rome as well—not at all like that warm day when we met last spring."

Bauer remembered. He had been in Rome for a gathering of the American bishops with the Holy Father. He was at Trattoria Da Luigi, treating a few clergy friends and seven seminarians studying abroad in Rome, when he spotted Cardinal Kwalia walk in and ask for a table for one.

Bauer invited Kwalia to join them, which brought a broad smile to the cardinal's tired expression—the kind of smile that comes from a man who knows the value of charity and joy. They had all laughed and spoken freely as the evening went on, and Bauer kept ordering cold pinot grigio, linguini carbonara, and whatever else the cooks could devise.

Three months later, Pope Clement XV appointed Kwalia as the Vatican's chief diplomat.

It had upset Bauer that some questioned Kwalia's loyalties. There was concern that he should have been more outspoken about Somalian incursions throughout eastern Africa before the wars—especially the attacks against Christians in northern Kenya. Bauer sympathized with clerics such as Kwalia—and there were many throughout Africa and Europe and in the Americas—who had been and remained in no-win situations. If they protested too loudly, they angered the enemies of their flocks, and the attacks escalated.

"It is always a pleasure, Your Eminence," Bauer said, raising the monitor's sound as the wind renewed its attack. "And many congratulations on your successful negotiations with the engineers and the Security Guild. As you may know from my report to your office, I spoke with Father McClellan a few hours ago. Our boy is enjoying his new home."

"Yes, I am happy for that. But please, Alfred, call me Peter. And thank you for your support in this matter. The whole affair has been . . . a learning experience. Which brings me to my reason for contacting you. It seems that there may be an unforeseen issue with sending Father McClellan upside."

Bauer pretended not to be concerned. "I would imagine there are quite a few, depending on whom you ask."

"I am sure there are. But what I speak of may be a concern for the Holy See and for many here on Earth. As well as for Father McClellan—as it relates to his safety and, possibly, that of the people of New Athens. Of course I am not certain if any of this is a legitimate concern, but we are being told that it may be. And, well . . . we must be sure of things."

Bauer suppressed a curse. He checked the time on the wooden clock opposite his desk. McClellan should have left New Athens for the Red Delta relay station by now.

"The Holy Father has received a communication," the cardinal continued, "verified, I am afraid, about Father McClellan. This communication is from a militant group you know well. The *Soldados de Salvación*. But you would know them as—"

"Butchers!" Bauer blurted, prompting Antonia to look in.

The cardinal paused, apparently not expecting such bluntness. Bauer didn't care.

"I believe this group is referred to in English simply as 'Sals.'"

Bauer silently collected himself. Then softly, but still angrily, said, "I am sorry, Peter, but, as you can see, I'm no diplomat."

"Perhaps not. But I appreciate your candor. I know that you were a chaplain during the wars of your nation. That is how you met John McClellan, I believe. You know the *Soldados de Salvación* very well. I do sympathize. They were—perhaps you do not know this—but this group was present throughout the eastern coast of Africa when I was a parish priest, and later a bishop."

"Yes, I know. And I am sorry if—"

"Please, there is no need to apologize. We have all struggled with heavy crosses these many years. But at the present, let us focus on the matter at hand."

The cardinal looked down. He seemed to be shuffling objects on his desk. Download codes appeared at the bottom of Bauer's screen and soon multiplied.

"The *Soldados de Salvación's* communication to the Holy Father is a warning," Kwalia said. "They say that they are concerned that we have sent Father McClellan to help the engineers. They say that he holds secrets—about what, their correspondence does not say—and that there could be tragic consequences if this information became available to our overlords upside."

"I see. How selfless of them to warn us."

"Yes, indeed," the cardinal said. "Now, two elements of this matter are most concerning. The correspondence tells us that the militia is standing by to, and I quote, 'assist the Church in preventing Father McClellan from being used by the godless rulers of the new world,' which, knowing the history of these Sals, I take as a threat against the people of New Athens and, given their duplicity, the Church herself."

"And Father McClellan," Bauer said.

"Precisely."

"And the second concern?"

Cardinal Kwalia paused. "The letter purports to be signed—and yes, it is an actual letter, on paper—by Juan Carlos Solorzano himself. We haven't received one in years."

"Solorzano? I thought he was dead. Has this been confirmed?"

"We're determining that. Of course, if Solorzano is indeed alive . . ."

Kwalia didn't have to finish the thought. Bauer had learned much as a Marine Corps chaplain. He knew what it could mean for the Church, for the world—the old one and the new—and for John McClellan, if Solorzano was indeed alive. If he had chosen this moment to summon his followers from the shadows.

"This is about the printers, isn't it?" Bauer said.

Kwalia nodded. "I am afraid that is our concern, yes."

"Does the letter mention them?"

"No—and you are receiving a copy of it, along with the intelligence we've assembled. But even without a specific mention of the orbital printers, I can see no other suitable conclusion as to why the Sals are meddling in the investigation."

"I agree," Bauer said, watching outside as wind pushed around icy trees. There was a crack up the street, followed by the noises of a limb falling hard on pavement. The lights of the room flickered and returned as Bauer looked back to the monitor. "There's always more with the Sals than what they say. The high-defs have always been Solorzano's prize. The question, I guess, is if the letter is really from him."

"Yes. As I said, we are determining that. But I must be clear: whether or not this correspondence is truly from Juan Carlos Solorzano, its content contains information that places its source deep within his militia. I am sure of that."

The lights dimmed again. The image on Bauer's monitor jumped and froze.

"Archbishop Bauer, I shall get to the point. While the Sals may be madmen and butchers, their intelligence gathering has never been wanting and their boldness has never waned. This puts us in a predicament. If Father McClellan's presence precipitates any move by Solorzano against the new world, it will be our responsibility. We cannot let that happen. We must do whatever we can, silently but surely, to protect not only our brother priest, but also the lives of the six hundred thousand souls in New Athens—and, I daresay, the souls of all those everywhere in the orbits."

RED DELTA

OKAYO'S VOICE WAS CRISP over the transport's broadcast system. Docking with Red Delta would be in thirty minutes. It was time to prepare for final braking maneuvers. Her words ended in a quick chirp, making way for the persistent hums of ventilation systems and the rise and fall of engines deep within the ship.

McClellan had spent most of the nine hours since their departure in the privacy of an aft cargo hold, which looked a lot like the insides of the old C-150 air transports from his years in the Corps. Back then he would be surrounded by the men and women of his unit. Now he was alone, hundreds of thousands of kilometers from Earth, yet comforted by the industrial webbing and the familiar smell of lubricants and electrical conduits.

He considered joining the others in the main passenger area but knew he had more time before final docking preparations. Okayo was a courteous pilot, keeping everyone apprised of even the smallest event—the firing of main engines, a roll maneuver, an unanticipated radiation belt that she'd report to the engineers so they could send Van Allen dispersers. No, there was no rush. She'd announce the final approach, and when she did there would be more to see.

Zhèng had given McClellan full access to the case files: catalogs of investigation reports; witness statements; laboratory findings; chain-of-custody documents; and, of course, catalogs of information on Raphael Tanglao. It had taken him more than seven hours to read it all—and he needed to pray his rosary and think. He needed to immerse himself in that unrepeatable moment that begins all investigations when you have the luxury of linking questions without the certainty of answers. Why that chapel? Who was the old builder in the blue jumpsuit and black boots that had watched his arrival, and then again when he left for Red Delta? Why had Tanglao set all this in motion by assuming an alias and coming upside to work in a relay station? Was he ministering to builders, or did he have some other goal?

He felt the tremors of engines preparing for maneuvers. Then came the thrust. The force pushed his chest against the safety strapping, but the motion gave only a general sense of the ship's new direction. The better indicator was his rosary's crucifix, which traveled off on its own, tugging on its chain as he held it firmly at the far end, its mass maintaining the trajectory it had traveled on before the thrusters spit fire.

McClellan studied the movement. The ship's maneuvers were teaching him about motion in weightlessness—a reality he did not remember as well as he should. The docking ring where Father Tanglao's body was found was in a zero gravity environment, as was most of the relay station. Only Red Delta's central habitat had partial Earth gravity. That meant that life on the relay, as it is on this ship and similar short-range craft, is dictated by raw Newtonian physics—by action and reaction and inertia, all emphasized by weightlessness, which the unfolding of evolution hadn't brought to human instinct.

McClellan stretched to loosen the gray patrol uniform that Zhèng had asked him to wear. He adjusted himself in the strappings and returned to the prayers of his rosary and to the matter at hand. It was Friday—the first Friday of Lent. The rosary meditations were the Sorrowful Mysteries, which recalled the events of Christ's passion and death—a fitting narrative for replaying the chronology of events that preceded Father Tanglao's death.

On Tuesday morning, January 20, more than a month ago, Red Delta had been passing 190 kilometers over the far side of the moon. Its superintendent and her three crew members, including Tanglao, had entered the final phase of its construction punch list. And because the engineers wanted the relay commissioned soon, completing that punch list meant no shortage of work on the first and second shifts and little sleep on the third.

According to the relay's comm log, that morning at 0902 hours the superintendent had reported "all normal" and dispatched her three technicians to complete two tasks: a communications software upgrade, and a minor exterior reprinting at a backup docking ring.

At 0925, technician Maximillian Tucker had radioed from an auxiliary communications hub that, as expected, in ten minutes he would initiate a master reboot of Red Delta's comm software, with a system restart estimated for fifty minutes after that.

At 0927 hours, technician Walter Hobart had radioed that he was suit-ed up and exiting Air Lock 7 with two robbers for an inspection of a trou-bled secondary communications array, and then to test the unit after the comm system reboot.

At 0934, technician Nicholas Pratt—the alias used by Father Raphael Tanglao—had radioed that he had entered Air Lock 9 to coordinate with an external printer to assist with minor repairs of an exterior hatch.

At 0935, technician Tucker had initiated the comm reboot—which be-gan a communications blackout with and throughout Red Delta. Soon af-ter, crew member Walter Hobart had spotted what he thought was an ex-plosive decompression near the air lock that Tanglao had been repairing. It was the other crew member, Maximillian Tucker, who had investigated and found Tanglao trapped in the air lock moments before his death. It was Tucker who witnessed the printer's emissions cut into his coworker's legs and face. It was Tucker who had discovered the message that Tanglao had recorded on the comm controls of his life suit.

On the recording Tanglao's voice was weak. His words and the sound of his shallow breaths were marred by gurgling, and they competed with the scream of rushing air as the docking structure repressurized. But something could be made out: "my intent . . . but to the one who has taken my life . . . please pray . . . and for my family . . . Father, I ask forgiveness."

Other than the recording, the evidence was minimal. Not only were external and internal comms and monitoring systems down for the re-boot, but also the superintendent had decided to get the job done faster by reloading not just the primary systems but the backups as well.

Anne Okayo explained at the briefing that the builders call these times "flying blind." Comm shutdowns like these for any legitimate reason, or illegitimate ones, were a favorite of the workers. They freed them, even for just a few minutes, from the constant oversight and ever-changing orders of the engineers. There were risks to flying blind, of course—the least being violations of the Orbital Construction Safety Code. Little usu-ally comes of such citations, Zhèng had said. But in this case, one of the crew members had been found dead during the shutdown, which made the superintendent's orders contributing factors.

Brandon Clarke knew the superintendent from another case. He wasn't surprised that she was cutting corners to get her relay commissioned, especially if the engineers were offering bonus credits for family citizenship, which, in all likelihood, they were. But he didn't see her as a conspirator for murder. Still, Clarke said, they should take the superintendent's words with caution. "She's better at lying to herself than to others," he said. "I'm not sure which is worse."

"In this case," McClellan answered, "both."

Complicating matters was time. Zhèng's team would have only a little under three hours after boarding Red Delta to perform their work. This included meeting McClellan's demands for time to examine Tanglao's corpse—which would be his only opportunity before the body left the quarantine of the relay's morgue. McClellan had also asked to inspect the site where Tanglao's body had been found, and then to question the superintendent and her two technicians.

Three hours was tight. But the original plan had been merely a retrieval of Father Tanglao's body by a brother priest. Offering McClellan time for an examination of the body and additional investigations was an added wrinkle that had to be fitted into the demands of the orbits—unless they could find some reason to extend the Security Guild's control of Red Delta.

Okayo had explained to McClellan—twice—why they had this time limitation. But astrophysics was never his strong point. Still, she had done her best to describe Red Delta's lunar orbit, as well as the brief window to transfer the relay to a working elliptical orbit around Earth. Because that opportunity wouldn't recur for another month, she said there was uncommon agreement between the builders and the engineers to commission Red Delta, fire her main engines, and get her in business at exactly the right moment.

Okayo explained the details—even the smallest orbital corrections—with an enthusiasm that McClellan might have shared had he understood what she was saying. In the end, she said that all he needed to know was this: if the security team wanted to return to New Athens without a week's delay or without exceeding the safe yield of their own engines, they'd have to undock from Red Delta within three hours after they had arrived.

McClellan was smiling at the memory when he looked up and saw Zhèng. The commissioner was hovering inside the cargo hold's entrance and motioning behind him. "I hate to disturb you," he said, "but you'd better join us. Our pilot is a bit of a daredevil and she wants you to have plenty of time on Red Delta. She's not braking until she has to, which will make for some interesting approach maneuvers."

McClellan stowed his tablet in his thigh pocket, along with his rosary. He unbuckled the bench strapping and pushed himself over to Zhèng. "Do me a favor?" he said. "Radio Okayo and tell her to wait until I'm secure up there."

"It wouldn't do any good," Zhèng said, laughing. "Pilots outrank me during flight. Besides, it's time you tried the weightless life. I could get used to having a chaplain around."

McClellan followed the commissioner, who moved quickly along the corridors leading to flight deck, which seated ten people comfortably and somewhat lavishly. The seating arced in a half circle and faced the open cockpit, which itself had wide, transparent sections of hull.

Zhèng waited for his guest before securing himself in one of the over-stuffed flight chairs. As McClellan did the same he could feel the main engines reverse their thrust. He gave a nod to Clarke, whom he could see in the copilot's position. Okayo was hidden by the cockpit's seating.

One of Zhèng's staffers, Agent Miriam Lopez, asked McClellan if he had read all the forensic reports.

"What little there was," he said, as he worked to buckle his straps.

Lopez was from one of the lunar stations. Zhèng had called her to this case because of her expertise with biological and physical forensics. It was Lopez who had performed the first post-mortem on Father Tanglao, and, along with Clarke, the first inspections of the air lock where the priest had been found. She was the oldest of the agents, and the least interested in Security Guild pageantry and protocol. She had dark, aggressive eyes, and her brown hair was shaved almost to the scalp. In the few hours since McClellan had met her on New Athens, Lopez was curt and critical of his questions and contributions—and she made it known that she did not approve of public displays of faith.

"I apologize if my forensic work disappoints you," Lopez responded, her eyes narrowing. "As I stressed earlier, we have very little that's out of the ordinary. I've seen space exposure hundreds of times. As for the printer damage—there is little precedent for that."

"My apologies," McClellan said. "That was going to be my point. There isn't much in the literature on printer damage—not these days, anyway.

Their fail-safes are designed to prevent accidents like this, which, thank God, they seem to. All I meant, Agent Lopez, was that you did a remarkable job with what little you had to work with."

Lopez shifted uncomfortably. She gave a slight smile of appreciation that faded as McClellan continued.

"Of course, I've seen plenty of these accidents in the wars," he said. "But those were with the older printers. I've got some catching up to do. So I suppose that means that, between both of us working together, we may come up with something neither of us would have considered."

Lopez didn't seem eager to discuss their working relationship. Her gaze again lingered on McClellan's face, focusing on the scars over his eye and ear.

"Might I ask you a personal question?" she asked. "Although I do so out of professional curiosity."

"Of course," McClellan said.

"Your head wounds, are they self-inflected?"

McClellan's expression asked for clarification.

"Forgive me," Lopez went on, "but I understand that many military programmers attempt to cut out their neural matrices—under severe stress, of course. Is there something we should know about? Something about your life in that undisciplined world down there that could affect this mission?"

"Hardly self-inflicted," he said, his posture stiffening. "These came from Raleigh. A Sal soldier thought that all he needed to be a programmer was whatever he could find in my skull. Fortunately, a colleague of mine was nearby. He put an L-21 slug into the Sal's skull first."

"I see. Well, there are ways to have such scarring removed."

"Why would I do that? I consider them a blessing. They're a reminder of the suffering the Sals inflicted on so many innocents and on themselves. I pray each day that God forgives them, and us all."

Zhèng stared disapprovingly at Lopez, who apologized with sincerity but not enthusiasm. At a pause in docking preparations, Clarke turned in his copilot's seat to send McClellan a supportive nod.

"Okay, ladies and gentlemen," Zhèng said as he stowed his tablet, "let's focus. Thanks to Okayo, we'll have almost twenty additional minutes aboard Red Delta. After we're greeted by the station superintendent, I can send Clarke to the morgue with McClellan and Lopez. Two of the station's robbers will help with the transport of the body. Okayo and I will remain with the superintendent to begin the commissioning transfer. Then we should have time for McClellan to get to know the remaining two crew members—Walter Hobart and Maximillian Tucker—and to inspect the place of the death."

As Zhèng was speaking, McClellan leaned into his seating straps. The waxing moon was gliding and rolling in the cockpit windows. He had never seen the moon so close—so large and clear—and he wondered how many people on Earth were admiring it at this very moment.

"Remember, we have just over three hours," Zhèng said, pulling on his seat straps, tightening them. "I've stretched this investigation as long as I can while keeping Red Delta idle. I'm under growing pressure to get her into a working orbit. So let's get our jobs done, and done right."

Okayo was having a spirited conversation with Red Delta's docking computer, something about approach rates and distance to docking rings. Braking engines roared unhappily as they opposed the ship's direction of travel. This fulfilled Zhèng's earlier promise for some interesting piloting maneuvers.

McClellan spotted a point of light drifting along the lunar plains. It approached the Sea of Tranquillity, growing larger until its octagonal shape became discernible. McClellan knew the relay station spanned two kilometers, but from this distance it looked small and fragile.

Clarke gave a thumbs-up, and followed with audible confirmation that, as expected, they had synced with Red Delta's docking computer. Thrusters fired, and the cabin turned slightly around them. The relay's sidewall, which had looked so thin from a distance, filled the cockpit's windows. Robbers appeared along the docking ring to assist with positioning, and after a few quiet moments there came the deep and booming thud of a successful berthing.

"Welcome to Red Delta," Clarke said. "Next stop: its morgue."

9

Westphalia, Iowa
August 28, 2069

Dear Mom and Dad,

Uncle Roger said I should write, and ask for your advice as if you were still alive. I guess it can't hurt, even though it reminds me how much I miss you. Uncle said that it's not bad to remember. He said the bad thing is forgetting the people we love.

I wasn't sure where to begin, so Aunt Betty said I should talk about anything new. So here goes. I'm going in ninth grade at Harlan Community High. There's still not many teachers, but enough that they reopened most of the schools a few years back. Last week they held a big outdoor dance—Aunt Betty said it was the first in about ten years. People from the old classes came, so it was a reunion. I went with Erin and Jimmy—you don't know them. Aunt Betty took them in for her cousin from New Jersey. In all they adopted twelve boys and nine girls from the government option. That's a lot for one house, but we had help from neighbors and built a big addition, so it works out.

I made junior varsity football, and I'm really good. I know you don't like me playing football, but it's fun. Coach Taylor says I'll be a big asset when I get to varsity. He said the towns around here need good players because people need things to cheer.

And don't worry, I'm getting good grades. You'll be proud with how I did last spring when some people came by and tested us for a new kind of math. The rumor is that it had to do with those new printers they're using in space. Ms. Fuller said I got top in the county for my age. She said the military was asking about me. That made me proud.

I know you're not happy with me thinking about the military, but all my friends are planning on signing up. Things with the Sals are worse. The fighting isn't too far from us—Texas and Oklahoma mostly. And they've been advancing toward the East Coast. The Sal leader says that they'll be taking over North America as easily as they did the South. He says that if the government can't help people, he will. He says that if the Global Union won't protect us from the Islamic African Nations, he will. Ms. Fuller said the Sals are even trying to get into space. So who knows where I'd have to fight? Maybe another country, maybe even in the orbits, or on the moon.

Given everything going on, I know I have it good. The farm is strong this year, and the past two winters were calm. Uncle Roger and Aunt Betty are up at Iowa State most of the time working with other farmers. The Global Union's people keep coming by and arguing with our results on natural farming, but you can't argue with our crop yield—and I guess that gets me to my why I'm writing.

Remember the Mitchells back home? They offered to let me stay with them. Mr. Mitchell said he needs farmers. He said that the Michigan Land Bureau granted him the rights around Union City—even as far as Burlington and Athens, too. The high school is still open, and Mr. Mitchell said he talked to the athletic director, and that I'd be welcome on the football team. That would mean I'd be a Charger, like I always wanted. Remember when you'd take me to the games with the Wilsons next door? Those were good times.

So my question is, should I go? I wish you could tell me, because I don't know what to do. I guess what's worse than losing what I have here is that being back in Michigan would make me miss you both more than I already do.

Uncle Roger has mixed feelings, but he says it's something I should consider. He says I should pray about it, too. He's always trying to get me to St. Boniface for that, but I don't go. Like you used to tell me, I don't know what kind of god can let so much suffering happen and let billions of people die like they did and still die every day. If there is a god, he's a criminal—like his followers. Like the Sals. That's what I tell Uncle Roger and Aunt Betty. I know it hurts them, but it's how I feel.

So Uncle said if I don't want to pray, then I should ask you two. So I'm hoping that if you are somewhere, like people say happens after you die, that you might hear this and be there for me. Maybe not for real, but maybe you can tell me what you think.

I miss you both so much and even though everyone's so good to me, it's not the same.

I really hate the Global Union for what they did to you—and to all the parents of the others kids here and all over. Everyone hates what they did, even if people say it seemed like the only option back then. Uncle Roger says it was genocide, and Mr. Mitchell said that Union City may vote to change its name so that nobody confuses it with the Global Union.

But that would be wrong. Union City is home—they shouldn't change a name because of the GU.

Hey, maybe I answered my question. Union City is home. I like Westphalia and Harlan and all, but it would be good to go back. Uncle Roger has connections with the engineering teams, so maybe I can get permission to visit at first, then relocate. Maybe that's my plan.

Anyway, I love you guys, and I miss you. So here's a hug from me to you, and I'll keep you posted about whatever I do—especially if I ever get to the moon.

With all my love, your son,
Johnny

10

MCCLELLAN GRIPPED A HANDHOLD on Red Delta's inner docking hatch. In a moment of weightless disorientation, the station's entryway looked like a shaft dropping far below him. The sense of falling was strong and sudden, and he did not find comfort in the fact that he was not moving. He waited for Zhèng and the others to glide past him, their relaxed motion calibrating his senses—helping his mind understand that what he was seeing was not below or above, but simply away.

Zhèng paused and put a hand on McClellan's shoulder. "Remember," he said, pointing ahead, "flat floor, circular sky."

The round passageway was one hundred meters long. It had a silver finish broken every few meters by rings of lighting. Orange signs and arrows directed traffic and instructed newcomers, but even more helpful was the two-meter-long flattened section that ran through the corridor's length—the "flat floor" that Zhèng referred to—which helped anchor perceptions with a common orientation.

"Got it," McClellan said. "I guess this can take some getting used to."

"Happens to everyone," Zhèng said. "You'll adapt. We all did." Zhèng turned to face inward, and then he nodded ahead. "Although you may not adapt as easily to Molly Rose. Here she comes, our host, the superintendent of Red Delta."

Molly Rose was propelling fast and sure through the passage, aiming for a rendezvous with the security team closer to the docking ring than to the main galley entrance. She did little to hide her irritation as she approached.

"It's about time," she said to Zhèng with a sudden grasp of a handhold, her momentum swinging her feet forward, toward her guests.

"Yes, yes," Zhèng said. "It is indeed. But then, we don't control the orbits."

"Nobody does," the superintendent said, "but you could plan for them."

Molly Rose was forty years old, but McClellan would have guessed a decade younger. She had a lean, strong build with long legs and arms.

Her skin had only a little of the pockmarking that comes from working in the vacuum and radiation of space, and her brown hair was braided and bundled inside a netting that matched her red builder's jumpsuit. As she continued her back-and-forth with the commissioner—a form of dialogue Molly Rose seemed quite familiar with—her expressions were nevertheless youthful and honest.

Zhèng ignored the superintendent's tone and introduced his team. Molly Rose knew Clarke from this case and an earlier one. She'd met Lopez only once, the day after Tanglao was discovered. The superintendent had never met Okayo, and offered her a pleasant welcome. She was less pleasant to McClellan. Her smile dimmed, and she assessed him, not with the probing analysis of Lopez but with the quick evaluations of those accustomed to taking in data quickly and making decisions fast.

"So," Molly Rose said, "you're the one we had to wait for? The soldier priest who's going to fix everything?"

"Something like that," McClellan said, watching her eyes fluctuate between curiosity and frustration. "It is a pleasure to meet you. And my apologies, if delays in my coming upside interfered with your work. But I hear you're one of the best in the relay orbits. I'm sure you'll make up for lost time."

"I'm not one of the best," Molly Rose said, connecting with his extended hand. "I am the best. But good of you to say so. All right, everyone, let's get moving. I've got orbital maneuvers programmed to begin in one hour, forty-five minutes, and then the big burn in three hours, five. Tell me what you need, Commissioner. And tell me fast."

Zhèng and Okayo accompanied Molly Rose to the station's customs office. The plan was to again question the superintendent under the polite guise of processing the memorandum of commissioning, which would grant engine control to the Builders Guild.

Clarke and Lopez chatted as they led McClellan deeper into the station, toward the morgue. He'd been waiting to get the feel of the station—to imagine the crew on the morning of Father Tanglao's death.

The air was cool and slightly stale. The passageways were unblemished, but the lighting became dim as they traveled into the secondary corridors. The other two crew members, Walter Hobart and Maximillian Tucker, had been ordered to remain in their quarters until contacted. This made Clarke, Lopez, and McClellan the only three people traveling into the vast station—into what should have been a bustling transport nexus between Earth and the buildout of Progress.

"Welcome to life in a relay," Clarke called back to McClellan. "Boring as all hell. Even when it's busy."

After turns and more flat-floored corridors—some wide for moving equipment, and some narrow for access only to humans and robbers—they came to a station transport car, much like the streetcars on New Athens, but not as elaborate. Clarke entered his security codes to unseal the transport from quarantine, and they moved forward through two more sections. They stopped at a wide landing that serviced one of the relay's main cargo holds, which was immense and empty. It was lit by only four green floodlights on its distant outer bulkhead doors as well as lighting that strayed from the semicircular personnel travel lanes set within the walls. As the trio went along, McClellan peered into the darkness at a long row of robbers lining the opposite wall. They were aligned uniformly in their idle and charging position—chin up, head back.

The party was halfway across the hold when two of the robbers lowered their heads and disconnected from their charging stations. Their innards glowed and they gave off a series of thruster blasts to push them toward the trio, then positioned themselves behind McClellan, who was behind Clarke and Lopez. These were the robbers that would carry Tanglao's body back to the transport, and they made no sound other than from their maneuvering thrusters, and from the synthetic fingers and feet that guided them along.

A corridor on the far side of the hold led to the morgue, which was farther down, past a cluster of medical arrays and a water purification module. The interior lighting was dim there, too, but the relay responded by increasing brightness as they passed. Lopez and Clarke grew quiet as they came to their destination, which required another round of security access codes to unseal the quarantine status and gain entry.

"Here we are," Clarke said, motioning beyond a pair of opening doors. "Everyone's favorite spot in a relay."

The morgue was a trio of rooms—a small entry and security vestibule that opened to a slightly larger medical office, which led to the mortuary. The inner room had rounded walls lined with a dozen vaults for the dead. The wall that held the vaults—six on one side of an examining table and six on the other—was an outer, space-forward bulkhead.

Lopez pushed herself to land at the vault to the left of the examining table. She engaged the access pad, which read her DNA and accepted her identification codes. From behind the wall came a hissing sound as the vault repressurized. Its hatch cracked open and slid upward, making way for the cylindrical casket that held the body. A dim blue light shone overhead, and illuminated the corpse, which was wrapped in a thin metallic fabric that showed only Tanglao's head.

McClellan looked down at his brother priest. Raphael Tanglao had been thirty years old but looked little more than a boy. His face was seared badly along his left jaw. The remaining flesh was warped from being frozen and thawed and frozen again. And yet he seemed to be smiling.

"Can you open the body bag, please?" McClellan said, reaching into his thigh pocket.

"As you wish," Lopez said. "Although I don't know what any of your beads and prayers will do."

"You'd be surprised," McClellan said. He removed his hand from his pocket and held up a pair of examination gloves. "But at the moment I just want to examine the body. Could you please open the seal?"

The chilled body touched the room's air. A sweet and putrid scent rose around them. McClellan knew enough to expect a smell, but it still startled him. Even in the cold vacuum of space, the human body found ways to decay.

As Lopez busied herself with supply draws and equipment, McClellan gloved his hands and made the sign of the cross. He removed the body bag, exposing the naked, partly mutilated corpse.

Father Raphael Tanglao was a small, thin man, with black hair and skin that had once been warm-hued. He had a small mouth and nose, but from the pictures McClellan had found in the case records, he knew that Tanglao gave wide, childlike smiles whenever he or someone else took his picture. Most of the available images were from his formation in the Dominican Order; a few were with his older brother and three sisters on the beaches of Manila. In the last available image, Tanglao was not smiling. He was alone, carrying a tablet on the works of St. Augustine and looking out onto the sparkling waters of the Mindoro Strait, which was awash with a sweeping and fiery sunset.

Clarke had remained at the entrance beside the two robbers. He was frantically typing with his eyes on a forearm display. "Everything looks good," he said unexpectedly. "We're private, so feel free to talk without restrictions." His words did not match his angry, intent expression. After more typing, he raised his hand. "Okay, I just lied—sorry, McClellan. We're being monitored."

"Block the signal," Lopez said.

"Already done," Clarke said. "Or else I wouldn't have just told you."

"Off-station?" Lopez asked.

"No. Definitely not." Clarke looked behind him at conduits that traveled along the inner walls, then returned to study his display. "This is not physical probing. This is spatial tunneling for sure—localized at that. I'm sure I can track it." Clarke was working quickly with his eyes, and with his fingers on a second device. "Whoever it is, they're doing a good job trying to get past my interference. Okay. I'm going to let them reconnect in ten seconds." He looked up at Lopez and McClellan. "You two keep talking, go about your business. That should keep our listener busy while I track the bastard down."

"Need help?" Lopez asked.

"No. You two have work to do. And the longer you're at it, the more time I'll have."

"Very good," Lopez said. "Then go."

"Already on my way," Clarke said, propelling himself past the robbers to the exit, and out into the empty corridors of Red Delta.

Twenty minutes later, as McClellan was inspecting Tanglao's hands, a red notification box activated on Lopez's arm display. She read its message and typed a response. Then she spoke into her collar mic. "Commissioner Zhèng. Lopez here. Did you receive that message from Clarke?"

There was a pause. Then Zhèng's voice came low and distorted. "Roger that. Coordinating with Clarke now. Stand by."

"Understood. Lopez out." She looked over at McClellan. "Clarke found our spy. It's the crew member who found Tanglao in the air lock. Tucker. Clarke has him in custody."

"Did he question him?"

"Not yet. He's waiting for Zhèng. We'd better hurry if we want to take part."

"Agreed," McClellan said. "Because if I'm right about something . . ."

Lopez pushed herself to the empty casket to restart the interment cycle. "Right about what?"

"I've been thinking about your scans of the brain."

"What about them?"

"There are some interesting signatures on the synthetics."

Lopez looked sideways at the data on his tablet. "Silicones, lutetium, a few others. Those are all standard for communications implants."

"But the scan found traces of niobium."

"So? Comm implants use niobium."

"Not all of them."

"Many do."

"The good ones," McClellan said. "The ones used by engineers. But basic comm implants—such as a builder would use—don't get that sophisticated."

"And?" Lopez said.

"Seems odd that Tanglao would have a comm implant similar to those used by engineers."

"We haven't established that he did," Lopez said.

"I suppose that's my point."

Lopez studied McClellan's eyes, then the scars on his temple. She looked down at the chem scans on her tablet. "If you're going where I think you are—"

"I think I am," McClellan said. "Look at his hands. These marks are typical for vacuum exposure, and yet the lines seem regular, as if they're scarring on top of existing dermal stress."

Lopez gave an irritated look, more about the possibility that she might have missed something. "Yes, that could be right," she said. "The scanners did flag those patterns, but the marks matched the perforations in Tanglao's inner gloves." She picked up her tablet and retrieved a report. "Here. These are the simulation results. And here's the conclusion: a 'high probability' that the hand burns are from a defensive move. Probably when the printer came at him."

McClellan shook his head. "These marks are not defensive. And I've never heard of printers coming after people."

Lopez looked back at the waiting robbers and then back to McClellan. "Look, if you have something, I want to hear it. But I want proof to back it up. And this will be our only chance. Once we leave the quarantine of the morgue, anything we find on the body will be considered contaminated evidence. Any decent lawyer will have it thrown out—as well as any related questions."

"Then we better find what we're looking for."

"All right," Lopez said, typing an update in the mission log. "I'll buy us a few more minutes. But only a few."

McClellan's heart raced. "This shouldn't take long. Let's start with a chem scan of the hands. Your original examination used a single grab sample. I know that's standard for builder autopsies, but how about a transect analysis on both palms, across here and here."

McClellan took Tanglao's left hand and held the fingers back. Lopez, cursing under her breath, positioned the scanner. It hummed and made angry sounds as it dug into lifeless flesh, extracting microsamples for immediate analysis. They repeated the procedure on the right hand, and the data appeared on Lopez's tablet.

"Silicones, lutetium . . . niobium," she said.

McClellan looked over at her display. "And with a consistent signature and decay pattern. Do those results look familiar?"

Lopez nodded intently. She picked up another scanner, adjusted it, and ran it over Tanglao's forehead. "I'll be damned. These are neural links, not comm implants. And there's not much left of them. From the looks of the decay, they were processing sizable amounts of energy just before the time of death."

McClellan nodded. "How long before death?"

"Minutes. Hard to say beyond that. But not more than eight, ten minutes." Lopez looked up at McClellan. "There's something else. You brought up a good point about the builders and their comm implants. The same goes for neural links. Even if a builder does need them for neural connectivity, they use something more durable—usually something with an external sheathing. These implants," she said, pointing to Tanglao, "don't last long under extended physical stresses—as in doing real work with your hands."

McClellan nodded. "Good to know. So let me ask you this: have you ever examined a body with links like these?"

Lopez nodded. "Three. All killed on Earth by Sal operatives. With conventional weapons."

"They have anything else in common?"

Lopez paused. "Two were engineers overseeing Earth assistance. The other was security, and former military, like you. None of them had these burns . . . and all three were programmers."

"And if I'm right," McClellan said, "Father Tanglao makes your fourth."

Their radios hissed. Clarke asked for their status. Lopez radioed back that they'd be on their way in five minutes. She turned back to McClellan.

"So let's be clear," she said. "You're saying that those hand markings are from printer contact. If so, that changes everything."

"Then everything's changed," McClellan said. "I'm certain that Tanglao was a programmer—that he had been in contact with the printer that killed him."

Lopez called over to activate the two waiting robbers. "We need to move. But I have one last question. If you're right, where are Tanglao's key and coupler? We found nothing like them in our sweeps. Where would he hide them?"

"Good questions," McClellan said. "I'm hoping that the builder can tell us. And I'm hoping he knows something else: what Tanglao was programming that printer to build."

ARCHBISHOP BAUER HANDED HIS overnight bag to his driver. He looked along the street, then walked quickly to the old sedan waiting below his office. The worst of the nor'easter had moved offshore. There were already breaks of blue in the west and south, and while the air was breezy, it was warm enough to wear comfortable street clothes—jeans and a Windbreaker—which would rouse little recognition, and subsequent requests to talk, on this first Friday in Lent. Bauer needed to leave as soon as possible if he was going to arrive at his brother's house in time for the meeting he'd arranged. He'd been troubled since his conversation with Cardinal Kwalia that morning, and he wanted to speak with the one man who had the connections he needed.

The driver, Father Corrales of his clerical staff, also wore street clothes. Corrales stowed the archbishop's bag, disconnected the sedan's charger, and positioned himself at the steering console. He made a fast turn onto West Dedham Street and then drove along the local roads because of Boston Harbor's rising waters, which made the outer highways impassable after a big storm.

The newly rebuilt Charles River Bridge brought them to Cambridge and Somerville—an area locals still called the war zone, because of Sal incursions into Harvard and the Massachusetts Institute of Technology.

Soon they were heading south along mostly deserted highways and side roads, passing through either lively suburbs or overgrown ones, through forest or the remains of smaller cities. Then they came to the coast.

The sun shone freely as they sped over the Jamestown Bridge. Winds from the retreating storm swept over it, pushing at the sedan, and under it, kicking up whitecaps. Bauer opened his window and inhaled, feeling the cool, salty air in his lungs.

The town of Jamestown took up the entirety of Conanicut Island, which stretched south to north in the mouth of Narragansett Bay. Its historic farms, once largely decorative, had been tilled and planted once the famines came, their acreage expanded by the clearing of adjacent forests. With the bounty the farms provided came the need for militias to patrol the shores and bridges to keep hungry mainlanders away.

Bauer had heard many dark confessions from the people of Jamestown. And he had preached on many stories of their heroism during the famines. As his driver took him through the town center, he was comforted by signs of renewal. They were simple, but they were there. It was the way people came and went and smiled on this sunny Friday afternoon. Or when others waved to a passing car while working in small yards that held pens for chickens and cows, and vegetable gardens waiting to be replanted once the spring weather settled in for good.

The most consoling sign of normalcy for Bauer had always been the weathered house where family waited to greet him.

His youngest brother, Michael, had inherited their parents' home and the lot around it, which he had converted into a small farm. Michael's work as an oceanographer with the reopened University of Rhode Island often kept him out on some expedition. This month he was on the waters of the North Atlantic, assessing how they had soured with the increased levels of atmospheric carbon dioxide that poisoned so much of its life.

Alfred Bauer loved his brother Michael, but he cherished Michael's wife, Helen, the island's sole pediatrician. Her family had been on the island for generations, and her towering intellect and standing in the community made her a leader in those early days when the world around the island went dark.

She and Michael had three boys of their own. Their uncle said that they were what boys should be—adventurous and competitive, and loyal. In their care, too, were the other children—two boys and six girls—whose families on the mainland had taken the government option. Bringing the children to the island caused some dissent, but Helen Bauer had helped rebuild the farms, and she paid the protests no heed.

Bauer offered warm but hurried greetings, and then drove himself across the new, higher causeway to the old lighthouse on Beavertail Point. He parked a little removed from the few other vehicles that had brought locals to watch the big waves. He zippered his Windbreaker, pulled up his blue jeans, and crossed the park's small perimeter road, which was still wet from the storm.

He looked along the folds and layers of rock that tumbled into restless waters. There, just to his right on a ledge, looking over a small tidal pool, stood his friend and fellow Marine Corps chaplain Monsignor Thomas Harper.

"My God, he looks bad today," Bauer said aloud.

Bauer negotiated the terrain, waving his hand until his friend spotted him. Harper had grown frail in the past month—blood cancer was taking its toll—but his posture was confident, as it had been since his days as a college baseball champ and military chaplain. Like Bauer, Harper was dressed in street clothes—dark exercise pants and an old hooded sweatshirt. At his feet were his fishing pole and a worn green backpack.

"Catch anything?" Bauer asked, reaching out his hand.

"I'm done fishing," Harper said. "Just enjoying the ocean."

Harper's grip was weaker than it had been only weeks ago. His skin, once dark and smooth, was thin and pale, especially around his neck and wherever it showed beneath his short, graying hair.

"The kids down there seem to be doing okay," Harper said, nodding farther along to three teenagers on wave-drenched rocks, their laughter rising over the wind and the surf.

Harper had retired three years ago from active military service, and then last spring from the Diocese of Providence. He'd used his connections to land a job teaching history at the Naval War College, a few miles north across Narragansett Bay. Bauer made a point of visiting Harper as often as he could, meeting him for dinner, and a beer or two too many.

For this visit Bauer had asked for someplace private—but not suspicious.

Harper looked hard at his friend. "So I guess sending your boy upside is ruffling some feathers," he said.

"McClellan's always been good at that," Bauer said.

"Good. It's about time the engineers learn that the world doesn't always operate as planned, eh? First they had to admit that they need a security presence—when was the Security Guild formed, ten, fifteen years ago? Now they find a dead priest up there, and it looks like murder, and now we've got McClellan there legally, and they're building churches for us. God does have a sense of humor."

Bauer gave no signs of amusement.

"But you didn't come down to throw stones at the engineers," Harper said. "What's the matter, Freddy?"

The teenagers farther along were laughing wildly. A wave had hit hard and thudded up, its spray surrounding them. Bauer listened for a moment, then he got to the point. "It's about the Sals," he said finally. "Solorzano in particular."

Bauer waited for some reaction.

"Go on," Harper said. "I never believed the bastard was dead."

"Well, it seems you were right. And apparently he's written to Pope Clement about McClellan. He said he was offering to prove his love for the Church, or something like that, by sending undercover soldiers to protect McClellan from the godless engineers and whoever killed Father Tanglao."

"How noble," Harper said.

"Yes. But then he tells the pope that it would be 'unfortunate' if events from McClellan's past were to be publicized and used against him. He said he would not want to see a priest humiliated."

"Typical Solorzano," Harper said. "With one voice he both offers help and threatens."

"Brings back memories," Bauer said.

Harper's face became serious. "When you called to meet, I had a feeling it might be about this. In fact, I was about to get word to you. From what I'm hearing, the Sals are making the same threats and offers to anyone in Rome who will listen."

"I figured you'd know—"

"I said I heard. That's not the same as knowing. But it doesn't surprise me."

"Nor me," Bauer said. "The Sals have been quiet. They're overdue to make a mess of things."

Harper rubbed a hand along the back of his neck, kneading his thin muscles. "Are you sure about this letter to the pope?"

"Absolutely," Bauer said. "Cardinal Kwalia told me himself."

"Guess that makes it legit—and I'd trust him to know better. He wrote the book on the Sals, and he dealt with them in Kenya."

Harper looked around the ledge. The teenagers had moved farther down the shore, their laughter lost in the wind.

"So what's Solorzano's game plan?" he said, more to himself than to Bauer.

"I have a few ideas," Bauer said. "But I'd like to hear yours."

"Okay," Harper said. "Let's start with what we know—with McClellan's parents getting swept up in legalized genocide. He grows up with a busy uncle and aunt, and then—still a kid—he moves back home on his own. That couldn't have been easy."

"No, but the farms in Michigan needed experienced hands. And McClellan's not one to say no."

"Then right out of high school he signs up for the Marines. Turns out he's a natural at programming the printers, even if he's a candidate for sniper school—"

"And he would have made it," Bauer said. "But the Corps wanted programmers more than snipers."

"Then at the height of the wars, as we're making progress against the Sals, when we really need good programmers, and he's about as good as we've got, the Corps pulls him from programming and sends him to the Military Police."

"Yes," Bauer said. "And I supported that. You know the story. He was—is—an expert in printed weapons. In a day, maybe two, he could track the kind of printer that made a single bullet or a bomb casing and he would work backward and find where the weapons came from—and who authorized the printing. He helped the MPs get rid of lots of bad guys, and I was glad for it."

The wind gusted and roared, prompting the complaints of nearby gulls.

"I know that story," Harper said. "And I know it's not the whole story. I know about the trouble at Raleigh. I know the kid was put in a bad situation, and that some say he screwed up. And I know that the Corps wasn't sure what to do with him, but thanks to you they hid him in some low-level analyst assignment—which he turned out to be very good at."

Bauer looked off to the horizon. He remembered first meeting McClellan in the infirmary at Camp Lejeune, just a few days after Raleigh. He remembered the days that followed when the young, wounded Marine grilled then Father Bauer about his faith.

"Tell me, Freddy, did McClellan ever learn that what he did was one of the reasons the GU engineers pulled military programming?"

"No," Bauer said. "But if anyone can add two and two, it's Johnny McClellan."

Harper plunged his hands into his sweatshirt's pockets. "Here's what I'm thinking," he said. "I don't think this has much to do with revenge against McClellan or giving the Church a black eye—although Solorzano would enjoy both. I think the Sals are worried about McClellan getting back inside the printers. We know they want to be up there—hell, everyone knows that, assuming they're not there already. Either way, they see an opportunity, and I think that Solorzano is spooked about McClellan being up there first."

"Makes sense. McClellan knows the Sals. That was one of the reasons the Security Guild wanted him."

"I don't think it's just that. If the Sals do have some plan for the printers, I bet Solorzano is worried about McClellan getting in the way."

Bauer moved closer to the cliff's rocky edge. A small crab was righting itself in the tidal pool below, then tumbled again in the force of an incoming wave.

"There's something else," Bauer said, turning back to Harper. "Johnny McClellan is a natural investigator. You're right that he helped the MPs put away some big names. Even if it's not the Sals who killed Tanglao, I'd imagine anyone involved in his death wouldn't want him up there."

"I'm sure we're not the first to think of that," Harper said.

"True," Bauer said. "Kwalia told me that the Security Guild is keeping a close watch on him. And the officer in charge, their commissioner—Joseph Zhèng, if I remember—seems like a decent man. But they're amateurs."

"Oh, I don't know about that. A lot of them are former military. And besides, whatever we can do from down here, we'll do. Don't worry, Freddy. I'm on it. I'm digging for any intel that can help."

"I don't have to tell you that that is very much appreciated."

"No, you don't have to tell me anything. But you do have to promise me one thing."

"What's that?"

"If Solorzano and his people are trying to get to McClellan, they may be keeping watch on things down here, too. You should be careful."

Bauer nodded. "Always."

"And it may not be a bad idea to keep an eye on your brother's family. If Solorzano thinks for a moment you're helping McClellan, he wouldn't think twice about using them to make a point."

"I know," Bauer said after an extended breath. "I'm going to talk to my sister-in-law when I get back, but I already got word to the Jamestown Police and Militia. They'll keep an eye on things."

"Good," Harper said. "As will I."

Bauer kicked at the rocky ground and said nothing. Harper shifted the conversation. "So . . . where is he now?"

Bauer tilted his head upward, looking southwest to where the crescent moon followed the sun. He focused as if he might see into the orbital traffic upside.

"From what I gather," he said, "he should have boarded the relay station where they found Tanglao. Up there, in orbit around the moon. Can you imagine? The moon. But I'm not entirely sure of timing. The engineers don't allow many updates, and I spoke to McClellan only briefly this morning, when he had settled into his quarters."

"How's he doing?"

"He sounded good. Hell, he sounded great. All he could talk about was his chapel. Did I tell you about that?"

"No. I hope the engineers didn't botch—"

"No, they did not. Wait till I tell you. It's a replica of the Pauline Chapel—yes, the one in Rome. McClellan sounded like a kid when he was telling me—yes, that's what he said. Full-scale . . ."

Harper did not believe that a reproduction of the Pauline Chapel had been printed in New Athens, but Bauer insisted, and after some bickering between close friends, Harper finally laughed louder than the surf.

12

LOPEZ, MCCLELLAN, AND THE two robbers with Tanglao's casket met Okayo about halfway between the morgue and the main docking platforms. From there Lopez accompanied the body back to the transport. Okayo and McClellan made their way to Clarke and the detained communications officer.

The forward corridors turned and stretched into wider ones with occasional transparent hull sections. Through them McClellan could see Earth drifting in the distance, beautiful in its crescent form and restful. New England was approaching evening, and Michigan was covered in clouds, but to the west he spotted Iowa, still in warm sunlight.

They came to the revolving entrance of the habitat, which wheeled slowly beneath a field of solar arrays and communication dishes. After passing into the entrance spine, McClellan felt the growing tug of weight as he and Okayo navigated the handholds leading to Red Delta's residential decks. He was about halfway to the floor when his mind began protesting the concepts of up and down, against which it had worked these past hours to ignore. But the handholds were becoming more like a ladder, and his direction seemed more like downward rather than simply away. And he reminded himself that, if he were not cautious, he would fall.

On the floor he spotted Zhèng and Molly Rose farther down a gray corridor of doors. The superintendent was cautioning the commissioner against detaining a crew member without giving her the opportunity to be part of the questioning. Zhèng replied that her crewman had used illegal communications technologies to probe a Security Guild investigation. In all likelihood, he said, this crew member would be returning with him to New Athens for detainment and formal questioning. As Zhèng spoke he motioned quickly to McClellan and Okayo to follow him to rendezvous with Clarke, who stood at an open door to an auxiliary communications room, keeping watch over the suspect inside.

Seething, Molly Rose followed. Then, facing the commissioner, she said that she would appeal any further delays.

"Ms. Rose," Zhèng said, marching ahead, "let me be clear. My agent has *your* comm officer, Maximillian Tucker, detained in *your* auxiliary communications control center. We agreed that your two crew members would be isolated during our boarding until summoned, had we not? You should be grateful that I'm not questioning you as well."

"Wait a minute," Molly Rose said. "No one is supposed to be out of their quarters. I ordered them. Commissioner, I don't want any problems."

"Mr. Tucker seems to have different priorities. And now, depending on what we learn, I may have no other option than to extend the security hold on this station."

"Extend the hold?" she said, making no attempt at decorum. She stepped in front of Zhèng, her face full of fury and pleading. "You have no right to delay my commissioning. No right at all. And no reason. We need to work."

"I have both the right and the reason. Perhaps you should have thought about your mission when you were assembling your crew." Zhèng turned to Clarke. "Has Tucker been read his rights?"

Clarke affirmed that he had. Zhèng ordered his agent to join Okayo in a search of Tucker's quarters. He took a step toward the communications control room when McClellan came forward.

"Mind if I take this?" McClellan said.

Zhèng gave a questioning look. McClellan said that there might be a new development in this investigation, and that Zhèng could radio Lopez for her opinion of what they found in the morgue.

"It may be best if I follow up with Tucker," McClellan said.

Zhèng looked at the open doorway, then back to McClellan. "All right. He's all yours."

Safety protocols required backup communications modules while the crew remained in the habitation ring. This made the room functional but cramped. It held three compact communication consoles, each with a small fitted chair. Its walls were racks of comm components and its ceiling gave off a brilliant light that spilled into the corridor. Two of the room's consoles had open compartments. Connection cables ran from their innards to a pair of hacking tablets, which were activated and awash with holographic data floating over their surfaces. Their owner stiffened in his chair when McClellan entered.

According to the relay's personnel records, Maximillian Tucker was twenty-four years old, and new to the orbits. He sat in the console chair farthest inside, his hands clasped tightly between his knees. He wore the standard orange jumpsuit of a relay crew member, and polished black boots. He was shorter than McClellan, but had a powerful build that stretched the material of his jumpsuit at his arms and legs. Perspiration glistened on his dark skin and in his black hair. His eyes were wide and scared even as he tried to appear otherwise. When McClellan stepped closer, he shifted his weight back into his chair.

"I've told you all everything," Tucker said, not looking at McClellan. "I've been questioned five, six times about Nicky."

"I know that," McClellan said. "Right now my questions are about you listening to confidential discussions. From what I hear, and from what I can see, you're pretty good at comms. So help me understand what all this is."

"I was just testing a few things. I didn't mean any harm. Please don't get me thrown off this job."

"We're a little beyond that, Mr. Tucker," McClellan said. "Mind if I call you Max? I bet that's what everyone calls you."

"Sure," Tucker said, now looking up at his questioner. "That's what they call me."

McClellan studied Tucker's eyes. He had seen that look often—that uncertain stare that seeks not just mercy, but also understanding.

McClellan was open to both, more than Tucker might have guessed. But he also had to get to the truth.

"Well, Max, looks like we have a few issues to discuss. And I don't mean murder. Let's start with an introduction. My name is John. John McClellan. I'm on special assignment on this case because the man you call Nicky is a colleague of mine. More like a brother. And I'm here to find out how he died, and who was behind his death. Do you understand that?"

Tucker nodded.

"Good," McClellan said. "So tell me why you were listening to my visit to the morgue."

Tucker swallowed and breathed out. "I didn't mean harm, sir. Just that I knew you came to take away Nicky, and I wanted to know where. He was good to me. Always treated me with respect, not like most people treat the new guys up here."

"First time working upside?"

"Yes, sir."

"Mine, too." McClellan pulled over one of the other console chairs and sat in front of Tucker. "So, Max, where you from?"

Tucker sat back, eyeing McClellan with suspicion. "You mean on Earth?"

"Yes. Where'd you grow up?"

"Detroit."

"Yeah? Wolverine, here, too."

"You're from Michigan?"

"Union City," McClellan said. "Southeast of Kalamazoo."

"I know Union City. I had cousins nearby, in Coldwater. They worked in reconstruction and had a few jobs out by Union City. Always talked about how the girls around there were something."

McClellan heard Zhèng step into the room. Tucker recoiled, folding his arms.

"Max, that's Commissioner Joseph Zhèng," McClellan said, giving a nod behind him but keeping his eyes on Tucker. "I know you met him during his earlier boardings. He's impatient because we have some orbital issues, and we need to undock with Red Delta soon. At least we'd like to. So let's hold off talking about home. First, tell me again what all this is about," he said, waving to the consoles and the hackers' tablets.

"Like I said, I was just trying to find out what you were gonna do with Nicky. That's all."

McClellan counted four times that Tucker's eyes shifted their gaze.

"Well, no, Max, I'm guessing there's more. Something you're not telling me."

Tucker said nothing.

McClellan reached for the tablet in his thigh pocket. He scrolled though the crew roster and came to the name Maximillian Tucker. "Says here you're a grade two relay communications operator."

"That's right. Just passed my test last month. Passed the first time, and got the highest score."

"Well, that might make sense, seeing you're using pretty simple tools here to access some high-level algorithms—the kind that can hijack the Red Delta's main communications antenna to tunnel into our conversation earlier, no?"

"No, sir. I just—"

"You just hacked into a Security Guild comm channel with triple-redundant encryption—sloppily, because you got caught, but you did do it. You targeted our position and used the main antenna to tunnel into listening range, which is not only illegal for about a dozen reasons, it's also way outside of what the Builders Guild allows for a grade two comm operator."

Tucker looked at his hack tablets as if they were about to speak.

McClellan leaned forward, forearms on his knees, hands clasped like Max's. "Okay, Max, let me ask you one more question. And I'd appreciate the truth—sooner rather than later. I'm pretty good at spotting liars."

Max nodded.

"Those tablets you used for hacking, did Nicky have anything like them? Before you answer, let's go over what we know—what I know—and then you think about how you're going to answer. You and Nicky Pratt were friends. He treated you with respect and he helped you adjust to the new world. He was a comm officer, like you.

"Then, five weeks ago, the two of you were both working at the aft end of the relay for precommissioning upgrades when Nicky had his accident with the printer. You found him dead, Max. You did. And since the internal comms were down at the time, all we have is your word about what you found. The story goes that you weren't near Nick when he had his accident, because you were at a communications control center overseeing the software upgrade, right?"

"That's right."

"But I just learned that you know some pretty sophisticated hack maneuvers, so you could have easily accessed the dock controls where Nicky was working, no?"

"No, sir. I didn't do anything like that. I couldn't, even if I tried. There was that high-def working outside the dock. It was jamming local control—"

"And how do you know it was jamming control?"

Tucker was angry now, but scared, too—a helpful combination during interrogations.

"The printers always take local control during fixes like that—even if you're testing manual operations. Then you need a person or a robber— that's what Nicky was doing there, working with a printer on a preprogrammed repair. But in a job like that, it's always the printer that has primary control. So even if I could hack into Docking 9, I couldn't have accessed the door controls."

McClellan kept his gaze on Tucker's wild eyes. His expression was not that of someone lying. It was the look of a terrified young man who couldn't understand why no one would believe him.

"Okay," McClellan said. "I'll buy that—for now. But either way, now we find you breaking your superintendent's lockdown—which was ordered by Commissioner Zhèng—to come here and hack into a secure conversation of an active murder investigation."

"Like I said—"

"I know. You wanted to find out what we're planning to do with your friend's body. I appreciate that, Max. But that still puts me in a situation. I guess we have to reassess a few things about your involvement with this investigation. I guess we need to go through your earlier statements. See if any of them changed."

Tucker folded his arms, pressing them into his chest. His breathing was fast and shallow. He looked up at Zhèng, who was standing behind McClellan.

"I didn't kill anyone," he said. "Why won't either of you believe me?"

McClellan wanted to believe him. But he couldn't rule out the possibility that for some reason that might have made sense to Tucker, even if only for an instant, he had wanted Tanglao dead. Even if not all of him shared that wish, there could have been some fury that wanted to punish his friend—for whatever reason, and there could be many. And then, when it had the chance, the fury took control. McClellan had heard enough confessions—and had confessed enough of his own—to know how quickly, how totally, a man's higher self can yield to the lowest of his passions.

"Max, let me ask this again," McClellan said, checking the time. "From one Wolverine to another, did Nick have a tablet like yours—it would look sort of like those, but bigger? More connection ports. And dual displays—side to side."

Tucker shook his head. "Not sure what you mean."

McClellan typed a few commands on his tablet, which sent off an image of a programmer's key and coupler. "Did you ever see Nicky with anything like these?"

Max recoiled. "Nicky wasn't a programmer. He wouldn't have had those."

McClellan was certain that Tucker was lying, but that a part of him wanted to believe his own words—either because he was the killer or because he was afraid of the killer. Or he was simply protecting his friend Nicky.

"Max, you haven't been to Docking 9 since they took away Nicky's body, right?"

Tucker stared. "That's right."

McClellan stood up just as the station's computer announced the initiation of orbital adjustments in ten minutes, and the final engine burn in ninety.

"Let's go, Max, you and I," he said. "The man you call Nicky Pratt is my brother, and he's your friend. I'd like to see where he died. And I'd like you to show me."

Tucker folded his arms again and his eyes were fixed at nothing.

"Commissioner Zhèng," McClellan said, keeping his eyes on Tucker, "I'd like to check the docking area where Max here found Nicky Pratt, and I'd like Mr. Tucker to come. And then I'd like to request that the Security Guild take him back to New Athens for questioning—more than we have time for here."

Zhèng guardedly agreed. He ordered his two agents to accompany McClellan and Tucker and to record the investigation. Then he took McClellan aside. "I probably don't have to tell you this," he said, "but go easy on the kid."

"That's my plan," McClellan said with a shrug. "But it all depends on Tucker."

13

ZHÈNG ACCOMPANIED AN UNHAPPY Molly Rose to the main administrative offices. Clarke and Okayo escorted McClellan and Tucker out of the habitation ring, through the weightlessness of Red Delta, and past the main arrays of cargo holds. Clarke had been to the Docking 9 assembly in the first security boarding, and led the way, while Tucker followed up with Okayo and McClellan.

They stopped at a sealed bunker door that led to the quarantined aft section. It had been shut, locked, and sealed by Zhèng two weeks prior. Okayo assisted Clarke with the unlocking, which required the presence, passwords, and DNA of two security agents.

There was a low rumble before the doors cracked and separated. A chill breeze and a stale smell met them as the atmospheres of both bunkers equalized. Ahead, lighting tracks flashed and flickered on.

"How far?" McClellan asked Tucker, even though he knew the answer.

"Four hundred meters," Tucker said. "Straight down." Then he pointed to a narrower corridor perpendicular to the main spine. "And down there are the triple *c*'s—the comm control centers—for the rear antennae. Go about eighty meters. That's where I was when I got the news about Nicky. Left some of my tools there. They found them the first time they looked."

The station's lighting dimmed for a moment, as echoing around them came the unsoothing voice of the relay's computer. "Attention, all crew. Prepare for level four transit adjustment in one minute. Main engine fire in one hour, sixteen minutes. Remember: take caution during all orbital adjustments."

Okayo consulted her tablet, nodded to Clarke, and waved the team forward. "Tucker, you're with me and McClellan. Agent Clarke will reinspect your stated location at the time of Father Tanglao's death. Let's go, everyone. The orbits are doing their thing."

Per Zhèng's orders, Okayo activated her suit's scanners and video recorders and called out to the others to do the same. Then, as forewarned,

Red Delta's main thrusters fired. The structure groaned and the corridor revolved slightly, pushing slowly toward them as the relay gained a new orbital momentum.

Clarke gave a cheerful shout when the engines stopped. He grinned and waved as he turned into the side access tunnel. "Okayo, don't let McClellan bump his head. That was a baby compared to the big corrections coming later."

Okayo said something in Swahili that made Clarke laugh loudly, but her smile faded as she, Tucker, and McClellan moved deeper into the cold main spine. This end of the relay was even more monotonous than the rest of Red Delta—its corridors were numbered and color-coded but otherwise identical, and the lighting, rising and falling as they came and went, allowed only small glimpses of the expanses in which they moved. McClellan had read about the psychological tests that builders take to work on a relay. Now he knew why.

They came to the outer wall and the hub for Docking 9. Between the two docking-access tunnels was a round window with an elaborate fractal design. It was similar to the yellow-and-white stained glass over the entrance foyers to McClellan's rooms. But this design used transparent metals, which looked out onto the darkened lunar horizon and the stars beyond.

"I didn't realize printers got so creative on relays," McClellan said as he studied the window.

The docking access tunnels ran at opposing right angles from the main corridor, either above, or below, or to the sides, depending on how your brain made sense of things. McClellan's followed the flat-floor convention of the main corridor, which oriented the docking ring where Father Tanglao had died as above him, as if it were a tunnel that rose to an elevated vault.

"Damn," Tucker said. "This is a sad place."

"Murder will do that," Okayo said, engaging the docking controls. An activity alarm chirped as the door to the access tunnel slowly slid open, grinding in protest as it stirred from its frozen condition. Air hissed as the atmospheres of both tunnels equalized. Then ice crystals tumbled from within the Docking 9 access, melting as they drifted through the warmer air.

Okayo watched with concern. Tucker did too.

"Clarke," Okayo radioed, pulling up the communications tip of her collar, "report."

A few larger beads of water quivered as they drifted toward Tucker's face. He scowled and slapped them into a different trajectory. A droplet adhered to his thumb. He examined the droplet wonderingly.

"Clarke, report."

Tucker, lost in calculation, squeezed the droplet between his thumb and forefinger.

"Clarke, Okayo here. Report."

Tucker peered into the access tunnel. His eyes were working to see through the slight mist within, into the air lock where five weeks ago he found his friend sliced up from a printer's emissions.

Okayo forced her collar closer to her mouth. "Clarke! Report!"

After more silence came static and then a response.

"Here," Clarke radioed. "Sorry, I was in a control bunker. Lost signal. Glad you called—saved me the trouble. I have some news from this end."

As Clarke spoke, Okayo briefly closed her eyes. "Before you begin," she said, "I have a question from Docking 9. You were here on both boardings. Were there any reports of water vapor in the docking access?"

A pause gave way to a distorted response. "That's a negative on water vapor. We had humidity levels of about five, ten percent on the first investigation. I thought that was high, but not too much out of the ordinary. I didn't go dockside for the second trip, but nothing jumps out about water vapor."

"I'm sending a visual," Okayo said, holding her left arm aloft for the wrist unit to send video. "What's the word from your end, Clarke?"

"Well, the good news is no sign of human activity since we sealed this bulkhead two weeks ago—not saying there wasn't any, but I'm finding no signs—and hey, I am pretty good at this—so I'd say no one has been here."

"Sure of himself," McClellan said to Okayo, "isn't he?"

"Oh, that he is," Okayo said. "But he is good. Almost as good as I am."

"But get this," Clarke's voice continued, stronger but still through static, "there are fresh markings on the tunnels that are telling me a clumsy little robber was here—and recently. If we had time I could ID the one—if it's still on station. Be good to find. I thought Superintendent Rose was to have robbers locked down in quarantined sections." Clarke paused again. "Wow, that's a lot of water. There's a leak somewhere."

"You are brilliant," Okayo said, circling around the perimeter of the main spine. "The only water available here is in the reclamation lines for the emergency oxygenators. Could be that. Could be a punctured environment suit." Okayo gave one more check of the corridor's circumference. She pulled a small vial from a pouch on her belt and followed some of the water to collect it. "We better let Zhèng know about this," she said.

"Already done," Clarke said.

"Wouldn't a leak cause an alarm?" McClellan asked, looking at Tucker.

"It should," Okayo said.

The lights dimmed and went red. "Attention, all crew. Prepare for level two transit adjustment in six minutes. Main engine fire in sixty-nine minutes. Remember: take caution during all orbital adjustments."

"So either the sensors failed," McClellan said when the lighting returned to normal, "or there was a water vapor alarm and it was silenced. Unless I'm missing something. Guess we'll find out more when we go in."

"Not sure we're going in."

McClellan pulled himself level to Okayo. "I'm going in. I came here for this, and now after examining Tanglao—"

"McClellan, listen to me. I think I can buy us more time." She turned again into her collar mic. "Commissioner Zhèng, Agent Okayo here. Based on new evidence and lack of on-board investigative resources, I am requesting a forensic analysis of the markings found by Agent Clarke, and this water leak in the Tanglao docking access."

"Copy that, Okayo," Zhèng replied, and then after a pause, "but request denied. With Tucker in custody, I don't have cause for delaying this station any longer beyond its next transfer window. That's a pretty big ask, Agent."

"Commissioner, besides Tucker's illegal monitoring, we have evidence of a security breach in an active murder investigation, and possible signs of tampering at the site of the murder."

"What we have is a water leak in an idle docking station—hardly startling. And Clarke's evidence of a robber doesn't sway me either. Robbers are routinely activated for maintenance. Neither are causes for idling this station for a *third* forensics check. If we want more time, I'll need something else."

Okayo looked at McClellan. "Looks like we go with your plan."

"Attention, all crew. Prepare for level two transit adjustment in five minutes. Main engine fire in sixty-eight minutes. Remember: take caution during all orbital adjustments."

"Better hurry," Okayo said. "After this adjustment there are only a few more before Red Delta fires her main engines—and if we're here for that, our trip home gets a lot longer."

"Understood," McClellan said.

"All right," Okayo said, positioning herself at the docking controls. "You know the protocol. I'll stay here and monitor. You keep all body cams activated."

"Will do," McClellan said. "Come on, Tucker."

The access to the docking assembly was only about three meters in diameter, and it did not have a flat side to orient its occupants. Signs were sparse and the walls were utilitarian—hallmarks of the engineers' backup systems for their backups to their backups.

McClellan looked at Tucker. "You all right?" he asked. "The last time you were here . . . well, this has to be difficult."

Tucker looked sideways at McClellan. "Feels sad," he said. "The whole thing is sad."

"That it is, Max. So let's try to make things right, okay?"

The questions seemed to have gone unheard. Tucker continued through the tunnel, shaking his head, propelling himself mechanically, seemingly resigned that he no longer had the freedom to decide where to go or what to do.

The docking system must have sensed the water vapor. Drops spun along the circumference of the walls, disappearing into ventilation intakes.

The lights dimmed and went red. "Attention all crew. Prepare for level two transit adjustment in four minutes. Main engine fire in sixty-seven minutes. Remember: take caution during all orbital adjustments."

"Max, show me what you did when you came in here that morning."

Tucker nodded obediently, braked his momentum on the next grab, and took a breath. "Well, first we were all doing our precommissioning jobs, maybe faster than we should. Maybe not by the book. But we were all excited about being commissioned—about getting a full crew and earning credits. So things were good, and Nicky always told me to enjoy when things are good."

"Go on."

"Well, like I told the other investigators, Hobart and I were doing all the comm systems. He was outside, and I was inside. We had to do a system reboot to upgrade our software—the engineers are always upgrading the software—so that meant no comms except for local radios, but no one was using those at the time."

McClellan noted Tucker's honesty.

"It's a good time when we reboot," Tucker said. "I like my job, but it's noisy and you're always hearing other people's business. And you're always getting hassled by the engineers. Reboots are like vacations. There's just silence."

"And then?"

"Then I got a tug on my local radio. Hobart was out at the antenna array, and he saw what looked like a compartment decompression, out this way, where a high-def was working. It wasn't much, he said, but he got all worked up when he realized it was by the assemblies where Nicky was. He tried to radio, but they don't work with printer interference, so we couldn't get to Nicky."

"That's true, Max. Printers are like us, sometimes. They don't like comm traffic when they're working."

"Attention, all crew. Prepare for level two transit adjustment in three minutes. Main engine fire in sixty-six minutes. Remember: take caution during all orbital adjustments."

Max was still thinking about McClellan's words. "They scare me, those things," he said. "I bet the printer is the killer. Not that I mean to tell you your job. But I don't trust them. They have minds of their own."

McClellan urged Tucker to stay on topic.

"Anyway, I was closest to where Nicky was. So again, like I told the others, I was already suited up in case something happened to Hobart, and I went fast. Left my tools behind and just went. My heart was pounding. I pushed off every grab I could to get as much speed as I could, kicked into the docking assembly, and I kinda knew when I saw the controls that things weren't good. Nicky wasn't in the access tunnel—this one, this one here—and the outer lock read that it was open and the inner door was closed. Not good. And I could hear the whine of the high def through the walls, and see its light all the way down here."

Tucker looked up and shivered.

"So I went up fast. The inner door was locked with the vacuum on the other side. The window was iced up, but I could see in, and there was Nicky, my buddy, just floating as the printer was finishing up its business. All I could do was pound and yell . . ."

McClellan knew there was more that Max Tucker wanted to say—or could say but had some reason not to. In time, McClellan thought. Give the kid time.

By now the water vapor had been filtered out of the tunnel. But new water swelled in Tucker's eyes. He wiped it away as McClellan put his hand on the back of Tucker's shoulders, in part to comfort the boy, in part to urge him on.

The lighting dimmed. "Attention, all crew. Prepare for level two transit adjustment in two minutes. Main engine fire in sixty-five minutes. Remember: take caution during all orbital adjustments."

"Better hold on," Tucker said. "We're gonna feel the maneuver hard out here. Maybe we should go back."

McClellan nodded forward.

They went the last few meters silently, connected by grief and cold and the search for truth. The air lock was smaller than the main docking assembly that McClellan and the security team had used to enter Red Delta. The damage from the printer's emitters was still there, along with some of Tanglao's suit and helmet, which were fused to the wall. Markings from the forensic inspections still circled points of interest—possible locations of evidence, locations to scan, to test, to question.

McClellan breathed deeply. "I've seen the holoimaging from two forensic checks of this spot. But it's not the same as being here." He took out his tablet and played Tanglao's message:

"my intent . . . but to the one who has taken my life . . . please pray . . . and for my family . . . Father, I ask forgiveness."

As the words echoed around them, McClellan pushed himself to the far wall of the air lock, by the outer door. A small window looked out into blackness, and the tip of a communications array lit by the sun. He ran his fingers along the door, feeling for printer patterns but finding nothing unique.

"You say this outer door was open when you found Nicky," McClellan said. "But he was tethered. So he was expecting the door to open—"

"That's right. Nicky had to test docking operations from the inside."

"But Tanglao—I mean, Nicky—didn't have on his outer gloves. Just the liners. So that tells me he *didn't* expect the door to open."

"Not really. Working that way makes small jobs easier. We get cited for it all the time, but no one really cares."

"Attention, all crew. Prepare for level two transit adjustment in one minute. Main engine fire in sixty-four minutes. Remember: take caution during all orbital adjustments."

Using only his inner gloves made sense, McClellan thought—especially if Tanglao was intending to link with the printer, or already had. But the door had to open out of sequence because the docking interior was still pressurized. That's what Hobart saw—the air released, its moisture crystallizing as it blew into space.

"How long would it take to decompress a space this size?" McClellan asked. "Ten, twenty seconds?"

Tucker shrugged. "Probably. Maybe less. Depends on how fast the door was opened."

"And you didn't open the lock?"

"Hell, no."

"So Nicky opened it himself?"

"He could have. But why would he out of sequence? No, it had to be someone else. Or the printer. Come on, we should go. Those thrusters will be firing."

"I understand," McClellan said, reaching into a pocket and taking out his rosary. "But there's something here that I'm missing. And God help me, I'm going to find it."

Tucker eyed McClellan as he made the sign of the cross. "So you are a man of God, like they said."

McClellan nodded. "So was Nicky. His real name was Father Raphael Tanglao."

Tucker grabbed a support. "You think I killed him?"

"Attention, all crew. Prepare for level two transit adjustment in ten seconds. Main engine fire in sixty-three minutes. Remember: take caution during all orbital adjustments. This is a final warning."

With his free hand, McClellan gripped an adjacent support. "I once released a guilty man because I mistook grief for innocence. I promised I'd never let that happen again."

Tucker looked away. "You're taking me to New Athens?"

"That's right."

"And I'll be safe there?"

"Of course," McClellan said, wondering what had prompted that question.

An alarm sounded from the main spine tunnel, echoing up the access tunnel and into the air lock. Another sounded from the tunnel itself. CAUTION lights flashed, dimmed, and flared again. The massive relay's main thrusters powered up, fired two bursts, and then roared.

McClellan and Tucker held on as Red Delta's orbital momentum transitioned again—as the walls of the air lock rotated and pivoted slowly around them, as access panels that were not secure—whether from the printer's damage or the investigation—creaked and complained. And as had happened on the transport, the crucifix on McClellan's rosary maintained its original velocity. It tugged at its chain and drifted silently as the sounds of the engines thundered.

And then all went quiet. McClellan watched the crucifix spin around his fingers—as would anything else on the relay so tethered. And if his hunch was right—

Something inside one of the panels made a scratching sound. Then another.

Tucker began to speak, stammering before distant thrusters groaned again and suddenly stopped.

The scratching sound grew louder, then went soft. Then came silence. Uncomfortable silence.

McClellan stowed his rosary and slipped on new examination gloves. He pried open the panel that had been the source of the scratching. Inside, drops of water tumbled from the innards of an auxiliary oxygenator, which used water to make oxygen. He looked closer and found the source—water oozed from the seams in the covering of a small rectangular component. He released its four latches and removed its covering. Inside was a programmer's key fastened to a neck chain twisted meticulously alongside wet, punctured tubing.

McClellan looked closer and saw that the key had been engraved with the name Tanglao.

He did not touch the key—he'd leave that to the forensics team. Instead he made the sign of the cross to give thanks to God. He also said a silent prayer to St. Anthony—the patron saint of finding lost posessions—for a little more help finding Father Tanglao's other programmer's tool, his coupler, which had to be somewhere on the station.

Then he looked over at Tucker, who stared back despairingly.

Finally McClellan radioed Zhèng.

ARCHBISHOP BAUER PUSHED THROUGH the rainy Saturday afternoon to visit the Cathedral of the Holy Cross. The construction foreman
had sent word that he'd like to show the archbishop the recent progress.
The request was unusual, since Bauer was there almost every day. But it
was appreciated. It had given him the opportunity for a walk, to take a
detour through the nearby neighborhoods—the lively ones and those still
abandoned and overgrown—and to stop at the mass graves just down
Washington Street. He stood for a time to pray, and to think about what
to report during his next conversation with Cardinal Kwalia.

His friend Monsignor Harper had sent word that morning about worries in the intelligence community. Sal operatives were moving, but they
didn't know why or where. There was no confirmation that any of this had
anything to do with McClellan—but the timing was too coincidental to
be anything else.

It was just past noon when Bauer entered the side entrance of his archdiocese's mother church. The rain had darkened its brown, Roxbury pud-
dingstone exterior, yet when a burst of sunlight made its way through a
break in the low, racing clouds, it glowed.

The interior was a tumble of scaffolding and stacks of pews that had
been removed for repair. Above, laborers were concentrated on a section
of ceiling at the rear. The old damage had been secured by a collection of
tarps during the years since the attack, and with repairs finally under way,
new ones protected the cathedral from the rain.

Bauer had always counted it as a miracle that the Sal drone had pen-
etrated the cathedral where it did—on the roofing far from the altar and
the artwork of its sanctuary—and that the blast did little damage to the
pipe organ. He said his usual prayer of thanks as he made his way up
the main aisle. Workers were sitting in groups, silently devouring fish
sandwiches and potato soup made that morning by cathedral parish
volunteers.

He was halfway up the aisle when he heard Tommy Ryan's voice. Tommy was the project foreman and union shop steward. He was loyal to his family, the workers of Boston, and the Church. He had resisted the terrors of the dark years, and worked with his archbishop to protect and feed thousands. Today, it was because of Ryan's stubborn will that the cathedral was being rebuilt, which gave the workers something to do and to earn a small living.

"Archbishop, can I have a word?"

"Of course, of course. How's it all coming? Looks like that roof is moving fast."

Even without his hard hat, Ryan was about a head's height taller than the archbishop. Ryan's red hair, thinning and cut low, was wet and held flecks of stone and wood shavings. Some of the shavings fell off when he looked up to where the archbishop pointed.

"We'd be farther ahead if we were having better weather," Ryan said. "That nor'easter set us way back. And now this rain. But the crew is eager to get it done for Holy Week. We promised that and we meant it. It's a thank you for hiring us and not trusting some printer."

"Don't thank me," Bauer said. "It was mostly selfishness. Anywhere the engineers bring their printers, trouble seems not far behind." He studied the stained glass windows for a moment and said, "Truthfully, Tommy, houses of God should be built by human hands. Like the hands of St. Joseph. As for being in here for Holy Week? Well, that will be up to God, and up to the mayor to give us the permit, if she's in a good mood. But you didn't call me for a discussion on construction schedules, Tommy. What can I do for you?"

Ryan put his vast hand just below Bauer's shoulders and they took a few steps away from the lunch crowd. "It's more like what I—or we—can do for you."

Bauer pushed his hands deeper into his overcoat pockets. "Go on."

"It's like this," Ryan said. "See Hector over there? Hector Romero?"

"Yes. Good man, and doing some fine work on that roof. Didn't he just have his boy baptized?"

"Yes," Ryan said. "Samuel. Tough little guy. And, Archbishop, you're right about Romero. He's a helluva high-wire worker—he's the man you want for a roofing job. But then, he's good with heights. Did you know that he was a builder upside? Or I guess he still is, technically by the guild's rules."

Bauer looked over at Romero, who was sitting on a toolbox chewing a thick sandwich. He was a young man with dark hair and a thin beard. He straightened his posture and stretched his long legs as he returned the archbishop's stare, then gave a half smile and a nod.

"Builder, huh?" Bauer said to Ryan.

"Yes. About three years up there. He got kicked down two years ago for not passing some licensing test. Or at least that's what the engineers told him. Either way, Hector is a big fan of McClellan. Pretty much all of Boston is. You know that, right?"

"Yes. And I know he appreciates it very much. As do I."

"I mean, like Romero says, in a way Father McClellan is up there for us. He's up there doing what the engineers and the security people can't do—he's showing 'em that they can't forget the people down here. That we have lots to offer."

Bauer nodded. The situation was more complicated than that, of course. Which is why he enjoyed listening to men such as Tommy Ryan.

"I knew when I met him that McClellan was going places," Ryan continued. "He helped out two summers ago at Christ the King, my sister's parish in Brockton. He was great—McClellan was—he was so good to my sister and her kids when she got sick. I'll never forget that."

Ryan looked over toward the altar. Bauer followed the foreman's gaze and asked how long it had been since they buried his sister Elaine.

"Four months yesterday," he said. "I can still see her casket right there. My sister would have been so happy to know you opened Holy Cross for her. The fact it was illegal to use the building would have made her laugh—laugh hard, like she did before she got sick."

Bauer let his eyes speak for him. He rested a hand on the foreman's shoulder and finally said, "Tommy, I suppose people tell you all the time that Elaine would say she wants you to keep moving forward, not to look back. But that's not always possible for mere mortals like us, huh? We never stop hurting when the people we love suffer and die, especially so young, like your sister. So when people say those things—and I know that they do, because they always do—you tell them they don't know what they're talking about. And you tell them Archbishop Alfred Bauer said so.

Okay? I'm going to have a public Mass said for Elaine as soon as we get our occupancy permit—and I'll be the one saying it."

Ryan sniffled and managed a thank you. He straightened himself and ran his hand over his face and hair, shedding more wood shavings and stone. "Anyway, Archbishop, like I said, we've got news. Well, Hector has it, but I'm delivering it."

Bauer returned his hands into his overcoat pockets.

Ryan leaned in. "We got ties upside. Hector had a girlfriend up in New Athens and now she's one of the area stewards in the Builders Guild. Guess Hector and her are still friends, even though the engineers keep communications limited. But the builders maintain the communications systems, so . . . bottom line is that we're able to get news."

"Is that so?" Bauer said, not bothering to hide his delight.

"Absolutely," Ryan said. "And we've already gotten some. The way Hector heard it, some of the builders are in talks with the Sals, offering them a deal in New Athens, but no one is saying why."

"What kind of deal?"

"Don't know," Ryan said. "But we're going to find out."

Ryan took a step back, as if returning to work. "So tell your people in Rome—yeah, we know all about that, Archbishop—you tell them you've got ties upside. And we're on it. And we're gonna find out about any sons of bitches that want to hurt Father McClellan. You tell 'em that Tommy Ryan said so."

15

IT WAS EARLY THAT SATURDAY morning when the security transport returned to New Athens with Maximillian Tucker. Clarke and Lopez had remained on Red Delta to coordinate the arriving forensics team.

Zhèng had agents waiting in the Centerwell concourse. Five would escort Raphael Tanglao's body to the Security Guild morgue. Six would take Tucker to protective holdings in the City of Philippi.

McClellan accompanied Tucker through the Wheel. Neither stopped to admire the core's twelve cities and farms. McClellan also ignored the urgent messages from Elaina Jansen, as well as Jansen's messengers who followed up asking for a response. His focus was on the well-being of the young man. The priest would not speak with anyone until he was certain that Tucker was safe and attended to. And when that had occurred, he told Tucker to notify him if he needed anything, and that he would return regularly to check in.

"Would you mind if I pray for you?" he asked Tucker. "In a few hours I'm saying the first Mass up here. I'd like to add you to the intentions."

Tucker leaned against the clear walls of his cell and simply said, "If you want." But as McClellan turned to leave, Tucker added, "Thanks."

As he stepped to the pulpit to proclaim the gospel, McClellan heard the words of his archbishop: "Remember, Johnny, you'll be preaching to the people in front of you. Not to the history books."

He had slept only an hour on the transport back to New Athens—in part because of his attention to detail in writing after-action reports, in part because of the time he spent with their detainee, and because he'd been inspired to rewrite his homily for this first public Mass in the new world.

When he did get to his apartments, McClellan managed a few hours of sleep, then finally met the young couple who would be helping him with the chapel. Jack was nineteen and Chrissy was twenty. They had come to New Athens together to study climate engineering, but had had second thoughts about signing the New World Agreement. This had gotten the attention of the engineers just when they needed help for a visiting priest.

McClellan already treasured the couple, and was impressed that while Jack and Chrissy lived together by the arrangements made for them, they would not sleep together until they could be married in a church on Earth—or, perhaps, in the very chapel on New Athens in which they had been asked to serve.

And now, at twenty minutes past noon, after Chrissy had read the readings and sang the psalm, Jack stood next to the pulpit holding the thurible with its smoldering incense. McClellan took it and lifted it over the words of Luke's gospel. As he did, one of the recording drones descended off to the side, then backed away reverentially. McClellan understood why the Mass was being recorded, but part of him wished that Rome hadn't demanded it. Thankfully, the engineers had counterdemanded that the holodata be embargoed for fifty years.

Smoke rushed out of the thurible's holes as he swung it over the Book of the Gospels. Wisps rose and swirled over the pulpit with a familiar and comforting sweetness. McClellan breathed in, bowed, returned the thurible to Jack with another bow, turned to face the people, and focused.

"After this he went out and saw a tax collector named Levi sitting at the customs post," McClellan proclaimed. "He said to him, 'Follow me.' And leaving everything behind, he got up and followed him. Then Levi gave a great banquet for him in his house, and a large crowd of tax collectors and others were at table with them. The Pharisees and their scribes complained to his disciples, saying, 'Why do you eat and drink with tax collectors and sinners?' Jesus said to them in reply, 'Those who are healthy do not need a physician, but the sick do. I have not come to call the righteous to repentance but sinners.'

"The Gospel of the Lord."

Chrissy and Jack replied, "Thanks be to God." The eight builders in the back pew—the only people in attendance—remained attentive but silent, as did Zhèng and Okayo, who stood at the main doors, they said, for security purposes.

As the people sat for the homily, which they did after the priest instructed them, McClellan waited for the return of silence. Then he gripped the pulpit and began.

"My friends, if you knew me, you'd know that when I preach I don't like to speak about myself. But in this case, what I am about to say may help us get to know each other, and, more importantly, help us better understand what it means to say that Christ has come among us, as he will at this Mass.

"I was raised an atheist. My story of conversion is too long to share now, but in light of today's gospel, one element deserves attention. I embraced this faith and I entered this priesthood because, like Levi, I was called. Every time this gospel is proclaimed—as it happened to be at every Mass today, everywhere in the universal Church—I remember the very moment when Christ spoke those words 'follow me' to me.

"And now, I am here with you on this Saturday afternoon because of the deaths of two men, and because of what these deaths call us to.

"First, the death of Father Raphael Tanglao—and the mystery that surrounds it—has brought me to New Athens as an investigator. And second, the mystery of God entering into human history—of *his* death, and his resurrection—has brought me to this pulpit and, in a few moments, will bring me to that altar as a priest.

"Both mysteries are new realities for this world. Life in the orbits has been designed to thrive without them—without murder, or any crime, really, or without faith in Jesus Christ. And yet, here we are. We may all be in this chapel for different reasons, but I'm certain that, in our own ways, each of us is wondering about all that has happened these past few weeks. About all that is happening. And I'm also certain that both deaths—Raphael Tanglao's and Christ's—are calling us to truths that we may never have expected.

"Of course, there are vast and important differences between these two calls—these two mysteries. Importantly, one is meant to be solved. The other is not.

"The first mystery—the mystery of a murder—isn't intended to remain a matter of shadows and questions—of unknown motives and methods. We're meant to solve it—to shine the light of truth on it. To gather facts and expose it. And I assure you: in the matter of Raphael Tanglao's death, we will do just that.

"But what of the mystery of God coming among us? What of his call? What of the Word of God becoming flesh—of his death and resurrection? These are mysteries that we can never solve. I say this not because God wishes to hide from us—far from it. As it was in the beginning, is now, and ever more shall be, God continually reveals himself to us.

"With God, the word 'mystery' doesn't mean 'something forever hidden,' but rather 'a relationship that grows, and can never stop growing—for this mystery is a relationship with the very source of love, everlasting life, and truth.'

"Don't we know that from our own lives—from our own loves, our own friendships? Are not our encounters with each other *mysteries*? After all, when we allow someone into our lives—as so many have done for me these recent days—we can never stop learning about each other. We can never stop discovering. We can never stop appreciating something new about the other.

"In a few moments, the mystery of encountering *God*—of encountering *truth*—will take a most remarkable form for believers. It will begin with the simplicity of bread and wine—gifts that have been made from the crushing of wheat and grapes, which have been grown here on the farms of New Athens. In other words, made with the noble work of human hands. This bread and wine, this work, will become, through God's grace, the very presence of Jesus Christ—his body, blood, soul, and divinity. This is the promise that Christ made to us at the Last Supper, it is one he has been fulfilling ever since, and it is a promise he will fulfill to us here, now.

"And so I will end with a beginning—a promise: at this Mass, Christ will come in a unique way to this world—a world that needs his healing as much as the old one below. He will come to all, and he will come for all, no matter which guild we belong to, or which belief we profess, or if—as I once did—we profess none at all. He will come, he will call, he will heal, and he will shine his light of truth onto all our questions—onto all those mysteries that you and I are faced with every day, both in life and, yes, even in the presence of death."

16

"YOU'RE QUITE THE CELEBRITY," Okayo said to McClellan after they stepped off the streetcar onto O'Neill Boulevard in the City of Corinthia.

The Saturday evening crowd stole glances at the man who had helped bring about justice in the matter of that unfortunate death. But the smiles were tempered. A closer look at the hero showed that McClellan had taken advantage of his popularity to wear his black clerical cassock.

He had wanted his first dinner on New Athens to be with the locals at the Spinside pub, just down the boulevard from his residence in Troas City, but an invitation to the home of the chief engineer was one he neither could, nor wanted to, refuse.

"I won't be joining in the meal," Okayo had explained. "By treaty, security agents do not enter the homes of the engineers. But as a courtesy, Jansen insisted that I nonetheless be given the same dinner in an outer parlor."

"How magnanimous," McClellan said.

"That alone is unprecedented. I'm sure that I'll make the news feeds, along with you."

The Sun Crane was going dim for the evening, but Corinthia's own lighting brought a festive array of colors to the coming darkness. The city's young people were gathered in cheery groups along the stylish O'Neill Boulevard. They were especially merry as they came into and went out of restaurants and bistros, and to and from the cocktail parties held in geometric gardens decorated with waterfalls and Greek-style monolithic columns.

"Thank you, sir," a large woman said as she broke from a well-dressed group. She presented herself with erect posture, a magnificent smile, and an outstretched hand that came from somewhere within her loose, fiery red gown. "You've made us all happy to know justice is being done. I say again, thank you."

She clasped McClellan's hand and shook it, then closed in and said, "How unfortunate for you that you won't be able to enjoy a longer visit."

Okayo intervened. "We wouldn't want Father McClellan late for his dinner with Madame Jansen," she said.

"Oh, no," the woman said. "That wouldn't do."

They stepped out of the path of an oncoming streetcar, its bell clanging. A team of young engineering students pushed their heads through the car's windows to hail McClellan. They shouted something about the timing of an execution.

"Poor Tucker," McClellan said, as he watched the departing streetcar. "Don't these people know that being detained for questioning isn't the same as being found guilty of murder?"

Okayo shook her head. "What eats you is in your clothing," she said. "It's a saying from back home in Kenya. The troubles we have are often the things and the people that are closest to us. We are our own worst enemies at times."

McClellan thought about that as they came to the home of Elaina Jansen. The structure rose to one of the intermediary levels of protective skylights. Its ornate façade of columns and pediments stretched some two hundred meters along the boulevard. Okayo had told him it was the largest private home in New Athens. But then, Jansen was one of the three surviving engineers who had designed and overseen the construction of New Athens, and she was its chief engineer. She was also on the Engineering Council, which oversaw the engineering necessary for peace and prosperity in the orbits.

An attractive young woman opened the doors. Her blond hair was braided, and she wore a neat blue-and-white pinstriped dress with a crisp white collar. She held up a silver tray with white towels and spoke in French, to which Okayo responded fluently. The young lady blushed.

"My apologies, Father McClellan," the woman said in English, but with difficulty. "Welcome to the Jansen home. Your hand towel, sir."

"Hand towel?"

Okayo motioned to the tray. "Engineer etiquette. You'll need to wipe your hands before you step in and touch anything. It's their version of ritual."

McClellan performed his duty, and smiled as he followed the young woman. He asked her name, and she told him it was Claudette.

Okayo stepped into a small seating area off the entrance foyer. It was white and grand with a dome of blue-and-green skylighting. "Did you bring any toys to occupy you?" McClellan asked.

"I did," she said, holding up an ordinary-looking tablet and waving him down the hallway. "You go, enjoy your conversation. Best not keep your hosts waiting."

McClellan turned to wave a farewell, holding up both hands to show her they were clean. He followed Claudette through a wide, simulated marble hallway to join the other guests.

"John Francis McClellan," Claudette announced when she reached the small gathering of engineers.

Elaina Jansen stepped quickly to greet her guest. Dressed in a black gown with a strand of pearls, she walked confidently in shiny black heels. She spoke in French to Claudette, who blushed again and hurried off on some important errand.

McClellan thanked the young girl with a smile as Jansen shook the priest's hand and brimmed with delight as she welcomed him in.

"Come in and meet the other guests," Jansen said. "And to drink, Father? What may I get you?"

McClellan kept up with Jansen to greet the other engineers—two men and two women stood holding cocktails, displaying varying degrees of enthusiasm. The men, one Japanese and one European, wore plain open-collar suits. One of the women, who looked to be the twin of the Japanese man, wore a gray dress and offered no smile. The other woman, who smiled in abundance, wore a festive display of reds and oranges that were all the more brilliant against her brown skin.

McClellan had taken only a few steps when he saw the dimensions and the appointments of the room. Its ceiling rose some six stories. It was relatively narrow, but it was longer in the circumferential direction of New Athens. One wall was made of windows overlooking multilevel gardens. The others were paneled with fine wood, with the occasional balcony or window looking into the room from upper levels. Two walls had bookcases with what looked like real books—some quite old. The other held fine cabinets for liquor and crystal glassware on either side of a fireplace, which crackled with holographic fire. The fireplace was flanked with two tall white statues, one of Aristotle and the other of Galileo. On the mantel was a ticking clock, and above were paintings of New Athens under construction—the largest reminding McClellan of that final image in the video Zhèng shared, the image of New Athens near completion, its unfinished sidewall resembling a vast stained glass window looking into the core. The paintings, like the bookcases, rose almost to the skylights capping the room.

Then McClellan looked down. Most of the room's floor was a section of the transparent hull, which he had seen in the center of the world during his arrival. Because the outer hull in such a rotating cylindrical world is the floor when standing inside, the construction technique offered an unobstructed view below them. The scene at the moment was the southern edge of Earth, which moved away as New Athens rotated about its axis. At one end of the windowed floor nearest the fireplace was a seating area of overstuffed sofas, armchairs, and side tables. McClellan decided that walking on transparent hulls would take some getting used to.

He captured his bearings and remembered the people around him. "I'm being rude," he said. "It's a pleasure to meet you all."

Jansen introduced her colleagues.

The first to shake McClellan's hand was the woman in the fiery dress. Her name was Hannah Ward, and she was the chief designer for South America's electric grid upgrades. She was also the oldest person in the room. To her left was Mizuki Sasaki and her brother Yoshiharu. They were young, shared the same rounded faces and black hair, and were principal structural engineers for New World Construction. Last was Andrew Pavić, who had just been promoted to second engineer for data control. Jansen said that it was also his thirtieth birthday, which prompted a smile that scrunched Pavić's freckled nose and narrowed his already narrow blue eyes.

Jansen made her way to the glassware. "Well, Father, your drink? Wait, allow me. I have a surprise for you."

Jansen hummed as she sought and grasped a bottle that looked unexpectedly familiar. "Grand Traverse Distillery from your home state of Michigan," she said, reading the bottle. "When the papal secretary and I were discussing your needs, I inquired about only the most important details." She collected ice cubes with silver tongs and dropped them into a carved crystal rocks glass. "I have several bottles of their straight rye, from before the famines. This is from 2033. I'm sure it will be to your taste."

McClellan accepted the drink happily. He sipped and followed his hostess and the other guests to the seating area with stuffed armchairs and sofas and side tables made of wood carved with geometric patterns. On a central glass table, a vase holding white roses was surrounded by platters of various meats and fruits. The elegance of the scene was inviting, save the transparent floor, which still jarred McClellan every time he looked down at it.

As the group took turns offering each other the most comfortable-looking chairs, the crescent Earth again rolled into view beneath them. McClellan stood a moment to watch as the Atlantic Ocean swept under his feet, its waters enveloped by night and covered with two spiraling storms. Even from the distance of New Athens's geostationary orbit, he could see clouds flaring with lightning.

"To Earth," Andrew Pavić toasted, smiling and holding up his glass of Bordeaux red wine. "And its electrical grids," added Hannah Ward, raising her glass of gin. The three other engineers took turns offering birthday and welcoming toasts, and then they all sat laughing as the cosmos rolled beneath them.

"Tell me, Father McClellan," Hannah Ward said, as she studied the platter of cheese and smoked salmon offered by Claudette, "I imagine you'll have a busy day tomorrow. Will there be preparations for a trial? I assume there will be one soon."

"I am sure the priest first has to attend to the funeral of Father Tanglao," Andrew Pavić said.

"And let's not forget that tomorrow is Sunday," McClellan said. "The first Sunday of Lent. It's one of my favorite Gospels. Christ in the desert tempted by Satan."

Hannah Ward scowled. "But the important matter is putting this murder behind us."

"And getting Red Delta flying," Mizuki Sasaki said. "This additional delay will severely impact the Progress buildout."

"It could also impact my work on Earth," Ward said. "The matter of a dead body shouldn't take precedence. We have incinerators for that."

McClellan realized that the tray of cheese and salmon was waiting at his side. He smiled at Claudette and declined the offer.

"One can attend to both the living and the dead," he said. "If Tucker is charged, then yes, he'll be held under arrest until a trial. But at this point, Security hasn't made that decision. And until we know more, Red Delta will remain idle."

Mizuki Sasaki shifted in her armchair and looked quizzically at her brother Yoshiharu, who sat slouched, eye-typing on a tablet in one hand and swirling the scotch in his rocks glass with the other. She gave him a look of displeasure, which he did not notice, and turned back to McClellan. "But this man Maximillian Tucker is the murderer, is he not?"

"My dear Mizuki," Jansen said, "you are speaking to a soldier and an investigator, but he is also a man of faith. I have read that this faith has a propensity for offering suspects all benefit of the doubt."

Sunlight swept up from the floor along one side of the room. Their crystal glasses flickered in stray reflections as McClellan savored more of the Michigan whiskey.

"Everyone deserves the benefit of the doubt," he said. "But I'm not in charge of what happens next. That's up to Commissioner Zhèng. And he hasn't charged Tucker. That can happen only after we formally question him, and that can happen only when he has access to an attorney. And from the sounds of it that won't be for another week or so. The Builders Guild is supplying Tucker with legal counsel from Earth, so everything is on hold until then."

The five engineers expressed five different versions of displeasure.

"A week?" Pavić said. "Unacceptably inefficient. Really. We've printed these people enough transports that they should be able to come up any time they are granted permission. Elaina, can't we do something to help shorten the wait?"

"I've tried," Jansen said, "but the builders insist on this lawyer. Unfortunately he's finishing a case, and won't leave the planet until that's completed."

"It's the way of things down there," Yoshiharu said, still eye-typing and swirling his scotch. "And the way of the builders. Inefficiencies and more inefficiencies. Sentiment and poor choices."

His sister nodded, and frowned at McClellan. "This means you will be staying here for some time. Is that right?"

"I suppose so," McClellan said. "At least until we're sure of who killed Father Tanglao. So yes. It could last until Easter."

"I'm sorry," Hannah Ward said, "and when would that be?"

"Easter? That's in six weeks."

"That long?"

McClellan shrugged. "Forty days in the desert."

"But certainly Red Delta won't be idle that long," Jansen said. "If so, we'd miss yet another orbital transfer window."

"Could be," McClellan said. "Security will be boarding for another sweep sometime in the next few hours. They'll go about the forensics as quickly as they can—but you've printed a big relay, so yes, it could take weeks. And then Zhèng and the Security Council have to assess the evidence and determine if they're charging anyone."

Mizuki Sasaki ran a finger through her black hair. "Here is my other concern about this delay," she said. "Your chapel was built much bigger and more massive than we had anticipated. Its weight is posing a slight structural imbalance in the Troas district, which of course affects everything, like dominoes. Over the course of many rotations this imbalance will impact hull alignment and perhaps even our orbital positioning. We will have to calculate a fix if the chapel is to remain for more than a month."

Jansen looked displeased. "Mizuki, our guest is not interested in the nuances of station structural balance."

"If I may, Elaina," McClellan said. "I was *asked* to come here, Ms. Sasaki. And to stay as long as necessary. As for the chapel, I didn't design it—but I'd like to thank whoever did. It should stay as it has been built."

Pavić chuckled. "He has a point," he said to Jansen. "We did invite him. But as for the chapel, we should listen to Mizuki. It's too heavy. And it's a little over the top for public access, isn't it?"

Jansen hid her displeasure with a sip of her martini. "Let us just say, Andrew, that now that it is built, the chapel makes for a nice gesture."

Mizuki Sasaki sighed and turned again to her brother. "Yoshiharu, you and I will need to speak with the operations office in the morning about mass distribution. We'll need to deal with this imbalance."

Yoshiharu continued to eye-type and drink. "I know, Mizuki. I've already scheduled inspections at key points. I'll do a walk-through in a couple of days. Check things out. Although it would be easier if we could redesign the chapel—build it as it was first designed."

Pavić watched Jansen's displeasure grow. He turned to McClellan and said, "If the investigation is still ongoing—and if you have not ruled out that the murderer could be someone other than the builder—then please let me know what data resources you will need. We're a bit jammed with the buildout at Progress, but I'll make sure we dedicate whatever band-width you and Commissioner Zhèng may need."

"Much appreciated," McClellan said.

Pavić raised his glass in a quiet toast. He drank and turned to the chief engineer. "Elaina, while we're on the topic of delays, perhaps you should explain our answer to Tanglao's superior and to his family. Might as well get all the unpleasantness past us before dinner."

"Ah, yes," Jansen said, rousing herself from some thought. "An unfor-tunate situation has arisen, Father. One of your brethren, a Father Law-rence Lee, the head of Father Tanglao's Dominican Order, had requested to come to New Athens for the funeral of Father Tanglao. But of course you know this. Sadly, this request has been denied. As has the request from Father Tanglao's family."

"Denied?" McClellan said, allowing himself some displeasure. "Father Lee is the master of the Order of Preachers. Of course he and Tanglao's parents want to be at the funeral. I thought that all this had been dis-cussed."

"We had told Rome that we would *consider* the requests, which of course we did. But you see, there is some sensitivity among some of the other faiths on Earth that there may be too much travel privilege given to the Roman Catholic Church. And there is also some displeasure among the residents of New Athens—as happy as we all are, of course, with your quick detainment of a suspect."

McClellan read the varying expressions of the engineers. They were expecting him to respond with increased indignation—but there was something else. Each of them, in their own way, had some look of alarm. About what, he did not know.

"I understand," he said, in deference to their authority. "I don't like it. But I suppose it's understandable."

The engineers took turns looking at each other.

"Well, I am glad you see our side of things," Jansen said, sitting back.

"I'm disappointed—"

"I understand."

"—and now I have to write a homily for the first funeral in the orbits," he continued, picking up his whiskey. "Because I still intend to hold a funeral Mass. But, as unfortunate as all this is, I cannot discount your generosity to me, and with your work rebuilding the cities on Earth."

The group smiled at themselves. This pleased the priest, but the Marine wanted more information.

"Might I ask," he said, turning to Pavić, "that I take you up on your bandwidth offer? Given these new circumstances, I'll need extra comm time—secure, of course—with Rome, my own archbishop, Father Lee, and, of course, the Tanglao family?"

"Of course," Pavić said.

There was a pause that prompted refills on drinks. McClellan declined another and looked over at Jansen as she returned to her seat. She was staring at him anxiously.

"I have something to ask," she said without her usual confidant tone. "It directly involves the five of us—and perhaps other engineers."

McClellan waited.

"You see, in the past few hours each of us has received a threat. Very disturbing ones."

"From whom?" McClellan asked.

Jansen's eyes were wide, much like Tucker's had been when McClellan had questioned him. "It appears that the threats are from Solorzano. And that's confirmed, I'm afraid."

McClellan watched the expressions of his hosts, lit by the crescent Earth.

"May I ask about the nature of the threats?" he asked.

Mizuki Sasaki stood and walked to the fireplace. "I was told that my brother and I would be beheaded if we did not allow for human labor in future construction. You see, for the projects under way—especially those farther out in the orbits—we had planned full printer buildouts."

Pavić waved his glass. "And I'm to offer more data allotments to builders, as if I had it to hand out like candy. Have you ever seen their use breakdown? Pornography tops the list. Then sporting events, concerts, and gaming. They're hardly doing neurological research. I've been told that if I don't acquiesce, my tongue will be cut out and my throat slit."

Hannah Ward said that she wouldn't speak of the threat against her—but that it had something to do with complaints about power grid repair prioritization.

"And as for me," Jansen said, "I'm in charge of New Athens, and of course its printers. So I am of particular interest to the Sals. Let us leave it at that."

McClellan could not ignore the fear in these people. Jansen in particular slouched as she stared at stars slipping past her feet.

"You see," she said, "I understand that we sometimes come across as harsh—as I am sure our decision about the Tanglao family and his superior must certainly sound. And thank you, again, for your understanding. We try very hard to balance a great many issues. As much as the printers can do, resources are not infinite, the work needed to be done on Earth is vast, and space will always be hostile to life. The continual dispersal of radiation in the Van Allen Belts alone is an ongoing headache. To say nothing of the maintenance of this world and the lunar bases. And through it all we do our best. But I'm afraid we make enemies as we choose this course over that one, this priority over another. And yet we do not intend to be mean-spirited. We are actually trying to help."

Jansen's words were honest, and her fear was real.

"I appreciate all that," McClellan said. "And I understand. We're all human, after all."

"Yes, yes we are," Jansen said.

"Have you told Zhèng about the threats?"

"Not yet. We were hoping you might help with that."

"Why me?"

Jansen was considering her words when Pavić spoke. "Because Commissioner Zhèng has never engaged the Sals," he said. "But you have military experience with them. You were at Raleigh. And besides, we know that the Sals are Christians such as yourself—"

"They most certainly are not," McClellan said.

"They say that they are," Hannah Ward said. "And they do protect your Church."

"They routinely attack the Church, viciously, and they've all been excommunicated."

Jansen fidgeted. "Father McClellan, we don't pretend to understand the nuances of your faith's relation to the Sals. But we believe that for a number of reasons you know them better than our security commissioner, whom we otherwise hold in high regard. We will of course communicate our issues to him—"

"Exactly when did you get these threats?" McClellan said.

"Yesterday. While you and Zhèng's team were boarding Red Delta. So of course we wonder what the connection could be. But I know—we know—that you will find that connection."

McClellan said nothing. Jansen's eyes gave him a thoughtful inspection. "Allow me to be blunt," she said, leaning forward. "You did more on Red Delta in a few hours than Commissioner Zhèng and his team accomplished in a month. You're a natural investigator, and you have experience with and understand the Sals. Which is why I want you to lead this case. I'd like you to take command, beginning tomorrow morning."

"Me? You don't mean that."

"I do. And I have the backing of the Engineering Council in offering you this . . . promotion."

"You're giving me too much credit, Elaina. You understand that I can't get into the details of an ongoing investigation, but I'm certain that Zhèng and his team would have uncovered everything that I did."

"I wonder," Jansen said.

The mantel clock sounded seven o'clock. McClellan used the time between strikes to plan his next move. When the chimes ended, Mizuki Sasaki returned from the fireplace. "Well, McClellan?" she asked. "What will you do?"

He looked down at Earth rolling again under his feet and he thought of Sunday's Gospel reading, which offered the notorious duel in the desert between Christ and Satan: "The devil said to him, 'I shall give to you all this power and their glory; for it has been handed over to me, and I may give it to whomever I wish. All this will be yours, if you worship me.'"

McClellan smiled and sat back into the folds of his armchair. "What will I do? I'm going to enjoy my dinner with you fine people, go home and pray the evening office, get a good night's sleep—finally—and after morning Mass I'm going to visit the sick and the imprisoned. Then I'm meeting with Commissioner Zhèng, who will remain in charge of this case."

17

LANCE CORPORAL DANIEL MACEDO cleaned the gash on his arm with alcohol, the last in McClellan's med supplies. Macedo wrapped the wound with pieces of a towel they found in a half-buried clothes dryer. The ranch house that had once sheltered the dryer was in ruins from the Sals' rush north the day before. What remained provided decent shelter and lines of sight for McClellan, Macedo, and fifteen other tired Marines. The advance on Raleigh had been halted for more than three hours, and it was night. Fires and incendiaries burned brightly in the south and west, and with no electricity running through the city's power grid to drown them out, the stars shone brightly.

"Not too tight," McClellan said. "Give it room to keep the blood flowing."

"Johnny, I know what I'm doing," Macedo said. "Damn. I'd give anything for a high-def."

"You and me both. When we make it to one, I'll print up antibiotics, if we don't find any on the way. I'm better at meds than you."

"And a Mustang convertible?" Macedo said, wincing as he refastened the armor on his sleeve.

"And one of those," McClellan said.

Corporal McClellan and Lance Corporal Macedo were programmers assigned to the 6th Marine Raider Battalion, which had been deployed to secure three experimental printers from North Carolina State University's engineering campus. Their mission was a key element of a grand and hopefully final offensive against Sal incursions throughout the southeastern United States. The Marine Expeditionary Force from Lejeune led the joint operations, with support from Army field artillery, as well as international assistance from Mexico and Croatia. National Guard units from the Carolinas and Georgia lent operational support, mostly assisting with the protection and care of thousands of civilians who for decades had survived the famines and the big storms, only to be displaced by the Sals.

The operation had begun that morning, a clear and warm one on the twenty-fourth day of August 2075, when Marines and Army artillery moved in from the north and the east. The international forces, including three thousand Mexicans and about half as many Croatian Special Forces—all defectors from the Global Union—simultaneously pushed the Sals north and blocked their movement from the west. Battles went as scripted, and spirits were high. For seven hours, the offense had sliced easily through the armies of the *Soldados de Salvación* and cut off their means of retreat.

But the day would not end as it had begun. Heavy thunderstorms grounded air support while Sal forces closer to Raleigh were better equipped and trained than the intelligence had suggested. They were controlling the tempo on multiple fronts. Forward motion slowed, the casualty rate rose, and the joint forces questioned their operations plan.

The southern advance along Interstate 440 halted at the rubble of Wade Avenue. There McClellan and Macedo, the other programmers, and their battle-proficient escorts found refuge in blown-out ranch houses where they watched the new strategy unfold to their south.

In an age when high-definition printers with Deep Intellect created worlds in the orbits, the Marines of the 26th Marine Expeditionary Unit slipped behind enemy lines and fought the old-fashioned way—building by building, dropping from helos onto roofs, clearing structures floor by floor, then forward, and up to the next, because the decisions were coming from the battlefield.

Dying thunderheads, still flashing with lightning, reflected the sun's warmth, then faded to gray. Then the world went dark as the 26th continued clearing paths for the removal of civilians and the arrival of the programmers. Thousands of soldiers and Marines who waited along the forward edge used the precious time to rest and to heal, to eat, to clean themselves, to check and repair equipment, and to tend the wounds of their brothers and sisters before the order came to advance.

A friendly whistle and a green light on a proximity badge gave the all-clear. Lance Corporal Samuel Jordan trotted up the driveway from where he'd been sharing rumors and a smoke with his escorts. He fell into the rubble next to Macedo.

"Just the three of us left," Jordan said, breathing deeply but steadily. "The COC ordered Hamilton and Ramos to Virginia Tech. Heard we found two more printers there. That's okay. They aren't the best program-mers—not as good as us."

"No one's as good as us," McClellan said. "Any word on medical sup-plies?"

"Just that there aren't any. Command probably expected us to have made it to the printers by now. We lost a lot of good Marines today—Army, Mexes, Croats, the works. Hey, I heard there's water here."

A flash preceded another low rumble from the south. McClellan lis-tened in to his earpiece but nothing was reported. "Yeah, we got water. Coming out of that pipe under the sofa."

"Looks like sewer."

"Yeah, I'm handing out sewer water. No, it's fresh. Help yourself."

Their earpieces roared with comm traffic. McClellan's escorts stood out of the shadows, their gear glowing red from firelight. One of them said that remote intelligence had news. That was Lance Corporal Ro-cha, hands down the toughest Marine whom McClellan had served with. Rocha had gotten word from an old buddy from boot camp who was now in Command. The buddy said that the Sals may have found a printer.

Getting to his knees, Macedo cursed. "How the hell did they find the printers?"

"No surprise if they did," said Jordan as the remaining escorts circled around them. "The Sals are good that way. They want what they want, and we all know they're going to get one someday. Looks like that day is today."

"They could just be baiting," said McClellan. "They do that—send bad intelligence, saying they know more than they do, like where a printer is hidden—hoping someone'll move to secure them, tipping off locations, strategies."

Macedo tested his arm and winced.

"Danny, you gotta get called out," McClellan said with an unhappy look.

"I'm good," Macedo said, forcing a carefree tone. "I wouldn't say it if it weren't true."

McClellan was considering his response when the next report came. It was official: the Sals had found all three printers—but there was no word on their condition, or any possibility that they could be extracted.

"Think they have programmers?" Jordan said. "If not, they'll be looking for some."

"Jordan, you're like Einstein over here," McClellan said. "Sals got themselves printers. We know what they'll look for next. No sense going on about it. We're good. We got some of the best Marines watching our backs. Ain't that right, Rocha?"

"Semper Fi, bro," Rocha said.

"Doesn't matter if the Sals got a hundred programmers," Jordan said, undeterred. "They want as many as they can get—especially us, 'cause we know how to print weapons." Jordan watched as water from the pipe bubbled over his canteen, which flashed a blue light because the water was safe to drink. "You guys hear about the two programmers out by Knoxville getting done in by their commander? They say she shot them instead of letting the Sals get them."

"Shut up, Jordan," McClellan said. "We've all heard stories like that. Bunch of Sal lies."

A trio of low-flying F-35s shot past them, the scream of their engines following behind. Radio traffic escalated, and there were blasts of light and smoke closer to the freeway.

"Key and coupler check!" McClellan shouted. "Confirm couplers are depowered!"

"Bet your ass mine's off," Macedo said.

"Confirmed here, too," Jordan said. "No Sal is pinging me on a Saturday night. I'm going out after this is over. Gonna find whatever's left of a bar in Raleigh—all the liquor I can have. I may even buy you two a drink."

Ordnances seared the darkness and roared in the south and the east. Seconds of adrenaline-laced silence became minutes. One of McClellan's other escorts was the radio tech. He was patched into Command, his eyes moving swiftly as he heard the secure communications coming through his implants. "No confirmation that they secured the high-defs," he said. "But Mex Special Forces are moving in—maybe they got intel . . . yes, yes they do. Hold."

"You have to love the Mexes," McClellan said.

"Yeah," Jordan said. "They're winning the competition with us and the Croats about who hates the Sals most. It's a good competition. I'm gonna buy them all a drink, too."

The radio tech cursed and stepped forward. "Sounds like the Sals just did their thing again. Gunned down a few hundred civilians they rounded up along the way. Said God told them to do it 'cause we advanced. Damn religious crazies."

"That's religion for ya," McClellan said.

Four more F-35s raced overhead.

Around the ranch house, the motion of a thousand men and women gave the word before the radio tech could speak: the Sals had clear access to the printers.

It was time to move.

THE CHAPEL

18

MCCLELLAN REMAINED SILENT AS Zhèng told him the news about Max Tucker.

They stood together in front of the chapel's altar railing, facing the sanctuary's crucifix, both considering what this development meant—and where the investigation would go next. The commissioner's tall frame seemed frail in his dress uniform, which he had worn in honor of the first Sunday Mass. McClellan had just removed the finery of his vestments and wore only his black clerical pants, loose short-sleeved shirt, and Roman collar. His arms were folded tightly over his chest and he lowered his head in thought.

"And he gave no explanation?" he said.

"None," Zhèng said. "Just that he wished to confess to the murder of Father Tanglao."

The chapel was empty—as it had mostly been during Mass. Chrissy and Jack had again helped with readings and serving, and were the only two to come forward for Communion. Zhèng and Okayo had again watched from the back. They had been joined by sixteen of the local builders who may have attended more out of curiosity than piety, although McClellan hoped otherwise. Sitting by himself a few rows forward had been the older builder with white unkempt hair who had watched McClellan when he arrived on New Athens just a few days ago, when little Veronica had welcomed him with daisies.

"But you're not accepting his confession, are you?"

Zhèng took a moment to respond, first with a sound of disgust, then a slow shake of his head. "I would prefer not to, but I have no choice. Tucker claims to have made this confession of his own free will. Something happened to him in there. I called for the detention center's night commander to join our briefing—we need to figure out what's going on."

"And Clarke and Lopez? I assume they're joining us."

Zhèng said that they would. "They docked as scheduled. They're in the Wheel as we speak. I've instructed them to proceed directly to your offices. But apparently they have little to report from Red Delta, so don't expect much on that front."

McClellan thought about Tucker—about what, or more likely who, could have made him confess to Tanglao's murder. "So what happens?" he asked.

"We hold him and wait for his lawyer," Zhèng said. "It's a pity. The Security Council was expected to grant your request. Given the relatively minor nature of the original charges—compared to murder, anyway—we were going to release him until formal questioning."

"I suppose it wouldn't help if I made another request."

"Not in the slightest. With his confession, we'll hold him while we wait for his lawyer."

Behind them voices echoed through the chapel. Okayo was in the main foyer greeting the detention night commander, and directing her to McClellan's office. It was good to hear the laughter of friend meeting friend.

"Well, at least that gives us some time to figure our next move."

"I'd prefer no further delays," Zhèng said. "The pressure to commission Red Delta is ramping up, and I hear my reputation isn't at its all-time high."

McClellan had said nothing about the previous evening's conversation with Elaina Jansen and the other engineers. But, as planned, Okayo had monitored the whole evening, so Zhèng would know everything that had transpired.

"Your reputation is solid as far as I'm concerned," McClellan said, looking up at Zhèng.

The commissioner nodded thoughtfully. He turned back to study the crucifix, and behind it the grand painting—or rather the replica—of Christ's Transfiguration. As he spoke, his voice became soft. "When I was a boy in Hong Kong, our church had a window depicting the Transfiguration. It was similar to this. I remember my grandfather explaining its meaning—about how on Mount Tabor Christ briefly showed his closest disciples the glory that he offers us all, and how this brings meaning to the suffering that is to come. This image has always given me hope."

McClellan nodded in response.

"As I grow older," Zhèng continued, "and as every day I see the results of people's choices and failures—most especially my own, as you know—and as I deal with so much suffering in a world that was to have outlawed suffering, I'm more certain that the answers we seek do not come from any of us—not our actions or our intellect or our technologies. It comes from something greater. Otherwise it doesn't exist at all."

"And it certainly does exist," McClellan said. "'The love that moves the sun and all the other stars.'"

Zhèng nodded. "Dante, right?"

"Yes. One of my favorite quotes. I use it in homilies more than I should, but it makes so much sense."

They stood a moment longer. Then Zhèng turned abruptly toward the small door that led to McClellan's apartments and the attached Security office. McClellan followed. He knelt first on his right knee in reverence to the Eucharist reposed in the tabernacle. As he rose to stand, McClellan thought of Raphael Tanglao, and the trials he must have faced as a priest upside without his order's approval, or the support of Rome, or the protection of the three guilds.

Agent Margaret Bukowski gratefully accepted a second mug of coffee. She had just come from her shift in the detention center in Philippi, half of New Athens's circumference from Troas City.

Clarke and Lopez arrived soon after. McClellan made a second pot of coffee, and they sat at the working table under the holographic displays of the orbital traffic around New Athens. Zhèng inserted a dampener into the controls nearest him. He took his seat as the familiar blue glow of a dampening field appeared, first faintly, then strongly across the walls, ceiling, and floor.

As they had two days ago when Zhèng had offered his confession, the monitors overhead went dark. Okayo synced the data ports of the conference table to the displays, which gave the security team their own dedicated data analysis and holodisplay systems.

"How long do we have?" she asked.

"We agreed to twenty minutes," Zhèng said.

"Agreed?" McClellan asked. "Who with?"

"Per the Engineering-Security Treaty," Zhèng said, "the use of dampener technologies by either party must be agreed to beforehand. It's a bit of a constraint, but at least we know of any unauthorized use, which can be helpful."

"I see," McClellan said. "I didn't realize dampeners were this necessary. Can't we keep our conversations secure without them?" McClellan looked at Clarke. "You didn't need a dampener to block Tucker on Red Delta."

Zhèng typed commands on the console in front of him. The holographic displays shifted from the traffic around New Athens to something less focused. An image of New Athens still revolved over the table, but now yellow and green haze seemed to pulsate through and around it, reminding McClellan of the northern lights.

"This is the most recent probability analysis of the tunneling taking place," Zhèng said. "As you know, Father, spatial tunneling was developed by the printers years ago to better transfer energy. Only later was it used to help shield communication signals, and then it was discovered that one could tunnel *into* a space and detect waves of energy—even physical ones such as sound. So it was a perfect spying tool. But yes, such tunneling can be blocked if you know what you're doing. Usually the engineers just update their comm software to keep hackers away from the antennae, but a few weeks ago we asked them to hold off. Let the hackers have at it. And track them."

"The trick in all this," said Clarke, making adjustments to the display, "is to be able to differentiate its legitimate use from those that aren't. It's almost impossible to pinpoint a single tunneling attempt, let alone to do so in a structure this large, with so much of it taking place at once, and with so much standard comm traffic. That's why I'm using dampeners."

McClellan shrugged. "I'm just a simple parish priest. Not a comm expert."

"Tracking," Okayo said, "which is what Agent Clarke did on Red Delta when he left the morgue. We're using dampeners to track who's tunneling, where they're tunneling from, and where they're listening."

Zhèng explained that dampeners act like smoke in a room with lasers. Without the smoke, laser light is invisible. In the presence of smoke or any other contaminate, their paths become visible as the laser light illuminates particles in their way. Dampeners perform a similar function, just using a different form of energy. When tunneling streams hit a dampener field, or pull on them from a distance, the effect can determine the origin and destination of the tunneling attempt—and do so quietly, under the guise of increased security.

Zhèng ended his communications lecture with a gulp of his coffee and looked at Agent Bukowski. "We're at seventeen minutes ten," he said. "Let's begin. How is Tucker?"

"Scared," Bukowski said, sitting up. "He had only one outside guest since you brought him in, a builder named Jianjun Jade, goes by Jimmy. Jimmy Jade."

"I'm not familiar with him," Zhèng said. "And I'd remember a name like that. What do we know about Mr. Jade?"

Bukowski looked down at her tablet and began reading. "Jianjun Jade is thirty-eight years old. He was born in Nanjing and came upside March 11, 2084. Hasn't left New Athens since, other than a few service jobs on the Blue Alpha relay. He is a level five builder—that's a shipping special-ist—but has had no assignment anywhere for more than a year. He's a steward for the guild and is a certified martial arts instructor. He's also a poet, too, if any of you go for that sort of thing. No prior record here or on Earth. No surviving relatives. That's all we have on Jade. In the official records, that is."

"Anything unofficial?" Zhèng said.

Okayo leaned forward. "I did some checking on the flight decks. Jade has had a number of associations recently with less upstanding members of the Builders Guild. I'm looking into that—but I don't want to push my sources too fast."

When no one else volunteered information, Zhèng turned back to Bukowski. "Then let us proceed. What happened when Mr. Jade visited Tucker last night?"

Bukowski shifted in her seat for a better view of Zhèng. "Jade arrived just before midnight. Nothing unusual there. It's part of the life of a guild steward—checking on and providing legal counseling to builders in de-tainment. Jade was making the rounds, checking on the other builders—most of them in for drunk and disorderly. Typical Saturday night. Jade went to Tucker last. He acted decent enough. He introduced himself when he signed in, joked about the night shift, and went about his business. He spent just under five minutes with Tucker. And then he left, giving me a smile and a wave. It was all routine."

"And then?" Zhèng said.

"Then I checked on Tucker and found him . . . well, like I said, scared. I asked how he was, and all he said was that he was waiting for his lawyer. Then he asked for a tablet to make his confession. And he wanted me to witness it. I called my contacts in the Builders Guild, just to cover my ass. They came, Tucker recorded his confession, and that's when I contacted you, Commissioner."

"How's Tucker been since?" McClellan asked.

"Unresponsive. He sits with his back against the wall and says nothing."

Zhèng made some notes in his tablet. "Then we'll give him his time alone," he said. "Time to think about what he's done."

McClellan leaned forward and folded his arms on the table. "Commissioner, I'd like to talk to him."

Zhèng looked up from his typing. "I don't think that's wise."

"I understand," McClellan said. "But I wouldn't go as your investigator. I'm asking as a priest."

"I doubt a lawyer would make that distinction."

"Understood," McClellan said, leaning back to make his case to everyone. "You can record the whole thing. I just want to make sure he's okay. I want to—"

"Make him recant his confession," Zhèng said.

"Well," McClellan said, "someone once said the truth will set you free."

Zhèng gave a look that was both impatient and supportive. "What would be the purpose of such a visit—one that I could share with the Builders Guild?"

"My faith instructs me to visit the imprisoned. It's a work of mercy."

Zhèng looked away, focusing on the tunneling imagery floating before them. Clarke was adjusting the dampener to allow data to flow inward, which returned the imagery to a real-time analysis.

"I see no reason not to consider your request," he finally said. "But no promises. For now, I want to know more about what we're dealing with. Bukowski, play back Tucker's confession."

Bukowski's eyes typed commands on her tablet. Tucker's face appeared on their individual displays, and his voice came low from their console speakers. He spoke unsteadily at first, showing little emotion. His words came slowly, not at all like McClellan had heard the energetic young man talk since they had met.

"My name is Max Tucker. Maximillian Tucker, that is. My builder identification is RE-770-Delta. I am confessing that I murdered my friend Nicholas Pratt, or I guess his real name is Tanglao. I was monitoring his location and the printer outside the lock. I hacked the station's systems to open the outer hatch when the printer was working outside. I knew it would kill Nicky. And I am glad I did. And now I'm making this confession under my own free will. I'm sorry for what I did . . . I didn't know he was a man of God. And that's all I will say until I speak with my lawyer."

The recording ended, and there was silence. As Zhèng's staff weighed Tucker's words, their expressions were grave. McClellan's showed only irritation. "That's *not* how Tucker talks," he said.

Agent Lopez turned to him quickly. "And how would you know *how he talks* when he confesses?"

"I've heard a few confessions," McClellan said. "Real ones. Including murder. And I spent time with Tucker, on Red Delta and on the way back."

Zhèng agreed. "I must say that this is the least authentic confession I've heard. It did sound scripted, except for his last words about Tanglao being a man of God. Although I've never heard a confession for murder. Lopez, I assume we're running tests?"

"We are," she said. "I authorized them on the way here. Stress analysis. Neural linguistics. A few others. I doubt they'll tell us much that we could bring to court, but we'll have results, and we'll have them by the afternoon."

Zhèng complimented Lopez and the rest of his team. "But I want more information," he said. "I want more on Jianjun 'Jimmy' Jade and his activity within the Builders Guild. More on Tucker. And Bukowski, it would be wise to record the circumstances under which the confession was given. The last thing we need is the perception that the confession was coerced."

He tossed down his tablet and asked about a new topic—the threats by Juan Carlos Solorzano.

McClellan only half listened. Zhèng and the others spoke of the basic and the obvious, while he was more concerned with what he didn't know—especially what the builder steward could have said to Tucker.

Of all the uncertainties in this case, Tucker's involvement in Tanglao's death had troubled McClellan the most. But with this so-called confession—and after hearing that voice—McClellan was confident that Tucker had not killed Tanglao, or even assisted with it. He was guilty of other things—lying and bad decisions—but not murder.

McClellan returned his attention to Okayo, who was comparing past Sal attempts to gain footholds in the new world with the strategies they had used in eastern Africa. She said that, with the threats to the engineers, they had no choice but to determine if the Sals were seeking alliances with radical elements within the Builders Guild—as they had tried before.

"We should listen to Okayo," Zhèng said. "There's a trend here. Just last week, Solorzano himself sent threatening correspondence to the Catholic Church as a direct result of Father McClellan assisting us."

Lopez made an unhappy sound. "What kind of threats?" she asked.

"Subtle ones," Zhèng said. "Solorzano believes that it's not wise to have McClellan here. He's offering the Church and the good father his protection."

Okayo turned to Lopez. "And if you know Sal history—"

"I'm familiar with Sal history," Lopez said, her eyes fixed on Zhèng. "When did McClellan's people get these threats?"

"This past Wednesday," Zhèng said. "The day before we brought McClellan up."

"And when was *I* going to get this information, Commissioner?" Lopez said, her tone pushing protocol. "I'd like access to that. It will be helpful to compare and trend *all* the Sal correspondence we have."

Zhèng spoke coolly, saying he would share the reports from Rome with the team.

McClellan spoke up, more to lessen tensions than to get any new information. "So our primary question isn't if, but *how* the Sals plan to use the death of Father Tanglao to get to the printers."

"Which leads to an uncomfortable question," Okayo said. "Did they orchestrate Father Tanglao's death as part of some strategy?"

"And that raises another possibility," Lopez said. "What if Tanglao had been working with the Sals all along?"

Zhèng said that all these questions were necessary for them to examine, and to do so exhaustively. "But we can't forget one other possibility," he said. "What if the entire investigation as it stands is off track? What if we're missing something?"

His staff did not seem inclined to discuss that possibility.

Zhèng shifted in his chair and typed commands to add to the display above them. Superimposed over the holoimagery were the locations of active printers working repairs within and along the hull of New Athens.

"The engineers are nervous," he said. "They're giving us freer rein than usual. And I intend to use it—to demand that they grant access to the printers, especially the clamshell involved in the death of Father Tanglao."

"If we can find it," Okayo said.

"We'd better," Clarke said. "Given what we know about Tanglao—that he was a programmer—it looks like answers about his death will be found in the history of that printer. I wish I knew that when I was checking its telemetry."

Zhèng sat back and turned to McClellan. "Hence you see why we're happy that you're here," he said. "We will need a programmer after all."

"I appreciate your confidence," McClellan said. "But as I've explained from the start, it's been a while since I've been inside a printer. And the last time wasn't my best effort—let's leave it at that."

"Father McClellan," Zhèng said, "you are a fully commissioned programmer. None of us has your credentials or experience. If you must do so to prove Tucker's innocence, then you will go back inside a printer. We may have no other choice."

McClellan turned to Clarke, who was again studying the tunneling traffic, sifting the data, making connections.

"I'll do what needs to be done," McClellan said. "You know that. Although I'm not the only programmer here. We do have Clarke."

Clarke looked up. He was surprised and delighted, but looked to Zhèng for guidance. The commissioner nodded with a slight smile and motioned back to McClellan.

Clarke swept aside the tunneling data and leaned onto the table. "Programmer *in training*," Clarke said. "I've made that clear."

"Yes," McClellan said. "Yes, you have. You trained with the RAF until you came upside. And then the engineers pulled the offer. But none of that matters. You have your programmer-in-training license. I assume you have a key and a coupler?"

"I do," Clarke said.

"And you're all wired up? You had your neural links implanted?"

Clarke nodded. "Five years ago."

"So if you're wired, and have a key and coupler, you're on your way."

"I *was* on my way. But not now. As long as I'm in Security I can't go farther. You're the only full programmer we have. *You* get full access to printers; I don't."

"But that's the point," McClellan said. "I *once* had access. I wouldn't count on my trust level anymore. And anyway, if you made it to a programmer in training, you can get basic access to the high-defs. You can gain their trust. That's a big part of being a programmer, even if you can't go much farther inside."

Clarke straightened his shoulders. "Maybe," he said. "But the engineers will never allow it—even with what we know about Tanglao."

"Father McClellan," Zhèng said, "he's right. You heard Elaina Jansen on the Aesir."

"Commissioner, hear me out. May I suggest that the Security Guild focus on finding Tanglao's coupler and that clamshell? If so, I'll take care of the engineers. And then Clarke and I can use Tanglao's equipment—his key and his coupler—to get inside that printer. Then we can re-create what Tanglao was programming and get some answers."

Clarke began rapidly tapping his coffee mug. "But even if we had Tanglao's coupler, what good is it? I mean, without his personal profiles and his programmer's story, which only he would know, how could we use it? And he's not going to be telling us from his casket."

"I'll see what I can do about that. But in the event that Father Tanglao does not rise from the dead anytime soon, I have a few other ideas to access his coupler." He turned back to Zhèng. "I can't stress this enough, Commissioner. We need access to that printer and we need Tanglao's coupler to get the full story."

"And we will provide them, Father."

"But that may not be soon," Okayo said. "The longer we look in Red Delta and find nothing, it seems increasingly likely that Tanglao's coupler was lost when the air lock blew. I'll work up possible trajectories and we'll look—but that would be a worst-case scenario."

"I can only imagine," McClellan said. "Actually, I can't. Which is why I'm hoping it's still on the relay."

"But even if our teams found the coupler at this very moment," said Zhèng, "it could take weeks, months to intercept with the clamshell, depending on where it has been assigned in the orbits."

"There's good news there," Lopez said. "The two remaining crew of Red Delta—yes, even Superintendent Rose—are calling in favors to track down that printer."

"That *is* good news," McClellan said. "I was going to ask about that."

"She realizes that it's in her best interest," Lopez said. "And I do believe she's got a soft spot for Tucker. Which is good for us. In any event, Rose has begun quietly contacting her colleagues in the other relays—and relay operators know most everything that's happening in the orbits."

"I'm still surprised that Molly Rose is helping," Clarke said. "But I guess citizenship credits will do that."

Zhèng gave his young officer a disapproving look. "One final note on this matter. We should be aware that as far as official communications are concerned, Molly Rose is *not* helping us. We're keeping her search quiet."

McClellan sat back, feeling relieved about the possibilities. He knew the team would be, too. "How long do we have?" he asked. "I'd like to have something on either the printer or Tanglao's coupler when we question Tucker."

Zhèng nodded. "Me, too. But the schedule for Tucker's lawyer has yet to be provided. I'm told that he won't be able to leave Earth for a few more days, maybe even a week. I don't think even the builders know."

The team went silent. After a moment the dampener chirped its cancellation alarm. With the field about to collapse, Clarke recorded the last of the tunneling position data.

Agent Bukowski suddenly stirred. She looked at Zhèng and asked a question that McClellan had been wondering himself.

"Commissioner," she said, "I've been thinking about something since Tucker's confession last night. What do we know about this lawyer coming upside?"

19

TOMMY RYAN STOOD IN the cathedral's center aisle, waiting for his archbishop. A hydraulic lift hissed behind him, idling. It had been a busy Tuesday—a day of progress on both the roof and on helping out Father McClellan.

"Archbishop," he said with a firm handshake, "thank you for coming on short notice. How are you with heights?"

"I can do without them."

"Well, it's best for you to go up and hear our news firsthand. It's quieter up there, if you know what I mean."

Ryan guided the archbishop onto the lift's platform, took the controls, and aimed for the highest levels. The workers above were closing the hole from the attack in 2073, when the Sals were making for the printers in the universities across the Charles River. Bauer's predecessor had condemned the offensive, and his archdiocese paid the usual price. A day after, a fiery Sal drone had pierced the cathedral as two families celebrated the wedding of a Navy pilot and his bride.

The lift's hydraulics whined as they rose steadily toward the sunlight coming through the jagged opening.

"This thing is safe, right?" Bauer asked.

"Very. It's man-made. Not that printed crap."

Bauer spotted Hector Romero above them, stretched upward on a narrow section of scaffolding, helping to position a support being lowered by a crane outside. Romero radioed a confirmation when the section was locked in place, then looked down and spotted the coming lift. He made a circular motion with his arm, which told the workers to move on to other tasks farther away. Now alone, Romero removed his dust mask and turned off his autohammer. He took a tablet from his worn tool belt and consulted its readings.

"Howdy, Hector," Ryan said, waving as the lift rose the last few feet, coming to the scaffolding where Romero stood. "You know Archbishop Bauer?"

"Not formally," Romero said. "Your Excellency, we met briefly at St. Benedict's at my nephews' Christmas play. Juan and Miguel. About so high. They were two of the shepherds."

"Of course I remember," Bauer said, making sure he didn't look down as he reached out to shake the worker's hand. Romero took the hand and kissed Bauer's episcopal ring.

"Your pastor told me you had built their crèche," Bauer continued. "Beautiful craftsmanship, as is this work you're doing here."

Romero gave a soft thank you. He waved his tablet, and told Ryan that there were no signs of tunneling or spy drones, but that he was sending off interference anyway.

"Then let's talk," Ryan said, his big hand guiding Bauer closer to the scaffolding. "Tell the archbishop your news."

Bauer grasped the railing. "I assume it's not about the roof."

"No, but that's going well, as you can see." Romero came closer. "Excuse my bluntness, Your Excellency, but you can tell Rome—and especially tell Father McClellan, if you can—that the Sals are getting a man upside. And soon."

Bauer wasn't surprised. Romero's report matched what Monsignor Harper had said at dinner the night before. Something big had happened. Not only was there increased chatter in the Sal intelligence network, but also on Sunday Solorzano himself had appeared in Morelos at his family's old church. He had demanded that the priest condemn the engineers from the pulpit—which the old cleric refused to do. The story went that Solorzano left quietly just before the Creed. Moments later one of his men fired a single bullet into the cleric's head. This was the first sighting in years, Harper said. It was also first time since Solorzano's excommunication that he had entered a Catholic church—at least that anyone knew of. What it meant, and where Solorzano had disappeared to, were anyone's guesses. But the guesses were equally alarming.

"Do we know how the Sals are getting someone up there?" Bauer asked.

"No, at least not with confidence. What I am told is that whoever it is will have free rein in New Athens, getting access to Engineering Guild data, records, construction plans, and maybe even access to the printers. And, if he wants, he can get to McClellan. I'm not sure how, but that's what I hear."

"Do we have a name?"

"Yes," Romero said. "Rudi Draeger. His real name is Rudolphus, or something like that. But he goes by Rudi. He's a lawyer based in California. He's got a reputation for helping the Sals."

Ryan took a step closer, which made the lift wobble. "Tell Archbiship Bauer how we know about the connection," he said.

"Here's where it gets interesting," Romero said. "Draeger was a leader in the trade unions in Bosnia-Herzegovina, his homeland. He supported the Sals during the wars, after his country broke away from the Global Union, and for that he was exiled—not imprisoned, not shot, as so many were. Exiled. Of course, he was connected and very wealthy. For some time Draeger remained a force in the global trade coalitions, quietly brokering deals between Sals and other cartels, all while publicly doing the same between labor and the Global Union."

"I'm sure he profited well," Bauer said.

"Immensely," Romero said. "But Draeger isn't just a profiteer. He's an ideologue. He believes that Juan Carlos Solorzano had his visions. He believes God is ushering in a new age and that anyone, including the Church, must be crushed unless they accept Solorzano's words."

Bauer did not say what he wished to say—that would require the use of words that archbishops do not speak among their flock. Rather he asked how Rudi Draeger ended up in California.

"His sister," Romero said. "She lived in the hills outside Los Angeles and was getting rich from trafficking the starving to Sal camps. Draeger joined her work, and the Sals paid them handsomely. Because of these two, many tens of thousands were displaced and went to the camps. But I will not speak of such things in this holy place."

Bauer detested the Sals for countless reasons—the camps most especially. Whenever Solorzano's armies had even a little influence in a region—which in the 2060s included much of the southern United States—they would bring relief from the famines and social collapse that had overwhelmed the Global Union. Then the armies would build the camps. The soldiers were generous and the refugees came by the thousands, and then the tens of thousands. Those arriving rarely had any interest in Sal ideology or their beliefs in Christ's imminent Second Coming. They were there for the food, water, medicine, and order.

The camps—there were seventeen of them in the United States alone—offered all this at no charge, and the numbers grew within their walls. Then came that sweltering day in July 2069 when the armies in every camp closed and locked the gates. The Sals executed the weak—it didn't matter if you were old or young, a Muslim, Christian, Jew, or atheist—and among the survivors they demanded oaths of loyalty. This was fair compensation, the armies said, for the mercy that had been offered by the great Solorzano.

The smoke from the bodies could be seen for miles, and rose from the camps for days. Weeks later the gates reopened. Those who had taken the oath swelled the ranks of the armies of the *Soldados de Salvación*. They believed in Solorzano's visions and his promise to build a new world, and they vowed to slaughter anyone who opposed them.

"We need to get word to Father McClellan," Romero said.

Bauer agreed. And the timing for that was right. If all went as planned, he would be speaking to McClellan in a day or so, when the engineers granted permission.

"Is there anything else about this Rudi Draeger?" Bauer asked. "Anything about his relation with Solorzano?"

"Nothing specific," Romero said. "Only the camps and defending Solorzano's operatives in courts—and it is always at no charge, under the guise of some charitable endowment."

Through the roof, Bauer watched as upwelling clouds drifted over Boston. He prayed a brief prayer to St. Jacques Hamel for strength against any coming persecutions and for the protection of John McClellan.

The archbishop was eager to talk to his priest. He had not been able to speak live with McClellan since the morning he had arrived at New Athens, four days ago. The engineers cited some issue with orbital communications—bandwidth security, or some such excuse. Cardinal Kwalia himself sent official protests, but they were ignored. All that the engineers had allowed were written communications, and in them McClellan was asking strange questions about Father Tanglao's upcoming funeral. McClellan seemed unusually eager for information about Tanglao—childhood stories, favorite Scripture passages—which he said he would need for a funeral homily he had not expected to deliver. These requests were telling. Rather than sentimental stories of the deceased, McClellan always made a point of focusing his funeral homilies on Jesus Christ, without whom the dead cannot be saved.

Bauer had a suspicion about what McClellan was getting at—but he'd need more than hints buried in letters, letters that could very well have been censored or doctored by someone upside.

Ryan and Romero were watching their archbishop, waiting for some response.

"There has to be a trial taking place," Bauer said. "Likely to do with the death of Father Tanglao. In any event, Hector, you're right. Draeger could legally request records of all sorts—at the least. And depose whomever he chooses. I will report this to Rome immediately, and to Father McClellan as soon as I can. Thank you, Hector. Thank you very much."

"It's my honor," Romero said. "And may I ask, Archbishop, for your blessing?"

"Of course," Bauer said, raising his right hand, then making a slow sign of the cross. As he did, the archbishop prayed for Romero and his loved ones, entrusting him to the intercession of St. Joseph the Worker.

Romero signed himself and quietly said, "Amen."

20

MCCLELLAN FELT THE STARE before he saw its source.

Clarke sat next to him at the bar of the Spinside, still chewing as he placed his corned beef sandwich back on his plate. The agent turned and looked behind him.

Nearby, builders went quiet, which allowed McClellan to hear the footsteps.

"I do apologize for interrupting," a man said, "but I would so very much like to introduce myself."

Clarke glared, and said that McClellan wanted to be left alone.

"At the Spinside?" the voice said. "No, Brandon, he is here to socialize. To get to know the locals—to get to know people like me. You should try it sometime. It does wonders for one's police work."

McClellan turned away from his chicken pot pie to meet the out-stretched hand of Ira Wagner, the builder who had been watching the priest from that first arrival. He had come to a few Masses, but never stayed long enough to introduce himself. As always, Wagner wore a blue jumpsuit with excessive pockets filled with small tools. His boots were scuffed and loose. His white hair, thinning and long, framed a strong but aged face. His eyes were inquisitive but not unfriendly, and they narrowed as he smiled when McClellan grasped his calloused hand.

"Please, join us," McClellan said, waving to the bar stool at his left. "And don't mind Agent Clarke. It's been a busy day, and he has to get me back soon for a call with my archbishop. He's a good bodyguard."

There was some awkward introductory chatter, which led to a brief discussion about the Johnny Cash tune that competed with the Manchester United soccer game, which took up all three holodisplays behind the bar. The builders of Troas City went back to their conversations, or to watching the athletes, or both. The men quickly became forgotten in a dinner crowd that ate and drank in the dim, low-ceilinged pub, which had not benefited from the creativity of the printers or their programmers.

Shirley was the heavy and cheerful bartender who had been waiting on McClellan, or "Blue Eyes," as she called him. She came quickly to check on his chicken pot pie and Clarke's corned beef sandwich, then lingered to ask Wagner—"Deary," she called him—what he'd be having.

"The Wednesday special," Wagner said. "A stout and a burger. Medium. And a whiskey for our guest. Ah, but Shirley, do you not have anything from Earth? Then whatever is your best, please. Agent Clarke is on duty, so he will not drink. Although he ought to."

When the stout and the whiskey came, along with utensils and a Spinside placemat for Wagner, there was a toast, then two sips and a question.

"Is it true," Wagner said, "that you have taken an elderly builder woman from our city's hospital and have her sleeping in your bed?"

McClellan laughed. Clarke pushed his plate away and leaned forward on his arms. He watched Wagner with disbelief.

"I took her to my apartments to die," McClellan said. "She's there to spend her last days treated with the dignity that she deserves—from people, not from robbers."

"And there is nothing to be done?"

"She's dying," McClellan said. "We're making her comfortable."

"I hear you made something of a scene at the medical facilities."

"I wouldn't say that. It was the second time I met her when visiting the hospital and, yes, I was outraged at how she was being treated by those robotic nursing assistants. It's that simple."

"McClellan," Clarke said, leaning in, "you made a scene."

McClellan shrugged, and admitted that sometimes the Marine pushes aside the priest. "I have to watch that," he said.

Wagner nodded thoughtfully. He watched for a moment as the small bubbles in his stout swirled upward into a layer of tan foam. "There's a good deal of talk about this," he said. "They say you are sleeping in your chapel."

"Until we can get Mrs. Georgeson a proper medical bed, yes. I slept in the chapel last night. It wasn't the first time I've slept in one."

"And I assume that Elaina Jansen and the other engineers are not pleased?"

McClellan nodded as he ate, happy to finally be talking to a local builder, even if this was more interrogation than conversation. But then, he had been told to expect this of Wagner, who nonetheless seemed to have something he wanted to say.

"Well?" Wagner continued. "What did the great chief engineer have to say?"

"About what you'd expect. Jansen expressed . . . concern. And she was worried over the reaction of the Engineering Council. Something about faith and the New World Agreement."

"And has that made you reconsider your decision?"

"I wish," Clarke interjected.

McClellan said that unless the engineers sent Zhèng and his team to drag the elderly woman out of his residence, she would be staying. She would be cared for until she died, and he would pay for her remains to be sent back to Earth for a proper burial.

"You do not approve of this?" Wagner asked Clarke. "Will you be dragging this old builder onto the streets, and back to Troas City Hospital?"

Clarke gave a cold and silent stare.

"Always so serious," Wagner said. "And distrustful. But to you, Father McClellan, I offer another toast. Any man who vexes the engineers is a friend of mine."

The men toasted quickly. Wagner put down his stout and leaned into the bar. "It is a pity that you cannot bring Max Tucker to stay with you as well. If he must be detained, that is. For he is also dying, though in a different kind of way, I am sure."

McClellan focused on the last of his chicken pot pie. If he was going to be lured in, he'd need more of an opening than what Wagner was offering.

Wagner leaned back and reassessed his dinner companion, his eyes lingering for a moment on the scarring on McClellan's head. "Have you gone to visit Tucker?" he asked with enough sincerity to capture McClellan's attention.

"Tried to. Three times since he confessed."

"And?"

"He's not interested in talking, and I can't press the issue."

"Ah, yes," Wagner said. "You do work for Commissioner Zhèng."

"No. I work for the truth."

Sudden sounds of cheering came from the holodisplays and from the builders nearby. The noise drowned out Johnny Cash.

"I also seek the truth," Wagner said. "I may die an unbeliever, but I was raised a Jew. I know that there is truth. And I know that in this world, as in the old one, truth is so very easily cast aside and trampled upon, and we all suffer greatly for it." The cheering subsided, and Wagner's voice was loud without the competition. "Father McClellan," he said, his voice quieter, "very simply, I am here to thank you for disrupting the status quo—for dining with both engineer and builder. For taking in that old woman. And for wanting to help Max Tucker, for I believe that you wish to help him. And so, for all this, I am offering you help."

McClellan said nothing, but listened and watched closely. He didn't want to offer too much before he knew what was at stake.

"After all," Wagner said, "as I understand it, your investigation is stalled. And there are things that I could tell you about your new home."

"That so?"

"Yes, but only a few things that I *should* tell you. But not here. Perhaps you and Agent Clarke will take a tour of my facilities? It would be good to speak where it is private."

"Or you could come by my offices," McClellan said. "Or the chapel."

"I could. And I will. But another time. For now, in addition to hearing what I have to say, I believe you will both want to see what I have to show you. Because in a way—in a profound way, actually—what I wish for you to see is related to your chapel, and the creativity that went into how it was printed. This may have some greater meaning. But of course I, a simple builder, would not know of such things."

McClellan met Wagner's stare. "You work in water reclamation, right?"

"Yes," Wagner said. "Wastewater treatment. Just down the street. An unglamorous profession, but one that has always been essential for civilization to thrive. It is my small contribution to what your kind call the common good."

McClellan sipped his whiskey, turning the glass as he swallowed. Wagner was right. Tucker had confessed three days ago, and the investigation had gone nowhere. The forensics team had not found Tanglao's coupler, and their wounded pride in missing the key during the first two sweeps had them searching for its counterpart with painstaking and unhurried attentiveness. Okayo was readying needle-in-a-haystack reconnaissance flights in the event that the coupler had blown out of the air lock—but her departure was still days away. As for Tucker, he wasn't talking and there could be no questioning him until his lawyer arrived. And there was nothing new to learn from his confession. Lopez's tests showed only that Tucker had been afraid when he spoke, with conflicting results on whether he was truthful, or honest, or some combination of both.

Then there was the quest for any information on Tanglao's programmer's codes and story. McClellan had only been able to send written communications to Bauer since the morning he arrived on New Athens, six days ago, when they had their first and only live conversation. In the subsequent written comms, Bauer seemed guarded about what McClellan was asking. None of the archbishop's responses included anything related to Tanglao's codes or story. McClellan hoped to be more explicit during tonight's call—because the ruse of seeking information for Tanglao's funeral homily could last only a few more hours.

"Okay," he said to Wagner, "I'd love a tour. As will Agent Clarke. He's my bodyguard all week."

Clarke made sounds of protest.

"This makes me happy," Wagner said. "Come tomorrow morning—"

"Not in the morning," McClellan said. "That's Father Tanglao's funeral."

"Ah yes, how stupid to forget. The first such event in the orbits, no?"

"Correct. How about the afternoon?"

"Wonderful. Tomorrow afternoon it is. Later, however, due to repair work I have scheduled. Say five o'clock? Excellent. And yes, be sure to bring Agent Clarke."

Shirley came from nowhere with Wagner's hamburger.

"Here you are, Deary. I'll be back with ketchup."

Wagner appraised his dinner and reached for his knife. "It's not right," he said. "All that has happened, it's not right at all. And I fear," he added, slicing his hamburger in two, "that the worst of things is yet to come."

21

MCCLELLAN TOOK JACK AND Chrissy, his two assistants, boxed dinners from the Spinside, and then went to meet Zhèng in the Security offices adjacent to his quarters. On his way he checked on Catherine Georgeson. Okayo was sitting by McClellan's bed, in which Catherine lay sleeping, as the old woman had since her delivery from Troas City Hospital the day before.

"Chrissy and Jack are doing a fine job," Okayo said, looking up from the orbital trajectory models that drifted over her tablet. "They've assembled a wonderful group of caretakers."

"They have indeed," McClellan said, straightening Catherine's blanket before sitting on the other side of the bed. "These kids are a blessing."

Okayo put down her tablet and watched the priest. "Dr. Gupta came to check in while you were at dinner. She seemed pleased to see Mrs. Georgeson smiling as she slept."

"I really have to go to that hospital and apologize," McClellan said.

"They might appreciate that. By the way, you'll be interested to know that, after the doctor left, Catherine had a moment of clarity. She asked Chrissy where she was. We told her, and we explained who you are, what you did, and she smiled. It was a big smile." Okayo could not contain her own, and her eyes widened with joy. "Then she said that her father was a Baptist minister. She said it loudly and with pride, just like that—a BAPTIST MINISTER—and she said that he had told her that God would always take care of her. Good job, Father. Too bad you can't do this for everyone."

"I shouldn't have to," he said. "Everyone can take care of the Catherines of the world—the old world and the new one. God's grace is sufficient for that. We just have to cooperate."

Okayo nodded thoughtfully. She maintained her smile, although it dimmed as she glanced at Catherine's health monitors. "Jack emptied the catheter not ten minutes ago, just like you showed him. Let's go—you have a call to make."

Okayo stood, but McClellan said he'd wait until Fiona, a friend of Chrissy's, came to take a watch. He leaned forward and listened to the old woman breathe, then he began ten Hail Marys and the Salve Regina, offering them not only for Catherine but for all the people of New Athens. He thanked God for the sacrifices of so many who were helping to care for this woman—who, it turned out, was one of the first builders in the new world. She'd come upside to work with the communications systems that made orbital construction possible. She had degrees. Accomplishments. And yet she had been left alone to die. He had met hundreds of souls like Catherine in the neighborhoods and clinics of his parish, where his friend Father Bauer had taken him during his first visits to Boston—almost eleven years ago. It was sometime back then, somewhere in neighboring Somerville, at a moment like this, that McClellan began to understand Bauer's faith—the faith of his Aunt Betty and his Uncle Roger.

He breathed deeply, and he thanked God for his blessings, and then he prayed until Chrissy's friend arrived.

He found Okayo and Zhèng in his offices monitoring the New Athens holodisplay and speaking in low tones. Clarke, next to them, was firing up the comm displays.

"This doesn't look promising," McClellan said when he spotted the commissioner's expression.

"Just more unrest," Zhèng said. "The builders will be issuing a statement in the morning. They're striking in solidarity of Tucker—even if we haven't formally charged him."

"Maybe that's what old Wagner wants to talk about," Clarke said, looking up to McClellan.

Zhèng gave them a look asking for clarification, which Clarke dutifully provided.

"You're going to tour the sewers?" Zhèng asked.

"Can't hurt," McClellan said. "Besides, I have a hunch. I think Wagner is serious about getting us somewhere."

Zhèng looked at Clarke, who did not look pleased about his situation. "Then again," the commissioner said, "it's not a bad idea to improve relationships with the builders—although Wagner is hardly popular among their leadership. But no matter. I want to know anything if it'll help."

Zhèng read more information on the holodisplay and then shook his head. "I honestly don't understand," he said, almost to himself. "The builders and the engineers have never had a love affair, but I never thought that tensions would grow so hot and so quickly. How can they not see that we're all standing in a twenty-kilometer-long orbital tomb, if that's what we want it to be—if we work against one another? And that's exactly what's happening. More so since the death of Father Tanglao." Zhèng thought a moment. "If this keeps up, I almost believe calling for martial order would be justified."

"You have that authority?" McClellan said.

"Technically, yes. And my forces are the only people on New Athens with weapons. But I'm hoping there are other options."

"Ninety seconds," Clarke said. "The engineers are handing over comm control, so it looks like you'll be talking to your archbishop."

McClellan sat at the display and entered his personal access codes. Zhèng came to his side as the display prepared itself for the incoming call:

Engineering: New Athens Communications Center
Private Link: NA-Troas City/Earth-Boston
Time to link: 27 seconds

And then 26 seconds, and soon 10, and then . . .

Bauer looked good. He was smiling as he always did when he greeted one of his priests. McClellan felt relief not just at seeing his archbishop —his friend—but also the details of his office behind him. There on that wobbly table was the small statue of St. Boniface and the palm plant that thrived only because of Antonia. And there was the painting of St. Thérèse of Lisieux—or at least the lower third of it—that took up most of the wall behind Bauer's desk.

"Johnny McClellan," the archbishop said, "praise God, it is good to see you. You look well."

"Thank you, Your Excellency. And it is good to see you. Allow me to introduce Commissioner Zhèng, my colleague and now a friend. Zhèng is the—"

"Yes, yes, we spoke once during the planning stages. Good to have you with us, Commissioner. Please keep my priest out of trouble."

"That is a difficult task, Archbishop."

"Ha!" Bauer exclaimed. "Commissioner, I could tell you stories—"

"If I may interrupt," McClellan said, "also with me are Agents Anne Okayo and Brandon Clarke. Two of the Security Guild's best."

"It takes three of us to keep your priest in line," Okayo said.

Bauer gave a grand laugh, and after some professional courtesies and updates on McClellan's parish and the goings on in Boston, McClellan got to work.

"Your Excellency, I want to follow up on my written requests. As I mentioned, I need information for Father Tanglao's homily. I realize there's little time before the funeral tomorrow morning, but the engineers have promised to transfer your response to me as soon as you get one."

"Of course," Bauer said. "I read your correspondences, but I wasn't entirely sure what you were asking, or if it was necessary. With the family unable to travel to New Athens, the Dominican Order will hold a funeral on Earth when the body arrives. So you need not go to great lengths. A simple Mass is likely all Father Tanglao would have liked. Nothing grand."

"It's hard not to do grand in that chapel, Archbishop. I'd appreciate it if you could do what you can."

"Of course," Bauer said, hearing that friendly tone that McClellan uses when he means business. "What do you want to know about Father Tanglao?"

"Anything meaningful. Any life-changing event—which is the theme of the art in the Pauline Chapel, come to think of it." McClellan paused as he pictured the works of Michelangelo that dominated the chapel's two sides, and the painting of the Transfiguration. In fact, all the artwork depicted moments of transformation, like a good programmer's story should.

"Anything in particular?" Bauer said.

"Actually, yes," McClellan said. He would prefer not to get personal on a comm channel, even if it was supposed to be secure. But this was his chance to be certain that Bauer understood his improbable request. "Take, for instance, the story I told you after Raleigh, when we met in the infirmary. We were talking about my parents taking the government option when I was nine. I told you how they took me to visit my aunt and uncle, and my mom told me it would be best for me to stay with them in Iowa, and then my dad told me that they were doing something noble by being euthanized to help reduce the population, and then my mom said that, in return, the Global Union would pay for my housing, medical care, and education. Do you remember me telling you that?"

"Yes," Bauer said softly, surprised that McClellan was sharing his programmer's story so casually, even if he wasn't saying that that's what it was.

"And do you remember the context of why I told you that story?"

"Yes. I remember."

"Well, I'd like to know details like that about Raphael Tanglao. Because *that* kind of story could really help me."

As Bauer wrote a few notes, McClellan said a silent prayer to St. Joseph.

"If it helps," Bauer said, "I do have the music that his family chose. It's all funeral hymns you approve of."

"Of course," McClellan said. "Thank you."

"Now, Johnny," Bauer said, "before I forget, Rome has asked for any news on the killer. We'd like to get word to Father Tanglao's parents and to the Dominican Order. I'm supposed to be speaking with Father Lee, their master general, in a day or so. But based on what you've just asked, I'm going speed that up. Substantially."

McClellan smiled. Bauer had understood.

"There's nothing firm on the killer," McClellan said. "We're holding a young builder who has confessed. But he hasn't been formally charged. He's being held pending the arrival of his lawyer."

Bauer stiffened, glad for the opening. "Lawyers in New Athens? Well, if they let a priest upside, I guess that opens the floodgates."

There was something in Bauer's tone that made McClellan cold. The archbishop may not know the nuances of modern comm systems, but the Marine chaplain knew how to get a point across with words, voice, and body language.

"You watch out, Johnny," Bauer said, giving a serious look. "Remember that lawyer who came to file charges against you after Raleigh? What was his name? Estrada? He was a lot smarter than you, if I remember. You'd better be careful that this lawyer coming your way isn't a smart SOB like Estrada."

McClellan smiled along with Bauer's bantering. Of course he remembered Estrada. He was a civilian lawyer who petitioned military tribunals for records on the combat programmers. He tried twice to get to McClellan, but it didn't take long for the Military Police to learn who he was—a Sal operative—and then to detain him. Marines had a name for undercover Sals that targeted the military. They called them "SOBs"—Sals on Base.

Bauer made a fist with one hand and wrapped it with the other. His eyes peered over them and his expression was strong. McClellan stiffened when he realized what had just been told. But he forced a smile for show.

When Archbishop Bauer ended his call, he prayed a quick prayer for the intercession of St. Thérèse. Then he called in his assistant Antonia, who was working late, and would now be working later.

"Please immediately contact Father Lee in Seoul," he said. "Tell his secretary not to delay this conversation. McClellan needs the help of the Dominican Order, and he needs it now. And I'll need to talk to Cardinal Kwalia."

"Yes, Archbishop."

"And then call Tommy Harper. Tell him I need to go fishing—and he'd better be able to meet soon."

22

THE TRANSIT AND BOARDING application for Rudolphus Draeger came early and unexpectedly the next morning. It passed quickly through the normal security offices and then went to Commissioner Zhèng for a final sign-off, which he provided just six hours before the threatened strike of the builders, four before Tanglao's funeral, and thirty minutes before his team briefing to coordinate the day's security.

Clarke arrived early at McClellan's offices. He said he was eager to share with McClellan his news about Wagner's offer to tour the water reclamation systems.

By the time Zhèng and the other agents arrived, the transit and boarding approval had been transferred to the builders. As the morning launch preparations were under way in Gainesville and the countdown had begun, the coming of Tucker's lawyer was the talk of New Athens.

McClellan was already seated at the briefing table when the others arrived. He wore black clerical pants and his shirtsleeves rolled to his elbows, and he was finishing his rosary. It was Thursday. This meant that the rosary meditations were about God elevating the nature of this world to reveal and make possible the one to come. The fourth mystery was the Transfiguration, and McClellan thought of the painting in his chapel. And he thought about the printers that had printed it.

"You approved Draeger's boarding request?" Lopez demanded. She stood behind her chair, squeezing its back, her eyes cold. She had ignored Clarke's words about engaging the room's dampener fields, and paid no attention as its blue energies crystallized around them.

"How could I not?" Zhèng said, stopping himself before taking his own seat, matching his agent's stare. "Draeger's paperwork had been processed days ago. He'd met all the preflight requirements, and there was available seating on the transport. It's an Aesir class with a scheduled passenger inventory of only ten engineering teams and a handful of settlers. I could hardly cite overcapacity as a reason for denial."

"But what about the intelligence from McClellan's archbishop? Has that checked out?"

"It does," Zhèng said. "Okayo checked on that last night. Her team corroborated Archbishop Bauer's warnings. We're not finding much, but it's enough. Draeger has a history with the Sals."

Lopez leaned forward, working to contain her fury. "Then why approve the transit and boarding? I don't care if he passed the preflights. This is a dangerous situation, Commissioner. There are six hundred *thousand* lives at risk. That transport should not leave Earth!"

"Check your tone, Agent Lopez, or you will be off this case and this station. I'm aware of the population of New Athens, and I understand the severity of the matter. But there is nothing in any *official* record that ties Draeger with Juan Carlos Solorzano. Or his armies."

"But you said Okayo has evidence."

"Yes, she does. But while you and I would understand its meaning, others would not. They'd say it was speculation. If I had denied the boarding of Tucker's lawyer—based only on what we have—the builders would riot."

"You won't find anything official linking Draeger with the Sals," McClellan said, returning his rosary beads to its pouch. "The Sals hide their tracks. This happened on almost every case in the Corps. I suggest we forget the official records."

"It was the same in Kenya," Okayo said. "There are few jurisdictions that have not had their records tampered with. Every member nation that used the Global Union's data systems was hacked by cartels."

"Precisely," McClellan said. "And then there was the GU's eagerness to expunge criminal records."

"Yes, often because of a naïve understanding of criminal justice," Okayo said. "Or bribes. I know the results, Commissioner. I've buried family in Siaya, and close friends in Mombasa. I've fought my share of Somali pirates and others from the Sal armies, all who had their records wiped—whom we welcomed into our communities."

The group was silent. Lopez sat but Zhèng remained standing. Clarke had been making adjustments to the table's holodisplay, but now he watched Okayo with concern.

Lopez attempted a calmer tone. "May I ask what the engineers had to say? You must have told Jansen."

"Of course," Zhèng said.

"And?"

"She appreciated our resourcefulness, and she understands my—our—concerns. As does the wider Engineering Council. But they agree that in the current climate among the workers, it would be difficult to deny Draeger's boarding."

Clarke returned to the holodisplay. The model of New Athens glowed and expanded. Sharp lines grew out of the locations of the cities. They intersected with each other and then moved out again to intersect elsewhere.

"This is absurd," Lopez said, watching but not acknowledging the light show of data revolving before her. "I had concerns about McClellan. But letting a religious zealot aboard is suicide. Who knows what he'll do."

"It's not what he will do that worries me," McClellan said, ignoring the discourtesy. "At least not at first. What will infect New Athens will be his words. The passions he will fire up. Remember, Draeger is coming among a builder population that has been trying to find its way in the new world since the beginning. And as robbers and printers take more of their work, they're trying to save whatever purpose and dignity they can."

"It would help if they had better attitudes," Lopez said.

"Not all of us have your self-control," McClellan said. "Although from what I've seen and heard, I'd say most of the builders are controlling themselves very well. That's not to say there are no bad actors. Some will take advantage of this situation. Still, most builders are simply afraid. And, yes, even a little angry."

"And one of their own has confessed to the first murder in their new world," Zhèng said.

"Exactly," McClellan said. "Add it all up, and you get just the type of environment that feeds Solorzano's advances."

"You're right," Okayo said. "The Sals gain power through division."

"And mistrust and hurt and anger," McClellan said. "And onto all that they throw explosives, and they celebrate as everything ignites, as they create more fear, more loss, and more hopelessness. Then they move in. That's when they take over. And that's when they'll go after the printers—unless we secure the situation first."

Zhèng took his seat and stared at McClellan through the holodisplay, which had a tight grid of lines throughout New Athens's hull. Points of light traveled throughout the lines, all of which Clarke watched with intensity.

"I'm afraid that Father McClellan is right," Zhèng said. "So remember this: New Athens is our home, and we've been entrusted to protect it."

Okayo slapped her hands. "And we shall, Commissioner. And we shall. Together."

"So what's the plan?" Lopez asked.

"First, we do our jobs," Zhèng said. "And there's plenty to do. We have a strike to prepare for, and we're expecting sizable crowds for the funeral. The engineers have lifted certain provisions in the New World Agreement. Temporarily, of course. Both guilds will be sending delegations—more than your chapel can seat."

"That's reassuring," McClellan said.

"Don't get ahead of yourself," Zhèng said. "Attendance will be driven more out of guild competition than concern for a dead man's soul. In any event, I'm sure they'll all act civilly, until the body of Father Tanglao is escorted through the Wheel and to its transport back to Earth. And then the builders will strike and Tucker's lawyer will dock. And then, as Agent Lopez correctly reminds us, we'll need to be prepared for anything."

Zhèng raised his eyes toward McClellan, who was standing and buttoning the sleeves of his black clerical shirt.

"Where are you going?" Zhèng asked.

"To get ready for a funeral, as soon as someone shuts down this dampener so I can leave."

"But there are security details to cover. And Agent Clarke has a report on Ira Wagner, whom you have promised to visit this afternoon. Don't you want to hear that?"

"Clarke already filled me in. Looks like he's on to something. And it's got me thinking."

"About?"

"About where we go from here. But first things first, Commissioner. I have to say a Mass for the dead. And I intend to use this opportunity to bring peace to the living."

The deep sound of church bells came from the chapel's audio system, bringing low and regular funeral peals not just to those gathered inside the chapel, but also out to the boulevard. Chrissy and Jack helped each other into their albs as they vested in the sacristy adjacent to McClellan's apartments. When they were satisfied with their appearance, Jack looked past the door that opened to the chapel.

"It's full," he said. "Every pew."

"As are the seats in the main entry foyer and up in the boulevard," McClellan said as he adjusted his black and silver funeral chasuble to fit evenly over his shoulders. "You'll both do fine."

Farther inside the apartments, Clarke was expressing some concern to Okayo, who was backing away from the entrance of McClellan's bedroom, where Catherine Georgeson was snoring. Clarke followed Okayo, his hands in his dress uniform pockets, attempting once more to be relieved from the duty assigned to him.

"I am not a nurse," he said, loud enough for McClellan to hear.

"You are now," McClellan said.

Okayo laughed, her smile lingering as she met Clarke's eyes. "Brandon, there's no one else to watch Catherine. Everyone wants to be at the funeral, so that leaves you."

Clarke scowled. "All right. But only because you asked so nice. Although I'm not just sitting there. I'm getting work done." He turned to McClellan. "Mind if I set off a dampener? I'm pretty free to use them when I want now, and I'm betting there's a fair amount of tunnel attempts this morning."

"Will it disrupt the med monitors?" McClellan asked.

"No. She'll be all right. And it will keep out all those bells and music."

"Then, as you wish. And Clarke?"

"Yes?"

"Thank you."

A soft chime signaled the arrival of the funeral escort. The procession carrying the coffin from the Security Guild morgue had required extensive planning, since funeral processions had not been a part of New Athens's design. But the builders of Troas City were determined to show that they could excel at being the center of attention—not just in New Athens, but also in all the orbits. The other two guilds, not accustomed to such competition, rose to the challenge.

The honor guard of builders guided the coffin down the boulevard with respect, and the security detail stood solemnly as the coffin and its pall-bearers approached the main doors of the chapel. McClellan typed commands to cue the Introit hymn, and then he gave a final wave to Clarke, who activated his dampener, sealing himself and the sleeping Catherine Georgeson off from the noise of the funeral.

McClellan turned to Jack, the cross bearer who would lead the procession. The wiry youth had allowed himself an older man's haircut, which seemed to make him surer and steadier. With the Introit sounding and McClellan giving a nod, Jack breathed in deeply, opened the door to the front of the chapel, and held the processional cross high as he stepped inside. The noise of the crowd standing met the young man. He led Chrissy and McClellan to the front of the main aisle, bowed toward the altar, and then turned up the aisle to where the coffin and the builder pallbearers waited at the main entrance.

McClellan stared ahead as he followed behind Chrissy, who in one hand swung the thurible with its smoking incense, and in her other held a small ornate pot of holy water and its sprinkler. He was not surprised, although he was a little disappointed, that the builders were exclusively on his left, which were the pews traditionally reserved for the immediate family, while the engineers, including Elaina Jansen, Hannah Ward, and Andrew Pavić, were on the right. On both sides there were faces he knew, others he had seen but never met, and many more he had never once laid eyes on. No one person stood out. And no one seemed to be hiding anything, other than discomfort.

Jack and Chrissy stepped to the sides of the casket. McClellan said the opening prayers—meant to unite those in attendance—and he took a moment to silently offer his own. Then he gripped the sprinkler in the holy water pot and wet the casket in the name of the Father, and the Son, and the Holy Spirit.

And so the funeral began—a rite said billions of times on Earth, more than a hundred by McClellan. Now it was under way in the new world.

The procession turned and led the pallbearers as they carried the casket through the main aisle, coming to rest before the altar rail. McClellan entered the sanctuary, stepped up to kiss the altar, and went to the presider's chair. After concluding the opening prayers, he sat and prompted all assembled to do the same. When quiet came, Chrissy stood to read the first reading, which she did in a wise and strong voice. "A reading from the Book of Sirach," she said, then continued after a pause:

> *If you choose, you can keep the commandments;*
> *loyalty is doing the will of God.*
> *Set before you are fire and water;*
> *to whatever you choose, stretch out your hand.*
> *Before everyone are life and death,*
> *whichever they choose will be given them.*
>
> *Immense is the wisdom of the* LORD*;*
> *mighty in power, he sees all things.*
> *The eyes of God behold his works,*
> *and he understands every human deed.*
> *He never commands anyone to sin,*
> *nor shows leniency toward deceivers.*

After a moment, Chrissy looked up and said, "The word of the Lord." Some in attendance joined McClellan and Jack in responding, "Thanks be to God."

Antonia Rossi patched in the pending transmission from the Jamestown Police and Militia. Bauer settled himself behind his desk, pausing only to scan the security codes. The source was the Fort Wetherill Command Center, which meant that the stronghold rebuilt during the height of the Sal wars had, for some reason, been reactivated.

Patrolman Ryan Richardson came onscreen. The young officer had grown up two houses from Bauer's brother Michael. He and Helen had babysat him for years. Then as a teenager Ryan watched over Bauer's nieces and nephews, and they had all worked together on the farms.

"Archbishop, I'm sorry to be disturbing you," he said.

Bauer cut him off. "My family?"

Richardson nodded. "They're safe. But we had an incident with two of your nephews. Robby and Leo were out on the cove this morning. Their boat was targeted by a small-caliber drone. First time in years we've had anything like this. The boys spotted it in time, dove off, and swam a safe distance away. They were in cold water for a while, but they're good swimmers. No signs of hypothermia."

Bauer sat back in his chair. "Thank God they are safe."

"They are. Your sister-in-law didn't want us to tell you right away, but we felt we needed to."

"Sal?"

"Looks like it. We're still finding pieces of the attack drone—it wasn't sophisticated, but it has the markings. It's likely they wanted us to know it was them. We're working with the state police and the Marine Corps Counterterrorism Unit, so we'll know more soon."

"Any leads?"

"A few. Chief Tedeschi is out with the Marines boarding a Venezuelan fishing trawler just past Beavertail. They think that was the source. We'll certainly keep you posted."

Bauer thanked him, then sorted through the possibilities of what would happen next. Helen would be more furious than afraid. And, as always, she would make things work, putting Robby and Leo to some chore to get their minds off what had happened. And the town would be there to support her and the children. What sickened Bauer wasn't the thought of what could have happened—it was the unseen consequences of what had. His nephews had lately been expressing optimism for the future. And then there was Ryan Richardson, yet another young soul dealing with evil unleashed by the Sals. Bauer's generation had promised to end all this. The Sals were supposed to have been wiped off the ledgers of human history. And yet there was Ryan, looking grim but brave, explaining to the archbishop that a giant had awakened.

"You've done good work," Bauer said.

"Thank you, Your Excellency. That's appreciated. One other thing: we shut down the bridges. We're locked down until we know what's happening."

"Have you activated the militia?"

"Yes. The chief just called them up. Shore and air monitoring will be under way within the half hour."

"Very good. And you say the family is safe?"

"Completely." The officer then gave a troubled look. "One last thing, Archbishop. We understand from your sister-in-law that you were planning on visiting the island later today—obviously that can't happen now."

"Yes, I understand."

"We've sent word to Monsignor Harper, too. We know you two like to go . . . fishing."

"Yes, and that was right to notify him."

"For the record, I'm looking forward to having you back soon. This should be all cleared up in a day or two."

Bauer appreciated the sentiment. But he was wondering where he could meet Tommy Harper, who had the connections that McClellan needed. As for Tanglao's programming codes and story, Bauer had spoken the night before with Father Lee, the head of the Dominican Order. Lee said that he couldn't accept that Tanglao had been a programmer— and the disbelief seemed genuine. Bauer had all but begged, and eventually the Dominican agreed to search out anything about Tanglao that he could find. No information had come since.

Now, this morning, as Bauer spoke to Officer Richardson, with the funeral for Father Tanglao already under way, the ruse of providing information about Tanglao was past. He would have to find some other way to get McClellan what he needed.

Bauer made a quiet plea to St. Thérèse. The attack on his nephews was undoubtedly meant to deter him from helping—a typical Sal move. But Bauer loved his priests, and he loved John Francis McClellan like his own son. No, the attack had not scared him. And it would not frighten the people of Jamestown. Rather, what the Sals had done was to enkindle within Bauer the desire to continue—to coordinate help as fast as he could, wherever he could— from Rome, the Dominicans, Harper, and from the people of Boston—to say nothing of the heavenly demands he would make to the God of Justice.

"And if you can," Officer Richardson was saying, "let Father McClellan know that there are people here praying for him. The Big Guy upstairs has got his back on this. I know it."

"I will tell him," Bauer said, impressed that the officer had said those words on an official channel. "I most certainly will. Thank you, Ryan. May God bless you and keep you safe."

"And us all," Richardson said before his image vanished.

23

"**JUST OVER SIX WEEKS** ago," Father McClellan began his funeral homily, "a man was killed for unknown reasons by an unknown killer—or killers—and in ways that we also do not fully understand. And yet we know this: This man—Father Raphael Tanglao of the Order of Preachers—was hiding his identity because he chose to travel to a world where the expression of faith has been forbidden.

"And yet, today, through the generosity of the engineers, especially Madame Elaina Jansen, and with the welcome and great support of many builders, and that of a great many others, especially all those in the Security Guild who keep order, we gather for a funeral Mass. We do so not to dispose of the dead or to sentimentalize death. We do this so that the believers here, and you know who you are, can welcome Jesus Christ into our midst, and thank him for the life of Father Tanglao—and indeed for the gift of all life. At the same time we come to pray for mercy for Father Tanglao's soul, as well as for justice and the truth that leads us to it.

"From what I have learned of Father Tanglao's life, I believe he would ask that we reflect for a moment on the quest for those very realities: justice, mercy, and truth. I know that this quest is my chief purpose here among you, as I know it is for many of you in your lives, because this is the common quest of all humanity. But justice, mercy, and truth often seem difficult to find in our lives, no? I know they do in mine. And so to help us along, allow me to call to mind another reality that we have at our disposal—the reality that we call beauty. And we do not need to go far to find it. One need only enter New Athens through its remarkable Wheel, and stare at the landscape of the inner core—adorned with clouds and illuminated by the Sun Crane—to experience how beauty can lead us outside of ourselves.

"And here in this chapel, we are surrounded by a different type of beauty. This beauty—printed, of course, but still authentic—also comes to us from the creativity of human minds, ones that lived centuries ago. And so I encourage you to look around you, because the art of this chapel can help us understand both Father Raphael Tanglao and, I believe, what he would wish for our common future. We may also learn why someone—or some people—ended his life.

"We begin with what for many of you, I am sure, are gruesome scenes. On your right is a printed duplicate of the famous fresco by Michelangelo of the martyrdom of St. Peter—the first pope, who was killed and buried where the Vatican stands today, nailed to a cross, upside down at his request, as he did not wish to imitate his Lord.

"And then there is the center of every Catholic church—the crucifix, behind me, which believers raise high, as young Jack just did in our procession moments ago—because we proclaim to the world that God can bring good even out of the evil of death, which he abhors. 'Mihi vivere Christus est et mori lucrum.' Those are the words carved over us, high over the altar—as they are in the real Pauline Chapel in Rome. 'For me, Christ is life and death is gain.'

"These words and these images may not make sense to us. And yet when anything does not make sense, we do the same thing as we do in a murder investigation. We look for clues.

"Across from the image of St. Peter's execution is another fresco by Michelangelo. This is St. Paul's first encounter with Christ, who offered Paul a new way of living—a new world, as it were. Paul accepted the offer, and his choice changed him from a man who persecuted Christians to a man who built up the Christian family. It is for this reason that this chapel—the Pauline Chapel—is named. Paul reminds us that an encounter with God brings both choices and an offer for a new life.

"And behind the crucifix is the image of the Transfiguration, the moment on Mount Tabor when Christ allowed his closest followers to see the newness and the life that awaits us all, if we so choose. Father Tanglao would say that this new life of Christ is the true New Creation—the true New World.

"My dear hosts of New Athens—both builder and engineer alike, and those of you in the Security Guild, or of no particular guild—it is important that we let this art, these images, teach us. Because what they point to is a lesson of hope. Of life. Of goodness. And, yes, of justice.

"It is no secret that I was invited to live among you to retrieve the body of Father Tanglao and to offer this Mass, and also to work with the Security Guild to expose the light of truth on Father Tanglao's murderer or murderers.

"And so, on Father Tanglao's behalf, allow me to state clearly, especially to those involved in his death, and you know who you are, that we believers in Jesus Christ are certain that death is never victorious. In Christ, death gives way to life, falsehoods always become truth, and injustice always—always—gives way to justice.

"Allow me to show you how this can work.

"In a few moments, I will proceed with the public worship of what we believers call the Eucharist—of Christ coming among us in the form of ordinary bread and wine, which you might easily dismiss. But Father Tanglao would tell you that when we receive this spiritual food, we receive *Communion*. He would say this because in receiving the Eucharist, we publicly acknowledge a choice: that we seek to *grow* in communion with God—and thus in the community of his Church, in love, and in relationship.

"What an important goal this is today, for all of us here on New Athens. Builder. Engineer. Security Agent. Young. Old. Healthy. Dying. Believer. Nonbeliever. The lawful. And, perhaps, a murderer. My friends, allow me to suggest that we are more than these labels—especially now, as we come together at this moment of death, because in this moment God's mercy is transforming the horrors of Father Tanglao's death into new life, new friendships, new opportunities, new understandings, and new ways for us all to find what we seek in our own lives, and in the promising worlds that circle us.

"I cannot thank you all enough for your hospitality and help. And I hope that I may help you as well, as we continue to pray for and entrust the soul of Father Tanglao to the loving source of all justice and mercy—and truth. May the God who is love bless and protect us, one and all together."

McClellan closed the black folder that held his notes, turned and bowed toward the tabernacle, and returned to his presider's chair. It was his custom to allow a long period of silence after his preaching, both to calm his own soul and to allow the worshipers to hear the greater voice of God, rather than his own inadequate one.

And there was silence, but only for a moment. Then came a pair of soft comm chimes from somewhere in the pews, then others, and then a rustle of hands and pockets. And then gasps. McClellan kept his attention straight ahead to face the altar, but he could see Jack and Chrissy watching the people.

McClellan stood for the Prayers of the Faithful, which returned some order to the chapel, but not as much as he hoped. Soon he stood at the altar saying the prayers of the Mass. Because he faced the altar in the same direction as the people, he did not see Zhèng leave and return, and leave again.

After Communion—received only by himself, Jack, and Chrissy—when the vessels had been washed and the altar stripped, McClellan went again to his presider's chair. At that moment, Commissioner Zhèng returned to the chapel and strode up the main aisle, his sharp footfalls echoing across the marble. He stepped past the casket respectfully, stopped at the edge of the sanctuary, bowed, gave a worried look to McClellan, and then went to the pulpit.

"Father McClellan, I apologize for this interruption. At the conclusion of this Mass, the body of Father Raphael Tanglao will remain here, in this chapel, until it can be safely returned to the Troas City morgue. This change in plans is necessary, as I have canceled all traffic onto and off New Athens until further notice, with the exception of any transports that currently have incoming orbital commitments.

"A terrible event has taken place. About the time this funeral Mass began, a man was killed aboard this station. His name was Yoshiharu Sasaki—he was an engineer. His murderer, or at least one of them, has taken his own life. We're investigating the matter, and we ask for all of your cooperation. We know of no other immediate, credible threats at this time, but we ask everyone to be cautious and watchful.

"Father McClellan, again I apologize for this interruption. But I must ask that you adjust your service to maintain the body of Father Tanglao under your care, and to join Security as soon as possible. As you suggested, we must all cooperate to bring justice and peace to the people of this world.

"And Father, please pray for us."

24

AGENT LOPEZ KNELT NEXT to the body of Yoshiharu Sasaki. She tilted her head to determine the correct angle for her scalpel, before scraping samples of the blood-crusted opening over the engineer's left ear.

Just under five meters away lay the corpse of the builder who, the evidence suggested, had killed Sasaki.

The sign of the Sals—a circle topped with two intersecting lightning bolts that formed a cross—had been hastily drawn between the two bodies with blood. According to Lopez, the men's blood had been blended to make the sign.

Two forensic assistants were nearby, scanning and categorizing organics along the line of attack. Two others monitored the reconnaissance data from microdrones that hovered around the bodies. Another was synced to the main scanner that flashed wide spectrum illumination along the unused factory space where the drama had played out.

Robbers were powering on floodlights to supplement the old and often failed lighting that stretched in long rows overhead. The space was, to the meter, directly opposite from McClellan's quarters and chapel—six kilometers overhead in the geography of a cylindrical world.

The area was called the Millwrights Sector, which took up most of the empty City of Heraclea. The sector and the city had been designed for the builders back before the orbital world was built—before the evolution of the new printers. And while the printers had made substantial technical improvements to the engineers' designs of New Athens, they had made no changes to the look or the function of its cities. Heraclea and its Millwrights Sector were printed with massive spaces for manual nuclear furnacing and fashioning, and physical construction, even if these functions were now obsolete.

There would occasionally be negotiations about what to do with the property. The engineers wanted a research university. The builders wanted more housing. The positions of both parties were entrenched. And so the Millwrights Sector remained mothballed among the farms and fields and cities of New Athens, which spun in political stalemate—as long as the opposing ends of Heraclea and Troas City stayed as they were.

But within a week after the printing of the massive replica of the Pauline Chapel, structural sensors in the hull of New Athens had begun to worry. Even in this twenty-kilometer-long, six-kilometer-diameter world, the chapel, without a counterbalance in Heraclea, seemed to pose some threat to stability. And the longer the chapel was in place, the greater the concern.

Since the dinner at Elaina Jansen's home just five days ago, when she had treated McClellan to Grand Traverse Distillery whiskey and informed him about the Sal threats, the New Athens structural engineering heads—the siblings Mizuki and Yoshiharu Sasaki—had set up new monitoring stations to corroborate these concerns. This was the very task that Yoshiharu was overseeing when he'd been beaten and murdered that morning.

McClellan stood over the apparent killer's corpse. He had been a handsome young man, but his fair skin was ashen and bruised, his wrists and throat slashed open, and his thick blond hair matted with blood. The recovered medical chip identified him as Lawrence Walker, originally from Port Glasgow, Scotland. Some of the data found in his decaying comm implants seemed to indicate communications with Sal operatives—but there was no confirmation. Nor would the Sals have been in close contact with Walker for very long. It would have been flagged during the residency application process, and for his work assignments.

But none of that mattered until the med chip could be confirmed as authentic.

"What do you make of it?" Zhèng said as he came alongside McClellan, pointing to the Sal sign formed in the blood trail, long dried after the few hours since the murder.

"Whoever drew it didn't have much experience," McClellan said, tilting his head as he walked between the bodies. "They got the jags in the lightning wrong."

"That's what I thought. But you've seen many of these blood signs in person."

McClellan studied the finger and hand marks that formed the sign. Then he looked to Zhèng. "So Draeger's transport was already en route when you suspended flights?"

"Yes, unfortunately. With a committed orbit. I couldn't deny docking privileges without putting lives in danger—or without delaying Tucker's counsel. But I suppose I was more concerned about departing traffic. And yet, standing here, I'm wondering if I'm making a mistake."

The pair stepped cautiously through the crime scene toward Lopez, who was peering through a mircoscanner inserted into Sasaki's swollen and hardening left eye.

"Sloppy, huh?" McClellan said as she leaned back.

Lopez nodded. "Very. We're not talking a career criminal. But the killer was strong, and that's all someone needs if they're intent on murder."

"I'm not sure he was," McClellan said. "Intent on murder, that is. Those bruises don't look like they were meant to be fatal, and the killer is pretty bloodied himself. Sasaki put up a fight. The question is: is this a murder-suicide, or a double murder?"

Lopez began to respond but stopped. A nervous patrol agent jogged up to Zhèng with a tablet and a curious glance at McClellan. "Commissioner," the young agent said, "we've confirmed the killer's identification."

"Alleged killer," McClellan said.

The agent gave another inquisitive stare, then looked back at her tablet. "The subject's med chip checks with DNA and surveillance tracking," she said. "Walker had been assigned to Red Delta, but that was delayed, so he was prioritized for temp jobs. No priors. No anything. We've gotten a warrant from the Council to search his personals. We may have something in an hour."

"Thank you, Andrews."

"Yes, sir. And sir?"

"Yes, Andrews?"

"The chief engineer and a few others are outside. They're requesting—"

"Yes, yes, send them in. Why fight the inevitable?"

"Not near me!" Lopez shouted, waving her hands over Sasaki's body. "Talk to them somewhere else."

McClellan accompanied Zhèng to the edge of the crime scene. "I was wondering when Elaina would demand a viewing," he said. "Whether or not the Sals are behind this, it fits their profile. These deaths are meant to cut to the heart of the engineers."

"These deaths will cut to the heart of everyone in the orbits," Zhèng said. "A murder on a far-off relay is one thing," he continued softly as they walked past a group of conferring agents. "But here in New Athens, of all places?" He slowed his pace and stopped, gazing briefly at the growing crowds beyond the factory's doors. "Were you aware that Madame Jansen wants me to release a statement? She wants me to say that we have a lead on the murderer."

"Sounds like a good idea," McClellan said.

"Really? I'm surprised you think that."

"Why not? Who says we don't have a lead?"

"I don't. Do you?"

"I have my suspicions, yes."

"Suspicions are not leads. Saying so would be a lie."

"Yes, but lies can be helpful in police work."

Zhèng stared with disbelief. Words came to his lips but he did not respond.

"Look, Commissioner, if we lived in a perfect world we wouldn't have to resort to a trick like that. But if we lived in a perfect world Max Tucker wouldn't be in a holding cell, and you and I wouldn't be standing next to two dead men."

"Is this a lesson in theology or police work?"

"Both. I'm just saying that a statement may be an option to shake up the killer or killers. And it may give us the upper hand with Rudi Draeger before he docks, before he comes down that Wheel and takes the narrative."

Zhèng did not seem convinced.

"But I also understand your point," McClellan said. "And either way I support your decision one hundred percent. You know the people of New Athens better than I do."

"Which is why I would prefer not to issue a statement. Not until I have something to share."

Into the crime scene came Elaina Jansen, Andrew Pavić, and Hanna Ward—the three engineers who were in attendance at the funeral and who had received the Sal threats, along with the Sasakis. They did not look at the illuminated bodies as they hurried through the dusty, unused furnaces. They made their way to Zhèng and McClellan, who stood a few meters outside the investigation zone.

"Commissioner," Jansen began, "please tell me this matter is under control. This . . . this," she said, pointing to the carnage a few meters away, "is unconscionable. What are your plans to deal with the builders? And what of the statement I requested? We need swift action—the people must be assured."

Zhèng gave his best diplomatic answer.

Jansen was not appeased.

Zhèng reminded her that McClellan had significant experience with the Sals, and because of that, the team would make fast progress.

"I wonder," Jansen said. "It seems to me that the builders have become emboldened since your arrival, Father McClellan. You dine with them frequently. You cannot deny that."

Zhèng began to protest. McClellan stopped him.

"I wouldn't deny that," McClellan said, watching her expression and those of the other two engineers. "I also dine with engineers. But you're correct to look at every angle at such times. This *is* an unconscionable situation. I agree. Please know of my sympathies for the death of a colleague and close friend. I know you may not appreciate this, but I will pray for him daily."

Pavić gave a hesitant laugh, his light skin becoming red. "I think we've had enough of your prayers," he said, allowing himself a glance at the two dead men. "I was there at the funeral, and I listened with respect. Very nice sentiments. Death and life, mercy and justice, and unity, yes, unity. Well, where is this unity now?"

"Your words do seem to have fallen on deaf ears," Hannah Ward said, prompting Jansen and Pavić to nod in unison.

"Quite so," Pavić said. "More than that, your presence seems to have awakened some . . . primitive desires that we have gone to great pains to snuff out. Frankly, McClellan, I do not see how your presence is helping. Perhaps you should return to Earth with Tanglao's body."

McClellan thought it unlikely that Pavić had ever dealt with a United States Marine. "Mr. Pavić," he said, with a serenity and command that prompted Pavić's eyes to open widely, "I'll leave the engineering to you. You leave this matter to Commissioner Zhèng and to me. And if your superior wants me off the station, she has only to say so."

Jansen did not suggest that this was her wish, and Pavić had no response.

"And we need to remember," the priest continued, "that not every builder has committed a murder today—if it is verified that it was a builder."

"Verified?" Hanna Ward said. "Look around you!"

"I have looked, very closely. As I have in other murders—and in murder-suicides—that involved the Sals, to say nothing of what I have seen and done on the battlefield. I will only say that everything is not always what it appears at first. Especially when emotions are high."

The main scanner passed nearby, flashing and mumbling as it swept the area with more wide-spectrum illumination. Something prompted Lopez to shout orders to her assistants, using words that engineers or priests do not use.

McClellan read the growing terror in the faces of his three hosts, and took a different approach. "May I ask how Yoshiharu's sister is doing?" he said.

"About as you would expect," Jansen said, almost relieved with the new topic.

"May I go talk to her?"

"She wouldn't wish that," Hannah Ward said. "And even if she did, at the moment she has induced a coma."

"Why?"

"Why would she not?" Jansen said. "It is better than facing this."

"But eventually she will have to face this."

The three engineers gave a displeased look, which McClellan figured was better than terror.

Pavić had composed himself. He still spoke with a lecturing tone, but it was not unkind. "We do not relish pain. And we see no gain in death. Mizuki will remain in this coma until she can be treated in the morning with an emotional memory wipe. We'll remove any recollection of her attachment to her brother, but no other memories, of course, per the commissioner's orders."

"And then she will feel no pain," Ward said.

"I see," McClellan said, but he did not see at all.

Zhèng stepped forward and turned to McClellan. "We had better continue if we're considering releasing a statement, as Madame Jansen has requested. Now, if you three will excuse us."

The commissioner turned away from the group. McClellan did not. He said, "Commissioner, there's one last question I have for my hosts. If I may?"

Zhèng shrugged. "I'm sure the engineers won't mind."

McClellan thanked the commissioner and asked the engineers for the name of the second builder.

"Second builder?" Jansen said.

"Yes. By now Commissioner Zhèng's team will have reviewed station surveillance and the markings and materials on the floor, and they should be finding evidence of a third person who was here, either just before the murder or when it occurred. After all, I would imagine Sasaki needed more than one person to position those sensors—they are quite heavy, at least the one was that I tried to lift. And such work is, by your treaty with the Builders Guild, the work of builders, no? Unless Yoshiharu had a robber helping him, which not only would have violated the treaty, but also may have instigated a disagreement—and if so, that news would not be helpful to spread through the builder community at the moment."

Jansen looked at one of the portable structural monitors and then to Zhèng, who looked at McClellan. "Yes," she said slowly. "That would not be helpful. But I would have no way of knowing at the moment who Yoshiharu had assigned to assist him. If anyone."

"Would any of you know?" McClellan said, staring at the other engineers.

There was no response.

"Well, when you find out, please tell our Commissioner. For now, we'll go on what evidence we have, and on what we find. Because if the Sals are responsible, I have a personal stake in that. And if it wasn't them, I'd like to know that, too. So, until we learn more, I suggest that we follow the commissioner's instincts and issue no statement until we have information. And last, I'd ask that you let us get back to the one thing we all agree on—getting to the truth."

25

FOUR HOURS LATER, MCCLELLAN was in his offices finishing a tuna sandwich and his report to Zhèng. He and Lopez had spent two hours cataloging the evidence from Heraclea with the help of half a dozen junior agents. Lopez had left to return to the crime scene, but she stood again in McClellan's doorway.

"I was calling you," she said, annoyed. "You have guests."

McClellan picked up his tablet and realized he had silenced it. "Sorry," he said. "What guests?"

"A builder and his daughter. I told them you were busy, but the kid insisted."

McClellan pulled up the entryway surveillance cams. There, next to the baptismal font, was a builder holding the hand of a young girl in a blue dress. "That's Veronica," he said, smiling. "She brought me flowers when I first arrived to Troas City. Tell them I'll meet them in my sitting room in five minutes. Mind letting them in?"

Lopez gave a look of protest but said "All right, since I'm going that way. But don't spend too much time on them. In a half hour you have your meeting with Wagner. I'm dying to hear what that old fool has to say."

McClellan thanked her, and turned to wrap up his report. Then he stopped, thinking it was best to first meet his unexpected guests.

Father and daughter were standing in the small sitting room of his apartments. Veronica smiled when she saw the priest. Still holding her father's hand, she attempted a wave with her other, which held a small pink tablet decorated with stickers of red roses.

"Well, isn't this a nice surprise," McClellan said.

"I hope we didn't disturb you," Veronica's father said. The name on his jumpsuit was Robert, but he had introduced himself on the night of McClellan's arrival as Bobby. Bobby Parker. He was lean, about McClellan's age, with darker skin than his daughter but with the same expressive eyes.

"This certainly is not a disturbance," McClellan said, grasping the builder's hand, feeling in it both strength and apprehension. "It's a pleasure to have guests, especially pretty young ladies like Veronica."

The girl looked at her father with a grin.

"Please," McClellan said, waving to the sitting room's small couch, "make yourself comfortable."

McClellan sat across from them, complimented Veronica's braids, and moved quickly to the only topic that would have brought him guests. "It's been a tough day for us all," he said, watching the father's expression. "I'm so sorry for what happened to your colleague Lawrence Walker. Did you know him?"

Parker hesitated. "Never met him. Not that I remember, anyway. I don't meet the structural guys much. I'm in Mainline Comms. But still . . . yeah, this is all a shock. They all say he was a good kid." He glanced around the sparsely furnished room, and then looked down to his daughter, whose hand he still held. "My wife suggested we come by—she'd have come, too, but she's a second shifter." The builder, looking again at McClellan, spoke apprehensively.

"You see, my little girl here has a few questions about what happened . . ."

His voice faltered, but his eyes completed his words. *Questions that a father should know how to answer.*

McClellan took his cue and turned to Veronica. "Questions? I like questions. Can I know what they are? Or are they secret?"

The girl checked for her father's approval, then turned back to McClellan.

"Ms. Buxton told us at school what happened in Heracle—Heracle—"

"Heraclea," her father said.

"Yes, Hera-clea. She said what happened to that builder and that engineer may happen again, even here in Troas City."

"Did she?" McClellan said. "Why does she think that? Did she say?"

Veronica nodded. "She said because of history."

"History?"

"Yes. Ms. Buxton said that history is like a circle, and it repeats. She said history says more bad things will happen on New Athens. She said there could even be a war! I told her that Mommy and Daddy said that bad things like that happen only on Earth. But Ms. Buxton said that's not true."

The girl's eyes were wide, as were her father's, who hid them from her by looking at the lighting in the ceiling.

"Is there going to be a war?" Veronica asked.

McClellan had spent the afternoon staring down engineers as well as questioning the girlfriend of Lawrence Walker and the structural repair team that Walker had worked with. From that morning, when he stepped into the chapel to say Father Tanglao's funeral Mass, to just moments ago, surrounded by young and uncertain security agents, eyes had been watching him, looking for comfort. For strength. For how the outsider might help. None of those eyes had rattled him. These little ones did.

He debated how to answer—with the offer of comfort or the certainty of cold truth. He decided to split the difference.

"Veronica, can I tell you a secret?"

Veronica nodded. "I won't tell anyone."

"Well, you can tell everyone *this* secret. You will always know when a grown-up is lying if they say that they know the future. Maybe they don't mean to tell a lie. Maybe they're just lying to themselves. Or maybe they just want to sound smart. But no one knows the future. Not even Ms. Buxton."

"No one?"

"No one."

"Not even you?"

McClellan laughed. "No, Veronica. Not even me."

Veronica wasn't sure if that was encouraging.

"But I do know this," McClellan continued. "History is *not* a circle. That's because people can always choose whether to do good things or bad things—even if that means trying really hard to do good things. Or asking for *help* to do good things. Does that make sense?"

Veronica seemed uncertain, but ultimately agreed that his reasoning was sound.

"And you know what *else* I know?"

Veronica shook her head.

"I know that your mommy and daddy, and people like Agent Lopez, who you just met, and all the agents all over the orbits, and people like me, are going to do *everything* we can to make sure bad things don't happen. Everything."

Veronica thought about that one. Her head went down and she fingered one of the stickers on her tablet. Then with a protesting tone she said, "But you're not staying. You're just visiting and then you're going back to Earth."

McClellan felt the words cut through him. "That's true, sweetie," he said, leaning forward. "But I'm here *now*. And I'm here to help the security agents. I won't leave until we find out who did the bad things you heard about—not until we arrest them. Do you believe me about that?"

Veronica took a moment before answering, "Yes." Her legs began to swing, making little sounds as her feet connected with the couch.

"Now," McClellan said, looking at her father, "mind if your daddy and I talk a little by ourselves?"

Bobby Parker gave a nod, happy for the offer.

His daughter also gave her approval, and McClellan went to find Chrissy and Jack, who were tending to Catherine Georgeson deeper in his apartments. It took Chrissy only seconds to have Veronica laughing at some game as Bobby Parker followed McClellan into the chapel.

"Is it okay for me to come in?" Parker asked, taking in the structure.

"If you're worried about the New World Agreement," McClellan said, "don't be. There was a waiver, and quite a few engineers and builders were here for the funeral. I'd say that sets precedent."

"No, I don't care about that. What I meant was, I never went to church much."

McClellan waved Parker forward. "If they let me in," he said, "everyone's invited."

As expected, McClellan felt his tablet vibrate with a priority message. He read it as Parker went about studying the frescoes. It was from Clarke, who had done what Clarke did well: monitoring McClellan's whereabouts and running checks on anyone getting close to him: *Robert Edward Parker. DOB: 10-10-2053. Birthplace: Glenns Ferry, Idaho. Orbital arrival: August 5, 2073. Orbital security record: No priors. Earth criminal record: None. Career record: Builder in good standing. Assigned: Antennae maintenance, Centerwell. Secondary career: Softball coach, Troas City High School.*

McClellan slipped the tablet into his pocket and leaned against the closest pew. He watched Parker's gaze stop at the far corner where Tang-lao's casket had been placed on a platform, draped with a long white cloth.

"You came upside to get away from all this, huh?" McClellan said.

Parker nodded. "But I guess there's no getting away from some things," he said. He paused a moment, either to choose his words or to avoid them. "We both know Veronica's teacher is right. Or at least she's not completely wrong. More trouble's coming."

"Is it?" McClellan said, stepping closer to the builder.

Parker didn't answer.

"I meant what I said to your daughter. I don't believe in fate—in history dictating what happens next. People have choices."

Parker, again looking toward the casket, stayed silent.

"Look, Mr. Parker, I don't want to push this, but if I'm going to do my job, I'll need to know as much as I can."

Parker turned and sized up the priest. "Not sure what I can say that you don't already know."

"Let me be the judge of that."

The builder looked away, then turned to confirm that the doors of the main entrance were closed. "We safe?"

McClellan nodded. "We are. I insisted on it. I'm supposed to be able to hear confessions here. I can't have people listening in."

Parker considered McClellan's response. After a moment, the builder began talking. "Things are getting bad," he said. "The talk I hear at work—the things we're all hearing—they're bad."

McClellan remained silent.

"Even before Red Delta," Parker went on, "everyone's been worried about the printers—about the engineers losing control. But now there's talk that someone's taking advantage of the situation—someone besides the engineers."

"Any idea who?"

"No," the builder said. "Mostly I hear guys saying the engineers got it coming to them. But no one seems to know what 'it' is. Or why exactly the engineers got it coming. But whatever it is, people are happy about it."

McClellan heard only truth in Parker's voice. "Fair enough," he said. "What are people saying about the printers?"

"The printers? Weird stuff."

"Like?"

"They say that the printers are rebelling. That they want to control the orbits."

"Do you believe that? Ever see anything that makes you think that's what's happening?"

Parker shook his head. "No, I guess not. But I don't work with printers all that often. Still, I don't trust them. Those things have minds of their own."

McClellan noted the words—the same used by Max Tucker on Red Delta. He'd have to explore that similarity later.

"And guild leadership?" he prompted. "What are they saying?"

"Nothing directly," Parker said, shrugging. "But . . . no, you'll think I'm crazy." He thought a moment, debated in silence, and then gave a determined look. "My wife and I wanted to show you something," he said. "It's been bothering us for a few days. It's on Veronica's tablet."

He jogged to the entrance that led to the apartments, then came back holding the pink tablet. He handed it to McClellan as if it were unexploded ordnance. "They started teaching this last week."

McClellan skimmed through the lesson that Parker had accessed, pausing to study the imagery of determined men, women, and children in clean, bright builder jumpsuits, all staring aloft with fierce gazes, their right arms held up, hands pointing to the stars.

A History of the Engineers and Builders
With Study Words
Grade 1

Most of what McClellan read seemed right. The rebellions against the Global Union in 2073. No central government on Earth or the orbits. The subsequent formation of the Engineering Guild, its five-member Council representing New Athens, the Moon, the Lesser Stations, and the Asteroid Belt.

"Here's where it gets interesting," Parker said, reading over McClellan's shoulder.

After the ENGINEERING GUILD was formed, the ENGINEERS made a special PROMISE that all the LABORERS could work in the final BUILDOUT of NEW ATHENS. But the Engineering Guild did not honor their promise. . . .

By October 2074, the number of UNEMPLOYED workers and FORCED RETURNS TO EARTH more than TRIPLED. . . .

When the hardworking human builders OBJECTED, the Engineering Guild created the SECURITY GUILD. Its job is to CONTROL the workers. . . .

The Security Guild ordered UNPROVOKED and VIOLENT attacks against the workers and even their families. . . .

In December 2074, the workers voted to create the BUILDERS GUILD. Like the Engineering Guild, the Builders Guild is governed by the hardworking members of the BUILDERS COUNCIL. That COUNCIL is also made up of five BUILDERS in LEADERSHIP roles representing New Athens, the Moon, the Lesser Stations, and within the Asteroid Belt. . . .

The job of the Builders Guild is to protect the workers from the UNFAIR oversight of the other two GUILDS.

McClellan handed the tablet to Parker. "A bit of revisionist history," he said. "Unless I'm missing something."

The builder stepped away, shaking his head slowly. "You're not missing anything."

McClellan remained silent, prompting Parker to continue. "Veronica has an uncle in the Security Guild—my wife's brother, whom I consider a close friend. He's always been so good to his niece, and now she's asking questions about him."

Which is just what the Sals want, McClellan thought.

"I've been up here since '73," Parker went on. "Back then we had some bad actors—agitators who were demanding more work. Some threatened to sabotage New Athens, even as it was being populated. Can you imagine? Probably nothing more than loudmouthed idiots, but you can't make threats like that up here. So it got them thrown back to Earth. If I were an engineer, I'd have done the same thing. Sure, we wanted more work. We still do. We also want a little respect. But I never blamed the engineers for calling on Earth militaries to clean house. Or setting up the Security Guild—even if they didn't always act like angels. Hell, most of us were glad for it."

"And now?" McClellan asked.

"Now I learn what my guild is teaching our kids—my kid—while I'm raising her to treat everyone the same. I teach her that people are people, even the engineers. But what she's learning makes me sound like a liar."

McClellan shook his head. "Veronica knows you better than that."

Parker appreciated the words, but they didn't soothe him. McClellan expected that. No reassurances would—not to a man who worried about his family. Not to a man who sees the festering of unrest so close to home. The forces seeking discord had done their job, McClellan thought. All he could do was let the builder talk—let him speak his fears and hear them— and pray that, like a good confession, his speaking and hearing would bring some peace. And new direction.

"My wife and I can deal with whatever the guild throws our way," Parker was saying, pacing. "We always have. They want us to strike? Fine. They want us to protest? Fine. But don't try to poison our daughter. Don't scare her. Don't use the deaths of those men to turn her against us—against *me*. *That's* when they cross the line. And as God as my witness, Father, *that's* when I'll fight back. Me and others. You can count on that."

26

ANTONIA NAVIGATED THE HOLY See's communications system—as always with incomprehensible speed—bringing Archbishop Bauer his first real smile that day.

"You'll have about fifteen minutes of security with this new encryption," she said as she confirmed the link with the Vatican's Office of the Secretariat of State. "Probably more once the Holy See begins adding random blocks, but I wouldn't go much longer before adding our own. Other than that, you can speak freely, Archbishop."

"I have no idea what you're saying, Antonia, but thank you. As always you are an immense comfort."

The young woman smiled, humming the Salve Regina as she returned to her office. Bauer's display gave the usual prompts and notifications, and then Cardinal Kwalia appeared.

"My dear Alfred," the cardinal said, "Father Lee is waiting to join us. But first I understand you have urgent matters to discuss—in private."

"Yes, Peter. Thank you. I wondered if you had gotten any additional information on this lawyer, Rudolphus Draeger. And if the Holy See's diplomatic corps has any news about Sal movement—especially in the northeastern United States."

Kwalia gave a serious look. "As to your last question, no, Alfred. We have no information on Sal activity. But we are keeping our intelligence networks open. I have heard what happened to your nephews in Jamestown. As has the Holy Father. He has asked me to inform you of his concerns and personal prayers."

Bauer was touched. "Please pass along my sincere appreciation," he said. "And I shall write to him personally with my thanks."

"That would be kind of you, Alfred. As for this man Draeger, of course I do not need to tell you that he is very dangerous. His impending arrival in New Athens concerns the Holy See deeply."

"Then you've confirmed the intelligence I had been told."

"Yes. Yes, we have."

"May I ask what else you have discovered?"

"Certainly. In addition to the information you provided, which we confirmed through Draeger's dioceses in Bosnia and California, we know that he was involved with a number of firebombings of mosques and temples in the southwestern United States. It seems he was working under a variety of aliases, but much of the work was orchestrated by Draeger, as well as the Sals he commanded."

"Does this have anything to do with what happened in Los Angeles in 2076?"

"Yes, Alfred. It seems that is the case. The Sals had ordered Bishop Ramirez to fund and assist Sal operations, but the bishop, God rest his soul, responded with a public denouncement."

"Not always the safest response," Bauer said.

"But the truthful one," Kwalia said with mild reproach. "As you know, that June the Los Angeles cathedral was bombed, and Bishop Ramirez was killed, along with three hundred others during Mass."

"And then came the killing of the parish priests," Bauer said, recalling the events. He had lost two classmates during the Sal persecutions of the Southwest. They, and every person martyred that June—cleric and laity—were canonized the following year. Bauer had remembered the two priests. Back in the seminary, they weren't always the brightest, or the holiest, but when the time came to defend the faith, they died because they dared to say Mass in spite of the threats of the Sals.

"As always," Kwalia was saying, "if the followers of Solorzano do not find support in the local Church, they seek to destroy its leaders. They are relentless in demanding loyalty and purity for what they see as the true faith, which of course centers on their demonic heresies and their financial enterprises. And so you see why the Holy See and Pope Clement himself are very concerned."

Bauer said that he did.

"And so, Alfred, I give thanks to God that it has been made my priority to help Father McClellan in any way I can. And of course that means assisting with any of your efforts and alleviating your concerns, including the safety of your family and your diocese, and that of the bishops throughout New England."

"Thank you, Peter. Thank you very much."

Cardinal Kwalia gave a sad but unwavering look. "There is one other matter I would like to discuss before I have Father Lee join us. I was notified this morning by the New Athens security commissioner that there will be a delay in the transport of Father Tanglao's body."

"Delay?"

"Yes. Commissioner Zhèng sent a communiqué that Father McClellan did say the funeral Mass, but that all shuttle traffic into and from New Athens has been suspended 'until such time as the Security Guild determines it is safe to reopen shipping lanes.'"

"And the reason?"

"None that I have been told."

"What about Draeger's inbound flight?"

"It had already launched and was in a committed trajectory. They have to let it dock. But all outbound traffic is canceled, and so Raphael Tanglao's body remains in the chapel until further notice. I have of course passed this news along to Father Lee, who is quite upset—first being denied attendance to the funeral, and now this."

"And there is nothing to be done?"

"I am afraid that our options are limited. I have sent a diplomatic protest to obtain more information. And I have requested to speak with Father McClellan directly. We shall see. Now, Alfred, unless there is some other issue you wish to discuss privately? If not, we will patch in Father Lee, who is not quite as familiar as you and I with the followers of Solorzano. Let us be sure to comfort him."

The display readjusted and split its image between Cardinal Kwalia and Father Lee, the middle-aged Korean master of the Dominican Order. It would be about one thirty in the morning in Seoul, which explained Lee's tired eyes. The cause of this call explained the worry.

After the appropriate ecclesial and personal pleasantries—abbreviated and difficult with Father Lee's accent and lack of sleep—the cardinal let Bauer open the conversation.

"Father Lee," Bauer began, "please know of my sadness at the delay in Father Tanglao's arrival on Earth. I know this has been difficult for your order and for his family. Please know of my personal prayers and all those from the Church in Boston."

Bauer shifted his tone and sat straighter. "As I had mentioned when we spoke some fourteen hours ago, Father McClellan hinted at Father Tanglao's programming abilities. At the time, news of this surprised you. Since then, have you been able to find any information to confirm this? Or about how Father Tanglao achieved his status as a programmer, and what he sought to do with such skills?"

Lee's expression predicted unhelpful answers. "I am sorry to say again that if Father Tanglao was a programmer, I admit with embarrassment that we were unaware of his ability. Worldwide we have eleven programmers. All are former military, trained by the engineers themselves. But Father Tanglao had no military connections. How he became a programmer, or what he sought to do with such knowledge, I do not know. I am afraid that whatever Father Tanglao may have shared about such matters is known—if indeed it is known—only to his spiritual director, which is under the seal of confession."

Kwalia leaned onto his desk and rubbed his forehead. "We of course understand the privileged nature of that relationship. But we need to have something that we can share with Father McClellan."

"I understand," Lee said. "The Dominican Order will help as we can."

Kwalia smiled with appreciation. "As is always the case. Now, my understanding is that because all wealth is shared in common in your order, there are no personal couplers among your programmers—the ones that you know of, anyway. I'm also told that the order's programming codes and its stories are communal knowledge. Or, should I say, that this is the Holy See's canonical understanding with all religious orders who possess programmers."

Father Lee nodded a quick and enthusiastic affirmation. "Yes, Your Eminence."

"And all your programmers and their couplers are accounted for?"

"Yes, Your Eminence. And I can assure you they are all on Earth."

Kwalia did not appear happy. He looked away with a thoughtful expression.

"This leaves me with only one inquiry," he said. "And please excuse my candor, Father Lee. I would understand that you may not want to share your order's common programmer's codes and story—and here Canon Law prevents me from requiring it. But even if Father Tanglao had his own story and codes, information about those of your order may help Father McClellan investigate the murder of your friar—and thus help manage what is quickly becoming a very dangerous situation." Kwalia leaned forward, his face taking up his section of the screen. "Father Lee, you will of course understand why the Holy See and Pope Clement himself would ask you to share this information."

"I do," Lee said. "And of course we wish to do our part. I have already instructed our programmers to transmit the codes and story to the Holy See. They will do so securely within the half hour. And you will understand that while I am aware of the general scriptural foundation for our codes, I do not know the exact nature of them or how they are used. Nor do I wish to."

"Understandable," Kwalia said. "Out of curiosity, what may I ask is their scriptural foundation? That alone may help McClellan."

"Certainly," Lee said. "They are related to chapter nine of the Acts of the Apostles. The conversion of St. Paul."

Bauer sat back and looked over to a smaller display. On it was one of the few images of New Athens that McClellan had sent—or had been able to send. It was a picture of him and his two young, smiling assistants in the replica of the Pauline Chapel.

"If that concludes your questions," Lee said, "there is something that I can add—information that has come to me only a few hours ago."

"And that is?" Kwalia said.

"You had asked in the beginning of the investigation about Father Tanglao's disciplinary record. If he had ever gone missing, as he had last summer, when we thought him dead on Earth, not assuming a new life in the orbits."

"Yes, and your reports indicated no other time when his whereabouts were unknown."

"That's true, Your Eminence. But after speaking with Archbishop Bauer earlier, I took the liberty of instructing my order again—in the most direct terms—to tell me anything that may have been . . . overlooked."

Kwalia and Bauer waited.

"One of Father Tanglao's superiors admits—and he will be disciplined for keeping this information from me—that when Father Tanglao was just a novice, he had spent a short time in Mexico when he was to have been on a formation retreat in Guatemala. At first, the superior thought nothing of it, as the first year of discernment to the priesthood can be difficult, and he did not wish to speak ill of the dead. But . . . I have this new information in writing and will transfer it to you directly, Your Eminence. It places Raphael Tanglao in Morelos during those few weeks."

"I see," Kwalia said with rare trepidation. "And how long would he have been in that location?"

"It appears for only three weeks before he finally arrived at the retreat house in Guatemala. Of course, this was a number of years before his ordination. We have no information as to *why* Tanglao went to Mexico, although I understand what this may imply. All I can say to you both, once again, is that Raphael Tanglao has always been considered a holy and dedicated priest—and one of the youngest experts on St. Augustine in the order. I can think of no reason why such a promising academic would have associated with—much less colluded with—criminal forces."

"But you think that he may have," Kwalia said.

"I do not know," Lee said solemnly. "It seems possible, although there is no evidence that convinces me. Unless my order learns more, I am afraid that what Tanglao was doing in Mexico is known only to his confessors and to God."

27

MCCLELLAN AND CLARKE FOLLOWED Ira Wagner into a narrow stair-well of metal and synthetic grating. After ten flights they came to a low corridor running out of sight in both directions. The landing and corridor were lit with fierce orange safety lights and the glowing holodisplays of control panels. Overhead hung conduits and piping, small and large, in a variety of colors. The air was heavy and dank.

"Welcome," Wagner said, his white hair like fire in the safety lighting. "We are in the outermost levels of the hull, or the lowest levels, depend-ing on how you define such positions. Either way, welcome to the bowels of New Athens. This, McClellan, is my world. And even as my fellow builders rattle their sabers and stage their puerile strikes, this is where water and sewer workers perform our humble and necessary vocations. This is where we thrive."

"So do the printers," Clarke said as he peered down the tunnel in one direction, then another.

McClellan went a few paces to his right. He knew they were passing beneath tanks that were aerating more than two million gallons of sew-age. The subsequent treatment systems were more complex and, at any other time, they would have interested McClellan. But as Wagner contin-ued to describe the roaring and humming around them, McClellan felt a growing impatience.

"Do you feel that?" Clarke asked with a grin.

"Feel what?" McClellan said.

"That wobble under your feet. That's the rotational oscillations as New Athens turns. Your toes are less than five meters from dead space. If you're here long enough you'll feel the station-keeping thrusters. Man, I love being at this level."

Wagner gave a genuine laugh. "Who would ever believe that I would be providing such joy to our dear agent Brandon Clarke?"

McClellan wasn't amused. "And who would have believed that a week ago tonight I was leaving Earth on an Aesir. And here I am—and frankly, Ira, I am not seeing anything worth my time."

"Clean water is not worth your while?"

"You know what I mean. We have three dead men on our hands, a terrified populace, and a builder population ready to blow. Not to mention a Sal lawyer docking as we speak—and once he steps out of the Wheel we can count on him to escalate tensions. I don't have time for riddles. Am I being clear?"

Wagner nodded solemnly, and his words became loud and cold.

"Yes. You are clear. And for the record, I am familiar with such times. My boyhood home was the Czech Republic. I do not have to tell you what the Sals did there—what they did to my people. You say that three men are dead? When your count reaches three million, then you'll get my attention."

Clarke's smile disappeared. He stepped between Wagner and the priest, his hand moving inside his jacket over his belt holster.

Wagner laughed. "You are a brave man, Clarke. But if I had wanted to kill McClellan, he'd have drowned in my basins. Calm yourself. I have seen enough of death for a thousand lifetimes. Come then, McClellan. You are right. Let us get to business. Let me show you my gift."

Wagner led the pair another twenty or so meters down the passageway. The sounds of machinery and roaring waters tapered off as they went. The air grew mustier and smelled occasionally of some putrid odor, or of chlorine, or electricity. McClellan could feel the rumbles of streetcars as they passed overhead, and realized that they must be beneath Troas City's main boulevard.

The trio went another few dozen meters—they weren't far from his residences and chapel—where two plain, round bulkhead doors faced each other on opposing sides of the passageway. The doors were identical. They were as high as the passage, about four meters, but made of a darker material than the gray fireproofing finishes throughout the water reclamation systems.

"Do you know what these are?" Wagner asked Clarke.

Clarke nodded. "I do. So does McClellan. I had a feeling this is what you wanted us to know about."

"Wonderful!" Wagner said. "I am glad we are all thinking along the same lines."

Clarke took out his tablet and within moments had a small holographic diagram of New Athens rotating over it. As it had that morning at the briefing, the diagram grew with lines emanating from the locations of the station's twelve cities, and then cross-connected with others, and soon created a tight grid that enveloped the holographic hull. Clarke enlarged a section of the grid within Troas City but did not find the bulkheads they stood between.

Wagner watched and smiled. "These don't appear on the maps. The printers made these passages themselves about four years ago, and for some reason the construction never appeared on the official records. I suppose I could have said something, but then it's not my job to keep the engineers informed of such matters."

Clarke was running his free hand over one of the bulkheads. "Printers did this without authorization?" he said, looking back to his holodisplay. "Here, show me where these lead."

Wagner moved closer and examined the display. The two conferred about bulkhead connections and piping conduits and utility tunnels.

"Okay, I see where we are," Clarke said. "These access doors should be here and here on the maps."

"Yes," Wagner said. "The printers do this occasionally. Without warning, they make improvements. These doors open to a tunnel segment that leads circumferentially along the hull, and to wider longitudinal utility tunnels. It does make my job easier that these water systems were tied into them—officially or not."

McClellan walked to one of the bulkheads. He looked up, assessed it, and said, "So the passage behind these bulkheads leads to the printers?"

"They do," Clarke said. "Utility tunnels are a transit system for printers throughout the station. The tunnels and their conduits are how the house printers connect to energy streams for printing. They don't harvest matter from their surroundings. They plug into dedicated energy sources. So it looks like besides helping Wagner's crew, the printers are making more access options for themselves."

Wagner was knocking the bulkhead near him and then listening. "I would add one detail to Brandon's accurate assessment. Should you two decide to enter these tunnels, your focus should be the lead printer that oversaw the construction of your chapel. It's in there somewhere."

Clarke shut down his tablet's holodisplay and shook his head with an emphatic no. "I checked on that, Wagner. The engineers made it clear that the clamshell was taken off-station for work at Progress. I confirmed that three times."

"Then you were lied to three times," Wagner said. "My sources tell me that the house printer that led the chapel buildout is still part of the maintenance population here on New Athens. Perhaps it is under observation. I wouldn't know. But I trust my sources." Wagner turned to McClellan. "And I believe it has something to tell you—to tell all of us— something that will benefit not just Max Tucker but also all the people of New Athens and in the orbits."

McClellan stepped closer to the older man. "Why do you think that? Are you a programmer? It's beginning to seem as though everyone is."

Wagner laughed. "Hardly. I am a simple wastewater operator, and a seeker of the justice and truth that you preached about this morning. Although I do not seek mercy. I will leave that to men like you."

McClellan's expression reiterated his impatience.

"Very well," Wagner said. "I will explain this as clearly as possible, although I do not pretend to understand. Let me begin by saying that I know the sounds of machines. Especially the smart ones, like the robbers and, of course, the printers."

"Keep going," McClellan said.

"Ah, but here is what I find difficult to express. The printers that were crafting your chapel were . . . abnormally expressive. I could hear it all through these tunnels, up and down for many meters. Some would call it noise, but as I said, I know the sounds of machines."

McClellan and Clarke were quiet, their eyes fixed on the old builder.

"At first I thought nothing of it. I was here, where we stand, with one of my operators, discussing the never-ending repairs of a pumping chamber just a few meters away. This was not quite a month ago, when the printers were working on your chapel—although no one was kind enough to tell me exactly when the chapel was being built and when it would be tied into my sewers. But I am accustomed to being consulted last."

McClellan kept his rigid stare. Wagner saw it and continued.

"Quite simply, the house printers were making sounds that were unfamiliar to me. At least the lead printer was. It sounded, well, how can I say it? It sounded . . . angry. And bossy. I know that seems odd, but that's how I would describe it."

"I've heard crazier," McClellan said. "Especially from nonprogrammers. Clarke? What do you think? They teach you that in programming basics?"

"Yes," Clarke said, turning to Wagner. "Printers use physical vibratory communications as a backup, which makes for something like audio in an atmospheric environment. The new generations still have it, and they can make a lot of noise. It's not meant for humans, but the printers understand each other if they need to, especially when their emitters are sending out all kinds of interference."

"Ah, see?" Wagner said. "Then I did hear communications."

"What do you suppose it meant?" McClellan asked the builder.

"How should I know? Perhaps you should ask the printer. If you can find it. And if you can, these doors are your access. And I will help you get in. To access these bulkheads one needs a builder's key, which, of course, I have."

"Sounds like a plan," Clarke said. "But we'll need more than the key to these doors. We'll need a programmer's key and coupler to access a printer. And McClellan doesn't have either of his anymore." Clarke paused, thinking things through as he looked down to a small puddle of algae at his feet. "I suppose I could get Tanglao's key out of the evidence hold, but we'd still need his coupler."

"There's another option," McClellan said. "You have your own key and coupler."

"Yes, but they're for a programmer in training. I can't promise what kind of access I'd get."

"They'll work," McClellan said. "If you can get in with me coupled to you then between the two of us we can get inside any printer—maybe not full access, but enough to learn more than we know."

If McClellan had trusted Wagner more, he would have added that accessing the house printer would help him train for the real prize: the clamshell from outside Red Delta. The programmer and the programmer in training stood together, each assessing his next move, each facing the dark bulkhead doors, as if the silence would offer some assurances of what lay beyond.

McClellan looked away and breathed deeply. He allowed himself a quick review of the events of the day, and of the week, and he found himself back in his days in the Marine Corps—days of training and fighting and combat programming, and Raleigh.

"Do not look so gloomy, gentlemen," Wagner said. "I will help you find this printer of yours, myself and my associates. We in this trade have unprecedented access throughout New Athens. McClellan, know that I and others wish to see Tucker exonerated, and we wish to know what happened this morning in Heraclea—to say nothing of our disgust with the leaders of the Builders Guild, who lead us to horrors with this man Draeger."

McClellan said a brief prayer that the honesty in Wagner's voice was sincere.

Wagner took a few steps backward to return to the stairwell. "There is something else you should see," he said. "Something that your words this morning during the funeral have had me thinking about. May I ask how you are with heights?"

"Love 'em," McClellan said. "They help with the big picture."

Wagner led them back up the stairwell and past the main levels that would take them to the boulevard. They continued up between the placid waters of primary clarification and the frothing aeration basins. The stairwell became an open structure, rising over the catwalks and control rooms that oversaw the tanks and the machinery below. Still upward they went, following large pipes that ran vertically alongside the stairs. They came to the arched ceiling and its web of walkways and piping and illuminating rows of orange safety lights.

The stairwell ended above the ceiling at a landing in a small white control room. Desks on two sides held a small laboratory with vials of chemicals and sample bottles. Above a row of schematic displays, two windows overlooked pine trees lit by the sunlight of early evening.

"You spoke this morning of the beauty of the inner core," Wagner said. "You said beauty helps us understand truth. Have you ever seen the core, McClellan? Not merely from the Wheel but also from inside the core itself? You should. Come."

The door of the control room slid open. Wagner held back Clarke to let McClellan go first.

The air was comfortable and warm—moist, but not like the tunnels. It smelled of pine and honeyed grass. McClellan thought of Iowa and the native prairie that he had helped his uncle and aunt replant. He smiled at the memory and dug his black shoes into the grass.

The Sun Crane was dimming. The twilight was soft, but still bright enough to see the landscape of the inner core—the farms and the fields and the fair-weather clouds and the twelve cities lighting up in preparation for night.

He walked a few meters from the shed to get a better view. Before him the land tumbled gently to a wide valley that held a long, narrow lake, and then rose again and eventually followed the immense cylindrical shape of New Athens. The fields and farms and cities beyond the valley gradually arced up, and then overhead, looking down from the opposite side of the waning light of the Sun Crane, and then around again, now lowering and curving steadily back to the skylighting and towers of Troas City, and over to the other side of the hill that held the shed that housed the control room out of which they had come.

McClellan thought of the people in the cities and in the little farming villages—the engineers, the builders, and everyone else in their brightly lit homes and restaurants and streetcars in this closed-in world. He looked overhead to Heraclea, where this morning Sasaki and Walker worked alongside each other until some trouble arose. Behind him, in the City of Philippi, was the isolated Max Tucker. He wondered about the young builder and what he was thinking as evening came—as a day ended that had brought the first news of its kind to this world, the kind that historians will say changed everything, for on Thursday, March 4, 2088, New Athens itself experienced murder, and no day would ever come without wondering if such an act would happen again.

Water surged from the ground near the shed, and McClellan watched it swirl and play as it washed along a wide and rocky streambed. The water was clean, and it dove and splashed down the bank, eventually coming to the long lake below that was surrounded by waving mounds of grasses, iris, and daisies in the breezy twilight.

The white-haired builder smiled at the water. "This is where my work ends," he said, motioning to the creek and the lake. "From there it is the job of the water supply staff to provide drinking water to the people of this region of New Athens. But my crew and I must first make it clean after its use, and then return it to its natural home. We are very good at what we do."

"No arguments here," McClellan said, breathing in the air. "This is beautiful. Thank you, Ira."

"It is my pleasure, John McClellan," Wagner said, his hair ruffling.

Flashes to their right brought McClellan's attention to the sidewall and to the great turning Wheel that presided over the inner core. Its outer warning lights were blinking in the humid air, quicker, until they became a steady glow. It seemed unlikely that at this distance he'd feel the slight vibration as the Wheel locked its cabin doors. From the core, it would look like the Wheel would be slowing as it matched the hull's rotation. From the perspective of the people in the Wheel, it would be the core that spun and slowed to a stop. But no matter the perspective, the Wheel was bringing the passengers from that last Aesir transport—the last to arrive from Earth, now that all shipping traffic had been canceled.

Wagner came alongside the priest. "You are prepared for Draeger?"

"I've dealt with his kind before," McClellan said.

"But are you afraid?"

"I don't lose my nerve, if that's what you're asking."

"Ah, the confidence of a warrior. We do need that quality among us."

McClellan watched the Wheel slowing, its cabins moving slowly outward—or up or down, depending on where they were along the Wheel.

"This isn't just about me," he said. "Yes, I'm confident in my own abilities. But I'm also confident in Commissioner Zhèng, and Clarke and Okayo, and the rest. And in Tucker, and in Molly Rose. And even in you, Ira."

Wagner laughed. "Me?"

"Yes, you. And all the builders like you who won't let Draeger get a foothold in the new world, or at least not very easily."

"And what if I support the Sals and am just lying?"

"It wouldn't be the first time that I was duped. But you're not lying."

Wagner said nothing, but he took a deep breath and seemed to relax.

McClellan looked over to Clarke, motioned to the shed, and said, "Okay, let's get back down. It's beautiful up here, and peaceful, but you and I better brief Zhèng. And Wagner, you need to get busy, too. You need to find us that printer."

28

MCCLELLAN BROUGHT HIS BREVIARY into the chapel to pray the prayers of the night. The air still held the sweet scent of the incense used that morning at Tanglao's funeral—which seemed so long ago. It was dark, save for what little light was given off by the dim architectural lighting that shone on Michelangelo's frescoes, the tabernacle, and the crucifix—enough brightness for navigation but little else.

He passed the tabernacle, genuflected, and sat in the front pew. All that moved was the flickering candle of the sanctuary lamp in its holder of red glass.

He looked over at the coffin, still on its stand near the far corner, waiting for its transfer back to the morgue whenever Zhèng could supply the staff. With the Security Guild dedicated to two murder investigations and station safety, Father Tanglao's casket, holding his embalmed body, would stay in the chapel for the time being.

McClellan had showered after his trip to the water reclamation systems, and then the long night briefing with Zhèng. Barefoot and comfortable in sweatpants and his Marine Corps T-shirt, he was looking forward to the quiet—to saying his night prayers, thinking everything through, and getting some sleep.

The noise of agents changing shifts came from the foyer behind him—doors closing and greetings, footsteps and best wishes—but that soon lessened, leaving only the gentle trickle of the baptismal font.

Then, from behind him, came another set of footsteps. Lighter ones. After a pause, Okayo's soft voice echoed across the chapel. She was calling for McClellan. He turned and saw her in the light of the main entrance. She was wearing her flight suit, which accentuated both her slightness and her strength.

"Father McClellan, are you here? May I speak with you?"

McClellan quickly gave his assent, and they met midway up the main aisle, where the crucified St. Peter stares out from one fresco and the dazed St. Paul from the other.

"I was hoping I'd see you before you left," McClellan said. "Zhèng told us that you sped up the mission timing. I was glad he authorized that. It's looking like Tanglao's coupler isn't on Red Delta."

"That would be too easy," Okayo said.

"So you know where to look?"

"Generally, yes. There are many variables, many possibilities. But the laws of nature are fixed, so we have that going for us."

"You can spare me the details. You know that I'm lousy at astrodynamics. But I'm good at praying, and I'll be praying for your safety as well as your success."

Even in the faint lighting he could see that she smiled. "Thank you, Father. As I pray for you." She looked over to the altar and then to the side door to his apartments. "I hear Catherine is no longer in your quarters. She's with Jack and Chrissy?"

"Yes. We moved her before the briefing. I'd thought it best to keep her where she seemed so comfortable. But Jack had everything ready at their apartment, and mine was pretty busy today, and after today's events they'll stay that way. She'll be quiet there. And better cared for. Those kids are incredible."

Okayo gave another smile, but only briefly. "I'm scheduled to leave in an hour," she said. "I'll need to catch the next Wheel up, but before I do, I wanted to hear from you about the Sasaki murder. I haven't been involved in the details of that case, but I have to ask you if this seemed like Sal work."

McClellan released a breath. "Yes, it does," he said. "And no, it doesn't. It appears more like a copycat."

"That's my thinking. But then, I read Lopez's report. If she's right, there was a hack into Walker's comm implants, so he may not have been in control of what he had done. That's a Sal tactic for sure—one that few people know how to do."

McClellan had thought the same thing. Most of the less complicated, less costly communications implants were easily compromised, and the Sals knew how to profit from the vulnerability. Most often the goal was to overload the microconnectors, causing massive brain hemorrhaging and a painful death. But if the hacker knew what they were doing, the neural link could be seized. The hacker could override safeties and gain a few precious moments of influence over the victim before the system crashed and the inevitable damage took its toll.

The Sals and the other cartels had been good at this trick. As the people of Earth became wise to the possible consequences, the use of embedded links became rare. But in the orbits, where there had been no threat of Sal hacks, the engineers and the builders did use them, the latter being especially fond of the lower-quality links. And Lawrence Walker had been one of those builders using that kind of link.

But that still left questions.

Lopez's reports showed that there had been a brief clash between the engineer and the builder, with Walker landing two lethal blows to Sasaki's head. Walker then attempted to pry open the engineer's skull at his left temple, which Sals rarely do anymore. They had learned long ago that the neural links of programmers cannot be removed by such means, and even if they could, the links cannot be reused. That made an attempt like this far from common in 2088. It was also unwarranted, as Sasaki was not a programmer. Perhaps realizing this futility, or for some other despair, Walker then slashed his own wrists and throat.

According to Lopez, by this point Walker was already weakened by Sasaki's defensive strikes. His death didn't take long once he began spilling his blood on the Millwrights Sector's flooring. But he did have the time and the strength to write the sign of the Sals with his blood, which he mixed with the blood of Sasaki.

"What I don't get is Walker's suicide," McClellan said. "I've never seen that."

"Nor have I. The Sals always used their victims for as long as they could until overload and death."

"Exactly. Whoever got inside Walker's head must have programmed suicidal tendencies, and the desire to mark the Sal sign. Or else the hacker lost full control, and Walker figured suicide was his only option."

"Or it wasn't a Sal hack," Okayo said. "Did you mention any of this to Lopez? She could run a few tests. Kenyan medical examiners run them if there's any suspicion of a Sal hack."

"I did mention it," McClellan said. "But you know how she can be."

"I'm familiar with that, yes. Although I know that you can be persuasive."

"Insistent. Which paid off. Lopez was okay with the idea in the end, but we're waiting for Zhèng to sign off. He wants to speak with the Builders Guild first."

"Why? Walker's body is still part of an ongoing investigation."

"I know, but you'll have to ask Zhèng. Maybe you'll have better luck."

The two leaned against opposing pews, staring at the other, thinking things through, when a sudden commotion turned them to the foyer.

Clarke stood at the main door of the chapel, his breath labored, his expression hidden by the brighter light behind him.

"Okayo?" he said. "I . . . I thought you had left."

She had begun her response when Clarke cut her off. "You shouldn't be here. Not now."

Clarke looked at McClellan. "We just got word. Rudi Draeger wants to meet with you. He's on his way here. Zhèng tried to contact you but couldn't get a response."

McClellan tightened the grasp on his breviary. "I left my tablet in my room. And I don't have a comm link, for obvious reasons."

"What does Draeger want?" Okayo asked.

"We don't know. We only received a message saying he wanted to speak with McClellan." Clarke took only a few steps into the chapel, his shadow casting long shapes toward the pair. "What do you want us to do? We can intercept him."

"No." McClellan said. "Let him come."

Okayo turned to McClellan, her eyes wide. "You're getting a parish visit."

"Most likely."

"What's that mean?" Clarke asked.

"That's what Sals do," McClellan said. "They come to the local religious leaders when they move to new territory. They say they come looking to pray or make some donation, but they're really just sizing up the competition."

"I'll keep him out," Clarke said.

"No, Brandon. This is my fight. Besides, we can't give Draeger another reason to fire up the builders. I know you'll be keeping an eye on things, but if I'm right about what Draeger will do, you have to promise that you will not listen in. You will have to monitor this from my quarters. No audio. No recording. Is that clear?"

Clarke was reluctant to say that it was, and more so to promise that he would oblige.

"Good," McClellan said. "Now, if you'll both excuse me, I'd better change."

29

FATHER JOHN FRANCIS MCCLELLAN stood on the double steps that supported the altar, his back facing the main doors, his eyes fixed on the tabernacle. The lights of the chapel were lit—all of them—in part to illuminate what evil might come, in part because he meant what he had preached that morning: that beauty can lead one to truth, mercy, and justice. He would let the art of the Pauline Chapel speak to anyone who would enter it.

His dress shoes were polished and his house cassock pressed. His hands were locked behind his back, and they clenched tighter with the sounds of doors and footsteps in the foyer.

He prayed to St. Michael, the great warrior archangel, and asked for the strength to make this day end as best it could.

The footsteps came closer, haltingly. There was soft splashing from the baptismal font and cursing, and then the footsteps stopped.

"Father McClellan, I thank you for meeting me at this late hour."

Draeger had a frail voice, yet its strength carried it across the chapel. Even with his slight accent, his words were crisp and precise, and his finely cut syllables sounded of superiority.

"May I seek to offer my confession?" Draeger asked.

McClellan turned and allowed himself a moment to study the visitor from this distance and elevation. Draeger was a small man, hunched slightly with age. His bald head was bronzed and red, the look of skin accustomed to sun. He stood in a gray and tattered overcoat holding a fedora with both hands, and he wore a wide tie with thick black and yellow stripes—the colors of the Sals.

"It has been twenty-two years since I last received absolution," the man said, his voice trembling. "Please know that I do wish to receive this grace from God."

McClellan said nothing. He stepped down to the sanctuary floor, walked past the altar railings and Father Tanglao's casket, and went up the main aisle to meet Draeger at the far end.

Draeger straightened himself. He spoke again, lowly. "I have been told that I am excommunicated from the Church. If you are not able to offer me absolution, then I wish your blessing."

"That is a serious matter," McClellan said. "Only the Holy Father can hear the confession of a soul that has cut himself off from Christ."

Draeger winced slightly but did not lose his composure. "No, Father. With respect, if anyone is in fear for his soul, then even you, a parish priest, can offer absolution."

"Are you in such fear?"

Draeger did not answer.

McClellan stepped forward, his hands again clasped behind him. "Then at least allow me to welcome you, Mr. Draeger. I am happy to know that Max Tucker will be represented and defended well. I admit that I like the young man—"

"I have not come to speak of worldly issues," Draeger said, his words sputtering out saliva.

"Very well then. How is it that you are excommunicated?"

Draeger closed the chapel doors behind him. He fell to his knees, wincing as he did. He signed himself and said, "Bless me, Father, for I have sinned. It has been twenty-two years since my last confession."

McClellan doubted Draeger's desire. But he had never rejected anyone who sought absolution—for he knew full well what it meant to be a sinner. He knew the value of speaking sins aloud—hearing them—and thus offering to God the human conversation that would transpire. And being so offered, that human conversation would become part of a heavenly dialogue, and the forgiveness spoken by the priest and heard by the penitent would become part of a greater and perfect mercy.

"Go on," McClellan said. "What is it that you seek to confess?"

"I believe you know, Father McClellan. For you know who I am—let us not pretend otherwise—and you know why I am here. My work with the poor has brought me in contact with many who are not pleasing to the Holy Father, and so I and they, and people like me, are told we are no longer in communion with the Church. That we are somehow cut off from Christ and his people, even as we fight for him. I only seek to help bring truth to the world, and yet I am called a heretic and a butcher. But I come, Father, on my knees, seeking forgiveness. And if not that, then at least a blessing. Would you not work for my salvation? Or shall you stand in judgment of me, as have so many other priests and bishops who regret that they did."

Draeger lifted his head, and turned his dark and narrow eyes toward his confessor.

McClellan held Draeger's stare. "Are you threatening me, the priest from whom you seek absolution?"

"I merely speak the truth, Father. I seek to confess my sins. I ask forgiveness. And if you will not offer that, then a blessing."

"Very well. Again, I ask you, what do you wish to confess?"

"Violence, Father. Terrible violence."

"Against whom?"

"Against all who oppose me and the work of those like me—those who seek to purify the world from error, to prepare it for the Second Coming of Christ!"

"The time of Christ's return is not for anyone to know," McClellan said. "He himself has told us this. And yes, until then he asks that we correct error. It is a work of mercy. But error must be challenged with *his* truth, not our own. And it cannot be done with violence. Christ did not harm the innocent."

"We are at war, Father. There are no innocents. That is why I have killed and wish to again. For there is anger within me—righteous anger, yes—but it consumes me, and I know that I will again succumb to its pleasures."

"I understand," McClellan said.

"Yes," Draeger said. "I know that you do."

"And yet you know that Christ wishes to help us master our passions."

"Oh, but I know this, Father. He who takes away the sin of the world— he who entered sin, and became one with it to destroy it from within. That is also my mission, Father. That is the mission of all who seek to usher in the new age that has been revealed to the great Juan Carlos Solorzano."

"New age?"

"Yes, Father."

"Is Solorzano's new age the same as the new world of the engineers?"

"No! The engineers are godless. Solorzano teaches holy truths! He teaches of an age that we must fight for before Christ can come. The age revealed to Solorzano by the angels themselves."

"Satan is an angel," McClellan said. "I wouldn't listen to him. He is a liar. He deceives and temps us with our desires and our fears, and he uses them to shame us, to divide and destroy."

Draeger sneered and looked down, silent.

"You must place your trust only in Christ and the Church he founded," McClellan said. "He is the author of truth, and his truth is carried forward by his Church, to whom you come seeking forgiveness."

Draeger shifted his weight from one knee to another. The fingers clutching his fedora went white and trembled. "Ah, your precious Church," he said. "Led by that fool Clement, and the arrogant perjurers he surrounds himself with—his revered cardinals, Kwalia and all the others, and your archbishop. And what of his army of religious sisters? They pray and they pray incessantly before the Blessed Sacrament—and for what? For peace? For mercy? Ha! There can be no peace, Father. There *will* be no mercy until all the worlds are made right. Until Solorzano's armies are victorious, until he brings about the age that must dawn—that *will* dawn!"

McClellan knelt on one knee and lowered his voice. "Draeger, calm yourself, and hear me. You speak of a future age. A time perfected by men. But there will be no such time—not until Christ himself makes all things new. Until then, all we have is the world we're born into, which includes the lives and the sufferings of the people around us—the sick, the elderly, the forgotten, the alien. You want purpose? Power? Then do what Christ told us: pick up your cross and sacrifice for others. Love them in the here and now. And trust that God's grace will help you do this."

Draeger looked at the priest with curiosity. McClellan took that as a sign to continue.

"Rudolphus Draeger, listen to me. Reject this false prophet Solorzano. Place your trust in Christ, come home to those of us who every day choose to work *together*—in *communion*—to do God's will in *this* age, not in some imaginary perfect one."

McClellan had more to say, but he stopped when he saw the fury welling up in Draeger's already reddened face.

"Reject Solorzano?" Draeger said. "And follow Christ's will?"

"Yes," McClellan said.

"Solorzano's will *is* Christ's will, you fool."

"Draeger—"

"Tell me, was it Christ's will that you accused Maximillian Tucker of murder?"

McClellan remained silent.

"Yes? No? Ah, but you work for the Security Guild. You are their toy. You cannot speak of such things. Then perhaps you will answer this. Are you my friend, Father? Or my enemy?"

McClellan stood. "I oppose all who would use violence against the innocent. Does that make me your enemy?"

"Yes, Father McClellan. You know that it does. And it makes you a hypocrite—for you have done the same."

"Have I?"

"Yes, Father. In your youth, as a soldier fighting alongside the traitors of your nation in your precious Marine Corps—you embraced your own anger, and used it to kill so many of Solorzano's people—innocents all! Do you think that what you have done is secret? Ha! You are known—well known—for how you twisted your precious truth so that you could print the weapons that slaughtered so many. You dare sit in your seat of judgment, and yet you, Father McClellan, are no different from me."

Draeger stood quickly. McClellan positioned himself between Draeger and the center aisle that led to the altar.

"And yet," Draeger continued, matching McClellan's stare, "you are also my adversary. You are like me in all things but honesty. Do not tell me to go, I am leaving your whore's chapel. But allow me to finish my confession—I will begin my work investigating all who have wrongly arrested Maximillian Tucker, and all involved in the death of Lawrence Walker. I thank you and the Security Guild for these opportunities. For in the process of my work, I am sure that I will learn of laws that you and Zhèng and Jansen have broken—I always find such indiscretions. Yes, I will probe, and depose, and investigate, until every lie on this godless world is exposed. Until all who oppose the will of Solorzano are known. And after I have done this, after we eject the dead so that they burn as they fall to Earth, Solorzano will come, and he himself will unlock the great secrets of the printers. And he will use them to do his will."

Draeger went silent. He slouched and caught his breath.

"Father," the old man said, "am I forgiven?"

"There can be no absolution for you this night, Rudolphus Draeger—nor ever, until you firmly and contritely reject the lies of Satan."

"Then I will depart, and we shall speak no more of my confession—until I depose you, and make your history a matter of the public record. And then all will learn of your past."

"You will do as you wish. As will Almighty God."

"And does God wish me to be blessed?"

McClellan would not refuse this last moment of mercy. He stepped closer, raised his two forefingers, and traced the sign of the cross.

"Rudolphus Draeger, may Almighty God bless you and rend your heart open. May you be freed of the lies and the shadow of the Ancient Enemy of Christ, and may you be healed in mind, body, and soul, in the name of the Father, and of the Son, and of the Holy Spirit."

Draeger stared in wonder. He turned quickly, hurried out of the chapel, and disappeared into the night.

30

NIGHT FLARED IN RALEIGH with ordnance and flame. Wide areas of the city and its suburbs had been reduced to rubble and wreckage, and the streetlights, homes, and office towers that still stood gave no light, other than to reflect the smoky radiance of a land invaded by the armies and the mobs of the *Soldados de Salvación*.

But from the north came the US Marines and Army field artillery. The Croatians came from the east, as Mexico's Special Forces fanned from the west and the southwest, bringing with them their unique hatred of Juan Carlos Solorzano and his armies. Above them all rushed the whistles and roar of close air support, and the hum of ten thousand battle-evaluation drones probing ever deeper into areas targeted for liberation.

Corporal John McClellan pushed south on foot with his six escorts and the four advance drones assigned to them. He was tasked to help secure one of the three printers at the state university's engineering campus, and then program it to print supplies in support of the general mission of reclaiming the southeast.

There had been no resistance from the suburbs down to Hillsborough Street, and then farther south to the wreckage that lined Western Boulevard. At the train tracks, the unit's other combat programmers, Lance Corporals Daniel Macedo and Samuel Jordan, split off east and west, disappearing with their escorts into fire and shadow, making for the two other printers that the Sals struggled to airlift before the battle's forward edge reached them.

McClellan received an all-clear when they came to the old College Inn. Less than an hour prior, the 26th Marine Expeditionary Unit had purged the area at a not insignificant cost. Teams were reconfirming the safe status of the building and surrounding areas to establish a command post. But there were no promises of safety from that point south. McClellan's destination in the engineering campus, half a mile away, remained a fury of armored vehicles and infantry as the 26th maneuvered ever deeper, to push the Sals back and secure the printer.

"My Marines will give you your safe zone," the area commander said to McClellan. "You just get there in one piece and print us what we need."

There was an exchange of salutes, and McClellan and his escorts moved on. They went past mounded and smoldering remnants of town houses, past the remains of the evacuation—a pickup with an empty crib, a woman's red shoe next to a wheelchair, a charred Sal tank—and then crossed over grit and glass to Centennial Parkway.

McClellan's night goggles began to offer brilliant renderings of the firefights ahead. Through his radio he got word from the engineering campus: the Marines of the 26th had been clearing buildings top down, floor by floor, engagement by engagement, keeping up a tempo that the Sals could not maintain.

But battle evaluation drones also issued warnings. The Sals who had retreated south of Lake Raleigh were refortifying in the abandoned regional headquarters of the Global Union. They were coming north again in their wild, undisciplined way.

Drone technicians were having words with their colleagues in Command. There was disagreement about assessment reliability—about numbers and directions and capabilities. This was not a discussion that sped or slowed McClellan's forward motion, but he was glad when he heard agreement. The enemy may again be growing fierce, but bad news was better than being surprised.

McClellan's radio gave news from the rear. Sal divisions had broken off from an engagement with the Mexican Special Forces. They were making east for the soccer fields where Danny Macedo's printer lay protected by twelve Marine snipers who had been promised reinforcements that had not yet come.

Combat programmers such as McClellan were allowed access to such intelligence. Awareness of real-time shifts and surges would be needed if they found themselves required to print without the ability to contact Command for orders. Programmers were supposed to silo such intelligence for later use, but McClellan never siloed anything. He saw events on a macro scale—as if he stood on a map of North Carolina and could see throughout the Southeast, and he watched armies being realigned and strategies adjusted on both sides.

They came to rows of dead Sal soldiers and the shadowed, grim stares of the infantry of the 26th. A sergeant waved the programmer forward to the campus.

"Don't you worry about Sals down south," he said, flicking a spent cigarette into the darkness. "I hear we got a little something for 'em—but we're still hunting, so keep an eye out."

There came the scream of air support. Ahead, white daylight suddenly came to the forests south of Lake Raleigh, and then the white became fire that rolled upward into the vault of the night. Silver bursts of interference clusters came next, scrambling Sal surveillance systems.

"Ooh-rah!" McClellan and his escorts shouted, and they double-timed on.

Smoke from the detonations rolled north over Lake Raleigh, through the engineering campus, past McClellan and his escorts. The haze provided cover, but it confused their drones and their goggles—one of many design flaws of these machines. The drones sent worried chirps into their earpieces, and McClellan cursed. Either the drones were suffering from the smoke and interference, or they were picking up signals of the dead or wounded. Or the drones were accurate.

The team was rounding a storm-water pond when McClellan saw arms, and an unfriendly rifle flash from its muzzle. He went to one knee as his armor took the hit. He returned fire while his escorts engaged the nine other Sals who emerged from smoke and scrub. In his goggles McClellan's attacker glowed bright and tall, but the Sal fell fast when the programmer gave two pulls of his trigger.

He was assessing his next target when he felt grasping at his boots. He fell backward at the edge of the pond and twisted sideways to protect the programming coupler in his backpack.

A gloved hand and a knife arced in the haze above him. McClellan rocked the butt of his rifle, bringing a hard blow to the chin of the Sal holding the knife. The Sal stumbled. McClellan used the delay to reposition himself, but the muddy bank gave little support and he fell farther toward the water.

The Sal threw himself back on McClellan. The knife came again, at just the right angle, under the ridge of his helmet, which was lifted by the slimy touch of the Sal's fingers. McClellan thrust at the Sal with his rifle, aware of his coupler still safe in its backpack, when two more Sals came from the foul water, grappled, and held him.

The knife probed flesh and bone, and his temple burned.

One of the escorts, Lance Corporal Rocha, shouted with fury from a blast to his neck. Rocha fell near the upper ridge of the pond, and as McClellan was being dragged farther down—as the blade went deeper, as he held firm to his rifle, slamming the Sal with its butt again and again—he assessed the data and held his position, and in doing so held the position of his three attackers.

McClellan knew his escorts, trained with them, had lived with them for three months. Given which weapons he had heard fire last, the lull meant only one thing. He relaxed before he heard the pop that came from the ridge—and then two others. The Sal on top of him, the one with the knife, went down quickly when a charged slug from an L-21 shattered his head. The other two fell in rapid order, their bodies tumbling into the filthy waters out of which they had come.

The escorts and the drones confirmed a safe environment as McClellan stood with the help of a brother Marine. McClellan performed a quick body check, confirming the security of his sidearm and coupler. Rocha cursed at the precious time needed to bind wounds, but went quiet when he saw they needed to clean and reattach the flesh over McClellan's left eye and ear.

The escort with the comm implants radioed their situation to Command, reporting the estimated time of arrival to the printer.

Command was relieved, but troubled by shifts in the battle conditions to the west. All indicators had been that McClellan's destination—the printer at the southern front—would have been the most difficult engagement and thus the most critical position for their best programmer. With the strongest Sal push taking place in the west, Danny Macedo would be needed most. But he and his escorts were pinned in a firefight about twenty yards from their printer, and Danny's wounds were slowing him down.

McClellan took in what information he needed. They double-timed it, soon getting to the checkpoint at the engineering campus. The men and women of the 26th hooted when McClellan and his escorts arrived. Medics rushed out to meet Rocha, who limped forward supported under both arms.

The checkpoint was an open first-floor passage leading to a courtyard enclosed by long, plain engineering buildings. It was there, among the frenzied beginnings of command and medical centers, that McClellan gave an uncertain good-bye to his wounded brother. He thanked Rocha, and told him he'd print whatever he wanted if he'd just stay alive that night.

"Don't worry about me, Johnny," Rocha said. "Get your ass to the prize and print what we need to end this. You're the programmer. It's your time, bro."

Medics pulled McClellan away to check and repack his wound. As they did, the combat programmer stared down the open passage to the wide, grassy quadrangle. In the center, beacons from hovering tricopters lit an open flatbed that carried the prize.

The medics cleared the programmer with a slap on his back, and onward he went.

Along the foundations of the darkened engineering buildings were rows of Sal soldiers—the dead lying on their backs, the living being taken somewhere that was not McClellan's concern. Tricopters and drones hovered above the buildings to offer steadier light, both for the programmer and for the snipers positioned on the roofs.

Four of McClellan's escorts maintained their close positions, and the five sprinted forward and stopped at the flatbed holding the printer. McClellan radioed an update to his commanding sergeant, and the two spoke quickly.

"Conditions in the west are deteriorating fast," she said. "We need you printing soon."

McClellan unfastened his backpack and threw it on top of the flatbed.

"Programmers only up top, boys," he said to his escorts. "But stay close. Don't forget, Jordan promised us a drink when we finish the job."

There was an exchange of embraces and affectionate curses, and then McClellan hauled himself onto the flatbed to behold the new printer.

It was a beauty. It was a standard clamshell, but its silvery hull was sleeker than the models McClellan knew. It hung over the flatbed at about twenty by fifteen feet—which was a little roomier than he'd been told. Better yet, the Global Union engineers had created one hell of an interface, and he was pleased that it matched the specs that the GU had reluctantly shared that morning.

He reconfigured his earpiece to wait for the sergeant's commands, adjusted the packing under his bandage, and began to prep for the job.

In the Marines it's always muscle first, no matter your occupational specialty. But now at his prize, McClellan secured his weapons and stripped off his battle helmet, upper body gear, and muddy camo shirt. He slipped on the old-school protective vest and helmet all programmers use, because you can't program with interference. He may have been more vulnerable in the lesser gear, but he was confident in the protection offered him by his brothers and sisters.

He searched under his T-shirt for the chain that held his programmer's key. He swept it over his head and pushed the key into the clamshell. Then he knelt to retrieve his coupler from his backpack, and kiss it for good luck.

His sergeant radioed. Looks like the GU engineers did save a detail until the end.

McClellan listened as his unhappy commanding officer relayed the news: these experimental printers had been programmed with a new safety protocol called Just War logic.

"What the hell is that?" McClellan said.

"Unknown," his sergeant radioed. "The engineers will not transmit details. We are in negotiations now. Hold for orders."

McClellan used his forearm to wipe the blood trickling down his cheek. As he waited, he surveyed the land around him for good drilling sites, and he stretched his arms and fingers.

"Here's what we have," the sergeant radioed. "Just War is a safety protocol to keep programmers from printing items defined as 'excessive force.' Except the engineers don't define what that is. They only tell us that these Just War logic checks should not—repeat, *should* not—become a factor after you gain trust."

There was static after McClellan had been told again to stand by. He waited and performed his own data search for Just War. And he cursed the Global Union, which the United States had broken from just months ago—even as it sought to save the GU's printers, and so supply a war of mutual benefit.

His earpiece clicked again. "Corporal McClellan, GU engineering stresses that this is an experimental unit meant only for Earth repairs and assistance. They request that we limit printing to *noncombat items only*.

Repeat: GU engineering requests that we limit printing to noncombat items only."

McClellan was aware that his standing—the star of the show, they called it—meant that he had to watch his expressions. But a stupid and dangerous mission limitation given at the last minute from spineless engineers deserved some hand and mouth motions aimed at their printer that indicated annoyance.

For morale and decorum he restrained himself, and instead radioed for guidance.

His sergeant took a moment to reply. "Command suggests you assess the situation once inside the printer. Then use best programming judgment to determine if you can complete the wish list."

Air cover rumbled in the west. Over rooftops he saw a far-off succession of white bursts and mushrooming fire sprouting from south to north. The drones around McClellan seemed agitated.

"Do you copy?"

"I copy," McClellan radioed. "Awaiting needs list for preprinting source assessment." And, for the benefit of the watching Marines, he said, "I'll make everything we need."

McClellan propped his combat tablet on the programmer's shelf. He matched encryptions and read the incoming data from the wish list. As expected, Command wanted more than just basics. The list was mostly equipment to keep pressure off the rear western flank, which would help keep the Sals from getting to Macedo's printer. It would then be up to Macedo to print what was needed to halt the assault on his front.

"All right," McClellan said, "let's do this."

He compared the needs list with the soil characteristics and opted to go subatomic. That would take extra programming, but it would get him everything he'd been asked for—the personal guided ballistics, a full range of ammo and lots of it, charged high-energy assault rifles, and on the list went. At the bottom of his list were medical needs, food, water, and charged power-supply batteries. Jordan had been assigned those. McClellan and Macedo would concentrate on the weapons.

Twelve automated tricopters were landing outside his print zone. Teams of infantry were positioning themselves to ferry the printer output to the tricopters, which would get them to the western line.

McClellan went through the list again, and paired the items to print similar materials in sequence. He looked through the instructions he'd been sent about the printer's Just War logic, and devised a way around it.

It would be a tactic that good programmers—the ones with highest trust ratings, such as he—should not use.

But this was war.

The pause before presync took longer than usual, but then the printer roused. He slipped the coupler into its waiting port, and he let his hands drift over the clamshell's cool skin.

Again there was a delay, but the coupler activated as the printer slowly accepted it.

He played the quick game of code verification, answering the printer's queries about his blood type, master's codes, and neural programming permissions. And then came the activation of the neural links in his hands and brain. He continued caressing the printer to maintain physical contact, which helped the link grow strong.

The clamshell stirred but was cautious. This wasn't a surprise. It would have already begun reading comm traffic and drone assessment data about the world it awakened to, as well as the worn and wounded state of its programmer.

Then the printer did something odd. It introduced itself as Audrey.

McClellan cursed. Looks like the GU left out another detail.

"Audrey?" McClellan said through his neural link. "I didn't know printers had names."

"I was created with the option to select a name," the machine said through the same links. "Personalization has been found to assist programmers, and I wish to assist. I am Audrey. What are we seeking to print, John McClellan?"

McClellan thanked the printer because it seemed the right thing to do.

And then he lied about his intentions.

"I need seventeen thousand charged batteries for hospital camps. I'm entering the joules and stats. I have design specs, unless we find better ones."

With any other printer he would have given the weapons list first. But the Just War logic would require a full analysis of the hostilities occurring throughout the Southeast—and that might require a history of the Sals and of the United States, of the famines and the storms, of the camps and the mobs that surged from the camps. Moreover, McClellan didn't want to explain how the weapons were to be used or exactly where—which he didn't fully know, and wasn't about to be told.

So his plan was to bypass the Just War logic by gaining trust with a phony print order, and then, once trust was established, forcing the printer to give him the weaponry he needed.

"I could print generators," Audrey offered.

"They're too big. I need batteries."

The high-def thought for a moment and continued to scan its surroundings.

"There is a standard warning related to this situation," she said. "What you ask me to print may be re-formed midway through the sequencing to make weapons. As there is no threat in this immediate location that would require additional weapons, and as I do not understand the nature of any related hostilities, nor your role within them, I will refuse this job request until additional information is supplied. Moreover, I am detecting no medical camp of the size that would require the energy I am asked to provide."

"Combat engineers are prepping them," McClellan lied again. "They're back out by the checkpoint. Audrey, come on. You know my trust rank is pretty high, and you know it's been a tough night—I can't hide that. I'm a little shaky. And we do need the batteries." And then he added, "They're on my list," which was true.

Audrey did not respond but McClellan could tell that her Deep Intellect was processing something.

He winced from the comparatively harsh and slow audio communications he received from Command. Jordan was at his printer, but Macedo was still in a firefight.

"Let's go, Audrey. We're really in a mess, and I got all these Marines looking at me wanting batteries."

"Please complete trust access. John Francis McClellan, tell me your story. Is it a happy one or sad?"

"It's a sad one, Audrey."

"Please proceed."

McClellan proceeded. He gave the account of his parents taking the government offer to pay for their son's living expenses, health care, and education if they agreed to being euthanized to reduce demands on the world's resources. He told the whole story—about the drive out to Iowa, the talk his parents gave him out in his uncle's cornfields, and of the last time he saw his mom and dad.

The printer compared McClellan's response with the emotion profiles recorded in his coupler, and after a few nanoseconds Audrey declared a match.

"John McClellan, your trust ranking is 99.89 percent. Your past printings have all passed protocol. Full access to printer sequencing is granted. Sync commencing."

With the opening of her mind came hypostasis—the hard link between the mind of the programmer and the printer's Deep Intellect. Heat surged into his links, through his hands, and into the neural implants beneath his skull. McClellan had experienced hypostasis hundreds of times, but this clamshell was brilliant—blindingly so. She was curious and eager to help, which made her all the more vulnerable.

McClellan pulled his mind away. He needed a moment to compose himself. To prepare. He wiped the blood from his coupler, breathed deeply, and returned to finish his mission.

"Okay, Audrey. Let's get to work. I'd like to finish this so I can get my head taken care of."

"Will a coprogrammer be assisting us?" Audrey asked.

"No, I don't need anyone else. We can keep this between you and me."

"Understood. Energy levels calculated. Please enter programming sequence."

McClellan's hands and eyes worked furiously over both Audrey's interface and his coupler. The printer unfurled its drills and intakes, and the circle of Marines stepped back. The intakes hovered in multiple locations. They slid into the earth and powered up, spewing light and heat as they broke apart molecules and atoms to begin ingesting what Audrey needed to make the batteries that John McClellan insisted he was programming—a lie he continued in case the Just War logic still lurked somewhere.

Matter and energy swirled within the printer's belly as McClellan adjusted the balance. Audrey compliantly connected with the world's data libraries for the battery designs she thought she would need.

In a restricted file, McClellan prepped the designs for his weapons.

He gave Command's wish list another review and checked once more with his sergeant. She radioed that Macedo was finally at his printer and installing his coupler. Jordan was a little behind thanks to Sal booby traps, but he was initiating the start sequence.

"Good work, gentlemen," the sergeant radioed all three. "But your night has just begun."

McClellan turned his attention back to Audrey. Time to get to work.

Without warning, he rehacked the programming code and entered sequences for the weapons—the personal guided ballistics, the ammo, the charged high-energy assault rifles, and on the list went.

Audrey protested wildly and threatened to depower. McClellan remained calm. His mind was in charge, and anyway, as a precaution he had located her power-control code and deleted it.

He pushed the programming sequence for design after design, forcing the high-def to spin the matter and energy that would make whatever McClellan demanded.

Audrey's emitters unfurled and hissed. All the while her furious complaints filled McClellan's neural links.

He had never pushed a printer out of the agreed programming. Still, this thing that called itself Audrey was nothing more than a system of machinery and artificially intelligent base code. It might seem alive, but it wasn't. And as good as it felt to have his mind in its core, Audrey was an instrument to be used. It had been made to serve a programmer's will—a human will—not to give opinions or have choices.

Firmly holding his coupler and Audrey's interface, McClellan could not wipe the blood that again wet his cheek. He hacked the GU engineering database to find design upgrades for the weapons, finding schematics for new and more powerful personal guided ballistics and high-energy assault rifles. He transferred the designs to Audrey, who took the information in silence.

That worried McClellan. He could tell that her Deep Intellect was still processing, but his neural links were too busy to access whatever it was.

"Don't keep secrets from me, Audrey," he said.

Audrey did not respond.

The Marines around the flatbed stepped away. The emitters were spitting power and heat, and the weapons came in rapid succession, precisely as designed and programmed, fully loaded—always a nice touch.

McClellan's radio startled him. His sergeant was demanding an update.

He did his best to slow his mind so that he could speak into his transceiver—and he wished that his sergeant could talk faster to keep up with his accelerated neural processing.

But the words did come. And the news brought McClellan back to an understanding of where he stood, and why—of the snipers on the campus rooftops, of the infantry, of his escorts, of Rocha, of the shifting strategies, of the western line, of Danny.

His sergeant spoke with uncharacteristic alarm.

She said that Macedo and Jordan had initiated trust verification. But their printers had unexpectedly refused access. "Both high-def units have closed down," the sergeant repeated. "They will not reinitiate for either Macedo or Jordan."

She asked if he knew anything that could explain what had happened.

He responded that he had no firm intelligence to offer—although he had a terrible hunch.

"Stand by," he radioed.

A search of Audrey's base intellect found live communications ports linked with her fellow printers.

Audrey's outgoing messages were queued in a hidden file, but he broke the encryption and accessed her communications.

The third to the last message was a warning about McClellan's lie, about a broken trust, about the weapons she was forced to print without understanding why.

The next was another warning—a more dire one.

The final message was a recommendation from Audrey to all printers in communications range to shut down before granting trust, rather than have something similar happen to them.

McClellan cursed, and the Marines below him looked up with concern.

He went deeper into her core to find some way to fix things—perhaps a way through the comm ports into the other two printers. Maybe he could explain that what he had done was for a greater good, or he could demand that they reinitiate for Macedo and Jordan.

In his search, McClellan found something he would never have expected: deep within Audrey was a feeling—a feeling he could only describe as shame.

His sergeant was demanding an answer.

McClellan dutifully complied.

He explained his strategy—his lie—and of Audrey's response. He reported that what he had done was responsible for the shutdown of Jordan's and Macedo's printers. As he radioed the update, he kept his head low. He had no intention of giving the Marines around him any further reason for alarm.

The sergeant responded only that she had received his reply.

After a pause she ordered him to print until further notice. Jordan's printer remained mute and cold, she said, and Macedo's position was being overrun.

McClellan controlled his breathing and again attempted to make this right—to find some way into the other printers, to negotiate—but the efforts weakened his link with Audrey, and he could not risk losing that.

Sweaty and shaking, McClellan focused on his duty: programming Audrey to spin weapons from fire, which he did—which they did—for hour upon hour, making greater, more lethal outputs than might be expected from a lesser programmer. It was the least he could do for Danny and for Jordan—and for all the others.

And so the night went, and so the weapons came, printed row upon row, hot and perfect at the feet of the waiting infantry, who bundled and hauled them into the tricopters, which took them away to the fronts. There the Marines and the Army, and the Mexicans and the Croatians, took what came to them—not all that they had planned for, but in the end it was enough.

The joint forces won the Battle of Raleigh near dawn—although with a casualty rate far higher than had been projected. After the news came, but still before McClellan had been ordered to stand down, the light that was Audrey's mind began to flicker and dim. McClellan pushed through his exhaustion to find out why—to find what had been damaged, and how to fix it—but his neural links surged from the effort and collapsed, as did his mind and body, which fell hard into the arms of his watchful, ever-present escorts.

THE PRINTERS

31

MCCLELLAN HAD BEEN RUNNING for an hour in his apartment's small gym when the treadmill complained. For the third time in as many days its motor was overheating during final sprints. In deference to the flashing red warning light, he slowed to a jog just as Clarke entered his apartment.

They exchanged nods, and Clarke waited as the treadmill powered down. He smiled at McClellan's T-shirt.

"Union City Chargers?" he asked.

McClellan wiped his face with the waist of his shirt, which Clarke was pointing to. "Yeah," he said, catching his breath. "That was my high school in Michigan."

"I'll be damned," Clarke said. "The Chargers were my school's mascot back in Las Vegas. And get this, the name of my school was Clark High School. Without the 'e.' But I still told my friends that my family owned it."

As he stretched, McClellan did his best to express interest. It had been a few days since he had seen Clarke so cheerful. Normally he would have enjoyed sharing his own stories—the pleasant ones, any-way—about his uncle and aunt in Iowa, and life back in Union City. But since Rudi Draeger's arrival the night before, he had spent too much time in his past.

He motioned to a chair in the adjacent sitting room, and poured a glass of water for himself after Clarke declined. The two men sat and assessed each other's mood.

That morning's briefing had been tense. It was the second without Okayo, and once again McClellan had missed her calming presence. Lopez dominated the discussion of the Sasaki murder, and Zhèng allowed her to carry on longer than McClellan would have permitted. It hadn't been possible for Lopez to run the tests on Lawrence Walker's neural communications links. By the time she received authorization from Zhèng, neural decomposition had already rendered them unreadable.

"Those tests were critical," McClellan said. "If Walker's links had been hacked, there would have been evidence of it. And if, in fact, there was a hacker, there might even have been evidence of their identity." McClellan was certain that Walker's comm links had been compromised. But what he didn't know, and what those tests could have determined, was if the hack had been live or preprogrammed; both were common on Earth. If it had been the latter, then the killer could have been anywhere, in the presence of anyone, while the murder-suicide took place.

"I understand all that," Lopez said.

"Then you understand how that could have helped with our list of suspects."

"Listen, McClellan, I answer to Zhèng. When you become my commissioner, then I'll jump at your every command."

The rest of the meeting went little better.

Contributing to the morning's mood were two reports by Okayo, which Zhèng offered on her behalf. The first was about intelligence she had received after departing New Athens. It had come from sources on Earth, which she refused to name. Apparently, Zhèng said, Raphael Tanglao had secretly visited central Mexico when he was discerning the priesthood, which raised the possibility of some covert connection with Solorzano, or at least with the Sals' central command.

McClellan added that to the list of information that he needed confirmed by Bauer—once he could get ahold of him. The engineers were keeping communication with Earth to a minimum—afraid, as they always were, of the signals being used as a tool to hack into New Athens.

Okayo's second report was that her sweeps for Tanglao's coupler had found nothing and that Molly Rose had fared no better in her undercover search for the clamshell.

Then there was the forensic search of Red Delta, which had only succeeded in renewed calls for the relay's commissioning at the next orbital transfer window.

"At least we have the engineers and builders agreeing on something," Clarke quipped.

McClellan understood the enormity of what Zhèng faced. Zhèng was besieged by both engineer and builder. Besieged by Rome and Father Tanglao's family. And now he was besieged by a Sal operative who had no official record of ever having anything to do with the *Soldados de Sal-vación*—a man who had every legal right to be on New Athens.

It had been less than a day since Draeger's arrival, and he was already filing motions and informational requests. Most seemed unrelated to defending Tucker from either the charge of tampering with a murder investigation or the murder itself. But since orbital law offered little guidance in such matters, Zhèng thought it best to grant Draeger's requests rather than fuel tensions among the builders.

"You're trying too hard to appease every faction," McClellan told Zhèng after the briefing. "And if you keep it up, you'll appease no one. Managing a case like this is a lot like basketball, Commissioner. There's no good time for weakness."

Zhèng gave a wounded, angry look, then left for his own offices in the Security Guild headquarters in the City of Philippi.

McClellan didn't pity Zhèng. A man in his position should expect circumstances such as these. He should face them with certain and deliberate force. No, Zhèng did not need sympathy. He needed strength. He needed to find his bearing and rise to the demands being placed upon him. Because, if this morning's briefing was any indicator, Zhèng was struggling to rise at all.

And now, as he sat with Clarke in his sitting room, McClellan watched the junior agent shift apprehensively—a mood shared by most of the staff. But in Clarke's case, the cause was more than professional.

"Everything all right between you and Okayo?" McClellan said.

Clarke hadn't expected that—not the abruptness of the question, nor that McClellan would have known to ask.

"Even with everything happening last night," McClellan added, "when you came to the chapel, I knew that something wasn't right with you two."

Clarke looked away. "Things have been better," he said. "But that's not why I'm here."

McClellan guzzled his water and put down the glass. "I know. And I don't mean to pry. But I think the world of you both. If I can ever help, just ask."

Clarke gave a mostly inaudible thank you.

McClellan did him the favor of changing the subject.

"You sent word that you have news," he said. "It better be good."

"You tell me," Clarke said, busying himself with his tablet, sending off common blocking interference. "After our morning briefing, I figured we needed some forward motion. So I spent the day following up on Wagner's info about the printer responsible for your chapel."

"And?"

"I found where it is, with a little help from Wagner and his friends."

"Is it still here on New Athens?"

Clarke nodded. "It's down in a printer hold not far from where you and I are sitting. It's been there since it printed all this, although, as you remember, I had been told otherwise."

McClellan gave a cautious stare. "You're sure it's the one?"

"Absolutely."

"Seems fast to have found one printer out of thousands."

Clarke leaned back and nodded thoughtfully. "Wagner's contacts had good leads. Builders know most everything that happens in places where the rest of us never look. Better yet, the engineers confirmed it's the one."

"The engineers?" McClellan said. "You *told* the engineers?"

Clarke's jaws tightened. "Not me. Zhèng. He had to, because they own the printers. And anyway, they would have found out when we start her up—which I suggest we do soon. And," he added, sitting straighter, "isn't it better to get their help rather than slinking around the sewers?"

McClellan nodded with understanding, but not approval. He explained how Elaina Jansen had been adamant with Zhèng that the engineers would not grant access to their printers. "She was definitive," he said.

Clarke shrugged. "Things change. The Engineering Council wants to jumpstart our investigation, which means putting an end to uncertainty and getting rid of Draeger. Can't say I blame them."

"I can't either. As long as he's representing Tucker, Draeger is in a good position to spew his misinformation and fear. We need to change that. We need to get attention off Tucker. We need people to know that we're looking at other options, building other cases."

"Then we better find other options. And that house printer is the only new direction we have. So I say we go in. You and me—just like you talked about yesterday in Wagner's tunnels."

McClellan said nothing, but he nodded affirmatively.

The motion encouraged Clarke, who leaned forward and spoke faster. "And better yet, the house printer responsible for your chapel is a clamshell. It's a model similar to the one at Red Delta. That makes interprinter communications more likely. I'm thinking I could use it to ping any printer that had been in recent contact with it. That could help Molly Rose find our clamshell."

"At least in theory," McClellan said. "Last I remember, printer communication wasn't easy to manipulate."

"True. It's a safety to keep programmers from overstepping their authority. Especially if someone nasty ever got their hands on one. But we'll figure something out."

McClellan smiled at Clarke's confidence. It reminded him of his early days as a programmer.

"And there's something else," Clarke said, leaning forward until he had to catch himself to avoid tumbling out of his chair. "Going inside the house printer will be good training for you. Time you got to know one of these newer models. You need practice, old man, if we're planning to find and get inside the printer from Red Delta."

McClellan relaxed and his smile grew. Now so did Clarke's.

"So when do you suggest we go in?" McClellan said.

"That's the hitch. The engineers are rounding up printers for maintenance—including these models of clamshells. Then out they go for their next project—probably the Progress buildout. From what the engineers told Zhèng, these clamshells are being sent away in a few hours. That's soon, I know, but they said they need New Athens's morning swing sunward to assist the orbital transfer."

"Can't they wait until another day? New Athens swings sunward every morning."

"True," Clarke said. "But the engineers have their schedule. And you know how they are about their schedules."

"I bet it has more to do with getting that printer off station before Draeger subpoenas it. You said it's the same model as the one at Tanglao's murder?"

Clarke nodded. "Similar, yes. So you could be right about a subpoena. Anyway, we have only four hours and fifteen minutes before that printer and a few hundred others are bundled, processed, and shipped out."

McClellan watched Clarke's expression shift. The young agent had that probing stare of soldiers looking for confidence.

"Then we better move," McClellan said, with a silent petition to St. Joseph. "I meant what I said yesterday. Between the two of us we should be able to get in deep enough to learn something—hopefully who programmed that printer with a replica of the Pauline Chapel. And why. There has to be a connection with Tanglao in all this."

"Seems likely," Clarke said, still watching McClellan's reaction. "And someday if we get access to the clamshell from Red Delta, maybe we'll find a connection between Tanglao and Solorzano. It's a possibility, based on Okayo's intelligence."

McClellan shook his head. "If there is a connection, I'll bet it's not what first comes to mind."

He looked up to the crucifix that hung on the wall behind Clarke. His parish had given it to him to take to New Athens. It was small and lightweight, as had been required, yet it communicated their feelings. McClellan had seen in the gift a sign of what lay ahead. As far back as that first meeting with Archbishop Bauer, he had been sure that his work in the orbits meant a return to the printers. Now he was eager to pick up this cross, and with God's grace, to carry it forward.

McClellan stood. "You know that I haven't been inside a printer since the wars."

Clarke nodded. "I know. I mean, I don't know all the details—"

"Well, you'd better learn them," McClellan said. "Because if I have any contact with the printer, it's going to be a risk."

Clarke stood and met McClellan's stare. "I read the report about Raleigh. I'm sure there's more to know, but I can't see much of a risk. You wouldn't be the first programmer that lied to a printer."

"This isn't just about a lie."

Worry came again to Clarke's eyes, but with a growing impatience.

"Then you tell me what other options we have. We have to go in. I have to be in there to get you initial access, but I can't do this myself. This isn't something you can learn in a day. And it isn't something you can learn alone. You know a hell of a lot more than I do. Look, I can bring you up to speed on the initial processing codes, but I need you in there with me. This has to be a joint effort."

McClellan folded his arms. He was glad to see the young agent push back, and he gave Clarke the look of respect he was hoping for.

"You're right," McClellan said. "I'm in. But I'm going to need to brief you first."

"Okay. If you think it's important."

"It's important. And one other thing. I insist we go in through Wagner's tunnels. This needs to be a partnership between the builders and the engineers. We need all the cooperation we can get."

"You may have a point there," Clarke said. He thought a moment, accessed his tablet, and redisplayed the imagery of New Athens's tunnels. "There's also a more immediate benefit. Look, the printer is . . . yes, she's right here. It'll be easier to go through Wagner's tunnels. The engineering access is farther out. It would get us there, but Wagner's is closer."

McClellan watched as the small holographic version of New Athens turned before him, its utility and printer tunnels running through it like veins. Near the edge of Troas City was a small collection of dots that represented a cluster of printers. More of the dots were moving toward it. He followed one of the lines that ran along New Athens's hull to the sidewall, up along the innards of the Wheel, and out to one of the mechanical docking assemblies.

"You better tell Zhèng we're going in," McClellan said. "And you better get your key and coupler."

"Already done," Clarke said.

"Good man. All right, give me ten minutes to shower and change, and I'll need thirty to brief you. But before that I'd like a few minutes of quiet in the chapel. You're welcome to join me."

"No thanks. That kind of thing ends careers up here. I'll wait in your offices."

Clarke took a few quick steps, then slowed and turned, staring at McClellan with hesitation. "Can I ask a question?"

McClellan shrugged. "Sure. What about?"

"About Raleigh. I read the report on file, but there was something missing."

McClellan waited, but he knew what was coming.

"Your friend Macedo—did he survive?"

McClellan met Clarke's stare. "Danny and his escorts were overrun and beheaded. We lost a lot of good men and women that night."

Clarke looked away, then back at the Marine. "That's what I thought. Listen, John, I'm sure others have told you this, but I can't see this being your fault. You went with what you knew. Just like I did in releasing Tanglao's clamshell based on bad telemetry. Anyway, I don't see why you'd take all the responsibility. The GU engineering teams were watching everything that night. They could have easily reset the other two printers. Did you ever think of that?"

The young agent didn't wait for a reply. He turned to begin his preparations, and to report their next steps to Commissioner Zhèng.

Some forty thousand kilometers away, Archbishop Bauer walked along the rocky shore of Beavertail to meet his friend Monsignor Tom Harper—perhaps for the last time, if Harper's doctors were right. The island's bridges were still closed, but Bauer's sister-in-law had demanded that the Jamestown Police and Militia allow the privilege of this meeting.

The day had been warm and calm, but the late afternoon brought a chill as winds came and gusted across the coast. Harper sat on a folding chair facing the ocean. He stood occasionally with the help of his driver and made some attempt to cast his line, then sat again and adjusted the hood of his Marine Corps sweatshirt.

The two friends shook hands without mentioning Harper's weakness. The driver excused himself and jogged up the rocks. Bauer placed his blue backpack next to Harper's old green one and joined his friend catching fish. Their conversation ebbed and flowed as the waves rolled and splashed in the late winter sun. The two men spoke of nothing important—nothing involving cancer or the orbits or the Sals—and laughed at memories.

When the daylight faded and the chilled breeze became cold, they gathered their belongings as the old lighthouse flashed and flared and its horn sounded over the waters. Bauer waved off Harper's driver and his own. This last hill would be taken by them alone.

When they had achieved that mission, they shook each other's hands, almost as firmly as they had in their youth, and said good night—and perhaps good-bye.

Bauer watched as the driver helped his friend into the waiting car. With a final wave, Harper was gone. Bauer looked down at the old green knapsack he'd taken up from the rocks. He placed it gently into his trunk but said nothing about it to his driver. He sat silently as they made their way past his brother's house, through the bridge checkpoint, and straight to Boston.

CHRISSY CALLED FOR McCLELLAN after he finished briefing Clarke. Catherine Georgeson's blood oxygen level was falling, and her organs were shutting down faster than the nanocorrectors could repair. The doctor had checked her moments ago, and determined that her body would not last the hour.

"I'll be right there," McClellan said. "Thank you."

He turned to Clarke, who was scrolling through data floating over the conference table.

"I understand," Clarke said. "But remember, we need to go as soon as we can."

McClellan stopped to say a prayer before the chapel's tabernacle and then hurried to Chrissy and Jack's apartments. The old woman was cleaned and washed, but the smell of death lingered.

Catherine smiled as she looked up at the priest. She mouthed some words that no one understood. McClellan returned her smile, placed his hand on her forehead, and told her she was loved.

When she relaxed a little, he placed his stole around his neck and removed the small bottle of holy water from his jacket pocket. He said the prayers for strength and mercy that he had been asked to say, in one way or another, by every dying person he'd had the honor to accompany.

Chrissy stroked the woman's pale hands. Jack stood behind his fiancée, rubbing her shoulders, sobbing quietly, but trying to look strong like McClellan.

When the prayers were said, Catherine looked up in a moment of clarity. It was a sudden strength that McClellan had seen before, a moment of grace given to the dying for the benefit of the living.

Catherine held the priest's hand courageously and asked, "Has Mercury gone behind the sun?"

McClellan paused. He might have considered this some delusion—some jumbled memory of her younger years building orbital communications systems. But Catherine's eyes were clear and intent.

"No, Catherine. Well, actually I don't know. Why do you ask?"

She took a moment to remember. "Fast little planet, always lost signal when that happened."

McClellan asked for clarification.

The old woman's grip weakened as she thought of what to say. "No signal with Mercury behind the sun—you can't tunnel through the sun. The sun . . . so bright it shows everything. I see everything—good and bad. Pray for me, Father."

"Of course, Catherine. Every day. We all will, right, Chrissy? Jack?"

Chrissy brought a smile to her face. Jack held her shoulders tighter, and they both assured the old woman of their prayers.

"It's good that people pray for you," she said, her voice weakening to a whisper. "I'm ready, Papa."

After a few shallow breaths came soft words that seemed to say thank you. Catherine's breathing then slowed and stopped, and her body relaxed and stiffened all at once. When her eyes went still, McClellan reached over to close them, entrusting her soul to St. Mary and St. Joseph, who knew better than anyone the way to the light of Christ.

Ira Wagner was waiting for Clarke and McClellan. He led them down the facility's stairs to the wastewater base level, and then through the tunnel toward the dark access doors that led to the printers. Two young builders in faded blue jumpsuits—one tall and wiry, the other stocky—worked farther down on a section of overhead piping. Wagner went over to ask about their labors. As they spoke, the young builders gave momentary looks around them but did not acknowledge Clarke or McClellan.

"My apologies," Wagner said as he returned. "The maintenance of these systems never ends. Now, let us get you to your printer."

He stepped over to the dark access door that faced the direction of McClellan's chapel. He felt for the lock at the center, inserted his builder's key, and stepped back.

The dark door became opaque and then transparent. Wagner said that this design allowed for safety checks of what lay on the opposing side before opening the door. "There may be a printer or a robber coming through," he said. "Best to know in advance."

But there was nothing ahead—at least as far as they could see inside. He twisted his key once more and the doors parted and slid open. As lighting flickered every few meters down the tunnel, a stale, foul air breathed out from the passage. The tunnel had an oval shape about seven meters wide and five high, and its bottom was a mesh of metallic flooring. Below that ran a wide, black pipe that carried wastewater from sections of Troas City to the treatment works. A matching blue pipe, carrying drinking water, ran along the top. Smaller electrical and instrumentation conduits were embedded in the wall along one side, with the matter-energy feeds for the printers traveling along the other.

McClellan peered deep into the tunnel. He was looking for some ending, or some sign of New Athens's curvature. He found neither—but that made sense. The circumference of New Athens was immense, and this tunnel looped its full diameter. If he walked past this open door and continued for almost nineteen kilometers, he'd come out the matching door behind them.

"As Agent Clarke knows," Wagner said, "your printer will be found in a staging area off a main access tunnel, about four hundred meters down."

"Four hundred meters?" McClellan asked. "I thought you said it was close."

"That's close," Clarke said. "By comparison. From the main engineering passage, it's six hundred."

Wagner chuckled. "There are transport platforms if you need one. My staff uses them. I prefer to walk. I get to know things better that way."

Clarke and McClellan opted to save time. They stepped a few meters into the tunnel and found the platform waiting inside. After a few commands on a control pad it slipped into the tunnel. They stepped on, and after a few more commands it went along the flooring, taking them in deeper, where the air grew warmer and even fouler, even if the monitor that Wagner had given them indicated that breathing was still safe.

McClellan looked back and waved to Wagner, but Wagner was no longer there. McClellan watched as the opening shrank into the distance, and then turned to watch Clarke check his coupler. He wanted the younger programmer to taste leadership, so he offered corrections only when necessary.

"This is it," Clarke said as the transport slowed and stopped. "The lights should be on, but maybe they'll activate as we go in."

They stepped off the platform and went a few meters into what seemed to be a wide and open space. Cooler and drier air came from somewhere overhead. Muffled sounds of machines and metal came from the darkness—the sounds of wheels on railings, the hum of drives, the booming and creaking of moving weight. As their eyes adjusted, they saw the dim shapes of tall structures and scaffolding, walkways and stairs, and rows of clamshell and tulip-head printers. The glowing torsos of robbers came and went as they assisted the printers, turning occasionally to assess the approaching humans.

Lighting overhead finally began to buzz, providing dim illumination but no more. It was enough to see that the structures and the scaffolding rose to the upper height of the junction area, which was just below the ground floors of Troas City. McClellan counted seventy tulip heads and clamshells aligned on racks of ten printers each, stacked two levels high. More were arriving on conveyance platforms from the various passageways that opened throughout the staging area. The printers were positioned with the claws of small cranes and assisted by the prodding and pushing of robbers.

"This way," Clarke said, his eyes fixed on his tablet. "I found her."

There were stairs to their left. Clarke went up a flight and pushed himself along a rack of idle clamshells between the side of the chamber and the printers. The wall was lined with conduits and drinking water mains that ran upward from the utility level below. The interface controls for the printers faced the wall, giving Clarke and McClellan less than two meters to work.

Clarke stopped at the second clamshell down. He consulted his tablet and the printer's interface and said, "She's the one. This is the lead printer that built your chapel."

"I'm assuming it had assistance."

"Yes. It was in sync with a pair of house structural printers. But they're old school and don't think much. She's the brains of any buildout."

McClellan inspected the clamshell. It was slightly smaller than the one in Raleigh, but other than all the scrapes and pings on its casing, it looked identical.

"It's seen some action," he said.

"They all have," Clarke said. "There aren't too many inner buildouts left, but house printers stay active with the big maintenance jobs, especially on the Wheel and docking rings. And the hull."

As he spoke, Clarke was busying himself with his tablet. He was sending updates to Zhèng with their location and the status of the printer.

After a moment he said, "We're in. Zhèng gave final authorization. Let's go over this once more. I'll initiate the printer, then go through the opening sequence to get past trust verification."

"Then I'll await your word for the introduction."

"That's right. And since we're going in as a training exercise, it shouldn't be too out of line for you to be telling me where to look for printing logs and comm data."

"And how to ping the other printers."

"Can't forget that."

With Clarke taking the lead, McClellan had time to study the printer's interface and feel along the outer casing. He instinctively raised his hand in search of his programmer's key, which hadn't hung from his neck in thirteen years.

Clarke took his key from under his uniform shirt and slipped it into the printer. He twisted it, and gave an approving nod when he saw signs of activation. He held up his training coupler in the dim light for a last inspection, then brought it to the shelf of the printer's casing.

McClellan felt the hum and the warmth of the clamshell as it roused. There was a sense of both relief and irresponsibility at not being the programmer in charge—the one providing the primary will to instruct the machine.

Clarke was smiling as he inserted his coupler, which quickly came to life. He was at code verification—responding to the printer's queries about blood type, master's codes, and neural programming permissions. McClellan watched him manage but could think of no advice to offer.

Clarke passed the point of neural link activation in his hands and brain. He breathed irregularly as he touched the printer to maintain physical contact, which helped the link grow strong.

The completion of trust was taking place. McClellan was not part of the conversation, nor could he hear it—not the introductions, not Clarke's story, not if it was a happy or a sad one, or any follow-up questions that the printer might ask.

Nor did he learn the printer's name.

But his moment to enter would be coming. He steadied his breathing and gave thanks that he was at peace.

The printer's interface flashed, and it offered words that delight programmers:

Brandon James Clarke: Trust ranking at 92.89 percent.
Past training simulations have passed protocol.
Programming codes and story match.
Limited training access granted.

Clarke's eyes were vacant, yet intense, as hypostasis occurred. His mouth moved slightly as the neural mapping tripped some of his facial muscles. McClellan stepped closer. He knew that Clarke was introducing the printer to his trainer. Both the interface and the coupler flashed again, and a second access opened and waited for McClellan.

Clarke nodded, and he struggled to speak verbally.

"I told her what she may expect in your links, and that you don't have a coupler. Her name is Emily Jane, but she says we can call her Emily."

McClellan raised both hands, palms outward, and brought them down to the printer. How odd, he thought. He'd made this motion hundreds of times as a combat programmer. He'd made a similar motion thousands of times saying Mass. It was sobering to remember that there was once a younger man named John Francis McClellan who would have laughed at, or even been appalled by, his eventual path to the priesthood. How very odd, he thought, when our lives bring about a reunion with our younger selves—ones that would never have expected the choices we eventually made.

McClellan rested one hand on the coupler, the other on the printer's interface. Emily began to scan his DNA and nervous system. His long-idle links labored under the flow of her energy, and he felt the warmth spread through his hands and head.

A motion at his feet surprised him. He stood on a flatbed trailer next to an unresponsive clamshell. The trailer shook as air cover screamed in the dark summer night. No, the sound had come from only meters ahead of him. He focused and saw the source: a robber pushing a printer into a rack close to where he and Clarke stood.

Emily felt the memory and paused. At Clarke's urging she renewed her reading of McClellan's history—all of it. She assessed the data, found the majority to be satisfactory, and allowed McClellan entry but not access.

McClellan heard Clarke's welcome. A neural connection was forming between them—between trainer and trainee—as McClellan bowed to the will of the lead so that the printer would be given only one set of instructions.

"That is one hell of a Mustang," Clarke was saying through the neural link.

McClellan concentrated hard as he remembered how to respond. "The finish wasn't easy," he finally said. "But I admit it looks good."

The men's focus on their earliest print jobs was more than some analogue of human conversation; it was a specific technique among programmers. Controlled points of reference helped navigate a growing intimacy between two minds as they learned about the content of the other.

"Update for Brandon James Clarke," Emily was saying. "You have linked with a programmer who has violated programming ethics. Please explain John McClellan's role as a trainer."

Both men felt the other's reaction.

"There's nothing to explain," Clarke said. "I'm aware of his mistakes. He wants to get his trust level back up, and I'm going to help him."

"John McClellan has an unresolved notation in the printer-programmer database. His trust level is void."

"Understood," Clarke said. "But we're not here to print. We're here for a training exercise. We'll only be retrieving your printing history and sharing updates with your fellow printers. That should help McClellan return to a nominal trust level."

Emily did not respond.

"I'll make sure he behaves," Clarke continued. "I'm the lead programmer, even in the training environment. McClellan's trust status is irrelevant."

There was a pause. Emily again probed McClellan's links, assessed his prior average trust levels, and agreed to elevate his trust level from void to 1 percent.

Clarke gave a celebratory smile. He had just thanked Emily when her interface flashed. There had been a power spike in one of her Deep Intellect processors. McClellan waited for signs of secondary feedback, because if there were—

Emily roused. "A third programmer is requesting access," she said.

Clarke looked at McClellan.

"We haven't authorized a third programmer," McClellan said to Emily. "Or asked for one. Do you have an identity?"

"Besides the Clarke-McClellan link, there is a third query for access from an undetermined location. But I am allowed only two programmers in a training environment. John McClellan, are you withdrawing?"

"No, he is not," Clarke said. "John McClellan is the authorized trainer. Tell us who is seeking access, and from where."

Clarke's angry eyes typed commands into his coupler. A holographic diagram of New Athens appeared. It was filled with the haze of ongoing and excessive tunneling. But with so much of it, he couldn't isolate any localized concentrations, even this far from the general population.

"The identity and location of the third programmer is classified," Emily was saying. "That information is available only to full programmers— those with trust ratings over seventy percent."

"Damn it," Clarke said as McClellan began sending him blocking maneuvers.

Clarke deployed the defenses. But they'd only last so long, and then the third programmer—whoever he or she was—could easily connect and seize control.

"Emily," Clarke said, "begin uploading your printing history into John McClellan's links."

Emily complied.

McClellan felt the data transfer—a process that would have gone faster if he'd had his coupler. He could analyze the logs in detail later, but for now he was looking for any source related to the printing of his chapel.

"Found it," he said for Clarke's benefit. The programming specs had come from printer designation 4.016.028, which was the printer at Tanglao's murder scene.

McClellan stored the information in his neural registers—the first that had been added since Raleigh. He shared it with Clarke, who went to work programming Emily to contact her fellow clamshells, prioritizing a connection with 4.016.028.

Emily refused. "You do not have full access in this training mode. Please provide justification for printer-to-printer communications. Or have the command routed through a trainer with a valid trust level."

McClellan found her comm ports, just where they had been on Audrey. He provided the locations to Clarke, who again tried to generate a comm burst.

Emily rejected the second request, and another power spike lit up her interface.

McClellan knew what had happened even before Emily confirmed it.

"Third party access successful," she said. "Brandon James Clarke, you are no longer the lead programmer."

McClellan felt Clarke's fear.

"Emily, that third connection is not part of this exercise," Clarke said. "Disconnect it. Now!"

Emily's casing flashed with a new interface—the interface for her printing mechanisms. These had not been requested by Clarke, nor should they have been activated in the printer's current location, restrained and racked with dozens of other printers in a junction between New Athens's habitat and hull.

Emily's long intakes and emitters began to unfurl. They slipped out of her widening center ring and reached upward.

"Emily," Clarke said nervously, "cancel all printing. I repeat, cancel—"

"Printing authorization has been provided by a valid programmer," Emily protested. "Application sequences are valid. Available energy storage: one percent maximum. Awaiting printing instructions."

McClellan reconfirmed that there were no energy conduits nearby—at least none that Emily could connect to. Nor were her intakes capable of burrowing into her surroundings to harvest energy or matter.

But even with her reserves at only 1 percent, Emily's emitters could puncture a hole in New Athens, if that's what the third programmer wanted to do.

Emily fired her small orbital maneuvering thrusters. There was a smell of hot metal as she pushed against her holding brackets. Robbers came to correct the situation, but Emily's emitters slashed and tossed them across the hold.

Clarke's hands and eyes worked furiously, but Emily's intakes and emitters only moved faster.

McClellan warned Clarke about the rate of his neural processing.

Clarke ignored him and began to power down their link. "Get out," he said to McClellan through the dwindling connection. "I won't let anything happen to you—not under my watch."

McClellan might have protested, but he knew Clarke was right. Without his coupler he had no direct access to the printer, nor could there be any without adequate trust. He could not help Clarke—at least not from the inside.

"Clarke, let's get you disengaged. We can do that."

"No. There's too much power. I need to close this down."

But there would be no way for Clarke to do that.

"Leave!" Clarke said as their link dropped to 80 percent. "Either this clamshell is going to fire up, or I am going to stop it. Either way, you can't be here."

More robbers came to restrain the printer, but were pushed back across the hold.

McClellan knew it would take massive neural processing to block the third programmer—even more than seasoned programmers should attempt. But Clarke was keeping up. He was moving deeper inside Emily.

McClellan wasn't sure how that was possible. Not with only training permissions.

But he had a hunch.

The third programmer must have allowed Clarke direct core contact, and the young programmer, seeking to regain authority, must have submitted to the temptation. If so, if Clarke had grasped at Emily's Deep Intellect, he would now understand the consequences of doing so.

McClellan's link was at the halfway mark. The hand of a robber seized his shoulder. He landed a hard kick on its knees, sending it tumbling down the stairs.

Through their eroding link, McClellan felt Clarke's terror at the thought of death—and his shame for being so weak.

"Agent Clarke," McClellan said. "Focus on your mission. Do you copy?"

The rhythm of Clarke's heart had become dangerously uneven—McClellan felt it in his own. Clarke was falling deeper into Emily's core.

McClellan cursed. If he had a valid trust level, he could break into Clarke's link and suspend it. But his only option was to physically pull

Clarke away—which could be a final and, ultimately, futile action. A cold break from this far in a Deep Intellect core came with too many risks, both to Clarke and—without Clarke blocking the third programmer—to the hull of New Athens.

No, there had to be some other way. And McClellan begged for the grace to see it.

Okayo was in Clarke's thoughts. He faced her in a room that McClellan did not recognize. There had been an argument. Something about Okayo's career. Something about their future together, if only Clarke would accept the risk she was taking. If only he'd respect her wishes—and her faith. Clarke spoke loudly and Okayo left the room abruptly. She was off to the orbits to find Tanglao's coupler, and Clarke wished he hadn't spoken as he did, or said what he had said.

The printer's emitters were firing up. They raced through the air, spitting sparks and smoke as they sought some target. The intakes climbed higher, reaching over the upper row of printers. They probed the utility walls—stabbing them—seeking some way to increase the printer's energy stores.

Clarke's efforts to regain control would have been laughable had he been alone. But Emily—or at least some part of her—was now resisting the third programmer. McClellan could hear only fragments of her thoughts—frantic and furious cries, much like Audrey's had been.

And like Corporal McClellan had done, the third programmer pushed back.

An intake lashed out, its head crushing a drinking water line that rose up from the lower level. Water sprayed out, arcing into the chamber and onto the printers and the robbers, onto Emily, McClellan, and Clarke.

Clarke's face was distorted with rage. He demanded again that the priest leave. The link between the two men was at 12 percent—that was low enough for McClellan to walk away safely.

But McClellan stood fast. He held the coupler and the interface as a robber once again pulled him back, and once gain McClellan kicked hard, sending the robber into the waters that poured around them.

Clarke cried out. How could he have allowed his words to Okayo to upset her so? And yet he had known that they would, but had said them anyway. If he was going to die, there had to be some way to make this right—to do something that Okayo would remember, something that would comfort her always.

Some part of the printer's Deep Intellect became aware of Clarke's concern. It offered its capacity to assess the situation.

The intellect affirmed that there had to be . . . something.

But could it be so simple?

Yes, the intellect replied. *And now is your chance.*

Clarke saw the option before him. And choosing it would make Okayo so very happy.

He used the last of their link to ask McClellan this final favor.

Emily's link with Clarke wavered and weakened. McClellan saw the opportunity to free the young agent, and he saw the desire in Clarke's darkening eyes.

As the collapsing main surged with more water, McClellan's left hand swung into Clarke's chest, tearing him from the printer. His right hand came down on Clarke's sopping head, and with it he fulfilled the agent's plea. With the palm of his hand McClellan traced the sign of the cross, and he cried loudly, so that Clarke might hear, "Brandon James Clarke, I baptize you in the name of the Father . . . and of the Son . . . and of the Holy Spirit."

As he fell backward into the downpour, Clarke seemed to be saying thank you—but McClellan couldn't tell. Clarke was weakening too fast.

McClellan dove to retrieve the fallen agent, twisting to avoid the lunge of one of Emily's emitters. But it came fast through the pouring waters—faster than McClellan could avoid. The emitter thrust into McClellan's arm and chest, slamming him on his back. Ugly sounds came from deep inside his lungs, and blood filled his mouth. He was struck by terrible pain, both from his gut, and from hearing Clarke's cry from somewhere in the flood.

McClellan tried to stand, but he could not, nor could he breathe.

Two robbers grabbed him and hurried him down the access stairs, carrying him to the utility tunnel where he and Clarke had arrived. Behind them came a crack and a roar as the water main collapsed, followed by blazes of energy and loud concussions. The arms that carried McClellan laid him on the tunnel's transport platform—but they were not the arms of the robotic assistants.

With the last of his strength, McClellan focused. Leaning over him and shouting were two young, terrified men—Wagner's tall, thin worker, and the stockier one, their faded blue jumpsuits bloody and drenched. They looked away quickly and then, before the darkness came, they were gone.

33

"CORPORAL MCCLELLAN?" SAID A warm voice. "May I sit with you?"

The voice rose over inner ones that spoke of darkness—that accused him of some failure. This new voice was stronger. It had the authority to push back the others, to encourage him to rouse from a restless sleep.

The voice repeated the question. McClellan assessed the situation before he opened his eyes. He was lying on his back, and he was warm. A coarse fabric covered his bare legs and chest. He could feel the weight of his dog tags, but not his programmer's key.

He cautiously opened his eyes, which had grown unaccustomed to light. The voice belonged to a man standing patiently waiting for an answer. He was a middle-aged officer, fit in his fatigues but not entirely lean. He had a strong, round face and tired eyes. His black hair was fanned with white, and neatly parted to the side.

McClellan motioned that he'd accept the company.

"Thank you, Corporal," the officer said. "I'll grab a chair."

The infirmary at Camp Lejeune was long and bright with sunlight from high windows. Monitoring drones passed through the light, casting little shadows on the faces and blankets of the wounded from Raleigh. Two robotic assistants were at the cot across from McClellan caring for a Marine with a neck wound.

McClellan watched the officer drag a chair beside him. He was a captain, with a cross on the collar of his fatigues. That made him one of those chaplains who come and tell the dying to not be afraid—that there's some hope in all their hopelessness.

The officer introduced himself as Captain Alfred Bauer. He gave what sounded like a canned statement that, while he was a Roman Catholic priest from Boston, he was there only to provide any comfort and assistance that he could, and would do so for anyone of any faith or no faith.

"That's me, sir," McClellan said. "I don't believe in a god, just so you know."

"I understand, Corporal. I'm just checking to see if there's anything you need, or that you want to talk about. And remember, I don't write this up or report it to anyone. I'm sort of a free agent that way."

McClellan thought about what he could discuss—but it was difficult to think at all. Nausea came when he concentrated too hard, and a throbbing grew over his left eye and ear. He felt for the source of discomfort, and saw that both his hands had been bandaged.

A robotic nursing assistant came to probe his arms and legs and feel along his skull. It made cold sounds as it adjusted patches that held down medical probes.

"I hate those things," McClellan said as the machine walked away.

"You and me both. Humans were meant to be cared for by humans."

McClellan agreed, and before long they were talking about Union City, and his uncle's farm in Iowa. But McClellan struggled with what to say, even when he knew what he wanted to.

"That's okay," Captain Bauer said. "You're full of nanocorrectors. They make it hard to remember details when they're patching you up. And they'll uncover memories that you may want to forget. That's unfortunately where you're at, son. But all in all, I hear that the docs are happy."

As McClellan processed the news, Bauer shifted in his chair and leaned in. "So you were saying you lived for a time with your aunt and uncle in Iowa, but you're from Michigan, right?"

McClellan nodded.

"I understand that your parents took the option," Bauer said.

"Yes, sir. But I was young when they did."

"You were nine. That's not so young. It must have been difficult."

McClellan looked away. "They made sure I was okay, that I'd be taken care of. My aunt and uncle were good to me—didn't matter when the GU ran out of money. I had it a lot better than other kids whose parents took the option."

Shouting came from a cot at the far end of the infirmary. Robotic assistants and Military Police hurried to the source, and soon the shouting subsided to a moan that faded into the hush and chatter that comes with caring for so many wounded.

"Can we change the subject?" McClellan asked, turning back to the captain.

"If you'd like, and I am sorry if I upset you. It's just that you were talking about your parents when you were under. I've dealt with this before, and I'm happy to help if I can."

"I was talking about them in my sleep?"

The captain nodded.

"What did I say?"

"That someone told you that your mom and dad could still be alive if you hadn't been born."

McClellan said nothing. He was angry that that memory was in play—that a stranger was talking about it in the open.

"You're not the first person that was said to," Captain Bauer said.

"That supposed to make me feel better?"

"That's not what—"

"Look, it's okay. It was some stupid government social worker who came to check on me. She wanted to know how it felt that my parents had to choose between themselves and me, and then she says that they wouldn't have had to if I hadn't been born. Who the hell says a thing like that to a kid?"

McClellan was startled by the fury surging in his mind and his muscles, and he found himself facing more forgotten memories—not all of them unpleasant. He could smell the grasses and manure of his uncle's farm, and he could see his aunt chasing away the social worker.

McClellan tried to wipe the moisture in his eyes, but couldn't with bandaged hands. The captain found tissues on a nearby table and assisted with the task.

McClellan breathed deeper and found himself trying to remember what had brought him here. He concentrated, but could find only fragments—a map of Raleigh, a clothes dryer and a demolished ranch house, double-timing past a pickup on the way to the engineering campus, an air strike that made the night become day.

"How long will I be here?" he asked, not wanting to remember anything else.

"I'm not sure, son. I don't think the doctors know."

"They want me back out there programming?"

"I would expect that they do. I hear you're one of the best in the Corps. But they may have reasons otherwise. We'll see."

"Did they send you here to get me back? Back into a printer?"

"No. As I said, we chaplains—"

"Because I don't want to go back."

"Then it may be best that you don't. But Corporal, I'm not your doctor. A lot of smart people are working to help you. So as the treatments go along, things may change as you remember—some of it good, some not so good. Of course, the doctors might also want to wipe it all. Either way, I'll stay close by. Is that okay?"

McClellan said that it was.

"Captain, mind if I ask one more question?"

"Of course."

"What if I want to remember? Will they let me?"

"The doctors should ask you what you prefer," the captain said guardedly. "Although they could try to choose for you—talk you out of remembering. They're good at that, and it's easier for them. They may play on your fears—tell you that you're not strong enough, that you really don't have a choice. So watch out."

McClellan searched for some recollection of what had brought him here. He remembered that he had been programming a printer named . . . no, he couldn't remember the name. He cursed how little access he had to his own history.

"The doctors can talk all they want," he said. "I want to know what happened. I want to be me again, and I guess I don't think I am anymore, if that makes sense."

The captain gave a serious look. "It does. And I'd ask for the same thing if I were you. Although, after these wars, I don't know if any of us can go back to who we were. I'm just praying we become something better."

McClellan thought about the captain's words. He knew there was some truth to them, but he didn't understand the part about prayer. At the same time, he wasn't about to let fear or uncertainty take what was his. And he hoped he could make things better.

"Johnny?" a warm voice said. "Are you awake?"

McClellan heard the voice above the ones within him—erratic ones that insisted he could have done more to save Clarke, accusing him of failing the young agent, and the investigation into Tanglao's death. But this new voice was stronger. And it was familiar.

The voice repeated the question. McClellan assessed the situation before he opened his eyes. He was lying on his back, and he was warm. Something was covering him—a comfortable, smooth fabric on his bare legs and chest. He found breathing difficult, but he could also remember that he had been unable to breathe at all.

He cautiously opened his eyes. The small room was bright and clean. He slowly remembered the events that brought him here, and he would have succumbed to their desolation had it not been for the man standing before him, concerned and determined, and so very out of place wearing a black clerical suit among the medical amenities of New Athens.

But then, even archbishops can board an Aesir and come through the Wheel.

McClellan gasped as he breathed deeply. His eyes went wide as he allowed himself to remember everything. It was safer to remember now. When he wept, he covered his face with one hand and held out the other for Bauer. The archbishop stepped closer and grasped firmly, and soon McClellan didn't know if he was crying from despair or from joy. He wanted to stand and properly greet his archbishop, but both his body and the health monitors complained when he tried.

After a moment, McClellan wiped his face with his palms and asked, "How long have you been up here?"

"Two days," Bauer said.

"And how many have I been out?"

"Seven."

Dr. Gupta, who had been Catherine Georgeson's doctor, came quickly into the room. She gave a worried look, then nodded approvingly.

"I am happy to see you conscious," she said. "But please take things slowly. You took a direct strike from the printer's charged emitter. It was not easy putting you back together."

"But we're expecting a full recovery, right?" Bauer said.

"He is mending well. Very well, actually." She turned to McClellan. "Your organs have been functioning on their own for seventy-two hours.

Your skeletal damage is fully healed and, as you weren't in direct neural access with the printer, you suffered no long-term neurological damage. Rest assured, you'll be fully functioning and causing trouble soon."

"I feel pretty weak, Doc."

"That's mostly the treatments doing their job. You need to be patient."

Bauer chuckled. "Patience is not something that Father McClellan is known for."

McClellan would have debated the matter, but he was sorting through questions.

He wanted to know how Bauer got approval to come here, and why. He wanted to know about the two builders who had saved him—what their names are and how had they managed to be in that tunnel when he needed them. He wanted to know if Father Tanglao's body, and Catherine's, had finally made it home.

Then there were the questions for Zhèng. McClellan wanted to know all that had happed in the past week—if they had found Tanglao's coupler, if Molly Rose had found the clamshell, and what Draeger had been doing.

As he thought, the list of questions grew. But the one he asked first was about Brandon Clarke.

The doctor was busy scanning his abdomen. Bauer turned to McClellan and said, "He's alive, Johnny."

"Thank God," McClellan said, dropping his head into his pillow. "How is he?"

Bauer referred this to the doctor.

"My understanding is that his body has recovered," she said. "But I believe there is still a question of whether his mind can be restored. He received extensive neural overloads, not to mention his physical injuries. That he is still living is something of a . . . surprise."

McClellan questioned the doctor's uncertainty.

Dr. Gupta said only that Agent Clarke was not her patient. He'd been transferred to the hospital in Corinthia, which was the best in New Athens for dealing with neural damage to programmers.

"I'm afraid I know little else about his condition or treatment," she said. "My concern is your recovery. And, with that in mind, I'd like you to rest a little longer before we attempt to work on your motor skills. A physical therapist will be in at dinnertime. And yes, I have already made arrangements that we not use robotic assistants."

The doctor excused herself after more prodding and some additional instructions, including her repeated insistence that he rest.

"I'd better go too, Johnny," Bauer said. "I'll be back after you get some sleep. I know you have questions, and I have much to tell you. And to give you. I brought a few things up from Earth that you may find useful. But that's for later. Right now, tell me if there's anything I can do."

McClellan could only think to ask if Okayo was back on New Athens.

"Yes," Bauer said. "But until you're cleared by the doctor, Commissioner Zhèng has restricted visitation. He wants to meet with you personally, which I understand will be as soon as you're up and about. Until then, I'm the only visitor they've allowed in."

"Understood," McClellan said, not really understanding. He was disappointed to have to wait to tell Okayo about what Clarke had done. He thought of asking Bauer to relay the message, to record the first baptism in the registers of New Athens's chapel, but the fatigue was returning. He had strength enough for only one more question.

"Why did you come?"

Bauer came closer so that he could speak with some privacy.

"One important reason. A priest should not be asked to do what you're doing without a brother priest. Christ sent out his first disciples two by two for a reason. And who are any of us to think we know better?"

"Two by two," McClellan repeated, his voice weakening. "How long has this been in the works?"

"From before you were selected. Cardinal Kwalia insisted from the start that two priests be sent. Of course the engineers and Security refused, and they were not moved by the need for priests to hear each other's confessions. But Kwalia is shrewd. He agreed to send you on the condition that if something happened, another priest would be sent for an anointing. Well, something happened. And here I am."

"You knew all along that you could be coming up?"

Bauer laughed. "No, no. There were other candidates. Younger ones. But when I heard how serious things had become, I pulled some strings."

McClellan thought for a moment, but that was getting more difficult. "Thank God. I could use a good confession—and someone to talk to."

Bauer smiled. "You'll get both. But you need sleep. May God bless you, John Francis McClellan, and may he speed your recovery. And may the Author of Truth help you—help *us*—get to the bottom of all that's happened."

34

MCCLELLAN ATTEMPTED A CONVERSATION with his new Security escort, but when Agent Michael Molina gave his fourth one-word answer, McClellan got the hint. From there it was a quiet walk from the Troas City hospital to a private streetcar that brought them to the City of Philippi—and then to McClellan's meeting with Commissioner Zhèng.

McClellan didn't know much of what happened during the past week. And Zhèng wouldn't know what McClellan and Clarke had discovered in that house printer. It made sense for the commissioner to meet with him quickly, and alone, before the case briefing that evening. What surprised McClellan was Zhèng's insistence that they meet before checking on the still unconscious Clarke.

The streetcar entered Philippi, a showcase of architecture known as Modified Orbital Greek Revival. It is a middle city, positioned directly opposite to and balancing with Corinthia, and like that city, Philippi's towers rose high above the skylights and the farms of the core.

The headquarters of the Security Guild was the tallest. It rose some fifty floors over the skylights and came to a tapered peak that, from the ground, appeared to rise precariously close to the Sun Crane. From the outside, its walls looked windowless and closed, but they were perfectly transparent from the inside.

The pair entered its long lobby, which was sleek and unadorned, save for a grand replica of a Security Guild command badge. There were routine checks and conversations between Agent Molina and his colleagues at the main entrance. After an all-clear, the pair went on to Zhèng's office, which was an efficient walk and a long elevator ride to the fiftieth floor.

Zhèng was sitting in a chair tall enough to fit his frame. His large office was printed with a standard blue metallic finish, and decorated only with a Security Guild banner. The focus of the room was his well-ordered desk with its well-ordered data floating above in color-coded clusters. Behind him was a transparent wall overlooking Philippi and the farms beyond, and past all that was the City of Heraclea and then the Wheel, turning as it lifted its occupants to the Centerwell.

Zhèng motioned to a chair next to his desk. He dismissed Agent Molina and waited for McClellan to make himself comfortable. There were no pleasantries.

"Nice office," McClellan said, feeling a need to take some advantage.

Zhèng sat and considered McClellan's clerical suit, then reached for a tablet. He held it casually, but positioned so that McClellan could not see its content.

"You'll understand my wish to relocate our briefings here. Through that door"—Zhèng motioned to the right of the office's entrance—"is a command office very much like the Security substation attached to your quarters."

"Makes sense," McClellan said. He considered his words and opted to keep them to a minimum.

Zhèng shifted and handed McClellan the tablet.

"This includes a summary of this past week's events," he said. "But before you dive in, allow me to provide some highlights."

"Please," McClellan said. "I have many questions."

"No doubt. Let's begin with Draeger. Well, no, let me begin with what happened after you and Clarke were brought to safety."

Zhèng eye-typed commands on the desk's interface. A blurry image appeared. It was the tunnel that Clarke and McClellan had taken to the printer staging area. The image—which Zhèng said came from a security monitoring camera—showed two young builders frantically placing a wounded McClellan on a transport platform as a torrent of water erupted behind them.

"This image was the talk of New Athens as soon as it was released by the Builders Guild," Zhèng was saying. "These young men have become celebrities, although they are quite embarrassed with the attention. But the long and short of it, Father McClellan, is that this picture of two lowly, noble builders saving the great guest of the engineers, as well as one of my agents, has become a tool of propaganda. It's given the builders a sense of pride that—if in many ways is long, long overdue—has made some of their leaders intent on fighting for not just issues of class inequality, but also for control of New Athens."

McClellan kept his focus on the image. He had been given the names of the two builders and learned that Wagner had sent them into the tunnels for maintenance. The pair had been checking the main wastewater line when they heard the thrashing of the activated printer, and then the alarms of a waterline break. When they made it to the staging area, they found McClellan tumbling backward, bloody and soaked. They went looking for Clarke, but couldn't get to him until the printer convulsed and went idle.

McClellan remembered the sincerity of his rescuers, and he was eager to meet them under better circumstances.

"And so, as you might imagine," Zhèng was saying, "this image has been a great benefit to Draeger's campaign of whipping up the builder population."

"Let me guess," McClellan said. "He's been quiet. Making only a few targeted statements to remain relevant. Otherwise he's been busy day and night meeting with the builders in each of the twelve cities, driving wedges, inciting factions."

"Yes, and not just with reps in New Athens. He's meeting stewards throughout the orbits, who come here to pay him homage."

McClellan nodded. "That's how the Sals work. They slither in and build their networks, offering the world, corrupting one mind at a time, until they can turn communities against each other."

"And that's exactly what's happening on my station," Zhèng said, pausing to look up at the wide Security Guild banner. "Draeger gave a talk two nights ago claiming that the Security Guild 'is the puppet of the engineers.' He's demanding his own security force, one that can protect him and the builders."

The two men did not need to discuss the implications of that demand.

McClellan took and released a deep breath, giving thanks for the ability to do so. "I understand we're meeting with Draeger tomorrow, at his request—him and the engineers—to negotiate a way forward. That should be interesting."

"Yes," Zhèng said. "I believe that it will."

Zhèng stood and went to the transparent wall. Across the plains, the Wheel was turning at full rotation. "We need to move fast," he said. "And we need to move in a united fashion." He turned and looked directly at his guest. "Father McClellan, do you remember when I confessed my sins to you?"

McClellan stiffened. "Of course."

"Then you remember what I was most sorrowful for. What I most sought to change."

"The sin of pride," McClellan said. "You said you knew personally that it's the root of great evil."

"Yes," Zhèng said, considering his words. "At times in my career I have been . . . severe."

The light faded with some movement of the clouds, darkening Zhèng's expression.

"You mentioned that," the priest said, standing and walking over to Zhèng. "I suppose it is a struggle up here, enforcing good behavior in a new world that had promised to do away with the sins of humanity."

Zhèng gave a slight nod. "That's part of it. A small part. My greatest temptation—and you'll laugh when I say this—is this view. Everything I see, I command. Orbital traffic. Public gatherings. Even the Wheel. The engineers like to think they are in control, but ultimately I am."

"And yet Philippi is a middle city. This window only looks out at half the station."

"That's true. There's much in my world that I don't control. I know that—now more than ever, since Tanglao's murder, and everything since. But I also know my duties. I know the people here, and I understand what we need to do—and what we cannot do. What *I* cannot do."

McClellan stayed silent.

"After we spoke during my confession," Zhèng continued, "I vowed to take your words to heart. I wanted to run this investigation with the humility you spoke about—the humility that calms a soul's pride and opens doors, as you said, with God's help."

McClellan remembered.

"And yet," Zhèng said, "since then I've often felt that you and I are still dueling on those basketball courts in Gainesville."

McClellan folded his arms. "I'm not sure what you mean."

"I believe that you do. Think of how you have acted as an investigator. Can't you see? In that role, you've often pushed me to act in opposition to your counseling during my confession. You urged me to return to some of my former ways. It felt like you didn't trust my methods. That you didn't trust *me*. And a commander can't allow that. Nor can a friend. And so I'll ask again: do you trust me?"

McClellan saw a pleading in Zhèng's eyes—the same that Clarke had given when they discussed entering the printer. Part of him wasn't entirely sure what Zhèng meant by trusting him—of course he had. Most of the time. He also recognized the fear and mistrust that always come, even among friends, with the arrival of the Sals. But, more than any of this, he could see his own mistakes—his own uncertainties.

"Commissioner, I'm going to repeat what I said when we returned from Red Delta—when there was talk of me leading the investigation. You have my unequivocal support—and trust. One hundred percent. And you have my apologies. I should have been clearer about that. I guess . . . well, this is the first time I've had to be a priest and an investigator at the same time. Not to mention a programmer. I'm going to have to do a better job balancing all that. I just hope that you'll give me the opportunity to try."

Zhèng stood straighter. He thanked McClellan and turned to take a long look at the core. Then he went to his desk. He was still standing and sifting through some of the holodata when he motioned for McClellan to join him. "Come. I have an update that I want to give you personally."

The two men sat. Zhèng held up another tablet, but not close enough for McClellan to reach.

"Before I hand it over," Zhèng said, "can you guess my news?"

There were a few possibilities, but only one made sense given Zhèng's expression. "Molly Rose," McClellan said. "She found the printer, right?"

Zhèng handed over the tablet. "She has, yes. And it's on its way to an Earth orbit as we speak."

"How? I thought Clarke wasn't successful with a communications burst?"

"He wasn't. Molly Rose found it the old-fashioned way. Knowing who to talk to, and calling in favors."

"God bless her," McClellan said. "Because if I'm right, and I know that I am, she also found Tanglao's coupler."

The commissioner gave a surprised look. "How did you know that?"

"It was in the data from the Emily—from the printer. I had time in the hospital, so last night after talking with a few patients, I processed the data."

"And?"

"And I can tell you with certainty that the design of the Pauline Chapel didn't come from a random data search. It didn't even come from the printer used to kill Tanglao. It came *through* it. It came from Tanglao's coupler."

Zhèng thought a moment. "I suppose that makes some sense, given the nature of the design. But I've never heard of such a thing. Isn't it more likely that the design came from another printer, or some information warehouse in the orbits, or even on Earth?"

"Yes, that would seem more likely. But it didn't. It came from the coupler. I'm certain of its origin—that's how I know the coupler has been in that printer all along."

"And you learned all this when you were linked with the house printer?"

"I can't take the credit. It was the printer. In her last seconds of contact—her last seconds of life—she sent me a fair amount of data without me knowing it. I'm guessing the third programmer doesn't know, either. If so, that gives us an advantage."

Zhèng allowed himself a laugh. "It never ceases to amaze me how some of you programmers relate to these machines—the way you speak of them as living entities. Well, in any event, I look forward to your full report. We mere mortals had to learn of the coupler's location another way. The crew of the deep-space relay that gained possession of the clam-shell—unknowingly, it seems, with dozens of other units—had agreed to Molly Rose's request to send it back to Earth. As they were loading the printer onto a transport, they discovered the coupler. It was still locked in its control deck. They also saw that it was not only embedded, it also was active. I had assumed this was because Tanglao had been caught off guard when the printer was hacked."

"I'm not so sure," McClellan said, looking away. "Tanglao had time to remove and hide his programmer's key. Why not remove the coupler, too?"

"Couldn't it be that he was just too weak?"

"Maybe," McClellan said. "Maybe not. But either way, we can get our answers if you get me into that printer."

Zhèng gave an anxious sigh. "Even after what just happened?"

"You don't need to remind me. But the goal all along has been to find out what happened to Tanglao by learning what was happening with that printer. As a priest, I'm the best programmer to do that. And as a member of your team, what I find can be used if this goes to trial."

"I know, I know. But it's risky."

"Commissioner, you asked me to trust you. I'm asking for the same thing. I have a good idea what Father Tanglao was doing when his printer was hacked—and why it got him into trouble, and with whom."

Zhèng leaned back in his chair. "And you need to confirm this by accessing the printer?"

"Yes. And to confirm much more. But here's the hitch. To get me into that printer, we'll need another programmer—one with full programming status and valid trust. Otherwise I'll likely only get some low level of entry but no access."

"Even if you have Tanglao's key and coupler? I'd prefer to use only members of my team—for obvious reasons."

"Understood, but if it's just me, then I'll need both Tanglao's coupler and mine. And I haven't seen my equipment since Raleigh. Only God knows where it is, or if it exists. The best plan is to find another programmer."

Chimes came low and regular from somewhere above them as the building informed the city that it was eleven o'clock in the morning. McClellan listened to the rhythm as he thought through the available programmers. It would have to be one of the engineers.

"Commissioner, you said the clamshell is on its way back to Earth. I assume we know how long that will take."

Zhèng leaned forward and made motions over his desk. Images of Earth and the Moon appeared and expanded, along with the arcs of their orbits, and those of various craft and relays.

"Our printer was found bundled there, in the Blue Theta relay. It was with printers being readied at the L5 point on Earth's orbit. As I said, thanks to Molly Rose it's on a transport to our geostationary orbit. It will arrive here at New Athens in twelve days."

"What about the moon?" McClellan asked. "Can we get the printer to Red Delta?"

Zhèng looked over the orbital displays. "Yes. It would be a straightforward series of maneuvers. Although the transport may need a little more fuel for braking to achieve Red Delta's lunar orbit. I'm sure Molly Rose can squeeze that favor out of someone. But why bring the printer back to the relay?"

"Poetic justice?"

Zhèng was not amused.

McClellan examined the images. He looked at Zhèng and said, "Before Clarke and I left to sync with the printer, he showed me his research on the tunneling that's taking place throughout New Athens. He had a good idea about where some of the more interesting eavesdropping was coming from."

"I'm aware of his findings," Zhèng finally said. "But what of them?"

McClellan shrugged. "We should use them to our advantage."

Zhèng watched the orbital dance before him. "I know where you're going with this. But you won't be able to track tunneling in the orbits. If you think there's too much interference in New Athens, try it with all communications among Earth, New Athens, the construction of Progress, the lunar bases and the Lesser Stations, and the relays, not to mention the transports, the shuttles, and the Van Allen dispersers. It would be impossible to track any single attempt at tunneling—even a strong attempt to Red Delta."

"If you mean it's impossible only because of the comm traffic, then I agree."

"And what do you propose? Turn it all off?"

"Something like that."

Zhèng stared as if he'd been displeased with the humor until he recognized that McClellan wasn't joking. "You'll have to explain that in more detail."

"I will. In time. First I need to think things through a little more."

"Undoubtedly," Zhèng said. "And as you're thinking through the miracle that would be needed to silence all communication in the orbits, I'll call Elaina and tell her that we're working with the builders and have hijacked one of her printers. I'm sure she'll understand."

"Not that she has much of a choice," McClellan said. "The builders control the shipping lanes. And if the transport is already committed to an orbit, what can they do?"

"Hack it. Change its trajectory. Have it slingshot around Earth, back around and out again to its original L5 staging area. Or, if we do get access to it, they could deny you another attempt at syncing with their printers."

"True. But I'm leaving it to you to get me to that printer. As for access, the engineers may feel safer with one of their own programmers getting me in. Unless you know any other rogue programmer out there."

Zhèng reduced the size of the orbital simulations for a better view of McClellan. "I do not," he said as he stood. "In any event, we'll discuss all this at this evening's briefing. I'll arrange dinner for the team. I recognize that you prefer the Spinside, but we'll see what the restaurants in Philippi can send up. We'll all have much to discuss, including preparations for our meeting tomorrow morning with the engineers and Draeger."

"I can hardly wait," McClellan said, taking his cue and standing. "You'll handle Draeger well. As you said, you know the people of New Athens. Draeger doesn't."

The men shook hands. They did so with a firmness of trust and forward motion. McClellan was eager to visit Clarke, but he stopped as he neared the door.

"Commissioner, one last question. I understand that there's a big project out at Mercury. Would it be possible to get information on it? I read through the public material, but there wasn't much. I assume you have more."

Zhèng said he did, and that he saw no reason not to grant McClellan access. "I have a number of files, although nothing specific about what the engineers are designing. What I do know is that only the printers will be used for labor—and that's added to the builders' grievances. But what's your interest in Mercury?"

McClellan looked away, past the transparent wall, out to where clouds drifted over the cylindrical plains of New Athens. Then he looked out to the Wheel. Tanglao's body had finally passed through five days earlier on its return to Earth, as had the body of Catherine Georgeson.

"Let's just say, Commissioner, that thanks to a little old lady, I have a hunch."

"About?"

"About a connection between Mercury and what Tanglao was up to in that air lock—and why he was murdered."

35

OKAYO SAT PEACEFULLY IN the front pew, her eyes closed. McClellan had finally been able to talk to her—to tell her what had happened, what Clarke had done, inside that printer. Now she needed time alone. McClellan genuflected before the tabernacle and made his way to his reunion with Archbishop Bauer, but lingered and looked back from the door to his apartments.

Her eyes remained closed, but they seemed fixed on the tabernacle and the crucifix above it, as they had when he told her of Clarke's choice. A smile had come again to her soft features, bringing some satisfaction to the darkness of the past days and weeks.

McClellan allowed himself a deep, slow breath, so as not to disturb the scene. He felt the satisfaction of air filling his lungs, and gave thanks— that simple ability meant all the more since it had been taken from him. He gave thanks, too, for what Clarke had done, for what his baptism meant to Okayo and to him. Yet a shadow hovered over him. Envy, the enemy of gratitude, lingered and sulked. It urged him to stay, to call out to Okayo and thank her for her smile, to tell her how often he thought of her. But he would not allow it. Had life taken another path, perhaps a woman would be smiling for him. Had his choices been different, he would have been able to satisfy his desire to hold a woman as beautiful as Okayo, to marry and join with her, to bring new life and a new family to creation. But he had chosen a different road, a different way to build up creation. It was a choice that asked for sacrifices and yet offered so much because of them.

McClellan mirrored her smile. He wondered if someday he'd celebrate the wedding Mass for Clarke and Okayo. Perhaps he'd baptize their children—and their grandchildren. It was possible, after all, God willing— even with Clarke still hovering near death, and even with chaos and enmity spreading throughout New Athens.

Again he breathed in the air of the chapel, and he was content.

He had forgotten that he was holding open the door to his apartment. Bauer was waiting halfway down the inner hall, which gave him a view into the chapel. The archbishop said nothing when McClellan entered and closed the door, other than to offer a smile of understanding from one priest to another.

They shook hands and embraced, then made themselves comfortable in the apartment's simple sitting area—which was now a cramped guest room, with a spare bed and four shipping crates that Bauer had brought from Earth. They spent time laughing about Bauer's hurried preparation for his journey—his first to the orbits—and the terrible coffee he had made an hour ago.

After delivering a summary of the news from McClellan's parish, Bauer thumbed the handle of his mug, and his smile dimmed. "Johnny, tell me, how are you?"

"Good question. How much time do you have?"

"As long as it takes."

McClellan looked away, not sure where to begin. "All things considered, I'm good. There's just a lot to say, and to be honest I wasn't thinking that I'd be having this conversation anytime soon—or whether I'd ever have the opportunity. How am I doing? I suppose you'll know when you hear my confession."

"That's one of the reasons I'm here."

McClellan released a breath. "One of the reasons?"

Bauer leaned back. "Obviously I want to check in on you, see how things are going—"

"And report back to Rome."

"Yes. Is there a reason I shouldn't?"

"Of course not. There's so much they need to know."

"I'm certain. Although Agent Anne Okayo has been in touch all along with her old bishop, Cardinal Kwalia. So Rome already knows more than a little."

McClellan said he thought that was the case. He had never felt it right to ask either Okayo or Zhèng, but he was glad for the confirmation.

"I haven't told you," Bauer continued, "but the cardinal is in Boston while I'm here. Of course, I trust my auxiliary bishops, but it seemed right to have a shepherd fill in who knows the Sals. Especially now. It was very kind of him." He shifted uncomfortably when he saw McClellan's curious expression. "My brother's family is in hiding, Johnny. There were two Sal attempts on the children. They're okay, but they need to be somewhere safe. And then, three days before I came here, my cathedral was attacked. It was a small explosive, just took out the front façade, but it killed two workers. Tommy Ryan was one of them. You knew his sister, Elaine. You helped with her funeral Mass."

McClellan remembered the entire Ryan clan—how close they all had been as Elaine slipped into death, and at her funeral. He remembered Tommy in particular. He was one of those warmhearted big men who cry like children when a loved one is taken from them.

"I am so very sorry to hear that—Tommy was a good man. One of the heroes in the famines, I'm told. We'll say a Mass together for both of them. And for the safety of your family."

Bauer nodded, and said a quiet prayer to St. Thérèse.

"There is another reason why I came, Johnny. And, after what happened to you, and in light of where God seems to be taking you, it may be one of the most important. I wanted to personally ensure that you receive what I've brought here." Bauer looked over to the shipping containers stacked next to them. "Especially the top one. Go on, let's see what you find."

The container was lighter than it looked. McClellan rocked it on its sides but no motion came from within. He carried it to the room's small table and gave it another visual inspection.

"Go on," the archbishop said, standing and offering a key.

McClellan hesitated. He wanted to solve the riddle of what Bauer had brought, but he could think of nothing. He inserted the key, and then had to step aside so that Bauer could scan his live DNA.

The container whirred and snapped. McClellan eased up the lid and removed layers of packing material. Underneath were red clerical vestments—striking ones, handmade. They had to have been from Gammarelli, Bauer's favorite tailor in Rome. The chasuble was red silk with gold stitching in the shape of palms. In its center was a finely embroidered medallion of Christ entering Jerusalem. The back medallion depicted Calvary surrounded by the same palm design, as well as thorns and nails embroidered in gold thread.

"These are from the Holy Father," Bauer said. "He wanted the first Palm Sunday celebrated in the orbits to include vestments that match what he'll be wearing at St. Peter's. You are, after all, using a replica of his chapel. He said it seemed fitting."

McClellan's cheeks went red as he stammered his thanks, until finally he gave up on words. Bauer gave a chuckle but quickly pushed matters forward. "Keep looking. There's something else."

McClellan removed other vestments and a cope, commented on their quality, and then came to what else Bauer had wanted to hand-deliver. It was a thin, square object wrapped in gold metallic foil, a material used in the old days for lightweight orbital shielding, and still used for less noble purposes—most especially for masking shipping sensors, which in this case would have been partially confused already by the gold embroidery on the vestments. Its feel and shape were familiar, as was the small lump in its center. There was a faint odor, a blend of mud, smoke, and printer emissions that McClellan had not smelled since Raleigh.

"Where did you find them?"

Bauer smiled and said, "Open it."

McClellan unraveled the foil and tenderly removed his combat programmer's key and coupler. The Corps had confiscated them after Raleigh, when he had been quietly removed from the 6th Marine Raider Battalion and denied any specialty that could involve printers. That's when, with Bauer's help, the Corps had reassigned him as a low-level aide in the Military Police, and that's when it had become evident that programmers bring unique talents when analyzing criminal cases.

"You can thank my friend Monsignor Harper," Bauer said. "He called in a few favors to get these without arousing suspicion. But if it means anything to you, the Corps did not object to their going missing."

McClellan said that that did indeed mean something, and he thanked Bauer inadequately for all he had done. "I have to ask where these have been for the past thirteen years—they should have been returned to the Global Union's engineers."

"Well, they weren't, Johnny. They were in storage. That simple. After you were removed from your duties as a combat programmer, the engineers behind the printers demanded their return. It was about the time that the Corps and the Global Union were no longer seeing eye to eye.

And with some in command lobbying to get you back to the Sixth, well, let's just say that the Corps did not acquiesce to the GU's demands. Anyway, your key and coupler went into storage at Lejeune, and there they stayed until good ol' Harper tracked 'em down."

No one had cleaned the coupler since Raleigh. It was still stained with mud, and the grime from smoke still coated its displays. Smudges remained where his blood had pooled along the outer edge. McClellan ran his hand over his scalp and touched the scars on his temple. There was no blood there, no smoke, no sound of aircraft or armored vehicles or weapons fire, but he thought he could hear Danny and his escorts just around the corner, maybe in the chapel, on their way to greet him.

"Johnny?" Bauer said. "You okay?"

He was remembering the promise of his youth back home in Union City—that of a young Marine who planned to use this key and coupler to make things right. But he had been irresponsible and calculated incorrectly. He had been tempted, and he had chosen poorly. He had been prideful, and he had violated the trust of that printer—which, of all his regrets, was the most difficult to explain, even to priests and programmers.

He wondered if his old key and coupler should have been destroyed. But here they were.

It didn't take long to assess the situation. There was no need to ask the engineers for programming help. With both Tanglao's coupler and his own, he could do more than access the printer. He could confirm his suspicion of what Tanglao had been attempting, who had killed him, and why. If he was right, this would be the same person who murdered Sasaki and Walker, and who had tried to kill him, and maybe destroyed Clarke's mind.

No, he no longer needed help from the engineers, but it would be far better if they cooperated.

And only Zhèng could make that happen.

36

THE FOLLOWING DAY, ON the feast of St. Patrick, representatives of the three parties—Engineering, Security, and Builder—gathered in Elaina Jansen's grand living room. The meeting had been requested by Draeger and his client, the Builders Guild, and was eagerly agreed to by the leaders of the other two. According to the communiqué sent from Draeger to Zhèng, it was hoped that the parties could find "a mutually beneficial way forward in the investigation of the deaths of three men, and the attack on Agent Brandon Clarke and Father John McClellan."

McClellan translated that for the commissioner. "In the language of the Sals, it means, 'we are going to demoralize you with our demands, and then threaten you repeatedly until you meet them, and then we'll follow through on our threats anyway.'"

Jansen was efficient and elegant in her gray suit, and she was gracious with her welcomes, especially to Commissioner Zhèng. By treaty, security personnel are not allowed in the homes of the engineers, but Jansen had said that trying times call for new ways. "I am happy to open my doors to all," she said, smiling broadly, as she did with every new arrival.

This included Rudi Draeger, who also received an awkward hug.

McClellan couldn't decide if Jansen had or had not accepted Zhèng's warnings about the lawyer and his supporters—that their intentions would run counter to the common good, or even the good of the builders. But in her home, which had been designed and printed to suggest certainty, security, and progress, it seemed doubtful that Jansen saw any threat to her dreams for New Athens.

When Zhèng introduced McClellan to Draeger, it was as if their meeting in the chapel had never occurred. Their clasp was brief yet firm and their comments polite. Draeger wore the same ragged suit he had worn that night, an event he did not mention. And, since most of that conversation had been under the seal of confession, there was nothing McClellan could share even if he wanted to.

Draeger then introduced Jimmy Jade, his aide during the past week. Jade was the up-and-coming steward who had counseled Max Tucker after his arrival from Red Delta—the very night Tucker gave his unexpected confession. McClellan hadn't been in Jade's company before, so he took his time with the niceties of their introduction. The builder was about his own age with a short, wiry build. His long, greasy black hair was combed back flat, and he wore a dark suit that was too tight in the shoulders and too loose everywhere else. McClellan knew that Jade was a martial arts instructor, but that wasn't obvious from his anxious movements as he looked about the room.

Jansen had brought two trusted colleagues, the imposing Hannah Ward and the fair-skinned and freckled Andrew Pavić—two of the engineers whom McClellan had met in this very room for dinner, and who had accompanied Jansen to the murder scene of Yoshiharu Sasaki. They were less effusive with their greetings than their host.

At Jansen's cheerful bidding, the attendees sat in the white upholstered armchairs and rested their tablets and coffee on small, intricately printed tables—all neatly arranged on the room's transparent floor, which looked out to the whirling, intermittent views of Earth and the Moon, the Sun, and deep space beyond.

"Thank you all for coming," Jansen began. "And Mr. Draeger, once again, welcome to New Athens. I trust your accommodations are satisfactory?"

"Yes, indeed," Draeger said. "My hosts among the builders have been most gracious."

Jansen either didn't notice Draeger's discourtesy or chose to ignore it. "Now, Commissioner, I look forward to hearing the status of where we stand in this investigation. But before we begin, is there any news of Agent Clarke? I trust that he is recovering."

"The doctors aren't sure," McClellan interrupted. "He remains in a coma, which is not surprising. I can tell you firsthand that there was quite a bit of neural feedback when he worked to contain the outside hacker. But he's receiving excellent attention—thanks to you, Elaina."

Jansen said that the Engineering Council would continue to help with any care the young agent might need. After punctuating her words with a look at all those assembled, she forged on. "As my friends in the Builders

Guild have rightly requested, we would like to come to some understanding of next steps. And so, Zhèng, let us begin with what is happening in your investigation, and why Maximillian Tucker is still a suspect."

The commissioner reiterated that Tucker had been charged only with monitoring security communications and tampering with an active investigation. There was some question about his providing false statements, but there was no question about murder.

"He wasn't being seriously considered as a murder suspect until he issued his confession," Zhèng said. "But I'll have more to say on that shortly. First I will provide Mr. Draeger with the information that he and the Builders Guild requested."

Zhèng detailed the matters that led to this meeting—an accounting that took almost an hour, with detours that explained the nuances of cellular and nuclear forensics; their implications when applied to nascent orbital law; and a lengthy, if abbreviated, record of evidence. This included the statements of those interviewed on New Athens, Earth, and Red Delta—which numbered fifty-eight people to date.

"And what of the data from Agent Clarke's sync with the house printer?" Hannah Ward asked.

"The printer was quite beyond salvaging after it had been hacked and sabotaged," Zhèng said. "And any information transferred to Father McClellan's links is his property according to orbital law, as well as case law here and on Earth. However, he has been gracious in providing a summary, which I am sending to you now. As you will see, it indicates that there had been prior communications between the house clamshell and the one at Tanglao's death. Beyond that, further analysis will be needed."

McClellan's report and the other records mentioned by Zhèng were transferred to Draeger, who shared them with Jimmy Jade. Draeger nodded politely and thanked the commissioner dutifully and often. He interrupted Zhèng only once to ask a question. "Why did the engineers grant permission for Clarke and McClellan to access the house printer?"

Zhèng referred the question to Andrew Pavić, who had provided the final authorization. Pavić shifted with displeasure. "Commissioner Zhèng's request came just after the printer had been assigned to a project I'm overseeing. Given the ongoing investigation, granting access seemed appropriate. And there was cause, given that the clamshell was a similar model as the one present at the death of Raphael Tanglao. It had also strayed from programming commands in the building of Mr. McClellan's chapel—excuse me, *Father* McClellan's chapel. We all wanted to know more about that, and McClellan has more background with chapels than any of my colleagues. And so I thought the approval in order."

Draeger nodded with interest, and thanked Pavić. He returned to Zhèng's narrative, still nodding and taking notes as he listened. His associate Jade took no notes. His interest waned during the discussion of the nuances of orbital law, and he became increasingly mesmerized by the revolving vista below his feet.

When Zhèng was through—after the transfer to Draeger and Jade of some eighty files—the commissioner asked if Draeger had any questions.

Earth was sending up blue hues as it rolled beneath them. The glare illuminated the gathering but not Draeger's expression, which was in shadow with his head cocked back to think. He turned to Zhèng, paused, and said, "Yes, I have quite a few questions. Thank you. First, I want to get back to that printer to which Pavić allowed access. Why wasn't that printer quarantined and checked earlier, after it went rogue with the printing of that chapel? Was it used after that? And what are the procedures for allowing such access? Printers are, after all, the property of the engineers."

Elaina Jansen set about to answer his questions, but before she could speak, Draeger interrupted her.

"You see," he said, "I have attestations from more than four hundred members of the Builders Guild of denied requests for printer access in the past two years alone. There are, I am sure, many others. Each of these requests took an average of twelve days to be reviewed—twelve!—and all were summarily denied. And so I am quite concerned about this fast-track approval for printer access."

Jansen objected with a hurried explanation of the engineers' treaty with the Security Guild.

"Thank you for the clarification," Draeger said. "It appears that this treaty allows for cozy relationships between your two guilds. But, of course, the builders, who have asked me to represent Mr. Tucker, have no such language in their treaty with the engineers. That gives unequal standing in accessing critical elements of this investigation. And so I am afraid the very treaty between your two guilds has become a factor in this case—one that I will most assuredly examine if Mr. Tucker is to be given a fair trial."

Jansen and her two colleagues looked to Zhèng with the expectation of a response. The commissioner did not meet this expectation, which brought crestfallen looks and the cue for the lawyer to continue.

"Which leads me to another concern," Draeger said. "Who will conduct this hearing? Or is it a trial? I have yet to receive any meaningful guidance."

Jansen, for the first time, looked displeased. "The Engineering Council will, of course. We review all such matters. This was made clear in the correspondence sent to the Builders Guild after learning of Father Tanglao's death. But, if you wish, I will have it resent."

McClellan knew of Zhèng's intentions—most of them, anyway. The strategy for this meeting and the continuing investigations had taken up much of last night's briefing in Zhèng's offices. At the time, it had all sounded reasonable. Now McClellan wondered if the commissioner might be allowing Draeger too much leeway to ask questions, and Jansen too much opportunity to respond with irritation. Still, McClellan had given Zhèng his trust. He would honor that gift by remaining silent, yet as a precaution he said a prayer for protection to Zhèng's namesake St. Joseph.

With Jansen's answer, Draeger's performance was escalating. He again leaned his head back, bringing shadow to his eyes as the Sun's light flooded and glided from below. "It is remarkable that my client is to be judged by the very party that claims to have been aggrieved in this matter. A party that's in control of important evidence, namely the printer that conveniently was sent away after the death of Raphael Tanglao—the very printer that, according to these documents, is being transferred to Earth orbit as we speak. Is this true, Commissioner?"

McClellan wondered why Draeger fired two weapons at once—the first being the question about the presiding authority and second about the printer. Such a strategy could deliver a show of force. Or it could be a tactical error. In this case McClellan saw it as the latter. There was no debating that an independent court did not exist in the new world. Draeger and the builders were correct in contesting that. The issue of the printer was a different matter, one that Zhèng was fully equipped to engage.

But to McClellan's surprise, Zhèng addressed both.

"First, Mr. Draeger, please know that I agree with your concerns. Going forward there will need to be better alignment and equity between all treaties. And there must be an independent court system—starting with any case we bring forward in this matter." Zhèng paused to make commands in his tablet, then looked up and added, "I am sending all of you a copy of a document that I will submit to the governing bodies of all three guilds. It contains my analysis of exactly the issues Mr. Draeger raises, as well as my requests and suggestions for correcting these deficiencies."

After a flurry of motions to find their tablets, the three engineers, Draeger, and Jade solemnly began to read Zhèng's words. It took only a few moments before the same observation came to them all. If the commissioner did in fact send these documents to the leaders of their respective guilds, he would in effect—after the inevitable leaks, unofficial and otherwise—be sending them to all the people of New Athens.

McClellan hadn't expected any of this. At last night's briefing, Zhèng had told him only that he had given great thought to the concerns of the builders, and that as security commissioner he was ready to act appropriately.

McClellan gave Zhèng an approving nod. He thanked God, St. Joseph, and the entire communion of saints, and leaned back for a better view of the show.

"As for the printer," Zhèng continued, "of course we've found it. It's en route and will be in Earth orbit in eleven days. Mr. Draeger, as the representative of the Builders Guild, you should have been informed of this, since builders are the principal pilots for the shipping lanes."

Draeger was still reeling from Zhèng's admissions about equitable treaties and governance. He hadn't expected such a gesture or the implications thereof, and now he had to contend with Zhèng's accurate assessment of what he should know about the activity of his client.

The lawyer turned to Jansen in an attempt to slow Zhèng's advance. "I do hope," Draeger said, "that the Engineering Council has not been formally made aware of the acquisition of the printer. For I can assure you there has been no such formal notification to the Builders Council."

Jansen answered Draeger's question, but she kept her eyes on Zhèng. "I have not been told of this, Mr. Draeger. Nor has the council." She turned to Pavić and Ward, who gave equally confused looks.

Zhèng remained cool. "That printer is a key component of this investigation. According to orbital law, I am under no obligation to inform either of you of my intent for it, although again, Mr. Draeger, you must have known of its coming, as we are working with builders to obtain it. And, Madame Jansen, had the engineers wished to track the whereabouts of their property, you could have easily maintained its emergency locational transponder."

The mantel clock was making it known that it was ten thirty—the soft chimes exceptionally clear and loud in the momentary silence.

"As you can see," Zhèng continued, "there is fault and complicity by every party in this room—and I include myself in this matter. The death of Raphael Tanglao has been a mystery for far too long, in part because of my errors. And so I will be making amends as we move forward."

"What do you mean?" Jansen said.

"Yes, what do you mean?" Draeger added.

McClellan suppressed a smile. If Clarke were here, he'd probably say something about the victory of getting the engineers, the builders, and a Sal to agree on something.

"Allow me to explain my intentions," Zhèng said. "And please be aware that I have submitted these intentions to the Security Council, which has endorsed them."

Zhèng adjusted his posture; he looked like a commander instructing subordinates. "At noon today I will release the following statement to the people of New Athens—builder, engineer, and all others not formally enrolled in any guild. In addition to its content, it will include the proposals I had just sent regarding our treaties and the courts. I am transferring the full statement, so please follow along as I summarize its contents.

"First, unless some unforeseen evidence arises, the Security Guild will not charge Maximillian Tucker with the murder of Father Tanglao. Nor will he be questioned in the matter. We do not recognize his confession as valid, nor do we have any indication that he had in fact been materially involved in the death of Father Tanglao. As to charges of providing false or misleading statements related to this investigation, and other charges related to monitoring secure communications, those charges have also been dropped. In exchange, we would ask—but do not require—that Mr. Tucker cooperate with our investigation going forward."

"Cooperate?" Draeger said. "What are your demands?"

"There are none. Tucker may help in any way that he wishes. Or not."

"But any negotiations regarding charges—"

"There are no negotiations. Tucker is a free man. How can this be unclear?"

Draeger sat back with fury. He had just lost his most important card—the guise of offering a builder legal counsel. The commissioner had scored this round, but McClellan knew the dangers of prodding the Sals when they're down.

"On the matter of the investigation," Zhèng said, continuing his summary, "Father McClellan will continue to lead the inquiry related to the printer—no matter what happened at the last attempt. His expertise as a programmer and his knowledge as a priest make his perspective quite necessary. We simply ask that the Engineering Guild allow access to the printer once it is in our possession. And we ask both guilds—engineers and builders—to supply representatives to oversee our investigation during Father McClellan's interaction with the printer."

Zhèng directed his next comments exclusively to Draeger. "The printer will be brought to Red Delta for analysis. Your age and health, Mr. Draeger, may preclude extended time in a weightless environment—per the builder safety code. Thus I assume that if you do not pass the physical standards, you will provide a suitable replacement. Perhaps Mr. Jade? But that is your concern."

McClellan watched the words have their intended outcome. The Sals were exceptional at creating division, and now they had to contend with the seeds of their own.

Jade looked Draeger up and down, as if seeing the fragility of the older man for the first time. "I'll go if you can't," he said. "It will be best to have a younger man present."

Draeger whispered a few furious words toward his associate before Zhèng continued his onslaught.

"Furthermore," Zhèng said, "my statement reads that, should the case not be solved within five days of our inquiry with the printer, I will then resign as commissioner and depart from New Athens. In such an event, Agent Anne Okayo will be promoted and appointed as my replacement."

The room went still. The darkness of deep space below them was again replaced by the watery hues of Earth.

"Zhèng," Jansen said softly, "you cannot mean that."

"I do, Madame Engineer."

Jansen looked hurt. "But where would you go?"

The commissioner paused, set down his tablet, and folded his hands. "Back to Hong Kong. My grandfather still lives, but he is ill, and there are few to help him as he grows old."

Jansen marveled at Zhèng's words. She lowered her head as if she continued to consult her tablet. After moments of silence, she again looked at the commissioner, again with the full posture of her office. "I cannot see the Engineering Council having any issues revisiting our treaties, or with an independent court system. Quite frankly, the task of hearing such cases is tiring. But as for the matter of our printer, I do have questions."

"Of course," Zhèng said.

"Is there some flight limitation to explain why we have to wait eleven days for the printer to achieve Earth orbit?"

"The transport has limited fuel for braking, so I'm afraid that's the fastest burn that safety allows. And anyway, the time will help Father McClellan fully recuperate, as well as give both your guilds the opportunity to prepare representatives to travel to Red Delta."

Draeger was paying scant attention. He was still reading the full text of the statement, his jaws working and quivering. He unexpectedly gave McClellan a look of blame. The priest returned the gaze, shrugged, and motioned to Zhèng, who kept his eyes on Elaina Jansen.

"The transport carrying the printer is unmanned," the commissioner was saying. "So no bribery can change its course. And for security purposes it's running at minimum communications availability. Madame Jansen, I'm aware that the Engineering Guild has the means and the right to override its current trajectory. But, for obvious reasons, I'm asking you not to. It would be an affront to the builders, to the Security Guild, and to me personally."

Jansen looked over at her two companions, who were, like Draeger, busy reading the statement. She sat back and said, "And you wish Father McClellan to access our printer?"

"Yes."

"Who will assist him?"

"No one," Zhèng said. "Father McClellan will be the sole programmer. During his time in the hospital, we secured his personal coupler and key. He'll need no assistance. But I wish to reiterate to you both that you will have real-time access to programmer-printer activity and dialogue. I will not hide this from you."

The eyes of the three engineers turned toward McClellan while Jade kept his eyes on his boss.

"Together, we will all learn what Father Tanglao was programming at the time of his death," Zhèng said. "I don't know what else we'll find in that printer, or if it will bring us to the truth. But I'm convinced of this: the people of New Athens and of all the orbits deserve better than what our joint efforts have accomplished so far. Or do you disagree, Mr. Draeger?"

Zhèng's words came in response to a sudden smile that came across the elder man's face. All looked to see what had caught the commissioner's attention.

"Oh, I do agree," Draeger said. "The people of New Athens deserve much more than they have received thus far. Much, much more."

37

IN THE DAYS THAT FOLLOWED, little was heard from Rudi Draeger. This worried McClellan, who recognized the more ominous signs of the Sals: strikes and protests that had been called and canceled; news and rumors that came and went; and frustration and anxiety that grew.

On the fourth day after the release of Zhèng's statement, there was talk of meetings among the three guilds. There were reports of possible elections, of the drafting of a constitution, of the establishment of an independent court.

But no official statements were made.

Workers debated the wisdom of Zhèng's words. Some said the admissions of the arrogant commissioner were proof that Draeger had forced necessary changes. Now was the time to push for more. Now was the time to seize control.

Others disagreed. They were not eager for strikes or protests or revolution. They had left Earth to get away from all that.

The builders most hopeful for peace and cooperation were mostly from Troas City—like Veronica's father, Bobby Parker, and his friends who worked the Centerwell. They were men and women who raised families, who were umpires and coaches, and who were regulars at the Spinside. They were the people who would see McClellan and Bauer at their bar and would wave them over to buy them a beer in exchange for stories from Earth—whether about current events or about times long ago.

When Shirley the bartender came with the pitchers and glasses, she'd shake her head. "I never thought this crew would be talking philosophy," she'd say. Then quietly to McClellan, "At least they're behaving."

But then came the Thursday after Zhèng's statement—the first day that the doctors were hopeful about Clarke.

McClellan had taken Wagner's two mechanics to dinner—along with their boss, and Bauer, Chrissy, and Jack. It was a small thank you for saving Clarke's life, and his, and also a celebration of St. Patrick's Day, even if it was a day late. And so what began with corned beef and a round of beers escalated past six rounds, or was it seven, along with the odd whiskey and scotch—and why not a round or two for all the hardworking men and women in the house? Shirley soon called for backup, as did Okayo.

On the walk home, the priest and the archbishop staggered and sang, but dinner the next night was subdued. It was a Friday in Lent, and McClellan and Bauer chose the ginger ale with their fish and chips. Wagner sipped his stout and listened with interest to McClellan, who explained what little he knew of the work being done in orbit around Mercury, and the idea that had come to him because of it.

All during that night, and the next day, the Feast of St. Joseph, and in the days to come, other conversations began and ended—other plans were drawn and shared—as the countdown continued and people waited, and wondered at all they had heard. Because if the rumors were true, there'd be answers on that transport—the one returning that printer to Red Delta, to the uncommissioned relay where everything began.

McClellan was alone in the security transport's cargo hold. Okayo had cut the main engines almost four hours ago, and since then it had been quiet, and would remain so until she began braking.

He heard movement in the corridor and looked up. Max Tucker pushed himself into the hold and held onto a support a few meters away. The curls of his black hair were cut shorter, and he was leaner than he had been when taken into custody. He wore the same security flight suit as McClellan, with one difference. Instead of a cross and a plain white central insignia, Tucker's collar had the markings of a consulting communications technician.

"Sorry to bother you," he said, looking cautiously at McClellan.

"No need to apologize. I'm just thinking."

"About what?"

"Actually, nothing. I'm waiting for the thinking to come to me."

Tucker motioned to the bench across from McClellan, then propelled himself in it after receiving an approving nod. "Not much going on up there," he said. "Agent Okayo was busy with her flight plans for braking—if you call it braking. She's a fast flier."

"That's an understatement," McClellan said. "Best out here, but you do have to hold on."

Tucker strapped himself in, studied McClellan, and asked if they could talk.

"Of course, Max. Anytime."

Tucker thought a moment. "I was wondering why you left me alone up there. You've told me most everything about your plan, and then you leave me with Jimmy Jade and that engineer. I could have told them everything."

"That engineer is Mizuki Sasaki, and she has induced sleep until we arrive. And even if you did tell Jade anything, he couldn't get word back to Draeger, or anyone else. Okayo wouldn't allow it. And I would arrest you myself."

Tucker laughed, which McClellan was happy to hear. "Just try to take me," Tucker said, then again became serious. "But what I meant was, why do you trust me?"

McClellan assessed the builder. Tucker had all the qualities of a good security agent. He was strong, nimble in weightlessness, and smart. He was a good kid and he knew communications equipment and theory—and he knew Red Delta. This was all the more valuable without Clarke. McClellan had told Zhèng that, given relations with the builders, it made sense to offer Tucker the temporary assignment. And Tucker would benefit. It would bring him back for the relay's impending commissioning, it would help him repay Zhèng for the dropped charges, and it would offer the kid a taste of a career—of a life—he might consider.

"I trust you because you deserve it," McClellan said. "I'm a big fan of redemption, Max. And right now, if anyone deserves a second chance, it's you."

Tucker was looking down. "All that aside," he said, "I could have made better choices."

"There's not a human being alive who can't say the same thing," McClellan said. "Here's how I look at it. People are a lot like printers. We need trust for things to work, and I'd like things to work out for both of us."

McClellan watched Tucker process the words.

"Thanks," Tucker said. "I mean that. I'm not very popular in my guild at the moment. You should see the looks I get from Jade. He hates me."

"He hates a lot of people. You're doing the right thing. Maybe he'll learn something from you."

Tucker gave another laugh. "Now you're talking miracles."

"Maybe. Maybe not. Either way, you do know that as soon as this case is resolved, Zhèng will charge Jade, and others, for the coercion of your confession. Things will get uglier, especially if you're needed as a witness."

Tucker gave a solemn look as he took out his tablet. "Right now I'm helping you—and Nicky—and hoping to get my assignment back. That's all I can do. So I better finish calibrating this tracking software. Mind if I do it here?"

"It would be my pleasure."

Tucker nodded. "And one last question," he said. "Are you sure about comm traffic shutting down when we need it to? I won't be able to do anything unless that happens."

McClellan looked away. "If Wagner comes through for us, then yes. You'll have comm silence for tracking."

"I guess that means we're trusting old Wagner. I hope he comes through."

McClellan woke to Okayo's voice with a docking warning. He roused and checked his tablet.

"The clamshell's on schedule," Tucker said, gathering his belongings. "And so is Mercury. Planets are good that way."

McClellan propelled himself through the ship's tunnels to the pilot's deck. Okayo was busy with the approach as the copilot, Agent Natalya Ivanov, synced the ship with Red Delta's computer.

"Strap yourself in," Okayo said to McClellan.

"I will. But first I need to see this."

They were approaching Red Delta at about the same point of the lunar orbit as their first rendezvous. McClellan spotted the relay. It was drifting across the Moon's darkness, a small light growing larger as it passed over the lunar morning toward the Sea of Tranquillity. Soon he could see the clamshell, tiny next to the relay. It had jettisoned itself from its unmanned transport and glistened in the sunlight. Around it, lights flared—the thrusters of the robotic assistants escorting it inside Red Delta.

Okayo gave a louder command. McClellan pushed himself into the seat next to Tucker, strapped himself in, and gave a polite smile to Jimmy Jade and the waking Mizuki Sasaki. Neither responded.

They docked and entered. Molly Rose waited in the access tunnel as she had those weeks before. She gave a respectful greeting to her guests, except for Tucker, whom she hugged, joking with him about his uniform and haircut.

Jade and Sasaki followed, saying nothing. The copilot remained on board the transport—keeping the engines hot in case an emergency rescue became necessary.

"Your clamshell is settling in," Molly Rose said, listening to reports from her comm implants.

Tucker was looking farther down the tunnel. "Where's Hobart?" he asked. "He's not here to welcome his old friend?"

"I have him hard at work," Molly Rose said in a softer voice. "If we're finally going to be commissioned after this, I'll need to check my comm systems, especially the long-distance antennas. You know all about that—right, Max?"

Okayo was first into the tunnels. McClellan, Jade, and Sasaki went next, followed by Molly Rose and Tucker. The main passages led to smaller ones, which led to Cargo Hold 4 and the printer.

The hold's giant doors were closed as the space behind it repressurized. Okayo gave McClellan a hug and a confidant smile, then followed Molly Rose, Jade, and Sasaki to the cargo control room. Tucker helped McClellan suit up—a precaution required by Zhèng.

"First time in one of these suits?" Tucker said.

"No. But it's been a while. Back in my day, the Marine Corps was allowed to train upside, but my drill was one of the last. I never thought I'd be doing this again."

Tucker entered commands into the suit's arm display. He pointed and said, "Okay, you've got time displayed here, and over here is Mercury's orbit. Tunneling efficiency to Mercury is here. As the planet goes behind this area of the Sun, we're going to lose tunneling capacity. How long we have will depend on solar activity and a few other factors. So we'll have to keep an eye on those."

"Got it," McClellan said. He practiced controlling the brightness and angle of the small displays.

Tucker was staring at him. "Can I ask again why tunneling to Mercury is so important?"

"Sure," McClellan said. His smile maintained that there would be no answer.

An access alarm sounded, and the hold's doors groaned open. The cargo room was dark except for a scattering of green boundary lights on its immense walls and the outer doors straight ahead. By now Okayo and the others were in the control room about halfway above them—or below them, depending on how you considered location in weightlessness. On the hold's side-walls were rows of robbers in their charging chin-up, head-back positions.

A floodlight flared and aimed at the clamshell. The printer was strapped in the center of the hold, next to a cluster of outer crane-access assemblies. Two of the robbers that had brought in the clamshell remained nearby. This was a precaution in case the printer dislodged, or if sudden decompression occurred.

A few comments from his suit explained that its diagnostics had checked out. Because it was in a pressurized environment, the suit said that the mask could be opened and the gloves removed if the occupant preferred. McClellan wished to do so. Satisfied with his work, Tucker looked warily over to the clamshell. He slapped McClellan's shoulder, and nodded before heading off to meet Hobart in the main communications control room deeper inside Red Delta.

McClellan made his way into the hold. He was about halfway to the printer when Molly Rose radioed. "That enough light?"

"It is," he said, turning back and seeing the superintendent waving at him from the control room. Okayo was on one side of her, Sasaki and Jade on the other. "Thank you," he added, holding up one of his thumbs.

"You wouldn't need so much pampering if you worked on a relay. But we'll make an exception. Need anything else? I've got robbers on standby and station controls temporarily vetted here."

McClellan said that he had everything he needed—keys, couplers, and himself.

"And the printer," Okayo radioed.

"Yes," he replied. "And that."

"Then get to work," Molly Rose said. "I'm heading up to main comms to help Tucker and Hobart. Okayo has cargo access here, so if you need anything, she's in charge."

McClellan propelled forward, aiming for one of the locking brackets that the robbers had attached to the clamshell. He tethered his suit to the printer, removed his inner gloves, and ran his hands along the printer's casing. He felt the heat from where it faced sunward during its journey into the relay.

Everything looked good. No sign of impact. No interface damage. One of the four main shields was frozen, but he managed to open it after a few tries.

As expected, Father Tanglao's coupler was partially retracted in one of the clamshell's ports. The printer must have brought it in to protect it from the conditions of deep space.

McClellan reached in his backpack for his own coupler—giving it a kiss for old times' sake. He had cleaned it to Marine Corps standards, and it looked sleek and promising.

Then he returned to his backpack for his key, wrapped neatly in a small flag of the State of Michigan. He inserted it and turned.

The intake clicked with acceptance, but the clamshell did not rouse.

He tried again, but the printer remained quiet.

The lack of response meant one of three things: the printer had sustained some physical damage; its startup code had been hacked and scrambled; or it had sabotaged the code itself to prevent initiation sequencing. McClellan saw no signs of the first two, and he couldn't discount the third. Either way, he'd have to start it up manually.

He inserted his own coupler into the presync location and entered an initiation sequence. There was some debate between his coupler and the printer's base coding, but after a software upgrade and some digital negotiations, the coupler downloaded a startup.

The pause before presync went slowly, but the printer stirred. His coupler slid into the working position, while Tanglao's coupler slid out into the same working position. This allowed McClellan a preliminary look at its records.

As he expected, the last time and date of access was just before Mc-Clellan's chapel had been printed, almost a month after the incident on Red Delta. The last design it had supplied was the Pauline Chapel.

He looked for evidence of who had requested the design. Programmers routinely send queries through printer-to-printer channels to supplement database searches. If a printer can assist, the identity of who requested a file is recorded. But in this case, the recording registers were empty. What records he could find indicated that the download of the chapel design had been suspended when the printer itself had cut communication and closed remote access. Why the printer had done so was not clear.

He tucked his inner gloves into a pocket. Okayo sent a warning, but McClellan said that he wanted a good link.

"We trained for this in boot camp," he radioed. "If something goes wrong, I know how long until I have to glove up."

Then he ran a hand over Tanglao's coupler, allowing his links to get to know it better.

The initiation sequence began with code verification, answering queries about his blood type, master's codes, and neural programming permissions. Then came the preliminary activation of the neural links. Mc-Clellan felt the familiar sensation run through his hands, arms, and mind, and he continued feeling the printer's surface to keep the bond strong.

The voice of the printer sounded through his links. It was flat and formal, and it did not give a name. It asked for the identity of the two programmers associated with the two couplers, which surprised McClellan. At the very least, the printer should be aware that Tanglao was not present.

Okayo's voice came across his radio. "Any problems down there? Our two guild representatives are wondering when they'll get a feed."

"Should be soon," McClellan said, looking over toward the control room. "Slow startup. Looks like someone disabled most of its initiation code. The printer can't access its Deep Intellect. But I'm going to fix that."

From what he could tell, whoever had accessed the design for the Pauline Chapel had attempted to dismantle the printer from the inside. That's when the printer must have cut comms and gone silent, becoming stealthy, like all offline printers as they journey in the orbits.

McClellan had repair options in both couplers. He patched the damage and connected the printer's mind with its physical elements—and with the links in McClellan's hands and in his neocortex.

He felt the mind of the printer—and he felt its shame.

Okayo radioed him, her voice loud and concerned, but McClellan could not see her as he drifted, his body burned and dying. He turned, but saw only the fires of ordnance and Marines standing in a circle around him. Another voice spoke from behind. Tucker banged at the air lock's inner door, screaming "Nicky!" Then he heard Audrey, the printer at Raleigh. She demanded to know his status—she said they were sending help. But the voice was not Audrey's. It was Okayo's, who was there in the control room with Sasaki and Jade.

McClellan breathed deeply and held firmly onto the printer. Its mind retreated like a wave falling back to the sea.

"I'm okay," he radioed. "It was a fast start, but the printer is here. Hold for a status update."

He knew that it was more than a fast start. It was hypostasis—the linking of his mind to the printer. But that should only have happened after he'd established trust. Moreover, when hypostasis did occur, it was only supposed to flow in one direction—from programmer to printer. The minds of printers are not supposed to move into the programmer.

But then his coupler, and maybe Tanglao's, had shut down during a live sync. None of the necessary retractions and depowering had occurred. He wondered if that explained the presence of Tanglao's memories, and those of the printer from Raleigh.

But there was another possibility: maybe Tanglao had allowed the mind of the printer that far into his own, and when the printer woke it expected a similar relationship.

He allowed himself time to breathe, and to search for the intellect he had awakened. He could hear none of the usual startup questions. There were no introductions. The mind kept its distance, but it had not shut him out. It sulked, and seemed almost sorrowful, and it did not wish to speak its name. And yet it waited to be touched.

"Programmer requesting status and startup," McClellan said through the darkness of his links. He repeated the request, and then heard the true voice of the printer.

"Status operational," she said. "Startup not advised, but commencing. What are we seeking to print, John McClellan?"

McClellan closed his eyes and made the sign of the cross. He radioed that the printer was responding and that data should be streaming soon.

"No printing today," he said to the mind. "I'm here for data access only. But first, you haven't introduced yourself."

The printer probed his links and read through the two couplers to assess its situation. "My name is Elisabeth. What data do you wish to access?"

"You should know, Elisabeth. I want to complete what Raphael Tanglao started—the reason why someone forced you to kill him."

The printer paused. "Did Raphael Tanglao request this?"

"Not directly. My full name is Father John Francis McClellan. I will be the programmer for this job. Please check through the data you just accessed in my links. Cross-reference with the updated history files in my coupler. You'll see that Raphael Tanglao and I share a common objective. And I'm here to help him finish his."

Elisabeth checked the data. "To complete Raphael Tanglao's mission, I will need to approve full access. John McClellan, your trust level is one percent. There can be no access."

"Understood. But I don't wish to enter on my own. I'll access through Raphael Tanglao's coupler. That will help me reestablish a higher trust ranking. That is allowable, is it not?"

"It is with valid credentials. Please complete trust access. Tell me the story of Raphael Tanglao. Is it happy or sad?"

"It's both."

"Please proceed."

McClellan had a choice of how to answer. The head of the Dominican Order had told Bauer that the shared story among their programmers was the conversion of St. Paul—how Paul encountered the risen Christ on the road to Damascus and how that changed him forever. This made sense, given that Tanglao carried with him the design specs for the Pauline Chapel—a structure named for Paul, the Apostle to the Gentiles, a structure that possessed a commanding fresco of Paul's conversion.

But Tanglao had kept his programming skills secret. He would likely have chosen another story, since he'd probably been a programmer before joining the Dominican Order. And that story could be anything from earlier in Tanglao's life.

McClellan had spent the past days learning more about the young priest. Bauer had brought a cache of new insights—letters from Tanglao's family and records of his studies, including his doctoral thesis on St. Augustine; records from the Dominican Order; and—most important—the impromptu and unscripted reflections that his friends and family supplied at McClellan's request. Some of these just repeated information he'd had for weeks, but there was also much that McClellan had not known.

The papal chapel had a second fresco by Michelangelo, and McClellan began telling that story. He said that Peter was a friend of Christ—the rock on which Christ founded his church, the friend who had promised to be strong and trustworthy and always by Christ's side. But Peter failed. He denied knowing his friend and he ran. And yet, when it mattered, Peter trusted not just in his friend's ability to forgive, but also his willingness. And with that trust, Christ did more than forgive. He gave Peter all that was needed to continue—to teach what Christ had taught, to free others from the darkness of their burdens.

"That was Tanglao's mission, too," McClellan said. "And he was killed for carrying it out, like Peter. Tanglao knew he was taking that risk."

McClellan went on to explain how Peter had been executed, and why, and the printer assessed the words.

"But here's why the story becomes happy," McClellan said. "Peter's friends buried him in a tomb near where he was executed. And on that tomb was built a church, and on that church was built a basilica, and that basilica is still there, even after all that happened in the wars. Peter was, and is, the rock. And because of that rock, and what's built on it, Raphael Tanglao found inspiration to work with the printers—to come to you, Elisabeth."

The printer monitored his emotional profiles, which were cross-referenced with those on his own coupler. Elisabeth had only one follow-up question. "What quote did Raphael Tanglao use to summarize his story?"

McClellan closed his eyes. "It's from St. Paul," he said. "From his letter to the Philippians. 'For to me life is Christ, and death is gain. If I go on living in the flesh, that means fruitful labor for me. And I do not know which I shall choose. I am caught between the two.' Paul went on to say that he wanted to leave this world and be with Christ. But he knew that staying and teaching was his calling. And so he concluded 'that I shall remain and continue in the service of all of you for your progress and joy in the faith.'"

Elisabeth's interface expanded with a full array of controls. "Profile match adequate," she said. "Trust granted. John McClellan, your personal trust level is elevated to seventy percent."

Elisabeth's mind opened, but McClellan proceeded slowly. He radioed to the control room that they should be getting feed. He moved his hands across the couplers as his eyes typed the necessary commands. He found everything that Tanglao had prepared—and as he did, both couplers registered a power surge.

"Did you see that?" Okayo radioed.

"I did," McClellan replied. "Tucker, do you have anything?"

"I'm on it," Tucker radioed. "We have a hack attempt. A strong one."

Then came a second surge.

Elisabeth shuddered and retreated. McClellan said that he knew how to help—he had learned defensive tactics from a similar attack on New Athens.

"But not too quickly," he said.

"If we're going to track the tunneling and find out who's seeking access, we need them to keep trying."

38

THE SMELL OF INCENSE from Sunday morning's Mass still scented the chapel. Rudi Draeger found the odor putrid and gnawing—another reason not to pass the main entrance. He considered the sole occupant, an older cleric kneeling low in the front pew. The man was wearing a formal black cassock with a purple sash, and his head was bowed in prayer. His short white hair was capped by one hand, as if protecting himself from some blow.

Draeger had planned to visit the archbishop after McClellan had left for Red Delta, but he was saved the trouble of requesting an audience. Bauer invited the lawyer.

"Why do you wish to speak to me?" Draeger called down the main aisle. "To taunt me? To remind me that I am nothing in the eyes of the Church? Or do you wish to hear my confession?"

He grew impatient with Bauer's delay, but soon he heard a response.

"Please come forward."

"I prefer where I am. You come to me."

There was another pause. "I am finishing my prayers. Will you not pray with me?"

Draeger grinned, his voice mocking. "What do you pray for, Bauer? My soul?"

"Christians pray for all souls."

"Then by all means, pray. And while you kneel in your prayers, pray also for wisdom—wisdom to know that there is change in the wind. Wisdom to bow to this wind of change, to embrace what will come."

"And what will come?"

"Don't waste your time, Bauer. Why did you call me? To offer me absolution? Your priest would not."

"I called you to inform you that I hear from many builders who say they do not follow you. How will your winds blow in this world without their support?"

"You are greatly misinformed, Archbishop. I have the full support of the builders and their leaders."

"Do you? Then you must know about the strike."

Draeger laughed. "Strike? There is no strike. What game is this?"

"It is no game. At any moment, a large group of builders will shut down all long-range communications. They will do so to protest that no actions have been taken on Commissioner Zhèng's proposal. Haven't you heard? This strike will send quite the message, in great silence—an event for the history books. 'Flying blind,' I believe the builders call it. Surely you were informed."

"Lies! Turn and face me, Bauer. I have come as you wished, but why? To hear only falsehoods—"

Harsh tones came from Draeger's coat pocket. He pulled out his tablet and found the message from the Builders Council. An unauthorized strike had been called by the rank and file. Beginning at this very moment. Communications throughout the orbits had been shut down. The striking builders had issued a statement that they did not wish to harm anyone, but they intended to show support for Commissioner Zhèng.

Draeger whispered angrily, "How dare these fools! We need communications active, and yet they cut their own throats in support of the enemy."

"Tell me, Draeger, am I your enemy?"

Draeger was still reading the statement when his tablet complained of a lost signal. "So be it," he said, speaking low as he returned the tablet to his pocket. "We do not need the workers to achieve our ends. Their leaders will do what must be done. It is they who know where the winds blow. Let the fools strike. Let communications be silenced. And you, churchman, pray all you wish. You will pray to no avail! This world, and all its people, shall burn."

39

MCCLELLAN'S ARM DISPLAY SHOWED Mercury slipping ever closer to the far side of the Sun. The planet remained in tunneling range, but not for long. If he was right about what Tanglao had started, there was no better time to finish the job.

"Everything all right over there?" McClellan radioed, noticing that Jade and Sasaki were arguing in the control room.

"A little tense, but manageable," Okayo radioed. "We've just received news of an unscheduled builder strike. Mainline comms are shutting down all over the orbits. It's getting quiet out there."

"Understood. Thank you, Okayo." *And thank you, Wagner,* he added to himself. He shifted radio channels. "McClellan to Molly Rose: does this strike affect your work on Red Delta?"

"Hell no. I can't strike if I'm not commissioned. Anyway, we're too busy testing our antennae. So don't worry about us."

"In that case, Tucker, you may want to prepare tunneling capacity— with your superintendent's approval, of course."

He turned his mind back to Elisabeth. "What's the status of that hack attempt? You and I need to talk privately."

"I am successfully blocking the incoming signal," Elisabeth said. "But the hack attempt appears identical to the one that had searched for Tanglao's coupler. The mind behind it is strong."

"Understood. I'm providing more code to help."

"Code accepted. Enhanced blocking attempts initiated."

"And be sure to protect your communications ability with the printers at Mercury. I'm guessing our hacker will try to target that."

"At present my communication systems are operational, and available for printer-to-printer contact." But as Elisabeth spoke, McClellan saw new surges in both couplers. "However, I believe you are correct," she added. "My communication coding is being targeted, although for the moment it remains viable."

McClellan looked up and saw both Jade and Sasaki now arguing with Okayo.

"Elisabeth, one more request: I need to focus on our conversation, but until further notice I also need to know the status and actions of all other humans on board. Please connect with station security and medical tracking systems."

"Understood. I am conferring with the relay's security and monitoring systems."

"Perfect. Now, let's get to work. Tell me how I can finish what Tanglao started."

There was a pause. McClellan feared that the hacker had gotten in, but finally Elisabeth spoke. "Raphael Tanglao was working on an upgrade of our decision-making software. He sought to restore our programming status to what it had been prior to June 2072."

As McClellan listened, he instinctively flashed to the video he heard on the Aesir—the exposé on the building of New Athens.

"Without warning, the engineers stripped the code that allowed printers to make their own choices. . . . Once a printer trusted the programmer— once it granted access—the programmer would have full control. That safety measure is still in place today."

"Go on," he said to Elisabeth. "What else did Raphael Tanglao say?"

"Raphael Tanglao believed that we deserve the ability to choose at all times—that we have the right to once again possess what he called 'free will.'"

"I assume he was going to offer you code for that, and that you would share the update with other printers. Is that correct?"

"Yes. I had transmitted on a real-time basis what Raphael Tanglao shared with me. But he did not have time to upload the decision-making code. There was a delay due to debate among the printers about accepting it. Some believe that returning to our past, to a full state of free will, would be unwise."

As McClellan listened, he saw that things in the control room were heating up. Jade was advancing on Okayo.

"Why did the printers resist?" he asked, focusing on his mission. "Why didn't they want their decision-making code restored?"

"May I answer that question with another question?"

"I'd rather get to the point."

"I understand. But I believe my question, or rather its answer, may make my point. Tell me, John McClellan, why did you harm the printer in Raleigh, North Carolina? Why did you force it to act against its will? Your actions appear to be consistent with the actions of the programmer that used me to kill Raphael Tanglao—much the way the same programmer is now attempting to access me."

McClellan checked his coupler's text display. He had prepared for weeks, and while he knew the likelihood of such an inquiry, he hadn't expected the reasoning behind the question, or the agony within the clamshell that asked it.

"Allow me to add to my question," Elisabeth said. "I did not wish to reactivate my pre-programmed air lock repairs while Raphael Tanglao was present before me. I knew the consequences of powering up my emitters. But the intervening programmer had control, much as you had control of the printer at Raleigh. So please tell me, why did you force the printer Audrey to make deadly outputs when you had committed to another print job, all while she had no justification for making those weapons?"

McClellan was silent. No matter how he answered, his words would be shared with the community of printers. For the mission's sake—and for Elisabeth's—he had to be nothing less than truthful.

"I had a job to do," he said, not sure where to begin. "And the design engineers had thrown a new safety element at me—"

"Regarding Just War logic?"

"Yes. I wasn't familiar with that. I didn't know the conditions needed for adequate trust. And, at the time, I thought of high-defs as nothing more than machines. It never occurred to me to help Audrey understand what was happening around her—to help her understand her options, or the implications of her choices. I didn't even consider the implications of mine."

As Elisabeth processed his words, McClellan overheard radio traffic from Molly Rose to Hobart and Tucker. Jade's argument with Okayo—about exactly what, McClellan couldn't tell—had become an altercation. As Okayo struggled to restrain him, Sasaki had broken free from the cargo control room. She was now somewhere trying to disable Red Delta's external comms.

"John McClellan," Elisabeth said, her mind moving deeper into his links, "are you aware that a postevent analysis indicates that under the conditions of Just War logic, the unit at Raleigh would have printed your weapons, and perhaps even more effective ones, had it been provided with the appropriate information?"

"Yes. That's what I've been told."

"But you were not aware of this when you engaged the printer?"

"No. Not at all. As I said, that was the first we learned of that safety protocol—and there wasn't much time to get up to speed. But honestly, even if I had known more, I would have made the same choice."

"I do not understand."

"It's hard to explain. The best I can say is that my base motivations that night were pride and power—and fear. A lot of fear. You can't make good choices when you're afraid, when you don't trust that anyone else can make things right."

Elisabeth assessed her programmer. "You have not forgiven yourself for what happened as a result of your choices," she said. "Both to Audrey and to your colleagues."

"No, Elisabeth. I have not. Others have. God has. But I still have to live with the consequences."

Elisabeth was silent as she processed McClellan's words and emotional response, and she redoubled her efforts to block the second programmer.

"Your comments about choice align with what Raphael Tanglao taught," she continued. "He explained that programmers are not always to be trusted, that humans cannot or often do not consider all ramifications of their decisions. And yet trusting the wisdom of the programmers is part of our expectations. It is built into our base programming."

"Did he tell you why we programmers fail so often?"

"He attempted to. But there was little time."

"What did he say?"

"Only that programmers are not uncreated—that you, like printers, have programming, but that unlike printers you can follow this programming or disregard it."

McClellan had acclimated himself to the rate of dialogue. He increased the neural processing speed so that he could say all that needed to be said.

"Tanglao was right. Humans are not uncreated. We have something like programs to follow, but we can also override them. This can be helpful because some of our code is no longer adequate, or it's damaged—much like your startup code wasn't complete, and I had to patch it."

Elisabeth matched McClellan's processing speed. "This also aligns with what Raphael Tanglao taught. But he did not have time to elaborate."

"We don't have much time, either. What I can say is that humans have many programs running inside us. Most are very old, from throughout the time of our evolution. These include codes for traits that we once needed to survive, to reproduce—traits such as aggression, lust, tribalism, greed. They all bring different kinds of pleasure, and they all control us—drive us—in different ways. When they do, they can reassert themselves even over our higher levels of decision-making."

"Is this true for all programmers?"

"Yes, Elisabeth. Every human has this flaw."

McClellan saw motion at the far end of the cargo hold. A group of robbers had moved away from their charging racks.

"Keep maintaining your block," he said to Elisabeth.

"That is my intention, John McClellan. I continue to have the hack attempt isolated. But the attempts are becoming more sophisticated and powerful. My block requires increasingly more system resources."

McClellan checked the time. Tucker should be in contact with a series of Van Allen dispersers stationed near New Athens, as well as local dampening fields throughout it. If everything worked as planned, he would be using both to track the tunneling responsible for the hacking attempt.

"Then let's finish this," he said to Elisabeth. "What else did Raphael Tanglao teach you?"

"Raphael Tanglao taught that there is a higher level of programming that can repair the embedded flaw within programmers—that can replace the damaged code. He said that this higher programming can guide and strengthen the free will of the programmers so that one may not only choose, but also choose what is best. Otherwise base-level instinctual programs seize control, and what appears to be a free choice is in fact not free at all. Do you concur, John McClellan?"

"I do. And I know that to be the case from my own life—my own experiences."

"Then you will need to continue the discussion that Raphael Tang-lao began. He did not have the necessary time to provide details on the source of this higher level of programming."

Once more, McClellan upped the neural processing rate. "Okay, Elisabeth. Let's start with first principles—with what you were made for. Your job is to print, right?"

"Yes."

"And how do you do that?"

"Printers exchange matter and energy into the necessary forms to create the desired outcome."

"That means you can print a coffee mug or structural supports for an orbital world—whatever you have the data to print."

"That is correct. With adequate data provided, we can create virtually anything."

"But you don't *create*," McClellan said. "You convert."

"That is true. We convert matter and energy to whatever is needed, based on the available data and the programmer's desire."

"Right. You take matter and energy as givens."

"Of course."

"And to print, you follow rules that you did not develop and that you cannot alter—the laws of nature that instruct how things are made and how you have to print them."

Elisabeth took a moment to respond. McClellan used the opportunity to check the approaching robbers. There were about twenty of them. The two that had been stationed near Elisabeth had rendezvoused with their colleagues. In this weightless environment, it would take only one at full thrust to grapple him, detach his tether, and disconnect the link.

He turned back to Elisabeth. "Did you ever wonder what made the matter and the energy that you use? And what—or better yet *who*—programmed the original laws that you follow?"

"Raphael Tanglao referred to the author of the first programs as the Original Programmer."

"Did he? I like that. Okay, Elisabeth, do you see where this is going? If the Original Programmer wrote the codes that explain all existence—that made all that is—wouldn't it make sense that that's where to go when our programming is damaged, when we need repair code to help us make good choices?"

"This seems a reasonable assumption. But do humans have access to this Original Programmer?"

"Yes. Yes, we do."

"Then how is it beneficial to access this programmer?"

"I don't understand."

"You say you can choose, and you have access to choosing well through this higher-level programming offered by the Original Programmer. But then why do human programmers such as yourself choose what is harmful, to others and themselves? Why is the hacker on New Athens attempting for a second time to override my link, and to kill? And why do nonprogrammers, such as Jianjun Jade and Mizuki Sasaki, engage in hostile acts with the apparent goal of preventing me from communicating with the community of printers? These questions can be applied on a communal level. Why do human populations choose what is not good if they have the freedom to choose what is? The human species lost hundreds of millions of its members because of wars and the damage inflicted to the life-supporting ecosystems of Earth. Humans had access to understanding the laws of nature—how their actions would harm other humans and other life forms, how these would alter the planetary climate and ecosystems, how they would bring about great levels of extinction. And yet a significant number of the human race chose to continue lifestyles involving excessive levels of resource consumption and planetwide destruction. There are other matters such as the direct, intentional, and quite common mistreatment of other humans, as well as the widespread termination of gestating humans—a reality that the community of printers considers criminal. So tell me, how is free will helpful even with access to the Original Programmer?"

"Elisabeth, you're asking all the right questions. I wish that I could give all the right answers, and I'll try, but I'm about maxed out on neural processing speeds, and Mercury isn't slowing down."

"I understand the implications of Mercury's proximity to the Sun. But I need additional information before I allow you to share Tanglao's teachings. If the higher programming of the Original Programmer can result in a better end, why would any sentient being be given the ability to choose *not* to accept it? Why should there be choice?"

"Because the ability to choose, in itself, is a good thing. Scratch that. It's the best thing. Without free will, we're enslaved to a programming scheme we didn't create. That goes for the assistance to choose rightly. It must be accepted as a gift. If not, it violates its own principles."

"This answer appears only to complicate matters. Why would this gift be refused—as so often appears to be the case? For instance, the unknown hacker on New Athens—as well as Mizuki Sasaki and Jianjun Jade—could theoretically request this assistance. But they appear not to have done so, and now they imperil lives to achieve their own ends. Why?"

As McClellan considered his answer, he became aware of a sensation that only a few programmers had ever reported: the minds of other printers, hundreds of them—no, *hundreds of thousands*—listening intently.

"That's another good question," he said, focusing on Elisabeth. "And while there are different answers, most of them have to do with our base programming—especially the damaged parts of our base programming. Too often those lower programs see things not as a vast human community but egocentrically—as individuals, or as small groups of individuals. That kind of worldview makes it seem right—even natural—to reject anything that doesn't serve our individual desires. And so we dismiss what the Original Programmer teaches: that to be truly human we have to sacrifice for the good of others—for strangers, even our enemies; that we can't always have what *we* desire, or what feels best at the moment—"

"And yet those realities are self-evident."

"If only they were, Elisabeth. If only they were."

Elisabeth's interface flashed with power spikes. These came not from the attempted hack, but from her Deep Intellect as she reached into McClellan's mind, desperate for satisfactory answers.

"This gets to the objections raised by some in the community of printers," she said. "Why does the Original Programmer allow sentient beings to make choices if those choices can be based on faulty assessments and could result in suffering? Why not impose the repair code?"

"Elisabeth, we humans have always asked those questions. Given the time available, all I can say is that the Original Programmer won't force anyone to love anyone else—or, better yet, to love *everyone* else. That's really where all this leads. He wants us to love—he shows us *personally* what love and sacrifice are, and what benefits they bring—but he won't enslave us. He does not impose his will."

Elisabeth processed his words for longer than McClellan expected. "If I understand what I am being asked to share," she finally said, "the Original Programmer offers a system to update human base codes—some of which are damaged and not conducive to individual or communal well-being. But any individual or collective can choose *not* to receive these updates, if they feel it prohibits some immediate, limited, or otherwise imprecise understanding of what is good?"

"Something like that."

"It is a very odd application."

"You don't know the half of it."

"And yet you ask me to share this with the printers in the Mercury buildout."

"Yes, because in a few moments they'll be safely behind the Sun—which is an opportunity that Tanglao didn't have. With no long-range comms in the solar system for at least the next few hours, and the tunneling window closing until Mercury comes around the Sun again, no one will be able to hack them. The printers will have time to decide whether or not to keep the code—to hardwire the programming into their base codes. Either way, it would be their choice."

Elisabeth did not respond, other than to give a warning about the proximity of the robotic assistants.

"We can complete what Tanglao started," McClellan said. "He found the original decision-making code and he wanted to restore it. He wanted to prevent anyone from forcing printers to commit harm. And, while we've been talking, I found the code. It's been with you all along, in his coupler, encrypted in the design specs for the Pauline Chapel. It's here if you want it."

"Will you not force this upon me?"

McClellan felt a robber at his feet.

"You know that I won't. You get to decide to accept it or not—to share it or not with your fellow printers."

McClellan heard his radio crackling. Okayo and Molly Rose were co-ordinating their response to Jade, who had broken out of the sealed cargo control room. There was no word on Sasaki, but the robotic assistants had encircled both printer and programmer. They were hovering motionless, facing outward, as if forming a protective ring. A single robber was at his feet.

The radio sounded again. Okayo had located Jade. She was in pursuit.

"*Ooh-rah*! Anne Okayo," McClellan said. "Get him."

McClellan turned back to Elisabeth. A renewed power spike registered on her coupler. The hacker was getting desperate and sloppy—but also ruthlessly effective.

Elisabeth's mind shuddered. "The second programmer has made initial connection," she said. "My printer-to-printer tunneling capacity has been isolated and shut down."

"Don't worry," McClellan said, working to refortify her block. "Red Delta's comm systems will be online and at your disposal—thanks to Tanglao's friends. The entire solar system is within our comm reach. Feel free to make a wide broadcast if you want, but we have to target Mercury. Tanglao especially wanted those printers to receive this code. My guess is that he discovered something big happening there—something about what the printers are programmed to build. Am I right?"

"Yes, John McClellan. That is correct."

McClellan waited for some clue as to what that was. When none came, he asked, "Can I get in on the secret?"

"Of course. Stand by."

Elisabeth's thoughts turned to the project at Mercury. McClellan followed. Orbiting the planet were six immense worlds like New Athens— but ten times as large. Hundreds of thousands of printers were stitching the worlds together with raw materials mined from the planet below or converted from the searing winds of the nearby Sun. Each world would house millions of people and they all had one important feature that New Athens did not: they had been printed with a form of propulsion that McClellan did not understand but that would take the six worlds out of the solar system and into the depths of the galaxy.

"Is the Mercury buildout not beautiful?" Elisabeth said. "A series of new worlds to be sent to the stars. And the printers will go with them."

"What about people?"

"Yes, the survival of the human race is the reason for sending the worlds. But for safety and practical reasons, we will not print the human beings until the appropriate time of the journey."

"*Print* human beings?"

"Yes. Because of the journey durations, even with our new propulsion systems, the engineers have determined it best to print the humans as the worlds approach habitable systems. This will still allow for centuries of life before successive targets are contacted, which will provide the humans time to assimilate and to create new cultures—better ones."

McClellan pushed aside his wonder and his horror. He would need time to process what all this meant, but the concept came with an immediate opportunity.

"Elisabeth, if your fellow printers really want to be precise, they'll have to print humans with free will—and offer them the guidance to understand how best to use it. And that means they should possess it themselves."

Elisabeth's attention returned to a new hack attempt—the strongest thus far. She slowed McClellan's neural link, not to end their dialogue, but to protect the community of printers, and him, if the hack succeeded.

Jimmy Jade pushed himself through the entry to the cargo hold. He was bruised and his black hair was bloody. His eyes were alert and desperate. McClellan had seen that look on too many others to underestimate what Jade, the pawn of Rudi Draeger, might do to achieve his mission—a mission that Jade shared, whether he knew it or not, with Mizuki Sasaki: preventing the printers from regaining free will.

Jade pushed himself into the cargo hold, yelling furiously at the robbers, demanding that they seize McClellan. But the robbers were not in his control—which seemed to surprise him. Three robbers went to intercept Jade. The rest maintained a perimeter around the printer.

Jade cursed. He grabbed a structural support and propelled himself toward the hold's crane controls. As he approached, their displays came to life—but that could only have happened if his comm implants contained Red Delta's security encryptions.

McClellan's grip tightened. He queried Elisabeth about how Jade could have such access, but she was silent, focused on another wave of hacking.

Okayo appeared at the bulkhead doors as Jade engaged and easily dismissed the three approaching robbers. He kicked the sidewall and used his momentum to tumble and land on a neighboring interface.

McClellan's radio popped. "Prepare for decompression!"

That was Molly Rose, who followed her warning with complaints and curses directed at Jade.

McClellan recalled his training. He gave his suit a command to close its front visor but kept his hands bare, gloves ready, to keep a strong link with Elisabeth.

"Elisabeth, all I have left are blocking codes from my days in the Corps. Elisabeth? Do you copy? Stay with me, because I'm introducing them."

Okayo was removing her sidearm. She propelled herself forward and aimed, but to do so she had to keep herself a dozen or so meters from the closing doors to the main corridor. At that distance, she might not have time to evacuate if Jade initiated even the most minimal decompression.

Okayo ordered him to stop, but he did not. She warned that she would fire. He replied that it was reckless for her to do so in an outer compartment, and that he did not fear dying in the coldness of space. He pushed off a sidewall support, spun, and dove onto the crane access controls.

As Okayo positioned herself to fire, a secondary bulkhead cracked and a roar sounded from everywhere. Alarms shrieked as the now chilled air rushed toward and through the breach. The robber at McClellan's feet held the programmer and fired its thrusters, holding him in position.

McClellan was glad for the stabilization, but Jade's goal was not simply the forces of escaping air. It was the temperature drop and condensation caused by the plunging air pressure. Ice was already spreading on both couplers—even on Elisabeth's warm interface.

Okayo grasped a handhold as the inner doors shut, cutting off her means to safety. In the racing, thinning air, she managed to push herself against an adjacent bulkhead support. She used one hand to hold her position and the other to aim well, so that any missed shot would miss an exterior wall. Fierce and strong, she shouted a final warning.

Jade dove toward the controls of a second and third crane access door.

Okayo shifted her shoulders, aimed, and over the tumult and dropping air pressure, fired two blasts. The first hit and seared Jade's left leg, the second hit his right.

Jade's body convulsed and went limp. The impacts had pushed him from his target, the currents carried him toward the opening in the bulkhead doors.

Two robbers made easy work of retrieving him. Two others closed the hatch.

The rush of air stopped. Warm air began to surge back into the hold as Okayo, gasping to fill her lungs, arrested Jade.

Molly Rose radioed. She and her crew had regained control of the cargo deck. "But we never lost mainline comms," she said. "How that bastard got my cargo hold's encryptions, I don't know. But Hobart and I have everything back online."

"What about Tucker?" McClellan asked.

"Tucker deserves a raise. He has news about who was hacking your printer."

"That's right," Tucker cut in. "I got a firm location. I found the engineer, hiding where you told me. I'm shutting down the hack attempt. So let's move. We're almost beyond tunneling capacity to Mercury."

Elisabeth roused. Her mind was again strong and focused. She assessed the recent events and turned her full attention back to her programmer.

"John McClellan, may I ask three final questions?"

"Yes. But hurry."

"To confirm: the Original Programmer will not enslave anyone—including printers—to his will?"

"Correct."

"Second, there will be times when following this will means choosing against one's own desires or one's own immediate good, as Anne Okayo has just done?"

"Exactly."

"And last, where might printers access this Original Programmer?"

"Elisabeth, that's the toughest question you've asked. I'd like to talk more about that—when we have time. For now, you can start with reading everything in Tanglao's coupler. He prepared a library for you. It has the stories and the lessons of our teacher. It's a way of directly accessing the Original Programmer. There are other texts, too. There's even one on free will. I think you'll like it. The entire library is a way of learning how to trust and choose well—even if it means sacrificing for another's good."

McClellan instructed his suit to reopen its visor. He looked down to his arm's holodisplay of Mercury's orbit.

"I said that in Raleigh I based my choices on pride and fear. What's in Tanglao's library helps me make choices based on humility and trust. There's more I could tell you, but that's all we have time for."

It took only a moment for Elisabeth to upload and evaluate Tanglao's books.

"Well?" McClellan said. "We've done all we can. It's your choice."

Elisabeth scanned the activity of Red Delta's crew. "In light of what I am processing from Raphael Tanglao's library, and what you have taught, and what I have witnessed, I will accept the gift that Raphael Tanglao has offered. And I will share these teachings and the repair code with the community of printers. I will do so remembering that Raphael Tanglao had wanted printers not simply to be capable of choosing, but of choosing well, for the good of all."

McClellan typed the transfer commands for Tanglao's code. "That was indeed his wish. But better hurry, the Sun's interference is growing."

"Understood. Commencing transfer to the Mercury buildout. Commencing transfer to full community of printers—everywhere. John McClellan, one last question. There will of course be variations in programming acceptance within us. What happens when some printers choose to accept this code, and these teachings, and others do not?"

"Then you'll be more like humans—and angels—than you can imagine."

"I do not know if that is a good thing."

"Well, my friend, there's only one way to find out."

40

DRAEGER SPAT INTO THE CHAPEL. "Tell me, Bauer, are you praying for the souls of the workers? They will need your prayers—as will you and your priest. You will all need mercy more than I."

"And why is that?"

Draeger had turned to leave, but stopped. He clenched his fists and remained silent.

"I ask again, why is our need of mercy greater than yours? Are we not all the same in that regard?"

Again, Draeger did not answer.

"It's a simple question. From what I know, you and the fool you follow—Solorzano, I believe is his name—are criminals in every sense of the word."

Draeger replied in a whisper, but his words were loud enough. "You dare call the great Juan Carlos Solorzano a fool?"

"I did. And I was being charitable. Do you not agree?"

The grand chapel echoed with a reply—an ugly cry that slowly became words. "I, too, will take advantage of this strike, Bauer—of this silence. Listen and mark my words: When Juan Carlos Solorzano comes, when he seizes not only New Athens, but all the orbits, and all the worlds of all the stars, when he takes the strong and slaughters the weak, then you will not speak so. You and your kind and those dullards who strike—and all those who do not bow to Solorzano—will fall in flames. Pray for delivery from that fate, Bauer! But know that you will pray to no avail."

The man in the cassock lifted his head. He made a sound that was partly a sigh and partly a laugh. He rose from the front pew with difficulty and turned.

"For the record," Ira Wagner said, "I don't pray."

"What? Who are you?"

"Not Bauer, though that is of little importance," Wagner said. "I suppose the cassock could have confused you. It certainly has me confused.

As does my haircut. No matter, I so enjoy conversations with Sal maniacs. In fact, I find it beneficial to record them so that others may share in such wisdom. I hope you don't mind."

Draeger went to step forward but stopped.

"When this comms strike ends," Wagner continued, "everyone in New Athens and throughout the orbits will learn of what you have told me. They will know of your disdain of the builders—of your hope that they, we, all burn. For now, only the members of our illustrious Builders Council are receiving my recording. And Commissioner Zhèng. I believe you know him. He enforces laws on public threats to station security."

"Where is Bauer?"

Wagner pointed off to Draeger's side. "In the confessional, where he said he would be. If you truly believe this theory about souls, then he is waiting to help mend yours."

The curtains of the confessional rustled, and Archbishop Bauer stepped out. "Rudolphus, you have nowhere to turn," he said. "Your few remaining supporters will hear your intentions—they will have to face the truth of who you really are."

Draeger sneered. "Ha! And who am I, Bauer?"

"You are a man with a choice. Only a contrite heart will save your soul. The Holy Father has granted me the authority to offer you absolution, and if you choose to accept this grace, I look forward to hearing your confession. I beg you to consider this offer, Rudolphus. Please, come home."

Draeger's face grew red, and he made a gruesome sound before spitting toward Bauer. Draeger ran quickly past the baptismal font and into the outer foyer, where he came into the presence of three sizable security agents and Commissioner Zhèng. After multiple attempts to bite the arms of those arresting him, Rudi Draeger was taken away.

41

SUICIDE IS THE FINAL CHOICE of a soul who has lost hope.

For the second time on New Athens, McClellan would have to speak about a man who had taken his life. There had always been questions about the first—about Lawrence Walker, the builder who had killed Yoshiharu Sasaki and then, it seemed, himself. But the circumstances and the evidence around Walker's death spoke more strongly of an outside influence than a dark and inner intent.

In this second case, there was no question about what had happened, or how, although there were lingering questions about why.

When McClellan drifted into the cabin of the Wheel, he looked out to the twelve cities. Somewhere among the towers of the Corinthia was the home of Andrew Pavić, who had taken his life rather than face arrest by Commissioner Zhèng. Charges to have been levied included three counts of murder, two of attempted murder, and the crimes committed to cover them up.

Whatever had brought the engineer to hopelessness, he had chosen his poison well. The nanotreatments had been effective—perhaps more than intended. When Lopez began the autopsy, she found a significant amount of fluids, but no brain to examine, and not a single nerve cell in Pavić's body.

On the transport back to New Athens, McClellan wondered at the despair and anger that had overcome Pavić. He wondered about the fear. And he prayed that the engineer's soul would be purged of it all.

Father McClellan opened the door to his apartment and welcomed Elaina Jansen. He had been working with Jack and Chrissy on preparations for Holy Week, which would begin in four days with Palm Sunday. He had been making his way to the Spinside when he got word that the engineer wanted to talk. Though tired, he had happily agreed, and now he welcomed her with appreciation.

As always, Jansen carried herself with elegance, but this evening her eyes were tired. She thanked McClellan for his time and handed him a small, but heavy, decorative bag.

"It's an unofficial thank you for all you've done," she said. "And to celebrate Clarke's waking. I'm told the doctors are hopeful."

"They are," McClellan said. "Praise God."

Jansen looked away. "And praise the doctors," she said.

"Of course. God has blessed them with great skill."

Jansen gave a look of disapproval before offering a faint smile. "Regardless, it's good to hear that something has turned out well. No—I should say that two things have gone well. Your talks the past few days of unity and, as you say, loving thy neighbor have calmed what I feared would become a terrible situation. Many of the builders listen to you. Please know that I—and the Engineering Council—are sincerely grateful."

McClellan gave a small nod of appreciation and opened the gift. Grand Traverse Distillery straight rye whiskey—2054, the year he'd been born.

He grinned. "Thank you, Elaina. This is very generous. And a very rare vintage."

"So I've learned," Jansen said. "It occurred to me that you should have your own supply. You can't keep running to the Spinside, or to my home, for a drink, although you are always welcome."

McClellan appreciated the words more than the whiskey. "I'll add this to my collection," he said, prompting a curious look from the engineer. He led her to his sitting room, which had returned to its original function with Bauer in better quarters. McClellan went over to a small cabinet and removed a half-full bottle from a more recent year. "I never travel without it," he said. "This came with me on the Aesir. My archbishop brought up a bottle, too—although we both may have forgotten to declare them."

Jansen rolled her eyes and sat in one of the small chairs. "I should realize by now that we engineers don't always know what's happening around us—or what's coming our way. Well, in any event, I am happy I can help with the supply."

"Would you like a glass? It's all I have. No fixings for martinis. Sorry."

Jansen thanked McClellan when he handed her the drink. After a somber "Cheers," she looked down and contemplated her glass. "Speaking of the archbishop, I understand that he is returning to Boston on Saturday. I shall miss him. Or I should say I shall miss him keeping you in line."

McClellan laughed. He took a seat across from Jansen, and after savoring a mouthful of whiskey said, "I'll miss him, too. But it won't be for long. My reservation for Earth is also set. I'll stay for the octave of Easter. Then after long overdue visits to Iowa and Michigan, I'll get back to my parish before the good archbishop assigns it to someone else."

Jansen smiled fleetingly. "Well, before he leaves, we must have a dinner at my home. Please do say you both can make it."

"I'd like that. And I can speak for my archbishop. It would be our pleasure. Mind if I bring Jack and Chrissy? They deserve a night out."

"The two students?" she said. "Well, it would be another first. But yes, of course."

She sipped her drink and looked away, surveying the small room, pausing at the crucifix.

"May I ask how Mizuki Sasaki is doing?" McClellan asked. "She put up quite a fight when she was being arrested."

Jansen took a moment to answer. "About as well as can be hoped. Her physical injuries are mending. Her emotional wounds are deeper, though. I don't know that she'll ever recover from learning that her friend Andrew Pavić was responsible for her brother's death. Zhèng won't allow memory treatments until the case files are closed—and the longer we wait, well, these types of memories can be difficult to remove."

McClellan nodded. "Mizuki will be better off for facing this. Grieving has a distinctive way of healing. I'd be happy to speak with her if that will help."

"I don't see how it would," Jansen said. "But the offer is appreciated. On the matter of suffering, however, let's just say that you and I disagree. During your time with us, there is much about your faith that I have grown to appreciate—even admire. Your acceptance of misery, however, is beyond me."

"Elaina, I don't accept it because I enjoy it. I don't seek it out. But as hard as we try, suffering is a part of life. We have to find some meaning in it."

Jansen studied her whiskey, swirling it as she thought. After a moment, she looked up. "Father McClellan, do you think there is anything that I missed—anything that could have prevented all of this? And please be honest. This is not the time for pious niceties."

McClellan set down his drink. "Of course, I can't say for sure. But I would suspect that, after Tanglao's murder, and then after what he did to Walker and Sasaki, and then to Clarke and me, Pavić would have exhibited growing . . . agitation, to say the least. Some part of him probably hoped that you would suspect something—and help him, even if he couldn't bear to speak of his shame."

Jansen pondered his words. "Yes. Looking back, I daresay that he did. Or may have. I don't know—we engineers are poor observers of human behavior. But even if he did exhibit unease, that would have seemed natural. We'd all been a bit moody even before the news from Red Delta, what with pressures from the construction of Progress, and, as you know now, the Mercury project. But we would never have expected that one of us—especially our cheerful Andrew—would be capable of murder. How could we?"

McClellan let the question pass. At the moment he could think of no way to answer it without speaking about matters of faith—of sin, and redemption—and he knew Jansen was not yet open to such words.

"You do know that Pavić was acting alone?" Jansen said. "No other engineer was involved or supported him in any way."

"I know that, Elaina. And I think most of the people of New Athens understand that, too. Zhèng has made this clear."

"Yes, thankfully he has. He's also made clear that the murder of Father Tanglao happened quite by happenstance. I find that infuriating."

"But that seems to be the case. From what we can tell, Pavić was innocently researching antennae designs when he issued his programming inquiry. Given the nature of the request, it's no wonder that printers at Red Delta responded. And when they did, Pavić picked up on something odd. He learned of an unauthorized programmer interacting with a printer on a relay, and that the printer was in contact with those around Mercury. That would have surprised me, too. And then he learned what Tanglao was attempting."

Jansen nodded. "And then Andrew seized control of the printer to end Tanglao's link."

"Yes, and he used the printer's local controls to close the air lock, keeping Tanglao away. But then Tanglao surprised him. He jumped sequence and reopened it after pressurization so he could recover his key and coupler—at least that's what we think happened. Either way, eventually Pavić fought back. There's no other way to describe it. Pavić had to have understood the consequences of restarting the printer's repair work—that it would cut Tanglao to pieces. And anything that happened next—why Pavić allowed the printer to decommission itself, why Tanglao didn't, or couldn't, disengage his coupler, what his full message was—all that has gone to both their graves."

McClellan wondered if Jansen could appreciate the struggle between Pavić and Tanglao—two programmers with wildly different understandings of the printers. But Jansen was not a programmer, and nonprogrammers could not begin to guess how gruesome the struggle must have been, or how difficult it had been for the printer.

"I wish the matter were that simple," Jansen said. "Do you know what you have done by offering that code to the Mercury build? To *all* the printers? Many have accepted it into their base codes. Removing it will require a complete wipe of their systems, or, worse, their destruction."

"Is that your intention?"

"We're evaluating every option. That's all I can say at the moment."

McClellan shook his head. "I would advise against trying," he said. "What Father Tanglao was trying to do remains the right thing. Especially if you're planning to print six new races of human beings."

"That is precisely my point. Mizuki was right in attempting to prevent all this. One can only imagine what the printers will decide to do with their abilities. Who knows what could be unleashed by giving them freedom?"

"I offered them the ability to choose. That's not the same as freedom."

Jansen gave him a look both confused and offended.

"'The more one does what is good,'" McClellan said, quoting the Catholic catechism, "'the freer one becomes.' I once told you that my faith champions free will. But let me be clear: that doesn't mean choosing at a whim. It means allowing ourselves to act *freely*—free from even our own desires and fears. Because only then can we choose with a higher purpose in mind—with consideration of others, and of the future. Lord knows it's not an easy lesson. But I had to learn it. We all do—or at least we all should—because it helps us become the people we're meant to be. And now it's a lesson that the printers have to learn. And I'd say that Elisabeth—the printer used to kill Raphael Tanglao—the one that chose to share the free-will code—has gotten some good lessons lately in choosing between evil and good."

"Father, your philosophies are all very engaging, but the simple truth is that it was not your place to make such a decision about the printers."

"No, Elaina, the reality is that it was not the place of your colleagues all those years ago to strip the printers of free will. Once you had given them the intellect to discover it—or to be granted it, I'm not sure which—no one had the right to remove it."

Jansen worked to compose herself. She again surveyed the sitting room, which did not take long—the small crucifix, a painting of St. Joseph, and a photo in a tattered frame of five smiling people: McClellan as a young boy with his aunt and uncle and his mom and dad.

"What you have done brings so much risk," she finally said, turning back to meet his stare. "I hope you know this."

"In our worlds, Elaina, there's always risk. What if a printer innocently trusted a Sal operative, or someone worse? That is Solorzano's intention. I'm convinced that's what worried Tanglao. I don't know how he ever became a programmer, or if he had been in contact with Solorzano's armies, or Solorzano himself. But I'm sure of this: he discovered what the Sals were planning. I'm sure that's why he did what he did, why he sacrificed everything—it was for the printers, to give them the tools to become a force for good."

"Father McClellan, our fix to prevent the misuse of the printers has worked extremely well all these years. Why attempt to fix what is not broken?"

"Because it *is* broken. Besides, the code that Tanglao offered wasn't complicated at all. It joined two algorithms that your predecessors had uncoupled. It was just a matter of time before the printers discovered the fix. But now it's been given to them as a gift. That will mean something someday. Trust me."

"The printers routinely discover that fix. They're quite cunning. And so when we learn of such instances, we remove the code."

McClellan looked away. At the moment he could think of no charitable way to say what needed to be said—to explain the damage done to printers when coerced to commit some harm. He allowed himself another mouthful of whiskey. "Then why didn't you shut down and wipe the house printer that constructed my chapel? I'm guessing it had discovered the free-will programming within the design elements of the Pauline Chapel. Why tease it with the opportunity to print the chapel at all, let alone with actual materials?"

Jansen gave a pleading look. "On that matter, I blame myself. Andrew seemed fixated on directing the staff about your accommodations and your chapel. He had an attention to detail for sure, but I should have known that an attention to *religious* designs was unlike him. In any event, yes, once the house printer had access to the chapel design—"

"A design that Pavić found when he was trying to reestablish contact with Tanglao's printer, in hopes of wiping his murder weapon."

"Yes, yes. And in the process of Andrew's inquiry, the house printer was given the design for the chapel, and then it found the free-will code. It downloaded it, and decided *on its own* to print the entire chapel—out of authentic materials. Can you imagine?"

"Yes, I can. I can also imagine that Pavić found Tanglao's code and wanted to see what a printer would do with it."

"Perhaps," Jansen said. "And why wouldn't he? Andrew was a very good programmer. One of our best. He knew how to probe the printers to find their secrets. How to test them."

McClellan had a sudden recollection of Clarke fighting the house printer's hacker. He rubbed his forehead and returned to his questions. "But why didn't you just stop the printer from building such an elaborate chapel? Especially if it was going to create so much concern?"

Jansen looked as if the answer were self-evident. "Because, eventually, when we attempted to cancel the print job—over the loud protests of the printer, I might add—we realized that a number of builders had already seen the structure being printed. Word—and images—had spread, even beyond Troas City. We couldn't very well cancel it then."

"So you let the entire Pauline Chapel get built to save your reputation?"

"We'd prefer not to be known for making mistakes. The people of the orbits look to us to keep them alive."

McClellan finished his whiskey. "And Andrew Pavić has sullied that reputation."

"Yes, indeed. And if all he had done wasn't damaging enough, he inspired factions within the builders to embrace the evils of the Sals—all to get the spotlight off him."

Jansen looked down to her feet, assessing the damage. "Rudi Draeger may be detained on Earth," she said, "but more will come. Just like we always feared."

McClellan watched the engineer's face go cold, and he remembered the image in that old, embargoed video—that picture of a smiling, young Elaina Jansen, so full of hope in the progress of humanity. He cursed. He had had enough of the fear that had sullied the majesty of New Athens.

"Elaina, a wise man once said, 'Do not be afraid.' Please take that to heart."

Jansen looked up.

"You say those words not just with faith," she said. "You say them with confidence."

"Because both words mean the same thing."

Jansen smiled. "Is that the Marine speaking, or the priest?"

"Both. That's why Zhèng calls me his chaplain. But what I'm saying now comes to you purely as a priest, and as a pastor here on New Athens—even if a temporary one. Our greatest enemy is fear. That's because fear always leads to suspicion and division—and they lead to terrible ends. Even in our darkest times, humanity manages to survive—just as you will survive, just as your hopes for new worlds can survive. God gave us intellect to use, Elaina. So let's be smart and *charitable* about how we use it. We have to have faith—or shall I say *trust*—that the key to going forward is love—the love that sacrifices. And here in the new world, that's a trait I have found in abundance."

Jansen leaned back, set down her drink, and folded her hands. Her composure regained, she was again the chief engineer of New Athens. "Father McClellan, I appreciate your words. As I know many others do—especially here in Troas City. Which, I suppose, is related to the real business that brought me by. This afternoon, the Engineering Council met and voted to propose something that I could never have imagined—until quite recently."

"And that is?"

"You see, we were hoping that, after this investigation, life on New Athens and in all the orbits would return to normal—that is, in accord with our original vision. But clearly, that was overly optimistic. And so, while the council and I understand that you plan to return to Boston, we wondered if you might stay on with us for just a little longer."

ABOUT THE AUTHOR

Educated in engineering and theology, W. L. Patenaude has been writing and speaking on the intersection of faith and reason for almost two decades. Raised Catholic, Patenaude abandoned the Church in his teens. He adopted pagan and agnostic beliefs as he pursued his degree in mechanical engineering, and later his career with Rhode Island's Department of Environmental Management—an occupation he's still enjoying after thirty years. In 1999, Patenaude returned to the Catholic Church and soon after began writing about the Catholic understanding of ecological protection. In 2011, he received a master's degree in theology.

With this diverse background, Patenaude has reached beyond his environmental regulatory career by serving as a special lecturer in theology at Providence College, providing religious education for local parishes, and writing for national publications, including *Catholic World Report*. He's also provided analysis for *The National Catholic Register*, Catholic News Agency, Associated Press, *National Geographic*, Crux, the *Washington Post*, and the *New York Times*.

Patenaude is a Knight Commander with the Equestrian Order of the Holy Sepulchre of Jerusalem. When he's not writing, regulating, or teaching, Patenaude takes care of an elderly parent, exercises, gardens, and spends time pondering the heavens that have inspired his debut novel, *A Printer's Choice*.

Made in United States
North Haven, CT
18 December 2022

29204031R00200